Judgment Day

Someone was standing to her left. She felt him as if he weren't behind a transparency at all, as if he were in the hall with her. But that couldn't be—they were all locked up.

Don't look up, she warned herself. *Keep your head down, keep mopping.*

And she did, without hurrying, without breaking her rhythm. She worked her way back to Jerry Wolfe again, and his voice picked up in volume as well as speed. . . .

Why can't he just shut up? she wondered peevishly. . . . And then something seemed to rush at her, from ahead and to her left. She started violently and looked up.

Right into the eyes of Prisoner MS-12.

He hadn't moved at all, he was impossibly still. His eyes were fixed on her. . . .

"He can't hurt you," Commander Bell was calling. "He's locked up, kiddo. Don't look at him. Just look at the floor again . . ."

"Shit," snarled Jerry Wolfe. "Beelzebub is just a Demon! I'm the Antichrist! I'm the one you should be scared of, I'm the one who's going to burn your soul in hell for eternity!"

BROKEN TIME

Maggy Thomas

A ROC BOOK

ROC
Published by New American Library, a division of
Penguin Putnam Inc., 375 Hudson Street,
New York, New York 10014, U.S.A.
Penguin Books Ltd, 27 Wrights Lane,
London W8 5TZ, England
Penguin Books Australia Ltd, Ringwood,
Victoria, Australia
Penguin Books Canada Ltd, 10 Alcorn Avenue,
Toronto, Ontario, Canada M4V 3B2
Penguin Books (N.Z.) Ltd, 182–190 Wairau Road,
Auckland 10, New Zealand

Penguin Books Ltd, Registered Offices:
Harmondsworth, Middlesex, England

First published by Roc, an imprint of New American Library,
a division of Penguin Putnam Inc.

First Printing, May 2000
10 9 8 7 6 5 4 3 2 1

ROC REGISTERED TRADEMARK—MARCA REGISTRADA

Printed in the United States of America

PUBLISHER'S NOTE
This is a work of fiction. Names, characters, places, and incidents either
are the product of the author's imagination or are used fictitiously,
and any resemblance to actual persons, living or dead, business establish-
ments, events, or locales is entirely coincidental.

BOOKS ARE AVAILABLE AT QUANTITY DISCOUNTS WHEN USED TO PROMOTE
PRODUCTS OR SERVICES. FOR INFORMATION PLEASE WRITE TO PREMIUM
MARKETING DIVISION, PENGUIN PUTNAM INC., 375 HUDSON STREET, NEW
YORK, NEW YORK 10014.

In memory of Mungy-Bungy,
cat and friend

ACKNOWLEDGMENTS

I would like to thank my writing buddies: Ernest Hogan (who brainstormed the original idea with me one day when we were washing windows), Chris Welborn (who asked pertinent questions about the Speedies), Rick Cook (for tips concerning gravity and Tipler Transporters), Cinda Smith and Diana Douglas (who keep me on my toes), Martha Casillas, Rosemary McVay, and Channette Wijangco (who kept reminding me that I'm a writer), Gia DeSimone and Myrk Tyva (for virus balls and hot chocolate), Diana Challis and Peter L. Manly (for advice about low gravity salt mines), Jennifer Heddle and Jenni Smith (who know what needed to be fixed), and Paul Schauble and Teddy and Dan Hogan (for computers that work). Any glitches or goofs in this book are entirely my fault. They've done their best with me, but I'm bad to the bonc.

FIRST WALTZ

The killer lives inside me
I can feel him move
Sometimes he's lightly sleeping in the quiet of his
   room
But then his eyes
Will rise and stare through mine
He'll speak my words and slice my mind inside
Yes, the killer lives

—Peter Hammill,
   "Man Erg"

Siggy was going down Monster Row for the last time.

In the movies, she thought to herself, *this would be the part where I got killed, after the lock opened and I pushed my mop and bucket into the hallway. Everything would look normal on the surface. I would be nervous, but unaware that anything was wrong. And I would get at least halfway through the job, or maybe all the way through it, but I wouldn't be allowed to escape.*

Siggy had seen plenty of movies like that, but she didn't like them. They lied, like any good piece of fiction; but they broke the rules and wounded when they lied. Siggy preferred musical lies. The kind with a happy ending, the kind you could dance to.

When the security lock opened, she pushed her mop and bucket into the hall. She glanced nervously at the officer before she crossed the threshold. He smiled at her, an honest, open grin, completely unlike the frozen stare of the Toady who had last held the job. The Toady was dead now, but Siggy still saw him out of the corner of her eye. He still sat at his old station, waiting to betray her.

The new officer closed the lock behind her. For the first week after the attack he had said, "Don't worry, I'm watching. I won't let anything happen to you." He was concerned when he saw her bruises and the way she had limped. Now the bruises were fading from her skin and she walked straight again. Now his reassurances were unspoken.

Siggy rubbed her short hair vigorously. *Don't cry,* she ordered herself; then she pushed the wheeled bucket along, bracing herself to begin her last chore at the Institute for the Criminally Insane. *He'll see if you've been crying. Don't let him.*

She didn't mean the officer, though she didn't want him to see her cry, either. The one she meant was near the end of the row, well away from the other inmates. He knew she was coming. He would have his piece to say, and she would have to hear it. They were recording everything, the investigators, the doctors. They wanted to hear if he would say something revealing, and Siggy was one of the few people he ever spoke to.

Probably George would be the only one, now that Siggy was leaving and Afrika was dead. Maybe George would leave too, and the Professor would be silent forever after.

Fifteen cells lined Monster Row, officially known as the Maximum Security Block. Only five cells were occupied now. Siggy passed the first four inmates without much concern; three of them were silent and the forth murmured threats she'd heard a thousand times before. A little further, and Siggy was almost halfway there. She pushed the bucket past cell MS-06.

Commander Bell had lived there. The janitors called him Dr. Jekyll or Mr. Hyde, depending on which way he was swinging.

Call me Joseph, he told Siggy. And eventually he had teased her own first name out of her, dissatisfied with the *Lindquist* that was on her name patch.

Joseph's cell had been empty for six years. The blood had long since been cleaned away. Afrika attended to that, so the cell was spotless. You couldn't even tell a man had bashed his head in against those walls.

I don't want to spend the rest of my life thinking of you as Lindquist, Joseph said. *Or even Lindy.*

Siggy pushed the bucket toward the end of the row. A blank wall waited there, her beginning point for seven years. Scrubbing the corners used to be her first priority. The Director had been a fanatic about those corners. Many times he had allowed her to complete the job, then sent her back to do it over; back among the Monsters, who scrutinized her every movement as she swished the mop back and forth, back and forth, almost waltzing with it. She was the only woman they ever saw, except for an occasional doctor.

She passed Jerry Wolfe's cell, MS-09.

The Tormenter. That wasn't a name the janitors had given him; the news media did it, once they had seen his home movies.

She didn't look in; he wasn't there. He had escaped two weeks before, killing Afrika, the Toady, three other officers, and almost Siggy. She never looked into his cell anyway, even when he spoke to her. She had despised him. He was a small man; thin, wiry, pigeon-toed. For seven years she listened to his grandiose claims, his convoluted reasoning; and she had been the recipient of his smug contempt. She wasn't alone in that regard. She had seen part of the mini-disc he made with the people, that man and the two children. He displayed the same smug contempt when they begged and screamed.

After all, he would have said, *I'm the Antichrist. That's the kind of thing you should expect from me. When I bring about the Apocalypse, you won't be surprised, will you Siggy?*

Yes! Siggy would have liked to snarl at him. *Yes, I would be surprised, you half-baked little creep.*

The Professor came into view. He was in cell MS-12. Siggy stopped, caught by his stare. Even after all these years, seeing him five days a week, she had never learned to take his gaze for granted.

He was waiting for her. He stood perfectly still, the way he always did; and as always, she felt she might have just missed catching him in some violent, purposeful motion, almost caught him doing something that would have astonished and terrified her. Spinning like a tornado, perhaps, or walking on the ceiling. If her eyes had only been quick enough . . .

She had never seen him in motion, not once. What human being had ever stood so perfectly still? Who else but the Professor could stare so intently you could hardly make your muscles move under his gaze? And what was it like for the people he killed, when he finally moved in their direction?

"This is your last day," he said, without inflection.

"Yes," said Siggy.

She was safe from him. The cell barriers were made
of a clear substance ten times stronger than industrial
steel, though it was only a millimeter thick. Its chemical
composition could be altered to allow air to flow freely
through it, and sound and light. But if the officer inside
the security lock thought the inmates were disturbing
Siggy he could make the barriers go black, shut out the
light and the sound. The Toady could have done that
back when he held the job. But he had never bothered.

The Toady had opened Jerry Wolfe's cell. Siggy was
sure of it, just as she was sure of who had ordered him
to do it. But no one could prove it now, and she had
been offered a fat settlement. She and the families of
the dead . . .

Siggy blinked. The Professor had moved. Now he was
standing so close to the cell barrier his nose almost
touched it. When had he moved? She must have looked
away for a moment, while thinking about the Toady.
Now the Professor was motionless again. Like a statue.

"You never belonged here," he said.

Some people might have been flattered by that remark, but Siggy knew it wasn't a compliment. The Professor didn't like her. He wasn't even a professor.
Nobody knew his real name, or where he had been born.
He had stolen the identities of some of his victims when
he used their credit cards, drove their vehicles, wore
their clothes.

The janitors called him the Professor because he
seemed to wear the same demeanor as the doctors at
the Institute, the same air of learned superiority.

Or did he?

He's like a mirror, Afrika would have said. She could
see him in her mind's eye, standing beside her, regarding
the Professor with a stoic expression. *He's cold glass,
Siggy, a mirror. He reflects stuff back at you, whatever
you think you're going to see.*

What would I see if I had no expectations at all? wondered Siggy.

But that was a hard question to answer; even standing
just a few feet from him, staring openly, clutching her
mop as if it were the rudder that would steer her out of
there. The Professor stared right back at her, not even

blinking as far as she could tell. Unless he was blinking
at the same exact moment she was.

He was a pale-skinned man, maybe forty years old.
Or maybe thirty, or fifty. He might have been Siggy's
height, or taller, or shorter. His hair was cut close to
his scalp, so she couldn't really tell what color it was.
His eyes . . .

Maybe they were mirrors, too. Right now they were
gray, like Siggy's.

"What's your real name?" she asked him.

"Do you think I would tell you just because this is
your last day?" he replied.

"I thought it was worth a try," said Siggy.

"Perhaps it was. Are you going back to your home
world now? To Veil?"

"Yes," she said.

"Don't fall into a Time Pocket."

Siggy almost laughed. That remark wouldn't make
sense to anyone but her. The doctors might spend
months trying to unravel what it meant, never realizing
how straightforward it really was. *Don't fall into a Time
Pocket.* Literally. Siggy had known someone who had
done that, long ago. . . .

She pushed the bucket to within a few feet from the
wall. The Professor was still staring. She used the
wringer to squeeze the mop almost dry, then regarded
the corners. The Director was gone now, he couldn't
send her back to do the job over again. She gave the
corners a perfunctory swipe, then swished the mop over
the already-clean floor. If she kept up this way, she
would be done with the hall in minutes.

"You can't imagine how startling it was to see you for
the first time," said the Professor, his tone indicating
neither startlement nor wonder. Siggy kept mopping, but
she couldn't help being careful. She was slowing down.

"You're quite beautiful," he said. "Or you ought to
be. Those gray eyes, in such a brown face. That white
hair. You look like an elf. Not one of those foolish fan-
tasy elves; the real thing, a wood sprite. One of the *huldrefolk,* that's what your ancestors would have called
them, the *hidden folk.* Separated from the ordinary

world by the thinnest of veils—so isn't your home world well named, Siggy?"

She didn't answer.

"Those Time Pockets you told me about—they go with elves, you know. You walk around an elf hill, and by the time you've found your way home again, a hundred years have passed."

"Nobody believes in the Time Pockets except me," said Siggy, then wondered why she spoke at all. The Director was gone, he couldn't blackmail her anymore.

It's very helpful to us when you talk to them, he had said. *They won't talk to doctors, but you plain folk don't threaten them. They know you're not educated, so you can't analyze them. They can't use your personal information against you, because you don't have the keys to their cells. But they'll reveal things about themselves in their interactions with you. You can help us so much, Lindquist. I do hope you will.*

Because if she wouldn't, he would keep sending her back again, to mop over, and over, and over. Or he would mark UNSATISFACTORY on her work report when she quit and tried to find another job, so she wouldn't stand a chance against the hundreds of other people trying for the same job.

Or he would make her watch the mini-disc again. The "special materials," with the police footage of the Professor's crime scenes, and the excerpts from Jerry Wolfe's home movies. Not that she needed to see it again. It was burned into her memory, every dreadful, pathetic moment of it. And now that Wolfe was loose, perhaps he would make another home movie.

"Jerry's dead," said the Professor. "Found burned alive on Tantalus. Did you hear?"

He had guessed what she was thinking. She could fool others, but never him. He had studied her too closely over the past seven years. He could see her thoughts swimming beneath the surface of her face like goldfish in a crystal pond.

"Just think," said the Professor, "if he had turned left instead of right, he could have ended up on your home world. On Veil. Perhaps he even stopped there briefly, on his way to Enigma."

Almost certainly, in fact. Veil was closer to Enigma than any other system, only three light years away. The Veil System formed from matter thrown out of Enigma billions of years before. Tantalus was ten thousand light years from human space; you couldn't get there anyway else but through the Enigma Fold, and you didn't go to Enigma from this sector without passing through the Veil System first. Period.

"I didn't hear," she said.

"Don't worry, he won't get any of your relatives. Someone used a plasma weapon on him. It destroyed the entire apartment. By the time they had put the fire out, there was only a bit of melted matter for them to identify."

Siggy stopped mopping and looked him right in the eye. "In other words," she said, "it wasn't him. It was some poor slob he killed in order to fake his own death."

Gray eyes looking back at her. Mirrors. "Do you really think so?" he asked.

Siggy started mopping again. The cleaning solution dried just as soon as you laid it down, so it was hard to tell what you had already done. Normally, she would have moved up two steps and re-done some of it, so she wouldn't miss any, so the Director wouldn't make her start over.

But he was gone, so she just guessed.

"How do you know he was found dead?" she asked the Professor. "Who told you?"

"My doctor," he said.

There had been something this time, almost a hint in his tone. Confidence? Triumph? Sleazy implication?

When Siggy turned in her resignation, she had tried to warn the doctors about the Professor. She hadn't tried to warn the Director, because he made sure he wasn't on the premises the day Afrika was killed; and he had stayed away once the news reached him, finally tendering his resignation from an extradition-unfriendly zone. Siggy hoped that since the staff doctors were no longer under the thumb of the Director, they might listen to her warnings about the Professor. It had gone pretty well until she told them he wasn't insane.

They patted her on the head. They waved their diplomas under her nose and told her everything would be all right.

So now he had apparently seduced one of them into getting him news from Outside. Strictly forbidden; the Director had controlled communication much more carefully. Information was the Professor's best weapon.

"You'll be back on Veil in time to celebrate Christmas," said the Professor. "You must be happy. All of those songs you like so much. I can see you now, going from door to door, singing your carols."

"Yes," murmured Siggy.

"Has anyone ever murdered Christmas carolers on Veil?" he asked. "Has anyone ever bashed their heads in and put them into trash compactors, and stuffed their bodies into tiny little Christmas packages?"

"No," said Siggy.

"Good. I would hate for someone to steal my idea."

"I don't think you have to worry about that."

Siggy was almost out of his sight. He was standing at the far edge of his cell, straining to see her. But she would still be able to hear him, even at the security lock.

"I hope you won't disappear, once you get back home," he said.

That could have been a threat. And the business about murdering carolers on Veil. She hoped the doctors were paying attention.

"I'm sure you're right about those Time Pockets," he called. She glanced back up the row at him. He had pressed himself into the sliver of space through which he could still see her. He looked as if he ought to have been stretched into the space, like people in old movies when they took the fifty millimeter image at the very end of the film and squashed it into thirty-five.

"People disappear into them," he said. "Your world isn't the only place where that's happened."

Siggy wished she hadn't told him anything about it. About the Lost Boy, whom only she remembered; or the Lost Fleet, whom everyone had good reason to remember each time one of the Speedy warships suddenly dropped out of jump-time and attacked her home world. Warships that had disappeared over a hundred years ago, in a war that was supposed to be long over. Siggy was only eighteen years old when she arrived on Agate to work at the Institute. She had been so full of her own strange past.

And the Professor had a way of getting information out of you.

"You have to go home, Siggy," said the Professor. "That's the only way it's ever going to make sense to you. Any of it."

And why should he care? There was some reason, she just wouldn't know what it was until it was too late.

That's the only way it's ever going to make sense to you. Afrika's death. The awful mini-disc, the weeping and the screams.

The Lost Fleet, who might even make an appearance for Siggy's Christmas. She could be blown to smithereens for New Year's.

"If you see the Lost Boy again," said the Professor, "tell him I said hello."

Siggy was glad, for once, that her Lost Boy really was lost. He was somewhere creatures like the Professor could never get at him, hovering at the edge of time, watching her, staying fifteen while she got older. If she could see him now she would warn him, "Stay away! Go back into your Time Pocket! It's not safe out here!"

"Good-bye," she told the Professor.

"Until we meet again," he promised, and smiled a cold and utterly sincere smile.

Siggy backed out of his line of vision. The other inmates had finally worked up the energy to assail her with a few choice words; one of them even rushed the barrier as if he had forgotten it was there. The officer opaqued it. He shut out the sound too, so Siggy didn't know if the inmate had slammed into it. The Toady had liked to watch the inmates crash into the barrier. He had liked to see if their remarks could make Siggy cry.

He died a Toady, Afrika would have said. *That's punishment enough.*

Siggy mopped the last few feet and signaled the officer. He opened the door and she stepped into the lock. She didn't even take a last look down Monster Row. The door hissed shut behind her.

Safe now, Siggy gave her head a good, hard rub. When she was done, she asked the officer, "Is it true, what he said about Jerry Wolfe?"

"Yes," he admitted. "You didn't know?"

"I haven't been watching the news." She ruffled her hair once more, for good measure. "So one of the doctors has been shooting his mouth off."

"Hers."

Siggy looked at the monitor. The Professor was standing perfectly still, looking right at the security camera.

"Don't let their stupidity get you killed, too," she told the officer.

"Don't worry, sweetheart, I won't," he said, emphatically. He looked away from the monitor and extended his hand. Siggy clasped it. "Take care," he said. "Write to us sometime, will you?"

"I will," said Siggy, but realized she didn't know his name. She had only met him two weeks before, and by then she wasn't taking in those sorts of details. She wasn't trying to make friends with people anymore. Friends only turned around and got themselves killed. Or they disappeared into Time Pockets, or waltzed away with strangers, and you never saw them again.

The officer turned back to the monitor. Siggy looked, too. The Professor had moved. As if he had known they had looked away for a second. But how could he have known?

It's not your problem anymore, Afrika would have said. He would have put his arm around her shoulders and walked her down to the cafeteria, where he and her other friends would have joked with her until she felt better, until she believed she could stick it out maybe one more day. But now he was gone.

Siggy pushed her mop and bucket out of the other side of the security lock and into the maintenance hall to the equipment room, where she dumped the cleaning fluid and hung the mop up. She closed and locked the door behind her, then proceeded down the hall to the second security lock, past the transparencies and the rooms full of equipment that had done absolutely nothing to stop Jerry Wolfe when he sauntered down this same hall himself. In a way, that was the Toady's fault. Jerry Wolfe was wearing the Toady's uniform when he came out of the security lock. Everyone hated the Toady, so no one could stand to look at him very long. Jerry Wolfe had been about the same height and weight as him, with the same color hair.

Siggy didn't look through the transparencies at the new officers. Two now; they had doubled all the maximum security posts. Siggy didn't want to get to know the new faces. She stood in front of the outer security lock and pressed her ID against the little screen.

The door slid open, and she was scanned. That was new, too. Before, they had only scanned you going *in*.

"Confirmed," said the new officers. They let Siggy into the lock, then let her out the other end, into the elevator. She rode up, for the last time. The door opened and let her out onto the main drag, a vast, echoing place of antiseptic smells, polished metal, and security cameras.

Siggy had already said her good-byes to those who cared. She made her way through the main security checkpoints. Everyone knew her by sight, but they checked her ID carefully anyway. Things had tightened up since Jerry Wolfe had managed to breeze his way through four checkpoints with the ID of a dead man.

Siggy went to the little storage room off the initial checkpoint, near the front entrance, where they were letting her keep her suitcases. She hadn't wanted to go back to her apartment again. The one Afrika had secured for her, the one across from his own family's. The one with the shared courtyard that they all helped decorate every year for Christmas and Halloween.

She walked out the heavy front doors and climbed out of the bunker that housed the Institute for the Criminally Insane, up the steps that had been carved out of the hard rock that was so plentiful all over Agate. The magnificent light of the sunset on Crazy Horse Mountain didn't snare her attention for long as she walked to the nearest transit stop. The transit would take her directly to the starport, to the ship that would take her home to Veil.

I'll never come back here, she told the shadow of Afrika, who walked beside her.

And then she was gone, too.

When Siggy was seven, she and her mother turned six pumpkins into Jack-o-lanterns for *Los Dias De Los Muertos* and Halloween. They would carry the two best ones to the graveyard to show Siggy's dad on the first day, and they would take him Halloween candy on the second. Siggy was sure her dad missed Halloween candy most of all. She certainly would have, if she had been the one who was dead.

Halloween was on the third night. On Halloween, Siggy and the other kids would dress up in costumes. The grown-ups would decorate their houses to look haunted, with cobwebs, skeletons, bats, make-believe graveyards, sound effects, boiling potions and black cats, competing to see who could do the best haunted house and giving candy and prizes to the kids who rushed from place to place.

Siggy's mom was going to be a black cat this year, with pointy ears, and whiskers and a long tail. Siggy wanted to be a mummy. She stopped drawing for a moment and glanced at her mom, who was bent over the pumpkins and carving away, her white hair trying to escape from her braids.

"Make the eyes real big," Mom said, "so Dad can see the candlelight shining inside them."

Siggy regarded the eyes she had just drawn. She decided they probably weren't big enough, so she drew bigger eyes around them. She liked *Los Dias* and Halloween the best of all, maybe even better than Christmas and Chanukkah, definitely better than Easter, Passover, Carnival, Midsummer, or even Walpurgis Night. Siggy's dad had felt the same way; Mom had carved his favorite Halloween poem on his gravestone. Lots of people had

Halloween messages on their gravestones. It was the one holiday that was as much fun for the dead as it was for the living.

Siggy finished drawing the face on the last pumpkin. It had big eyes (now), with eyeballs at the very top, as if it were seeing something scary in the sky. Mom had only finished the third pumpkin, but as soon as they were all done, Siggy was going to put candles in them. Then she would run up the hill and around the corner to Maxi's house, to fetch him back so he could see them too. Maxi was her best friend; they were in the same second grade class. He loved Jack-o-lanterns and Halloween candy too, so they had a lot in common.

"Pumpkin Number Four coming up," said Mom. "Almost there, Siggy. I'll bet we win a prize for these!"

Tomorrow it all started. It was just beginning to get cold in Red Cliffs; not so cold that you wished for spring, but cold enough so you would feel comfortable when you were running around in your costume. And both of the big moons were going to be almost totally full! How perfect could you get?

Siggy watched Mom for a while, but that just made her feel impatient. She wanted to ask for a sharp knife so she could help, but Mom had already said no to that (twice). So Siggy pulled a chair up to the kitchen window while Mom finished up the last two pumpkins. Four candy skulls grinned at her from the blue windowsill, with their names piped on them: Siggy, Marta, Kyle (for Dad's grave), and even one for Maxi. Siggy considered eating Maxi's skull, since he already had one at home.

The wind was blowing outside, making all of the chimes on the porch tinkle. Some of the leaves had already turned red or gold, brown or velvety gray. Siggy watched them dancing in wind whirlpools, like the way she and Maxi loved to waltz in dance class, or to polka— or even tango, though they weren't very good at that one yet. She glanced back at Mom, saw orange spotting the smooth brown of her cheeks.

"You've got pumpkin on your face," Siggy warned.

Mom laughed. "Of course it's on my face. And in my hair, and all over my hands! When we make pumpkin pies, I'm going to use the canned stuff."

Siggy turned back to the window and watched the mist creeping over the red mountains. It was boiling up in all the nooks and crannies; by evening it would spill out and drift down to Siggy's street, curling around the houses and trees, following all of the little streams and brooks that irrigated the fields and the terraced gardens. But the mist wouldn't be really thick until dawn. Most nights you could see all the way up the street. You could look up and see the light from the Enigma Nebula, glowing across the sky.

"Is it going to rain?" asked Siggy's mom.

Siggy peered up through the trees and the flowering vines. Fat clouds with black bottoms were drifting in a turquoise sky. Siggy opened the window and took a deep sniff.

"Yep," she said.

"Oh, that smells good," said Mom. "Better than raw pumpkin, that's for sure. After supper we'll make sugar cookies, and we'll decorate them with orange and black—"

A sound cut through Mom's words. Siggy cocked her head. It grew louder; rising, falling, then rising again.

"Mom," she said, "is that—?"

Mom dropped her knife. She jumped across the room faster than a ship jumping across the Enigma Fold, scooped Siggy off the chair and ran with her to the stairwell. She wasn't laughing anymore, and her brown skin had gone pale underneath. She dragged Siggy down the cellar steps, wrenched open the heavy door and kicked it shut behind them.

It was pitch dark down there. Siggy could hear her mom panting as she fumbled for the light button.

"Are the Speedies coming again, Mom?" Siggy asked, her throat tight with awe and terror.

"Yes, honey." Mom found the light button. Siggy blinked, and breathed a sigh of relief. The cellar was a nice place, clean and cozy, with a TV set, bookshelves, a roll-away bed, a couch, even a refrigerator and cooking unit. Mom put Siggy on the couch and turned on the TV.

Mom flipped through the first few hundred channels, but they all showed the same thing: a pattern that said TAKE COVER on it, with a countdown at the bottom.

Siggy read the countdown at 00:19:31, but the last two numbers kept getting smaller, and then they would start over at fifty-nine again.

"This is the real thing," said Mom. She sat down with Siggy and stared at the countdown. "We're pretty safe down here. We've got solid rock over our heads. They usually don't fire at civilian areas."

"Are they coming out of jump-time?" asked Siggy, feeling a little braver now that the lights were on.

"Probably just a few ships," said Mom. "Hopefully not too many."

Siggy sneaked a peek at her. Mom's face was calm again. Siggy wondered if she was thinking about the last time the Speedies had come out of jump-time, five years ago. When Daddy got killed. Daddy hadn't even been on Veil, he had been in orbit, on the communications array.

Something trembled under their feet, like an earthquake.

"Damn," said Mom. "God damn it."

Mom *never* cursed.

And then Mom started praying. She closed her eyes, and her lips moved, but she didn't fold her hands, she never did that. Siggy didn't either, as she prayed, too.

Stay away from us, she begged the Speedies. *Stay away from Maxi's house, and the school, and Dad's graveyard, and Mrs. Nielsen's house . . .*

The list went on and on, and the countdown got smaller and smaller. Eventually the numbers said 00:00:00. There was a *BLIP!* from the TV, and a reporter appeared on the screen. Siggy and her mom stopped praying.

"Good afternoon," said the man on the TV. "This is Oscar del Torro reporting from the VBS studio on the orbital array. No part of the array has been hit by enemy fire, repeat; we have *not* been hit by enemy fire during this latest attack by the Lost Speedy Fleet—however, there has been one direct hit on the surface, this one, sadly, in our world's capital, Desert Center."

Mom gasped. "Desert Center is one thousand miles away! And we *still* felt the impact."

The scene shifted to a view of the largest continental

mass, Prima. Siggy could see a large city with a scorch mark in the middle of it.

"The good news," said the reporter, in voice-over, "is that the casualties appear to be surprisingly low, with only three confirmed deaths so far, twenty-seven people still missing. This is our lowest death toll within the last hundred years, and a large part of the credit must certainly go to the city planners who moved the starport and other potential targets decades ago. As you know, the intelligence the Lost Fleet must have about our world is over a hundred years old; each time they strike the wrong areas, it confirms the assertion of the current Speedy government that the Lost Fleet really is lost, somehow, in jump-time."

Mom was leaning forward, engrossed; but Siggy was having trouble keeping up. She knew that stuff had been moved so the Speedies wouldn't shoot at it. She knew that no new stuff had been built where the old stuff used to be, so that was probably why hardly anyone got killed. She also knew that some people didn't believe the Lost Fleet was lost; people like Fredrick's dad, who said it was all a Speedy plot to attack humans without getting blamed for it.

"Mom, can I call Maxi?" she asked.

"Shh—" Mom was trying to listen to the news. The picture on the TV had changed to a man who was standing in front of a huge, smoking crater.

"—still so hot we can hardly stand here, and we're half a mile away from the edge—" he was saying, and there were all sorts of people in danger suits running around behind him, hover-ships in the air, ambulances and fire-sirens. Siggy sat back and let it all rush over her. She wasn't scared anymore. The Speedy ships had been destroyed, because the human ships outnumbered them, and now human computers were almost fast enough to make up for the difference between slow human reflexes and super-fast Speedy ones. She had learned all that in school.

The pictures continued to flicker on the screen, and now Siggy could see one of the Speedy warships. Only parts of it were left.

"Are they all dead?" she asked her mom, suddenly sorry for the Speedies.

"No honey, they said there's some survivors."

"Will they be mad at us?"

"I don't know," Mom said, slowly. "We still don't know very much about them, honey. Hold on, the man is talking about it . . ." Mom listened while the reporter used grown-up words Siggy didn't understand.

"Our government convinced them that the war is over," said Mom. "They beamed them a copy of the Treaty. That's what they always do. I guess it takes the Speedies a little time to analyze it, maybe two minutes. But the Speedies can do a lot of damage in two minutes."

There was a catch in Mom's voice, and Siggy thought about Dad again. Just a few minutes was all it took, and the people you loved most in the whole universe were gone forever.

"Mom, can I call Maxi's house?"

"You can try, but the channels might be tied up."

Siggy ran up the stairs. The pumpkins were still waiting on the table, grimacing and looking up at the sky as if they were afraid the Speedies were going to rain down more fire. Siggy ran to the phone and punched Maxi's number.

Nothing happened.

Siggy ran to the front door and threw it open. The rain was advancing in a solid curtain, eating up Siggy's town block by block. If she hurried, she could get to Maxi's house without getting wet.

Mom hadn't said she could go out yet. But they weren't doing the TAKE COVER on TV anymore, the sirens were gone. And Maxi was her best friend, and who knew if the Speedies had dropped some *little* bombs somewhere, some Maxi-sized ones? Siggy didn't even have time to grab her rain slicker, not if she was going to hurry. Was that Mom's footsteps on the stairs?

Siggy ran out the door and up her street. Sprinkles fell on her, the advance guard of the storm. She ran as hard as she could, as if beating the rain were suddenly the most important thing in the whole universe. Beat the rain, and Maxi will be all right, and the Speedies will read the Treaty, and they won't be lost anymore. Up to the top of the hill and around the corner, and Maxi's house would be the fourth one on the right.

Siggy started to climb the hill, but fell to her knees when the sidewalk twisted and wrenched sideways beneath her. She opened her mouth to scream, thinking another Speedy bomb had fallen. But there was no explosion, and the ground was still moving like a living thing. It curled around and up, then upside down; then around and over again, finally veering sharply to the left, where the street came to rest on its side. Siggy threw herself down and tried to cling to the sidewalk with her fingernails. It was as if someone had taken the world and wrung it like a wet rag; yet gravity still held her fast. Rain started to pour on her feet.

Siggy covered her head with her arms and stayed down. Her feet were getting soaked, but the rain didn't come any further; it had stopped at her ankles. And she wasn't falling sideways.

She peeked through her fingers. The street continued to twist around until it was upside down, and then it seemed to bend back toward where she was. She couldn't make any sense of it.

"Siggy!" someone was calling, from a distance. "Hey, Lindquist!"

It was a boy. Not Maxi; a teenager. He was crawling up the twisted street toward Siggy.

"Don't move!" he called.

Siggy stayed still. She looked at the boy, since nothing else seemed to make sense. In another moment she recognized him, and her heart began to pound. It was David Silverstein, the most handsome boy in the whole town. He was wearing his ROTC uniform. He was going to be a starman, everybody said so. Sometimes Siggy and the other girls would call to him and wave when he and his friends walked by, and sometimes he would even wave back. And he knew her name! He was coming to save her from . . . whatever the heck she had fallen into. Whatever the heck was twisting the street around.

Siggy kept her eyes on him. She waved, and he kept coming. Sometimes he was walking upside down, and sometimes he was walking sideways, but he never fell off.

And suddenly Siggy realized something. He wasn't rescuing her. He was coming *out* of the twisted place, *she* was the one who was at the very edge of it. She was the one who was rescuing him. He needed her to show him where to go.

"Over here!" she called, waving her arms as well as she could from her prone position. He saw her. He kept coming.

But somehow, he didn't get any closer.

The rain started to move up Siggy's legs. David was going farther away.

"This way!" she screamed. "Over here!"

She watched the sidewalk straighten itself out. It flowed back into its normal lines, and David Silverstein went away into infinity. He was gone, and she was on Maxi's street again.

Siggy got up. She didn't try to run anymore, she was already soaked. She went around the corner, back down her own street. She climbed up onto the lawns, peeked around the trees. She looked down Maxi's street, then ran a short distance along the lane that crossed and went down the other side of the hill. The streets didn't twist upside-down; everything was like it was supposed to be, only wetter.

"David!" she called. "Hello! Where did you go?" She wanted to go tell Maxi what had happened, but she knew something had happened to David. He hadn't come out of the twisted place. Where had he gone? Who would help him now?

She knew where he lived. It was a long way to go for a little kid, her mom wouldn't like her to do it. But David Silverstein was lost, and Siggy was the only one who knew it.

The rain was coming down so hard Siggy could hardly see. Her hair had mostly come out of her braids by then, and was sticking to her face. It didn't usually rain that hard. Maybe the sky had been twisted out of shape, too. Maybe the oceans were up there now, and they were falling down.

Siggy tried to run, but she fell down twice, hurting her

knees even more. After that she just plodded along, hoping she was going in the right direction. She and her girlfriends had followed David Silverstein to his block once, giggling behind their hands and trying to act like they didn't even know how handsome he was.

Siggy was crying; her knees really ached. But she marched up David's street and found his house, the big one with the fancy trimming and the great big picture window. At Christmas time, the Silversteins put their Christmas tree in that window, even though they were Jewish, decorating it with lights that made it glow like a fairy tree. Siggy and her mom always drove by and admired it, but Siggy had never gotten any closer than that. She had never gone up the front walk, through the little white gate and past the perfect rows of flowers.

Maybe David had found his way home already. . . .

No. Siggy knew it in her bones. He would never see his mom again.

That thought made Siggy cry even harder. What would his mom think when she knocked on the door, looking like that? Siggy didn't know, but she knocked on the door anyway.

It took a long time for anyone to answer. Siggy could hear the TV on inside. They were probably watching the news about the Speedy attack. Siggy knocked harder, and finally David Silverstein's mom opened the door. She was a plump, pretty woman with gray in her hair. She peered out at Siggy.

"Are you all right, dear?" asked David's mom. "Did you get lost during the air raid?"

Siggy swallowed, hard. She meant to tell David's mom what had happened to him, but her courage had evaporated. No one ever believed Siggy when she had strange things to tell them. So instead she asked, "Is David home?"

"Who?" asked David's mom.

Siggy shivered in the rain. "Your son," she said.

David's mom was frowning. She was standing on a highly polished wooden floor, and Siggy could see past her into a house full of beautiful furniture. It was just the sort of house you would expect David Silverstein to live in, the straight-A student who was in ROTC, who was going to go to the orbital military academy and become a starman.

"You have the wrong address little girl," said David's mom. "My son is named Barry. He doesn't live here now, he's away at college. Are you lost? Do you want me to call your mother?"

"No," said Siggy, ready to cry again, suddenly just wanting to get away. "I live around the corner. I'd better go home. Sorry." She turned and ran back down the front walk, past the flowers and out the little white gate.

"Wait!" David's mom was calling.

"Sorry!" Siggy called back, and ran away.

It wasn't raining so hard now. Siggy slipped a few times on her way to Maxi's house, but she didn't fall again. A feeling of tragedy had ballooned inside her. She tried to imagine what she would say to people about what had happened, but she couldn't think up anything that made sense.

When she saw Maxi's house, she slowed to a walk. She wondered if she looked ugly now, all bruised. Puffy from crying, with her braids undone. She liked to look pretty when Maxi saw her. She didn't used to care about that, but lately, in dance class, she had started to think of him as her partner. Maybe even, sort of—her boyfriend. She wouldn't say it aloud, but she thought it.

She knocked on his door. She heard someone running to open it.

"Mom," Maxi was calling from the other side of the door, "I bet that's Siggy!" And he wrenched the door open, just as he said her name. His brown eyes widened, and he grabbed her hands. "It is Siggy! Mom, Siggy is hurt!"

Maxi pulled her into the warm house, and she gazed at his handsome face, his brown-sugar skin and his glossy black hair. His eyes shined when he saw that she had been crying. Maxi's mom came and took them into the kitchen, where it smelled like cookies and there was one grinning Jack-o-lantern on the kitchen table. Maxi's mom got out her first-aid kit, and she patched Siggy's knees. Maxi started making hot cocoa for her.

"I fell in the rain," said Siggy. "When the street got all twisted up."

Maxi's mom didn't ask what she meant by that.

"The street got twisted," said Siggy, "and David Sil-verstein couldn't get up to where I was. He tried and tried, but he just got farther away. And then the rain came, and he was gone. Remember David Silverstein, Mrs. Fergussen?"

"Who?" she asked.

"Maxi," Siggy said, desperately, "remember David, the ROTC guy? Remember how he always wears his uniform, and we said we wished we could wear one like that?"

"I'm going to be in ROTC!" announced Maxi, spilling cocoa all over the counter.

"David Silverstein," said Siggy. "Remember?"

"No," said Maxi.

"Son!" said Maxi's mom. "You're making a mess! And you turned on the wrong burner."

"I can do it!" he insisted, spilling the milk.

Siggy sat still, watching them clean up the mess. She knew what had happened. David Silverstein hadn't just disappeared from the world. He had disappeared from people's memories, too. Siggy was the only one in the whole universe who remembered, because half of her had been stuck in the twisted place. Her feet had been in the real world, or she would have been swallowed, too. She would have been lost with David.

It all made perfect sense. If only she could tell people about it.

"It looked like a pocket," she told Maxi's mom. "Like a pocket that's been pulled inside out and twisted around."

"What did, dear?" asked Maxi's mom.

But Siggy didn't try to explain. Not yet.

Not for another seven years.

When Siggy was fourteen, Enigma shifted gears again.

Its cycles weren't apparently regular—not as far as anyone's supercomputer could determine—but they were always dramatic. It shifted back and forth between two states: Either it was spitting matter out, or it was eating it. When Siggy was fourteen, Enigma got hungry again.

Astronomers knew that Enigma had been doing what it did for at least ten billion years, because that's how old some of the matter in the Veil System was. There were three other (known) hub systems, each with its own version of Enigma; but Veil-Enigma was the only one that put on a light show. During a spitting phase you could see a steady stream of super-hot material flowing like a river through the nebula; but not *exploding* into it, like it would if Enigma were a quasar or a nova-phase neutron star. Most of the nearby systems had formed or were still forming from that river of matter, the vast clouds of asteroids that fueled the mining industry in the Veil System were Enigma flotsam.

Human astronomers had observed seventeen shifts since the discovery of the Enigma Fold; the last spitting phase had lasted seventeen years. The one before it had lasted 147. Astronomers saw the beginning of the new eating shift when they saw a plume of matter beginning to stretch out of Veil-Enigma's G-star companion. Within the hour, Enigma was in the news and Siggy's science teacher was in heaven.

"We can observe what Enigma *does*," she told all of her classes. "But so far, no one can figure out what Enigma *is*. The most popular theory is that it's a super-massive object, but it doesn't behave like any of the solar objects we've ever observed. For instance, if it's so massive, it should have devastating tidal effects on any object that approaches it too closely. Ships would be pulled apart by those tidal effects when they crossed the event horizon.

"But no one has ever gotten close enough to Enigma to feel any tidal effects at all. No matter how you approach Enigma, you always jump somewhere before you get near it. Only Veil-Enigma's G-star companion ever feels those tidal effects, because it sits at the event horizon, well beyond the jump point.

"We're not even really sure exactly *where* Enigma is. Ships can jump through the Enigma Fold approximately three light years from our relative position; but they can also jump across the fold fourteen light years from Tantalus, and that system is ten *thousand* light years from us."

"Excuse me, Mrs. Heyerdahl—" said Jorge La Placa, the smartest kid in Siggy's class, "but that's an oversimplification of the situation. The truth is, we still haven't mapped all of Veil-Enigma's jump points. You can reach four hundred twenty-six different star systems from our relative position, depending on your angle of entry, and we're *still* discovering new ones. It's so complex that humans and Speedies were both using Enigma for a couple hundred years before we accidentally encountered each other. That's why I think Enigma isn't a massive object at all; at least not a naturally occurring one. I think it's a Tipler transporter."

No one in the room was surprised to hear the name *Tipler.* With Enigma so close, and the Lost Fleet an ever-present threat, Physicists were as well known on Veil as movie stars were everywhere else.

"Right," said Mrs. Heyerdahl, "that's one of the more interesting theories. Did some ancient race build a stardrive device, a machine that warps space so ships can jump across an artificially created fold to destinations thousands of light years away? Lots of science fiction writers love that idea, but can anyone besides Jorge tell me what's wrong with it? What's the biggest flaw in logic?"

That was another easy one, so Siggy raised her hand.

"Enigma is so many billions of years old," she said. "Organic life probably hadn't had time to evolve when it would have to have been built, so no one would have been around to build it."

"No one from this universe," said Jorge, enigmatically.

Siggy got a chill up her spine, but it was a pleasant one.

Most other kids just wanted to know one thing about Enigma: "Will it eat *us*?"

"No," said Mrs. Heyerdahl. "It wouldn't do that even if it were a black hole. We're well outside its event horizon, so we can't get pulled in. But here's what's really interesting about Enigma: The matter it's spitting out doesn't just come from its companion star. That star is only four-and-a-half billion years old. So where did the older matter come from? And why do the spitting phases last so long? And why aren't they nova-like; why do they occur as a steady stream rather than as brief, massive explosions? Any theories?"

Jorge had plenty of theories. Some of the other smart kids in class had them, too. But Siggy had her own theories about Enigma. She didn't tell the science teacher about them.

Instead she told Maxi, in dance class.

"I'll bet the Time Pockets have something to do with Enigma," she said.

"The *what*?" he replied, as he expertly waltzed her around the room. She had to crane her neck to look up at him; he was already six feet tall.

"The Time Pockets," said Siggy. "You know, the thing that David Silverstein disappeared into."

"Who?" said Maxi.

Siggy sighed. No one except her could remember that name, no matter how many times she repeated it. "The Lost Boy," she said.

"Oh yeah." Maxi thought her theory was a good one—when he remembered it. Siggy had tried it out on a few others: teachers, her mom, the mayor of Red Cliffs. Their reactions ranged from amusement to mild concern. After all, Siggy had been seven when she had seen the street twisting up and taking David Silverstein away with it. Seven was a good age for hallucinations.

Siggy's Time Pockets were viewed in the same light as the monster under the bed and the thing in the closet. Even Siggy had begun to wonder if she had dreamed the whole thing up.

Until she found the proof.

It wasn't even that hard to find. David Silverstein had been a star athlete, he had been in ROTC and had won academic awards. There were pictures of him in the school yearbooks. Siggy had looked him up in the database at the school library and made hard copies of every page that mentioned him.

She presented the copies to her mother. "See?" she asked triumphantly.

Siggy's mom had glanced at the photos.

"See *what*?" she asked.

"The Lost Boy! That's him! He really does exist."

"Ohhh," said Siggy's mom, as if she really did see, but Siggy could tell that her mom wasn't even sure what she was talking about. She didn't remember that the Lost Boy had ever existed. And every time Siggy used the words *Time Pockets* she got that same puzzled look from Mom. From *everyone*.

Siggy tucked the printouts into a scrapbook she had labeled: THE TRUTH ABOUT DAVID SILVERSTEIN. Then she went to the library and started digging through old newspaper articles. She started looking eight years back, and she struck gold.

She found three articles, not just about David, but about his whole family. His father was an important physicist, his mother had nearly won a Nobel prize for microbiology. His brother Barry had been awarded a scholarship to Oxford—on old Earth!—and David Silverstein had been equally promising. Before he had disappeared, he had been rated among the top ten students in the whole *system*.

Siggy made hard copies of the articles and stuck them in her backpack. She had no idea what she was going to do with them, but she looked at the scrapbook every night, to remind herself of what had happened. If one guy could fall into a Time Pocket, why couldn't someone else? Who was to say that other people hadn't been falling into them all along?

Who was to say the Lost Fleet hadn't? That's what she asked Maxi in dance class.

"Wait a minute," he said. "I *remember* the Lost Fleet. You said people who fall into Time Pockets are forgotten."

"I haven't forgotten David Silverstein," said Siggy. "And you *can't* forget the Lost Fleet. They keep coming out again and shooting at us! That's how I know that the Pockets are pockets in time, because the Lost Fleet doesn't know one hundred years have gone by."

"Yeah, but—" said Maxi, stumbling as he tried to think his way around her argument, "I mean, shouldn't all the ships come out at once, if they all went in at once?"

"I don't know," said Siggy. "But nobody knows why Enigma does what it does, either. Or why it *doesn't* do what it *ought* to do."

No one could have argued with that. Thousands of ships jumped through the Fold every month, whether Enigma was eating or spewing, and no one knew why the shift never seemed to affect traffic. You could look up into the sky every night and see the glowing nebula outside Enigma's event horizon, but you could never see Enigma itself. You couldn't see if it was a sun, or a quasar, or even a big, mysterious gizmo built by a long-dead race; you couldn't get any data from inside that event horizon at all, no matter how much energy you expended.

"Maybe Enigma is a giant Time Pocket," mused Siggy as she and Maxi glided into a tango. "A big version of the little one I saw seven years ago. Like a big tornado that spawns little baby ones in its wake."

"You've lost me now," said Maxi, and Siggy let the subject drop. Maxi tried to understand her because he was her boyfriend. They were going to go to the freshman prom together. He had even given her a promise ring, and everyone knew what that meant.

Maxi didn't really want to talk about Enigma. He was satisfied to let it stay a mystery forever. He wanted to keep doing the tango, knowing full well that everyone was admiring them because they were the best dancers in the class, maybe even in the whole school.

Siggy gazed up at him and was suddenly so happy it took her breath away. Maxi got more handsome every year. Siggy's girlfriends said that they were a good couple. They looked like they should be standing on top of a wedding cake.

Maxi caught the change in her mood and smiled. Maxi always liked her best when she was happy.

Dance class was their last class of the day; afterward Maxi had football practice. So Siggy kissed him good-bye and watched him until he had disappeared into the boys' locker room, sighing at how straight and tall he was, how broad his shoulders. Then she ran out of the gym, her backpack thumping her shoulder. She hurried down Kay Neilsen Avenue and up the steep hill to Peco Street, feeling triumphant, clever, and privy to great mysteries.

The trees whose tops grew together on Peco Street were laden with gold and red leaves, but they hadn't dropped yet. A cold breeze blew down the street, as if someone had opened a giant door, then closed it again. Some of the leaves blew loose and rained on Siggy. *It's starting,* she thought; then wondered what she had just been thinking. About fall? Fall would always come around, always blow the leaves loose and bite the end of your nose. That wasn't anything bad. She trudged the rest of the way up the hill and started down again, before stopping dead.

She was on Cortez Lane; David Silverstein's street. How had she gotten there? She wasn't even headed in that direction, she had completely circumnavigated her own house. It was supposed to be down this hill and five streets over to Beowulf Road, then down another hill and around . . .

Around . . .

She turned her head painfully, slowly, and looked behind her. The street was curving. It went behind a tree and then disappeared. On the other side of the tree, Siggy could see part of Peco Street. The two were folded together, just like . . .

Like the Enigma Fold.

Siggy didn't move. It couldn't be happening again. Just

because she had been thinking about it? Or because Enigma had suddenly shifted gears again?

If she went into the Pocket, no one would know she was gone.

She must have already gone across it. For some reason, she hadn't fallen *into* it. Maybe that was what usually happened; certainly it was what happened when ships jumped across the Enigma Fold. Or it was what happened until the Speedy Fleet had gotten lost.

Siggy pulled a notebook out of her backpack. She tried to write down exactly what she had seen and suspected. She felt silly doing it; she had no proof of it. But David Silverstein might have been in there. He might still be trying to make his way back to where she was standing. He might . . .

He might! What would Maxi say if she told him? He would say that she had a good imagination. Everyone thought so; it was written on Siggy's evaluation reports from school. *Siggy has a vivid imagination; perhaps a little too vivid? Needs to be encouraged to develop a solid grounding in reality and academics.*

"This is why you're a B student instead of an A," her mother kept reminding her. Siggy supposed that was true. And what Mom said about jobs being scarce on Veil was true, too. The best jobs went to well-connected A students, then everyone else got what was left. By the time you got to the B students, all the good jobs were taken. It didn't matter that the county needed more employees; the government wasn't willing to pay for them. Siggy's mom had explained it to her a thousand times, trying to get her to knuckle down.

It was a good thing that she already knew what her future would be. She was going to marry Maxi and raise a family. Some day she would also prove her theory about the Time Pockets, but that would probably take a while. It might even take her whole life.

"Siggy!" someone called, and she practically jumped out of her skin. Cortez Street was back to normal, the Fold was gone. She turned and saw Mrs. Silverstein.

Guilt rushed over her in a wave. Mrs. Silverstein smiled and waved as she came up the street. She was only wearing a housecoat and was hugging herself to keep warm. "I've lost your number," she said, laughing, "so I had to rush out when I saw you. Are you still cleaning houses in your spare time?"

Actually, Siggy wasn't, but she said, "Yes. Do you need me?"

"We're having a party this Sunday. I thought perhaps Saturday you could come over after temple services . . . ?"

"Sure," said Siggy, fighting to keep the blush from her face.

"About three o'clock?" asked Mrs. Silverstein.

"Sure," Siggy said again, and grinned foolishly.

"All right dear, I'll see you then. I've got to get back inside before my toes freeze!" Mrs. Silverstein hurried back up the street, waving at Siggy over her shoulder. Siggy waved back, then turned and plodded away.

She had wanted to see what the inside of David's house looked like, so she had left a note on Mrs. Silverstein's front door, offering her services as a housekeeper.

It had worked. When Mrs. Silverstein gave her the grand tour of the house, Siggy made admiring comments about how beautiful the antiques were. And when they passed the gallery of photos that you could find in every house on Veil, Siggy had pointed to the ones of David and asked, "Who is that?"

"That's my son, Barry," said Mrs. Silverstein, even though Barry didn't look that much like David. But the photos weren't even the strangest thing. The strangest thing had been the room.

They had passed it in the hall. "Shall I sweep and dust in there?" Siggy asked.

"That's just a closet," said Mrs. Silverstein. "Don't worry about it."

So while Mrs. Silverstein was running an errand to the store, Siggy crept into the "closet." It was David's room. All of his things were still there. His life on hold, with a thick layer of dust over it.

Siggy looked down and saw her own footprints in the dust. They were the only ones. Hadn't anyone even opened the door since he had disappeared? Hadn't they tried to put a coat in the "closet"?

That was when Siggy did something her mother never

would have approved of. She took one of the Awards of Merit down from the wall and tucked it inside her shirt. When Mrs. Silverstein came back from her errands, Siggy was so nervous she could barely keep her hands from trembling.

"You've done a wonderful job!" said Mrs. Silverstein. "I'll call you again, dear."

And every time she did, Siggy felt so guilty about taking the Award of Merit, she knocked herself out doing a great job to make up for it. So Mrs. Silverstein kept calling her. It was a vicious circle.

Siggy stuffed her hands into her coat pockets and marched home, hoping that no more Time Pockets would develop on the way and no more mothers of Lost Boys would pop up to make her feel guilty.

Siggy didn't relax again until she had turned down Indianola Avenue and was climbing the steps to her own front porch and unlocking the door.

"Mom?" she called.

She could hear the sound of the TV coming from the back room. Mom loved to watch the news before supper. Siggy dumped her backpack in a chair and hung her coat up on the rack. She put her galoshes on the hearth to dry. The house felt wonderfully toasty, and smelled like enchiladas.

Exactly what I need after a day like this, thought Siggy. She walked down the hall to the family room, passing their own gallery of photos. Siggy's favorite was her parents' senior prom portrait. She always paused to admire it. Dad was eighteen in that one, and she always pictured him that way, even though he had been twenty-four when he died. He looked so handsome in his suit, his hair cut short, almost military style. She gazed into his smiling gray eyes and said a silent prayer.

". . . remains to be seen," came the voice of the TV reporter from the family room. Siggy went in to see what was up. She had a feeling it would be something about Enigma; that's all they talked about these days.

The reporter was saying, "Traffic parameters for Speedy and Human use of the Enigma Fold were clearly outlined in the Treaty, but many human officials are now openly doubting that the Speedies are sticking to their end of the bargain. This is not necessarily anything new, but for the first time in decades, scientists are publicly voicing their concerns, as well . . ."

Siggy glanced at the handsome young man on the screen, who was sitting at his studio desk with a graphic of the Enigma Nebula behind him.

"Sit down, Siggy," Mom said. "There's something I want you to hear. They mentioned it at the beginning of the program, it should be coming up soon."

"Okay," said Siggy, with a twinge of apprehension. It hadn't been that long ago that Mom would chase her away from the TV when something awful was being reported. Now it was just the opposite. Now she was worried about preparing Siggy for life; and what was worse, she always wanted to discuss things afterward. It wasn't that Siggy minded being included in adult matters, it was just that Mom always seemed to get so worried about things. Siggy hated to worry. She wanted to feel good about stuff, look forward to stuff.

She sat down on her side of the couch. She got a brief shock as she suddenly realized that she and her mom were the same size. When had that happened? They looked like a pair of bookends, especially since Mom had gotten her hair cut almost like Siggy's. The only difference was that Mom's eyes were black.

Just now Mom was frowning at the screen, listening closely even though the reporter was saying things that people on Veil had been talking about for years. Of course people wondered whether the Speedies were honoring the Treaty: The Lost Fleet kept attacking Veil. Despite that, the Speedies refused to put an ambassador on Veil, someone who could instantly negotiate with the attacking ships the moment they dropped out of warp, preventing any further death and destruction.

Siggy wished she could talk to the Speedies herself, tell them about her dad and how much she loved him, how much she and her mother missed him. Didn't they know about stuff like that? Didn't they have families, too?

"We know that the Speedies were mapping the Enigma Fold centuries before we were," someone new was saying on the TV, "probably at least two hundred years before we discovered it by accidentally jumping to Tantalus." The new person was a middle-aged woman with coffee-colored skin and hair cropped close to her skull. Something about her screamed "scientist," and she quickly confirmed Siggy's suspicion.

"To date, we have mapped four hundred twenty-six destinations from the Veil point alone," she said. "Three hundred seventy-eight from Tantalus, one hundred twenty-three from Quetzl, and twenty-seven from Philae. These are the hub systems of human space; jumping from any of those other nine hundred fifty-four systems will take you back to one of those four points, depending on your angle of entry. But by no means do we believe that those four points are the *only* hub points. We have seen too much evidence of Speedy expansion into space far beyond the capability of their star-drive technology, advanced though it is beyond our own—"

"Hold on a second, Dr. Ngoni," interrupted the reporter, his face appearing on the split screen beside hers. "How do we know that this expansion has occurred when we haven't yet expanded that far ourselves?"

"Because," she said, with strained patience, "by the time we get somewhere, they're already there sixty-five percent of the time, and they've already begun development. Often we've discovered evidence that they've been established in systems for decades before the Treaty was signed, yet there's no mention of those systems in any of the appendices of the Treaty. And even when we haven't traveled to various places, we have powerful telescopes that can tell us what's going on there; we can see signs of advanced technology in use, and that technology has the Speedy signature. And remember, what we see in telescopes is pictures of the past, it takes years for the light to reach us. They've gone so much farther than us, yet they won't share information—"

"I have to interrupt you again, doctor," said the reporter. "Our link with the Decider has been set up, and he is willing to respond to some of your issues. Mr. Decider?"

Dr. Ngoni had half a second to look both shocked and

excited, and suddenly the image of a Speedy replaced the reporter on the other side of the screen.

Siggy and her mother gasped.

They had never seen a Speedy in a live broadcast before, let alone one interacting with a human. Only a select few humans ever dealt with Speedies; the peace was too fragile, the interface too precarious to risk misunderstandings. Yet here was a Decider, who had no real equivalent among human beings; a person of such high status that his decisions were instantly accepted by other Speedies, only questioned by other Deciders. That much Siggy and her mother knew, that much had filtered down from human ambassadors.

And even though everyone on Veil had seen photos of Speedies, those static images didn't quite capture the reality. This individual had the characteristic pale skin of his species, and wore a one-piece black garment that hugged his lean, humanoid form. He sat perfectly still, like a statue; the only movement Siggy could detect was the sparkle of iridescent colors across his huge, multi-faceted eyes. His nose and mouth were remarkably human, and it was his mouth that revealed the most emotion. Though Siggy couldn't quite tell what that emotion might be, it was something profound, she was sure of that. But perhaps this impression was based on the fact that the dark, tapered tendrils that grew from his head, sensory apparatuses that combined both smell and hearing, were folded tight against his body.

In attack mode.

It was part of basic history, one of the biggest misunderstandings behind the war, a matter of simple body language. During all of the centuries of human and Speedy space exploration, plenty of other life forms had been discovered, but neither side had encountered *intelligent* life before.

There were two basic differences between Speedies and humans: The first involved the fact that those sensory tendrils on the heads of Speedies expressed a wide range of emotions and intentions. A Speedy who had peaceful intentions would spread his tendrils, allowing them to absorb the maximum range of sensory input, preventing him from banding together with a pack of other Speedies to attack, because the tendrils would literally get in the way of such an action. If violence was intended, Speedy physiology demanded a complete focus of perception into the visual cortex; so those tendrils flattened tight.

Human hair didn't move unless there was a good breeze, it was always inert; and to Speedies, this was as much an implied threat as bared teeth would be to humans.

The second thing compounded the first. The Speedies knew that humans must be put together differently, that their bodies must work differently, just as their minds certainly did. And they knew that their instincts might be misleading them, so they gave the humans time to dispel those first, hostile appearances.

Speedy time. Many times faster than human. So while the humans muddled around in slow motion, making many more blunders in the process, the Speedies waited with growing alarm for some clue about what humans intended, what they *were*.

Siggy knew the story by heart. Speedies existed in a speeded-up universe. The war had started before the humans knew it, but to the Speedies, it had been a long time in coming. It had only ended when cooler minds on both sides had managed to convince enough officials to stop and take a closer, slower look. Then hurrah! The war was over, the Treaty was established, and both sides were moving toward a future of increased communication, commerce, and understanding.

Or were they?

Siggy gazed at the face of the Decider and wondered if she would turn to stone under the glare of those eyes. He had no irises, no pupils, yet she couldn't shake the feeling that he was looking specifically at her, and her heart was pounding, her ears buzzing, it was suddenly hard to breathe. She was scared and mad and sorry and fascinated and—*awed*. Awed because his face commanded respect, admiration; there was intelligence inside that alien mask, superior knowledge, and emotions that you could almost, almost . . .

Doctor Ngoni's eyes had become very bright, but her jaw was firm. She had sat silently, waiting for the Decider's response to her earlier remarks; but he was apparently waiting for her to start the dialogue. Siggy watched her swallow and square her shoulders.

"Mr. Decider," said Dr. Ngoni, "As a scientist, my main concern is *not* the acquisition of territory, or the division of resources, or even the control of traffic through the Enigma Fold. What concerns me first and foremost is the sharing of scientific knowledge. We human scientists have hoped to establish and maintain an open dialogue with your scientific community. Why hasn't this happened?"

The Decider's answer was immediate; he hardly waited for her to finish speaking.

"We have no such community," he snapped. Siggy jerked at the sound of his voice, so harsh and seemingly angry. But his face did not reveal anger, it seemed more as if he were straining to form the words slowly, so they would be coherent to human ears. And his tone was surprisingly low; Siggy had expected it to be high-pitched, like the sound of a speeded-up human voice.

"You have no scientists?" Dr. Ngoni was asking.

"We are scientists," he said, buzzing slightly at the end of the last word.

"*All* of you are?" Ngoni asked, obviously intrigued.

"All have the skills," he replied. "We observe that you specialize much more. Communication is difficult. Knowledge must be earned."

Dr. Ngoni frowned, but seemed determined to carry this rare dialogue as far as she could. "We work very hard to understand the universe," she said. "And to understand *you*. We are capable of cooperation. And enlightenment."

"That is why the Treaty exists," snapped the Decider.

Ngoni nodded. "The war has been over for one hundred years. No one wants it to happen again. The purpose of science is discovery."

Iridescent color flashed across the Decider's eyes, then played over the dark sheen of his flattened head tendrils; and Siggy simultaneously caught sight of a subtle pattern in the weave of his black garment, a complex interweaving of geometric forms, suddenly there, then gone again. Like a mirage.

"Knowledge is dual in nature," he said, harshly, carefully. "Creation and destruction are the results of knowledge. These forces are both necessary for life to exist."

Dr. Ngoni had grown pale under her eyes and around her mouth. "Destruction grieves us," she said.

"We regret the death of your children in the war," said the Decider, and Siggy felt a stab under her heart, a tightness in her throat. As far as she knew, no Decider had ever said that before. No Speedy had ever expressed any kind of regret.

Why was he doing it now?

"Decider," said Dr. Ngoni, "Do you believe that you will ever be our partners? Will you ever be our allies?"

Those were not questions a human ambassador would have advised the doctor to ask, even Siggy knew that. But they were the same questions that were in her own heart, and she longed to have them answered; even knowing, as anyone on Veil knew so well, that bad questions could cost lives, rude questions could shut down communication for good and bring back the firestorm. Siggy looked at the alien face of the Decider, at those hard lines and fathomless eyes, and saw in it the acknowledgment of a challenge.

A human would have hesitated to tread in such dangerous territory. But this man was a *Decider,* who had no equivalent among human beings, and he did not hesitate.

"Partnership is still a possibility," he said.

Ngoni waited, along with Siggy and several billion other human beings, for him to say that they could be allies. Or even that they couldn't. No one expected friendship, not after the bloodshed, not with the gulf that lay between the races, wider than the gulf between the stars. Partnership implied cooperation, commerce; but *ally* promised more. It promised no more attacks, no more wars. It promised help in times of crisis.

But the Decider was silent.

Did he know what Ngoni was really asking? Could any Speedy know? Did they laugh and joke with each other? Did they play? Did they worry about the health of a neighbor, or send a fruit basket to someone who had lost a spouse; did they stop to help a perfect stranger change a flat tire?

We regret the children was all he had given them.
Maybe for a Speedy, it was a lot. It might even be too
much.

And Ngoni, at a loss for words but unwilling to let go
of the opportunity to really *talk* to a Speedy, to really
understand, was stuck with her original question: "Can
we count on you to share information with us, Decider?
As outlined in the Treaty?"

The Decider stiffened. "The Treaty was drafted by
Deciders," he snapped. "The Treaty is law. We continue
to pursue communication with you, within the limits of
our interface. You will demonstrate your worthiness to
us before we will tell you all we know. Your 'scientific
community' is guilty of crimes against us and against
your own kind. You do not share all information with
us, so you cannot expect us to do the same with you,
unless you believe we are fools—and we have given you
no reason to believe so. Your nature is still mysterious
to us, and so the Treaty stands, and will continue to
stand, until you give us reason to rescind it."

And suddenly he was gone. His image was replaced
by that of a very startled reporter, who quickly recovered his professional demeanor.

"Thank you for being with us today, Mr. Decider . . .
have we lost the connection? Yes. Well, that was a first
for us, a first for *any* network, to actually have a Decider,
live, in one of our broadcasts, and he brought up some
interesting points in his last remarks, Dr. Ngoni. What
do you think he meant when he said that human scientists have committed crimes against the Speedies, crimes
even against other human beings? Was he talking about
the war, or about human history in general?"

"I don't know," said Dr. Ngoni. "I'm an astrophysi-
cist. I spend my days wondering what makes the universe tick, not trying to find ways to destroy it."

"But you have to admit, during the war there were a
number of specialists: biologists, geneticists, neurologists
and so on, who were doing their best to find ways to
modify human soldiers so they could fight the Speedies
more effectively—some very disturbing facts about those
experiments have come to light in the last hundred
years, including vivisection of live Speedy prisoners, use

of human prison inmates for testing of procedures, viruses, implants—"

"You know more about that than I do," Dr. Ngoni said, wearily. "I'm just a telescope jockey."

"All right, Dr. Ngoni," said the reporter, "We're out of time, anyway. Thank you for joining us."

"Thank you," echoed Dr. Ngoni, and her image was gone.

"Coming up next," said the reporter, "the latest word on skin care: Cell reviving and elastin-rebuilding creams, do they really work? And we'll talk with some irate parents in the Bijapur System, their children are straight-A students, yet many of them aren't able to get into the sorts of colleges that will enable them to get good jobs; is it possible we have too *many* smart kids these days . . . ?"

Siggy looked from the TV screen with an audible sigh. "Was that good news or bad news?" she asked.

"I don't know," her mother said, softly. "I would like to think that his remark about the children means that they're capable of compassion, that they don't want to hurt us."

"But do they think *we're* the monsters?" wondered Siggy. "All that stuff about crimes against them . . ."

"In war," said Mom, "people do dreadful things. Some people do."

Siggy held her mother's eyes for as long as she could, until the loss they shared made it necessary to look away.

Soon the news would be full of reactions to what the Decider had said; official reactions from politicians and generals, unofficial reactions from ordinary people out shopping, or working. The kids at school would be talking about it, the teachers might even assign essay papers on the matter. But for the moment all Siggy could feel was numb. She couldn't even worry, or be hopeful or mad. She didn't know what it meant, probably even the Decider didn't. He was just guessing about human beings, for all of his intelligence. Just like everyone else always had to guess about people.

Or even sometimes about themselves.

This was what Mom wanted her to see, and now she

had seen it. Now she would think about it, long into the night, add it to the list of mysteries to struggle with: Speedies, Time Pockets, love and death.

Enigmas.

Siggy sighed again, and started to get up.

"Wait!" Mom said. "Here's the story I wanted you to see."

"Huh?" Siggy blinked at the screen, saw a jumble of dreadful images, a bloody collage that made no sense.

"This thing about the serial killers," said Mom. "You've led a very safe life up until now, Siggy; but who knows where you'll have to go to find work once you've graduated high school? I want you to know what's out there."

Out there was a good choice of words. Siggy could tell that the images were censored for public viewing, some of them blurred or blanked in spots to keep the most awful or obscene bits out of sight, but this precaution only added to the sense of horror and confusion.

"Just when it seems like Enigma is the only thing people can talk about these days," said the reporter, "just when the universe seems so full of mystery and possibility—reality reasserts itself with devastating force, and we're reminded that space is not the only place where enigmas exist. They can also be found in the human mind."

The scene shifted to the outside of a shabby little house in an equally shabby neighborhood, where several police officers were hustling a small man down a front walk and into a waiting van. The man wore leg manacles, which accentuated his pigeon-toed walk. He was handcuffed, and the burly officers had a very firm grip on him; yet he seemed unconcerned, even cheerful. He was grinning. It was a nasty grin, on a nasty face; a tight, vicious, rat-eyed face, full of self-satisfaction and gloating. Siggy was glad when the greasy hair fell down over the face to obscure its expression, and a moment later the little man had been swallowed by the van.

"Jerry Wolfe was arrested today in a small suburb of Parnassus, capital city of Tantalus," said the reporter, "and if you've never head his name before, you will certainly be hearing it again, because he is accused of torturing and murdering thirteen men, women and children, crimes which he allegedly recorded on mini-disc with his own home-movie system. Mr. Wolfe was arrested after accusations were leveled against him by a teenaged boy who claims to have escaped from Wolfe's house, a place that the boy described as 'a filthy torture chamber,' stuffed to the ceiling with debris; rotting food, weapons, books, electronics, old clothes, toys, power tools, and the bodies of his victims. Police have cordoned off the area, as you can see now—they are wearing safety suits and have been carrying bagged and labeled items out of the house for the past hour, including—yes, right there you can see that they are removing what looks like a body from the house in a body bag . . .

"But before we get any further into this story—we have yet *another* alleged serial killer to tell you about, and the circumstances of the crimes he is accused of committing are possibly even more dreadful, more bizarre than Jerry Wolfe's. The R-FBI have asked us to broadcast his image and ask if anyone out there can help them identify this man."

A static image filled the screen, of a man with pale skin, who might be thirty, or forty, or fifty; a man you would never notice in a crowd—unless he looked you right in the eye. Even from a photograph, his gaze was disturbing.

Siggy stared at him and thought, *No. This is not going to be part of my future. I'll never have to look out for men like this one. I'll forget him as soon as they take the picture away. I'll never see his face again, and I'll never have any reason to think of him again. I'm going to marry Maxi and live on Veil for the rest of my life. I'll never have any reason to know monsters like these.*

She gazed dutifully at the TV screen, as if she were really trying to memorize the man, trying to recognize him; but already she was forgetting him and thinking about better things, like supper, and Halloween, and Maxi.

The face of the Professor gazed out of the TV screen. It held the hint of a smile, as if he already knew what Siggy did not.

Some day she was going to know him better than anyone.

Calves are easily bound and slaughtered
Never knowing the reason why
But whoever treasures freedom
Like the swallow will learn to fly
            —traditional Yiddish folk song

Siggy didn't cry until they cut her hair.

She hadn't cried on the ship, not once during the two-month trip, space-time. It had been sort of interesting, actually getting a chance to experience jump-time in person instead of just getting three points out of four on a science test for describing the star drive as something like a needle poking through pleated fabric, with the fabric representing normal space-time. The part that Siggy had always had trouble with was the part where you explained what was in *between* those pleats, and why there wasn't any time there, and therefore no time dilation effects.

Because time and space are woven together, she had written, and was told her answer was incomplete. Experiencing space travel in person wasn't any more edifying. And she had to sleep in a small cabin that seemed built especially to compound the misery of eighteen-year-old kids who had never left their home town before, or slept in any bed except their own.

She hadn't cried when she had said good-bye to Mom, who had been so glad that Siggy had been able to find a job somewhere that paid decent wages and had good benefits, even if that meant her only child had to travel nineteen light years to get to it.

Siggy hadn't even cried on the night of her disastrous senior prom, when her whole world had come crashing down around her ears; and she hadn't cried during all the nights afterward, when she had lain awake in the dark wondering what had gone wrong, and what she had missed, and how you could possibly know a boy your whole life and then find out you never knew him at all.

She was only a little nervous when she got off the

public transport not far from the Institute for the Criminally Insane, her suitcases in hand because she had come
straight from the starport. The air of Agate was full of
unfamiliar smells and its gravity pulled hard on Siggy,
challenging her muscles after two months of simulated
half-g on board the ship.

She walked down the wide, clean sidewalk, toward
Crazy Horse Mountain, which loomed over the southern
half of Petra City. Crazy Horse wasn't like the red
mountains of home at all. It was blue and sharp-edged—
but breathtakingly beautiful, lifting her spirits as she
looked for the Institute, which she envisioned as a big,
white building with lots of trees and an understandably
high fence.

But she didn't see a place like that. Instead she saw
a massive granite block with an engraved bronze front.
It read: INSTITUTE FOR THE CRIMINALLY INSANE.

"Where?" said Siggy, looking in vain for the building
from her imagination. She saw plenty of other buildings;
impressive ones that soared into the sky, morning sunlight glittering off their beautiful colored metals and
diamond-hard glass. Birds flew up there in the silence
between the upper windows; big ones, like birds of prey,
probably hunting this world's version of pigeons. How
wonderful it must be to work in one of those fancy upper
offices, or live in one of those penthouses, and see such
creatures close up.

She would be seeing other sorts of creatures close up,
at the Institute for the Criminally Insane.

Siggy shivered, even though it was spring on this part
of Agate, a warm, dry spring like you would find in the
upper desert, the sort they had in Desert Center, back
home. But the hawks were different here. They were
brown instead of blue.

Siggy walked around the granite block. There was
nothing hiding behind it, only a huge parking lot with a
park on the far side of it. Siggy started walking toward
the park, thinking *maybe it's in there, behind the trees,*
but not really believing it. She was going to be late on
her first day of work.

She had gone perhaps a hundred feet when she saw
the hole in the ground.

It wasn't a round, natural sort of hole. It was square, and lined with cut stone, hard and ominously thick. Siggy walked to its edge and peered down. A wide flight of steps descended out of her line of sight. They were lit from above and the sides, and security cameras were trained on them at regular intervals.

One was even trained on Siggy.

Is it a dangerous job? Siggy had asked the job recruiter, nervously.

Are you kidding? the woman replied. *It's the top security mental ward for the entire Republic. It's probably the safest place in the galaxy!*

Standing there now, at the top of those steps, Siggy felt someone walking over her grave.

You're nervous, Mom would have said. *It's your first time away from home. You'll do fine, Siggy; people like you are worth their weight in gold. Reliable, intelligent, ethical—your dad would be proud of you.*

Siggy could picture Mom standing there, looking down the steps with her. Mom would have squared her shoulders and walked right down them, her chin high—but not so high that she would fall the rest of the way. Siggy laughed at the picture. Ever since she had left home, her mom had come to live inside her head, giving advice when she needed it, giving comfort and encouragement.

You won't know until you try, she would have said.

So Siggy descended the steps to the front door. Her knees didn't wobble at all, though the entrance looked like it belonged to a war bunker, built to withstand a direct hit from orbit.

Halfway down, the theme music from *Psycho* was going through her head.

She stopped in front of the featureless, metal doors. There was a keypad on the wall to her right, with a blank screen over it. Siggy set her bags down and peered at the keypad. It wasn't like any of the other ones she had seen so far. It had a lot of unfamiliar symbols and words. There was one marked SCREEN, which she pushed; but the screen just beeped and flashed a line of code too fast for her to read, then went blank again.

Siggy studied the keypad again. There was another

key that said ON, but it was followed by EXT. What was
EXT? Exit? Extension? She pushed it.

There was another blip, another line of code speeding
by, and the screen went blank again.

"Hey!" came a female voice, out of the air. "Stop
fooling with the keypad!"

Siggy jumped and looked around. The voice had come
from an intercom. She looked at the nearest security
camera and called, "I'm new on the janitorial staff. How
do I get in?"

"I know you're new," snapped the voice, halfway between annoyance and amusement. "Just stand still and
let us get a scan on you to match with our records. It
takes a couple of minutes the first time."

"Oh," said Siggy, and stayed obediently still.

After what seemed more like ten minutes, the metal
doors slid open, letting out a rush of antiseptic air. Inside
was a narrow lobby, an armored oblong space that fun-
neled into something that looked sort of like a transparent
airlock. Later Siggy would know that the transparency was
not glass or even diamond; it was the same super-hard
substance used to make the cell doors on Monster Row.
Six uniformed people stood outside the far side of the lock,
looking at Siggy. One of them was a stocky, brown woman
with short dreadlocks, who wore a pistol on her hip and
a no-nonsense expression on her face.

The woman's lips moved, and her voice came through
the speaker inside the lobby: "Move forward, Lindquist." Siggy grabbed her bags and rushed forward so
eagerly she almost dropped them again. The lady with
the pistol didn't laugh, but Siggy saw a smirk on the
freckled face of one officer, a fellow with red hair who
looked even younger than she was.

When Siggy was well inside the lock, the outer doors
closed behind her.

"Put your bags down and step away from them," ordered the woman. Siggy obeyed again. Once she was
clear, some lights strobed across her suitcases, sweeping
back and forth. Two of the officers watched a screen
intently while this happened. The others kept their eyes
focused on Siggy. She felt unaccountably guilty under
their collective gaze.

Siggy waited while the woman with the dreadlocks and pistol talked soundlessly with the two officers at the screen. She wondered if she ought to pick up her bags again. *Keep cool,* said the mom inside her head.

Then the inner doors opened with a rush of antiseptic-scented air. "Come through," ordered the woman, this time with her own throat. Siggy picked up her bags and walked in, trying not to look too relieved. The red-headed smirker was still looking smug.

"Tomorrow you'll have your ID with you," said the woman, whose name badge read THOMPSON when Siggy was close enough to see it. "Just press it against the screen and we'll open for you once we confirm a visual on you. You can bring stuff in as long as it's not on the restricted list, but be prepared for a search if you do. Everyone's stuff gets searched, no exceptions. From here you proceed on down this hall to the next checkpoint. They'll direct you from there. Any questions?"

"Is there some place I can put my bags until I'm finished today?" asked Siggy. "Jump-time got me here two weeks later than it was supposed to and I just got off the ship. I haven't had time to—"

"Everyone's putting their bags in our office for now," said Thompson. "That's just for today, don't get used to it."

"Okay," promised Siggy.

"Hoffman, take her back," ordered Thompson, and a tall, ebony girl with a long, black ponytail and the face of an Egyptian princess gestured for Siggy to follow her. Siggy hurried after, trying to match strides with the long-legged officer.

"Other people brought their luggage, too?" Siggy asked Hoffman. "So I'm not the only one fresh off the boat. That's a relief."

Hoffman didn't answer. She kept her chin up and her eyes on some point near infinity.

Maybe she's shy, Mom might have said.

Maybe she just doesn't like my face, Siggy would have answered.

The main corridor was lined with metal that gleamed like the snout of the blaster Thompson was wearing. It was well lit, but the effect was somewhat claustrophobic.

Siggy tried not to think it, but she was already pretty sure that she would be very grateful to leave this place at the end of every workday. They turned off the main drag, into a small hallway, and Hoffman stopped in front of another blank metal door, this one so nondescript that Siggy would have walked right past it without seeing it. Hoffman pulled her ID card out of her pants pocket and pressed it against a small screen. The door opened, and a man leaned out.

"Hand 'em over," he told Siggy. She handed him her suitcases, then tried to peer after him as he disappeared inside again. But Hoffman took her firmly by her elbow and steered her back down the side hall and into the main corridor again. Hoffman pointed toward the far end of the hall, where more armed officers waited at another checkpoint.

"That way," Hoffman said, her voice soft and non-committal, and she walked away from Siggy. Siggy looked after her for a moment, then proceeded in the direction indicated.

Siggy got fingerprinted and retina-scanned at the second checkpoint. From there they scooted her off to a medical examination, where they took tissue and blood samples, also for the purpose of identification; and where she received a health screening, which she passed with flying colors. Then she was waved through a third checkpoint and steered to an office crowded with other "support" staff, where she was instructed to fill out forms that she had already filled out back at the employment office on Veil. Hadn't they received them? Or the letters of recommendation she had submitted from Mrs. Silverstein and her other housekeeping clients?

"I know, I know," said the secretary, "I hear it a thousand times a day, 'I've already filled these out,' but you'll be filling out the very same ones again next year, so get used to it."

Siggy found a chair and started scribbling, hoping she could remember all of the information now that she didn't have her notes and her address book with her. Would they think she had lied on the other forms if she didn't fill these out exactly the same way? The fellow sitting next to her seemed to know all of his numbers and figures by heart.

"How many times have you filled these out?" she asked him.

"Ten," he said. "I could do it with my eyes closed."

He had an accent just like the meteorologist on channel 207 back home—what was the guy's name? Ahmed? Abdul? It was fairly easy to understand, there was a sort of drawling of the first syllables of words, and a flattening of vowels. It was much easier to understand than some of the accents she had heard on the ship. Siggy hadn't realized there could be so many versions of *Standard*.

He studied her with friendly curiosity. Lots of people stared at Siggy now that she was so far away from the Veil system. This fellow was a tall, sturdily built man with skin the same color as hers; but his hair was a mat of super-short black foam and he had brown eyes. "Where you from?" he asked.

"Veil System," said Siggy.

"Okay," he laughed, "I had a feeling you weren't from around here. I've never seen a person with your skin color who also had eyes and hair like that—if you don't mind my asking, are they real? Were you born with them?"

"Sure," said Siggy, surprised. "Lots of people look like me on Veil."

"Sounds like an interesting place," he said, and turned back to his forms, which he finished with a flourish.

Siggy scribbled as much as she could remember. They wanted to know everything about her, even her parents' names, the name of the nursery school she had attended, and her political party affiliation. But she couldn't remember some of the addresses—she had never needed them to get around in Red Cliffs.

"It's okay if you don't remember," said the man, peering over her shoulder. "They just need the important stuff for now, like Social Security numbers."

Siggy was glad to know that. She was beginning to feel a little overwhelmed. There were so many people in the room, and she was tired, had come right from the starport, and she hadn't had lunch yet, and there was still so much to do, and would they do a regular shift today, or would she get to go look for a place to live . . . ?

"My name is Afrika," said the man.

"I'm Sigrit." She shook his hand, which was big, warm, and callused. She wondered if she'd be growing calluses herself, soon.

"Sigrit," he repeated, having a little trouble with it.

"Siggy for short," she suggested, and he smiled.

"I like that better. This your first job, Siggy?"

"Yes." She blushed as if he had asked her if it were her first dance.

"Come on," he said, "let's take these up to the secretary and we'll get you going to your next stage."

So Siggy followed Afrika up to the front desk and got her forms scanned; and from there it was off to uniforms, name badges, and security IDs.

"But before you pull on your duds," said Afrika, "we'd better hit the barber. You don't want shaved hair falling down your collar all day long."

"Shaved hair?" asked Siggy, innocently.

"Better warn you up front, the Director is a clean freak. He sees dust where it ain't, he sees germs where they couldn't, and he has this big thing about hair floating around, like it's going to get in all the machinery and stop everything cold. Everyone on the janitorial staff has to get sheared, like me." He rubbed the top of his head.

"Okay," said Siggy, not all that concerned about it yet. She didn't see any reason *not* to get a haircut. It might even be fun to be short-haired for a change. She got in line for the barber and chatted with Afrika about inconsequential things until it was her turn to sit in the chair.

The lady barber was a middle-aged woman with orange hair and a big, permanent frown.

"I'm going to have to cut it down to an inch," she warned Siggy, as if she thought that news would make the girl bolt out of the building and run all the way home again.

"Okay," said Siggy.

Afrika winked at her, and the other freshly shorn employees waited to watch her transformation. *That's funny,* thought Siggy. *What's the big deal? I don't care if my hair is short. Maybe they think I'm vain about it. I'm not vain, I don't even have a boyfriend who would care . . . who would care how I . . .*

And that was when she started to cry. She did it silently, so the barber lady didn't know she was doing it, at first. Then the woman moved around to the front and said, "For heaven's sake! It's not like you're going into the marines or something!"

Siggy tried to stop crying, but now that it had started, it just came pouring out. At least she didn't sob; she kept her face perfectly still, trying to maintain as much dignity as she could. By the time it was all over, Afrika's eyes were shining and some of the other fellows were clearing their throats. Afrika dusted her shoulders off and rubbed the top of her head.

"You're initiated," he announced, heartily.

Siggy sniffed and wiped her eyes dry.

"You look cute with your new haircut," he assured her.

"Do you really think so?" asked Siggy.

He put a brotherly arm around her shoulders and walked her over to uniforms and name badges.

Siggy slipped into coveralls and pinned a badge on her chest that said LINDQUIST. After that she stood in front of a camera and got photographed. The new photo was stuck on a card with a bar code on it. Her new ID

By then she and Afrika had attracted some other people into their orbit, some old-timers and some other newbees, one of whom was anxiously wondering if they should wait in Auditorium D for the orientation speech by the Director.

"You can go and wait there if you want," said George, one of the old-timers, a tall, slim, cinnamon-colored man with deceptively sleepy eyes, "or you can come on down to the cafeteria with us and wait the extra hour it's going to take for everyone else to get through records and medical."

They went down to the cafeteria, and suddenly Siggy felt as if she were stepping out into the sunshine. The dark, metal walls that characterized the rest of the Institute were absent here. The cafeteria was cheerful and brightly colored, almost like home except that there were no animals, flowers, or fey creatures carved into anything. People were smiling and lingering over their food, and savory smells reminded Siggy that she was starving.

In short time they had gone through the buffet line and settled at a round table with their laden trays. Afrika and George had piled theirs high; that seemed a good sign. Siggy took a bite of potato salad and sighed happily. It was good, almost as good as Mom's. She had always heard that hospital food was awful. She spent the next half hour debunking that rumor.

"I could get fat in here," she remarked to Afrika. "Do they ever have tacos or pickled herring?"

"Not on the same plate, I hope." he said.

George looked at his pocket watch. "Time to go," he said, and Siggy wondered if she was imagining the grim tone that seemed to have crept into his voice. She glanced at Afrika, but his face was calm and unconcerned.

Auditorium D was half full when they arrived, so it was easy to find seats. But it turned out that they were among some of the last to arrive; within ten minutes the doors were being closed and everyone was hushing in anticipation of the Director's arrival. Siggy sat comfortably, wishing that she were there for a movie, instead.

"Listen," Afrika whispered, "whatever you hear next, don't take it too personal."

Huh? wondered Siggy. Personal? Was the Director that bad? Was he mad at her already? She hadn't even had a chance to do anything wrong yet. Except for touching the keypad at the front gate. She hoped they weren't upset about that. . . .

And then the Director walked onto the dais at the front of the room. He stood behind the podium that had been placed there and studied some note cards he had brought with him. He was wearing a headset with a tiny microphone.

Siggy watched him, anxiously. He didn't look so bad. He was somewhere between middle-aged and elderly.

He was thin and short, with shoulders that were too wide for his weight. His iron-gray hair was long enough to cover his ears, despite his alleged preoccupation with everyone else's length, and a lock of it kept falling over his eyes. He had a goatee, just like the stereotype of the Freudian psychologist, and he wore a beautifully tailored suit. He was frowning at his notes, which made him look intelligent. Siggy wondered if she might end up liking him.

And then he looked up, and that possibility vanished.

His face, when he regarded the audience of janitors, orderlies, and cafeteria staff, twisted into a grimace of distaste and contempt. It stayed that way throughout his entire lecture, changing only once or twice to reflect brief, malicious glee.

"I am the Director," he snapped, his voice amplified and projected into every corner of the auditorium. "Henceforth you will refer to me as *sir*. You will say, 'Yes, *sir*,' or 'No, *sir*,' or 'I hear and obey, *sir*.' Is that clear?"

Siggy wondered if they were all supposed to answer "Yes, *sir*!" in unison, but everyone maintained an uncomfortable silence. The Director flashed one of those malicious grimaces, then continued.

"As of this moment, you are officially employed at the Institute for the Criminally Insane. In case you've never thought about it, that's *criminally* insane. Meaning crimes have been committed by our inmates, violent crimes of a deeply disturbed nature; more disturbed, one presumes, than the crimes committed by 'regular' criminals. As you may expect, most of our inmates are restrained at all times, but fully thirty percent of them have limited freedoms and privileges that allow them to associate with staff such as yourselves with little or no restraints.

"These privileged few do not normally violate the rules of their confinement, lest they lose what slight freedom they have gained; but when they *do* violate the rules, they do so memorably. There have been six deaths at this institute within the last three years; of those six, four were staff members. As difficult as this may be to believe, even the insane can occasionally outwit the mighty intellect of janitors and orderlies. Do not fool yourselves into thinking you are smarter than the inmates just because they are insane and you allegedly are not."

The Director paused and looked down at his notes again. Siggy took the opportunity to lean close to Afrika and whisper, "My god."

"Told you," he whispered back.

"I don't believe this guy."

"You have to be nuts to want to be in charge of a prison full of crazy killers."

"What does that make us, then?" she wondered.

"Desperate," said Afrika.

The Director looked up again, twisting his face even more, if that were possible.

"Obey the security officers at all times," he commanded. "Do not argue with them, do not joke with them, do not try to tease them. They are armed for good reason, they will use lethal force if necessary. Do not bring contraband into this prison; acquaint yourselves with the restricted list you've been given and watch for posted updates. If you commit a stupid mistake, you will be fired. If you commit a criminal one, you will be prosecuted to the full extent of the law.

"Do not become personally involved with the inmates. Do not attempt to engage in dialogues with them, leave that to the doctors and the interrogators."

He stopped and shuffled note cards again.

Siggy whispered to Afrika, "Aren't there privacy shields on all the cells? They said so on TV."

"Sure," he whispered back.

"So why don't they just activate them when we have to be in the area? Then we wouldn't have to interact at all."

"That would be too intelligent."

The Director looked up and put his hand on the earpiece of his headset, as if he were listening to something. His eyes became unfocused for a moment, and then he looked directly at Siggy. He glared at her.

My god, she thought, *does he have this place bugged? Did he hear what we just said?*

"Some of you will be required to view some special

materials during your shift tomorrow," said the Director. "You will be notified. Those of you who are new will be instructed by your supervisors. You have thirty days to become competent at your job. Considering the nature of your work, this should be a more than adequate amount of time; but those of you who are especially slow will be terminated if you fail to live up to our standards. Those of you who prove skilled and diligent will be given a small raise. Continue to work well, and you will see regular raises every year.

"We are one of the best employers in this sector. I trust you will not squander the opportunity we've given you. Any questions you have will be directed to your supervisors. You will not be seeing me until next year. Be glad of that: Those of you who *do* see me will have cause to regret it. That is all—you may go to work now."

He turned and stalked out of the room.

Everyone let out an audible sigh of relief.

"Wow," said Siggy. "I don't know if I can stand to see him once a year."

"Just like Santy Claus," drawled George. "Only he uses a cat-o'-nine-tails on his reindeer." He stood and stretched, luxuriously.

Afrika was doing the same. Siggy was content just to rub the top of her head. It felt good. Why hadn't she ever cut her hair short before?

Siggy and the other newbees followed Afrika and George out of the auditorium and down to the maintenance office, where they would be assigned sections. Newbees would be paired with old-timers who would teach them their responsibilities. Siggy was glad they had finally gotten down to the real work; she wanted to know the ropes as soon as possible. She might even qualify for one of those raises in thirty days.

Because she had arrived with Afrika, she was paired with him. The two of them went off with a crew of six others to work on the third and fourth floors of the north wing. George was on their crew, too.

"Hey," he said to Afrika as they all got onto the service elevator, "what was all that about 'special materials' Mr. *sir* was talking about back there? You ever have to look at 'special materials' before?"

Afrika shrugged. "Just the stuff about body fluids and broken glass. This must be something new."

"Some other damned thing," said George. "We just better hope this place ain't bugged after all, like they say. We could get stuck with the shit jobs."

"Shit jobs?" asked Siggy, worriedly. "We have to clean up—you know—shit?"

Afrika laughed and rubbed her shorn head vigorously. "Sometimes, girl," he said. "But mostly we just have to take it."

Afrika's warning had been well-timed, because for the rest of that first day, Siggy had to clean some of the most disgusting bathrooms she had ever seen in her life. Many of the inmates apparently expressed their unhappiness with the universe in general and the Institute in particular by using their bodily fluids for vandalism. The stench was like a physical blow, and Siggy quickly found out that the first thing that had to be done was to attack the sources of that stench with odor digester and bleach. Only then could she and Afrika stand to get down to the detail work.

Siggy found fecal and urinal material in places she would never have imagined anyone could put them. But they weren't even the hardest substances to scrub off.

Those turned out to be dried snot.

"Sheesh," said Siggy as she and Afrika put their cleaning carts back in their storage area, "They should have given us biohazard suits to wear in there."

"They don't do that unless there's blood," said Afrika. "But make sure you always wear your sani-gloves, okay? No matter how uncomfortable they are. And don't touch your face at any time, until your hands are sterile again."

"Okay," said Siggy, lifting the industrial mop bucket the way Afrika had shown her to do it, tipping it into the drain without straining her back muscles.

"You're doing great," said Afrika. "You really work hard. I'm glad to see it. Any job worth doing is worth doing well, you know? It's like what Dr. Martin Luther King, Jr. used to say. If you're a street sweeper, be the best damned street sweeper there ever was."

"Yeah," said Siggy. "I think so, too. Maybe I'm just a clean freak, like the Director."

"You are nothing like him," Afrika said, almost a little too emphatically. Siggy shivered. *A goose just walked on your grave, warned the mom in her head, but Siggy didn't want to hear it. Not on the first day of her job, not when she was so far away from everything she had known.*

Silly, she told herself, *Afrika just doesn't like the Director. Probably no one does, no one in the whole universe.*

They walked out into the maintenance hallway and joined the exodus of workers getting off shift. Siggy saw George up ahead, but was too tired to call out to him. Her feet didn't hurt, even after six straight hours of labor; but the tendons that controlled the muscles at the very top of her legs ached. That usually only happened to her at dance marathons.

Well, at least this job would keep her in good shape.

They turned onto the main drag and started the long trek that would take them through the security checkpoints. Now more workers had joined them; it reminded Siggy of the final bell at school, with students filing out of the classrooms and heading down the long hall to the front door. Except these were grown-ups, and Siggy was a grown-up, too; and at the end of the day, grown-ups looked a lot more tired than kids ever did.

"Afrika," she asked, "how much blood does there have to be before they make you wear a biohazard suit?"

He didn't answer for a minute, and Siggy wondered if he had heard her. But then he said, "A lot of blood, Siggy. More than you've probably ever seen."

Or ever wanted to see, she was sure. But this was her job now. She would be facing a lot of stuff she had never imagined.

She just hoped that guys like Afrika would be around when she met the inmates. *If* she met them.

They were almost to the first checkpoint when the off-duty officers joined them. These people were easy to distinguish from the other workers. It wasn't just that they were dressed differently; they also moved differently. Their bodies weren't any harder, but their eyes were more watchful; and of course, they were armed. Siggy tried not to stare openly at their accoutrements, but she couldn't help wondering what some of them were. Though the blasters were easily identifiable, some of the other gizmos were not.

One-two-one-two, walked the officers, as if they were a military unit. They were almost marching. One-two-one-two-one-two-one-two, and Siggy, so tired from her first day of work, so overwhelmed (though she hardly knew it) by the Director's vicious speech, so grateful to have Afrika and the others for new friends, yet also a little fearful that they might prove to be false, just as Maxi had ultimately proven to be false. Siggy, weary and half asleep, felt the rhythm of the feet around her begin to shift, collectively, unconsciously matching the time of the off-duty officers.

One-two-one-two, swing your arms and stomp your feet, and Siggy began to hum.

One-two-one-two, stomp your feet, no need to think, and Siggy began to sing:

"A rooty-toot, a rooty-toot!
We are the staff of the Institute!
We don't smoke, or drink, or chew,
And we don't go with boys who do!"

That provoked tired laughter from the other workers, even some of the officers. Siggy started out of her half-trance, then grinned with relief as she realized that no one was offended. She hadn't even known she was going to sing, she had just blurted out the lyrics. But the officers weren't mad, they had even relaxed a little. Some of them grinned back at her. Afrika caught her eye and winked.

"Did you just make that up?" he asked.

"Heck no," said Siggy. "It's an old song, I just inserted the word 'staff' where 'girls' ought to be."

"I've heard a lot of old songs," he said, "but nothing like that one."

"It's probably seven or eight hundred years old," said Siggy. "Or even a thousand. From even before they started to make movies."

"Movies?"

"Vids," said Siggy. "Minis?" She had heard all sorts of words for *movie* since she had left home. Afrika nodded, so he must have understood one of them.

"I like the movies they made when they first started making them," Siggy said. "In the first fifty years. Those were the best ones, and you get to hear a lot of good songs in those."

Afrika looked at her sidelong. "You are full of surprises," he said. "I never met anyone who's seen a mini that old. *I've* never seen one."

"You don't have a classic movie channel here?" asked Siggy, unhappily.

"Sure," said Afrika. "Minis from a hundred years ago. Those are old, Siggy, but *you* like to watch stuff from the stone age. My son would be scandalized, he thinks *I'm* an old bone for listening to the music I liked back in high school."

They reached the first checkpoint, and sailed through. Siggy had thought there would be a long process involved, but apparently the checkpoint guards weren't willing to give tired co-workers too much hassle on their way out.

"Afrika . . ." Siggy yawned widely. "Are there any hotels nearby? I haven't had a chance to find a place to live yet."

"Don't worry about a hotel," said Afrika. "My wife and I manage the apartment complex right down the line from here, at Roosevelt and Fourteenth Street. Most of the janitors rent there. Free utilities and half off first month's rent."

"Wonderful," said Siggy, in the middle of another yawn. She was thinking that back home on Veil they had a Roosevelt and Fourteenth Street too. Only there they had a hamburger joint. "Are there fast-food places around there? Or a market?"

"Both," he said. "But you're having supper with my family tonight."

"Wow," said Siggy. "Thanks!"

"You're welcome," he said, and nodded toward some luggage that had been lined up against the wall near the last checkpoint. "You have gear over there? Let's grab it and get outta here."

The apartment complex had a swimming pool, a Jacuzzi, a gym, a laundromat, and an auditorium that could be rented for parties. It also had free Net hookup with three functions: broadcast, information, and communication. Siggy discovered this as soon as she walked into Afrika's apartment, as his eleven-year-old son was sprawled on the carpet in front of the TV, which was set on the broadcast function. He didn't look up when they came in.

"I'm home!" called Afrika, in a booming voice that must have reached every corner of the three-bedroom apartment. "I brought company!"

"How many?" called a woman's voice from the kitchen.

"Just one," Afrika called back.

"All right," called the voice, balancing somewhere between resignation and amusement.

The boy kept his eyes glued to the TV.

"Son," said Afrika.

"What?" snapped the boy, without looking away from the screen.

Afrika walked over to the TV and turned it off. The boy gaped at him in outrage. "I was watching that!" he said.

"TV does not come before family in this house," said Afrika, patiently.

"You didn't have to turn it off," said the boy, almost shouting. "I was watching it."

"Siggy," said Afrika, still patient and reasonable, "please excuse us for a moment."

"Sure," said Siggy, trying to sound cheerful, but she found herself feeling sorry for the boy, even though his rudeness was a little annoying. She hoped she would never be the recipient of that combination of soft voice and steel gaze from Afrika.

His son stared up at him for half a second, as if debating the possibility of resistance. But he quickly discarded the notion and got to his feet. He walked from the room, hanging his head, Afrika right behind him.

Siggy stood in the middle of the room, wondering if she should sit, or stay there, or even go into the kitchen and offer her assistance. She could smell wonderful things from that direction. But she hadn't been introduced yet, so she simply stood. She looked at the exotic prints on the wall, Egyptian tomb art and scenes of Haitian voodoo practitioners in the throes of religious ecstacy. There was an imitation tiger-skin rug on the floor, and the couch sported a leopard-skin print.

Afrika and his son weren't gone for more than a minute or two. Siggy couldn't hide her startlement when they reappeared so fast, and Afrika grinned at her. The boy walked up to Siggy and extended his hand.

"I'm Nathanial," he said.

"I'm Siggy," she said, and shook his hand, which was dry and cool, with bones that were too big for the flesh encasing them.

"Pleased to meet you," he answered, managing to sound almost cordial, except that his voice dropped out of audible range near the end of the sentence.

"Thank you," said Siggy, and let go of his hand, which seemed grateful to escape.

"Come on into the kitchen," Afrika said, his arm around his son's shoulders. "We menfolk have to set the table while the gals finish supper. Siggy, you get to sit and drink iced tea and be fussed over."

"Oh boy!" said Siggy, sincerely, and almost got a smile out of Nathanial.

In the kitchen, Afrika's wife was finishing supper; Siggy gave up the notion of offering assistance when she noticed that four daughters were there to help, one older than Nathanial, three younger. They were lovely women, slim and dark and carefully coifed in elaborate braids. They moved like a well-oiled machine, and Siggy was grateful to get out of their way and settle in the guest's chair at the supper table.

"Siggy, this is my wife, Kalisha, and my daughters, Electra, Sheba, Alexandria, and Topaz."

Kalisha and her daughters nodded politely to Siggy, but kept most of their attention on what they were doing. Siggy didn't mind that; what they were doing smelled heavenly. There was fried chicken, she could tell that much. Plus a couple of vegetable dishes, something that looked and smelled almost like cornbread, and something sweet for desert.

You'll have to ask for the recipes once you know them a little better, said the mom in Siggy's head.

I hope they'll like me well enough to give them, worried Siggy.

Of course they'll like you.

But Siggy couldn't tell whether they were going to like her that well or not, even when she had sat at the supper table for over an hour. The younger girls stared at Siggy when they thought she wasn't looking, seeming amazed at her coloring. Other than that, they were polite, they even smiled at her when she said something interesting or amusing; but there was an intangible reserve, and subtle holding back. There wasn't a definite warming until Siggy asked about the auditorium.

"Do you ever hold dances there?" she asked Afrika.

"Sometimes people have parties," he said. "Don't think anyone's had a party that was just for dancing, though."

"We have to throw one!" said Siggy. "I'll have to put up a sign on the bulletin board for dance lessons."

"To give or get?" he asked.

"Give," she said.

Suddenly, Nathanial's face lit up. "You know how to dance?" he asked.

"Sure," said Siggy. "I love to dance." From the corner of her eye she could see Afrika and Kalisha exchanging significant glances.

"What kind?" asked Nathanial. "You know how to do the Cool? Or how about the Dirty Done Deed?"

"Sure," she said. "Those are easy. I learned those

from watching the Dance Parade channel. I know some hard ones, too."

"Wow," he said, then suddenly got shy again. He looked down at his plate and pretended to be fascinated with his vegetables.

Siggy waited an appropriate amount of time, then glanced up at Kalisha, who nodded slightly in approval.

"Do you want to learn some dance steps?" she asked Nathanial. "I don't have anyone to dance with, now that I'm on a new world."

Nathanial's coffee-colored skin went a little pale, but he nodded. "Sure," he said, faintly.

"Okay," said Siggy, and let the matter drop for the time being.

By the time dessert was served, Kalisha's smiles had gotten a lot warmer. Her daughters elbowed each other and stifled some giggles, but they refrained from teasing Nathanial, and they seemed pleased with Siggy, too.

After supper, Siggy helped clear the dishes. When Nathanial had been sent to take out the garbage, Kalisha confided to Siggy in a quiet tone: "His first sixth grade dance is coming up, and he's worried sick about it. He knows how to move his feet, but when it comes to talking to girls, he doesn't know what to do with himself. He just needs to get used to the situation, you know?"

"Yes," said Siggy. "That's the first thing we learned in dance class back on Veil, how to ask each other to dance, how to look into each other's eyes and talk to each other—it's second nature for me now, but there were some new kids in school who were shy. I think I know how to draw Nathanial out."

Slowly, she thought to herself. *Don't try the fancy ballroom stuff at first, you'll just scare him off. He wants to do the dances all the other kids are doing, not anything new and strange.*

Though actually, ballroom dancing was *old* and strange. Siggy had been surprised to learn that not everyone in the galaxy liked to do it, or even knew what it was. She thought that was sad; they would love it if only they knew how, she was convinced. She was going to teach as many people on Agate as wanted to learn— and she hoped that would be a lot.

"Let me show you what apartments we've got available," said Afrika, and Siggy grabbed her suitcases and said her good-byes to Nathanial and the womenfolk.

But Afrika only showed her one apartment, one that was just across the courtyard from theirs. It was a studio, but it had a loft and a covered patio.

"Oh no," Siggy said, "this has got to be too expensive for me!"

"No," said Afrika, "it costs the same as the other studios, but it's got some extra features. The owner built it for his daughter when she was living here with him, helping him manage the place. She wasn't any good at managing, and neither was he, so they hired us and moved out a couple months ago."

He opened the front door and let Siggy in. One look through the front door, and she knew she was home.

"It's furnished!" she said.

"Sort of," laughed Afrika. "You've got a bed and a chest of drawers in the loft, a table and chairs in the kitchen, plus all your major appliances."

"And a couch!" said Siggy. "And a chair! And a *TV*!"

Afrika smiled. "It's already hooked up to the Net. I thought you'd like that. Have you got towels and sheets and stuff?"

"One set of sheets, two towels, and two washcloths," said Siggy, and she set down her suitcases so she could rummage through them.

"I'd better get you some coffee for breakfast though," said Afrika. "And something to eat . . ."

"I can run across the street to the store," offered Siggy, still rummaging.

"No, I've got some hotel samples," said Afrika. "We rent part of the complex for short stays. I'll go get some, be right back."

"Wow, thanks," said Siggy.

While he was gone, she pulled out her towels and sheets. She climbed up to the loft and made the bed, tucking the sides in where the sheets were a little too big; then put her towels in the bathroom. She unpacked the flatware her mother had given her, then an assortment of dishes and cooking tools, and finally her clothes and toiletries, plus her laptop music and book library, with its powerful mini-speakers. It was amazing what you could jam into two suitcases if you really had to.

Siggy drew out the laptop. It turned on automatically when you flipped it open, and offered a list of possible selections. Siggy's eyes read over the music column, wondering which ones would be suitable for Nathanial's lessons. Most would be out of the question for the time being. Siggy picked up the stylus and pressed the icon for *down*. The cursor slipped down the list, lighting each one in turn, until it reached "The Tennessee Waltz."

. . . *I lost my little darlin' to the Tennessee Waltz, when she stole my true love from me.* . . .

She had forgotten it would be there. Of course it was, it had been her favorite. She had loved the tune, but never paid the lyrics that much attention. Not until the night of the senior prom. And wasn't it funny when a song suddenly turned out to be about you, when before it had just seemed like a story, like a cliche? But that was why they called them cliches, because they were true so often.

"Here you go," Afrika said cheerily, startling her as he came through the front door with an overstuffed box, which contained some items that looked suspiciously non-hotel-sample-like. Siggy closed the laptop and went to help him, but she was mostly in the way as he hefted the box onto the kitchen table.

"I can't take all this stuff," she said with dismay.

"No argument," said Afrika. "It's yours. Who else would be willing to give my stinky son dance lessons?"

So Siggy accepted the things gracefully, and wrote Afrika a check for the first month's rent—at half off. Mom would be so pleased when Siggy wrote her.

"Most of us leave here at about eight in the morning," Afrika said after he had helped her unpack the box. "That way we can get to IFCI with plenty of time to spare, plus a little extra for sitting in the cafeteria and drinking coffee."

"Sounds good," said Siggy, gratefully. He patted her on the shoulder.

"You'll be fine," he said. "I get feelings about people. You'll be just fine. See you in the morning, Siggy."

"Good night," she said, and saw him out the door.

As soon as he was gone, she turned on the TV. Within a few minutes, she had found the local affiliate of one of the news networks Mom had always watched. It made her feel comfortable, a little less homesick. She sat down on the couch, which was covered in a lovely red plush that was only slightly worn on the arms. The chair was a complementary flower print, in almost perfect condition. Siggy watched TV for a little while, then remembered something else she wanted to unpack.

It was at the very bottom of the case, under her socks. Siggy had bound it in bubble wrap to keep it extra safe. She unwrapped it and looked at it.

It was a scrapbook with hand lettering on the cover that said THE TRUTH ABOUT DAVID SILVERSTEIN.

Siggy shivered. She had left so much behind, a lot of hopes and dreams; but this was something she couldn't leave, even if she wanted to. She couldn't forget David Silverstein.

She had seen him again, just before she had left. He had peeked out of his Time Pocket, still fifteen, younger than she was now.

She wasn't quite ready to think about that night. The Lost Boy had appeared just as Siggy's world was falling apart. But hadn't that been the way it was the first time? The Speedies had attacked, and the Lost Boy had fallen into his Time Pocket. Then Maxi had broken Siggy's heart, and the Lost Boy had called to her from out of that same Time Pocket, just long enough to say, *I'm still here, don't forget me, don't lose me, no matter how far away you have to go. . . .*

She could see him now, the Time Pocket curling away behind him. He called her name, but she couldn't hear his voice. He kept looking over his shoulder, as if he were looking for someone.

Or afraid of someone. She strained her eyes, but she couldn't make sense of the jumble behind him. Not then, and not now. Siggy settled down into the couch and tried to banish the image from her mind. Tried to banish all thoughts of Veil, but she couldn't.

She had gone far away, yet she could still see Veil from the corner of her eye. The Lost Fleet hadn't attacked since that day when she was seven, just before Halloween. Everyone said another attack was long over-due—Siggy might go back some day to find her world a smoking ruin.

Her heart said it couldn't happen. Veil had to wait for her, she was its daughter. Some day she had to solve the mystery of the Lost Boy and the Lost Fleet, but how was she going to do that? She was just a janitor.

Some day, she promised herself. *You'll find a way.*

She had no reason to believe that, but she did. She had her scrapbook right there in her hands, her proof, the evidence of all of her hard work and perseverance. David Silverstein and the Speedies would wait for her.

So comforted, she went to sleep on the couch, with the TV on.

In her dreams, she chased Maxi down an endless wind-ing street. "Wait!" she cried, and he looked back at her. For a moment, she hoped he would stop and take her hand. But he barely paused, and then he was running again, as if he had forgotten she even existed. She chased him all night, but she never caught up to him.

If anything, he only got farther away.

Morning on Agate was beautiful in a totally new way. It wasn't the mist-shrouded morning of Red Cliffs; it was clear and golden, with every detail of Crazy Horse Mountain etched sharply in the sunlight.

Seeing this every morning, thought Siggy as she rode the transit with Afrika and the others, *is going to make my days a heck of a lot brighter.*

She already recognized some of the people riding with them. Thompson was there, the security team leader. She smiled at Siggy, and made small talk with Afrika. George was there, and two other newbees: an older woman named Gong Li, who had jet black hair and freckles, and a pale young man with a perpetually tired face who introduced himself as Gustav von Holst. He tried to sit next to Siggy on the transit, and blushed when someone else took his spot. Afterward he tried not to look at her, and blushed every time that he acci-dentally met her eyes.

Uh-oh, thought Siggy, but he was cute. He had pale

blue eyes and a wry mouth. She hoped he really was
tired, and not sad. But in a way, she didn't want to
know. She wasn't going to fall in love again, not after
Maxi. She couldn't even think about it.

Afrika knew just about everyone on the transit. *Some
day I will too,* thought Siggy, looking forward to that
time when things would be comfortable and familiar. In
the meantime, she would just have to take it one day at
a time.

They got off the transit and descended to the front
door, showing their IDs to the viewer one at a time. The
lock admitted them in groups of five, and they filtered
through the checkpoints, down the long iron hallway.
Once they were all the way in, they went to the cafeteria
and sat with cups of coffee. Siggy could see that most
everyone else still had some waking up to do; but she
was bright-eyed and bushy-tailed. She barely sipped her
decaf, and tried to be friendly to Gustav without seeming flirty.

She was grateful when they got up to go to work.
Siggy liked to keep busy: working, studying, dancing,
walking, cooking, singing, preparing for holidays. She
was already making plans for her new life on this new
world; things that would please and entertain her new
friends.

That came to an abrupt halt when her crew had to
walk past an occupied cell block on their way to their
morning assignment. Siggy was startled when she saw
the inmates, and she blushed—an unfortunate reaction.
The prisoners were behind bars, rather than transparencies. Siggy felt their eyes on her as she passed them, and
some of them made semi-coherent remarks.

"Just think of them as mannequins," George whispered to her. "Just a bunch of dressed-up dummies who
can't think. Don't look 'em in the eye, and don't talk to
them. Why should you talk to a mannequin?"

It was an odd analogy, but it seemed to work. Before
long they were in another secured area, free to relax
and look wherever they wanted.

"You won't see many inmates the whole time you're
here," Afrika told her. "It's just that when you do, you

gotta get your psychology straight. You have to be prepared."

Siggy hoped she would be. She hoped she had the right psychology, the right stuff. She hadn't thought the job would be easy, but she had hoped it would be fairly straightforward. Now she was beginning to suspect that there wasn't a job in the universe that would fit that description.

As if to prove her right, a notice was pinned to the bulletin board outside the maintenance office. Afrika stopped to read it, George crowding in beside him.

"Shit," remarked George.

"What's wrong?" asked Gustav, anxiously.

Siggy had an ominous feeling at the pit of her stomach. It had begun to grow when they walked through the cell block; now it was making her breakfast feel like a sour lump.

"Special materials," said George. "I guess we're gonna find out what they are after all."

"Not everybody," said Afrika, and Siggy thought he sounded a little suspicious. "Just eleven names on this list."

"Who?" asked Gong Li.

Afrika took a deep breath and let it out again. "Siggy," he said, "you and me and George have to go at noon. The rest of you guys are excused."

"Ain't that interesting," said George. "And how come Thompson's on the list? And Rode and Ashmarina? They're security."

"Who else?" asked Siggy, an ugly suspicion nagging at one corner of her mind.

"Don't recognize the other names," said George.

"Me either," said Afrika. "We have to go to conference room H-7. Don't think I've ever been there before. . . ."

"It's in the west wing," said George. "I was there once. Got 'interviewed' for something I said to one of the doctors."

"What did you say?" asked Gong Li.

"I told him his eyesight would be a lot better if he'd take his head out of his ass."

There was a respectful silence.

"They grilled me for three hours," said George, finally. "I thought I was gonna lose my job that day."

Don't talk to the doctors, Siggy told herself, sternly. *Don't tell them what you really think of them, don't get mad at them, avoid them at all costs.*

It was good advice. It was too bad she wasn't going to take it.

When noon rolled around, Siggy was so nervous she couldn't eat lunch. Thompson and the others were already there when the janitors arrived: Siggy noticed that the others were dressed in security uniforms or the white outfits of orderlies.

Everyone wore the same grim look.

We all did something, thought Siggy. *We all said something that made him mad, and he heard us because this place is bugged. We pissed him off, and now he's going to punish us. But what is he going to do? Why didn't he just fire us?*

Stop it, warned the mom in her head. *It's psychological warfare. He wants you to worry, to work yourself up into a state wondering what's going to happen. Don't wonder, just be. Take it one moment at a time.*

But that was hard. Siggy tried not to look into Thompson's eyes and see the same knowledge lurking there, the same conclusions she had already drawn herself. And she averted her gaze from Afrika, because he knew, too, and he was as worried about her as he was about himself, like a big brother wondering if he would have to fight for his sister.

Finally the door opened, and an officer stepped out. He regarded them blandly.

His was the sort of face you could see in a crowd and forget instantly. He stood at an average height, with an average build; he had no distinctive mannerisms, nothing in his walk or carriage to set him off from anyone else. But Thompson stiffened as soon as she saw him. Her chin went up and her eyes became cold. Siggy gazed at the man, wondering what he had done to inspire that kind of dislike.

She didn't think of him as the Toady yet.

"Go in," he said in a toneless voice.

The room's metal walls shone dully in the dim light; its industrial carpet was roughly the same non-color. At one end, chairs had been set in rows in front of a large viewscreen hooked up to a mini player. Other than that, the room was bare, save for a lone chair by the door. The officer locked the door, then went to the front of the room, pulled a mini out of his pocket and slipped it into the player.

"What's this about?" asked Afrika.

The officer didn't answer. He went to the lone chair and sat down in it. Siggy glanced at him over her shoulder. He was staring at them the same way most people stared at their TVs. He simply watched, uninvolved, uncaring.

There was a *blip* from the sound system, and suddenly the Director appeared on the screen. Siggy started, then settled back, sheepishly.

"Congratulations," sneered the Director. "You are here because you have all been chosen for particularly hazardous duties. In short, each of you will have regular contact with the three most dangerous inmates currently incarcerated in this facility: Jerry Wolfe, Joseph Bell, and Prisoner MS-12. You have been chosen for thcse duties because each of you have displayed certain *talents* that would seem to indicate you might be particularly useful."

The Director paused to give one of his malignant grimaces, and Siggy heard Afrika expelling his breath as if he had just been punched in the stomach.

"We are required by law," said the Director, emphatically, "to make sure that you are adequately prepared for these encounters. That means that *you* are also required, if you want to continue working at this facility, to receive the training we deem proper for these circumstances." He leaned toward the camera and bared his teeth at them. "Any of you who attempt to circumnavigate this training will be terminated immediately, and a permanent blemish will appear on your record for your next potential employer to review. I trust this is very, very clear."

It was. Everyone knew how hard it was to get another job when you got fired. If you did get another one, the pay and benefits would likely be lower, and you would be on probation for the first several months, proving to your new employer that you weren't a bad risk. But if the guy who fired you also wrote a nasty explanation on your permanent record, the whole process got about ten times harder.

You could fight the blemish in court, of course, if you had about ten years to waste. And in the meantime you still had to earn a living, and if you were considered unhirable through regular channels, that meant a job at the government work farms. Most of them were in some pretty remote places; awful places, from what Siggy had heard.

"The materials you are about to view are audio-visual bytes from police documentation, as well as footage taken directly from the home movies of Jerry Wolfe. You will undoubtedly find them unpleasant. That's too bad; we all have to deal with unpleasantness at the Institute for the Criminally Insane, it is part and parcel of our calling. I and my staff have viewed many hours of the same footage, as well as materials from several other sources; we have found the experience instructional, and it is our intention to pass some of our conclusions on to you. You undoubtedly think you do not need this information. You are wrong, but if you feel you are not up to the demands of this job, you are welcome to leave this company now."

He paused, as if he could actually see them and gauge their reactions. Siggy could have sworn he was looking right at *her*. She didn't move, and neither did anyone else, but the uneasiness in the room was growing palpable.

"Those of you who have chosen to stay," continued the recording of the Director, "will hear my analysis of each incident directly after each segment. Listen carefully; this is not the time to let your minds wander. Your lives and the lives of others may depend on what you learn from these materials today."

And with no further ado, his image disappeared from the screen. It was replaced by a test pattern, inside which a countdown was moving. Siggy stared at the countdown, thinking, *I'm going to regret this. I'm going to wish I had gotten up and run right out of this room, never mind that the Director would sneer at me, or that I'd have to go home and explain to Mom how I managed to get fired on the second day of my first job . . .*

And then the images started.

At first, Siggy couldn't make out what she should be looking at. The footage hadn't been shot by a cinematographer, that was for sure. A man began to speak in the background, and he had obviously never been given speech or drama lessons.

"This is agent Michael Simon," he said, "October twenty-one-Philae Standard Time, at five hundred sixty seven East Surrey Avenue, Apartment Seven-A, registered to Ronald S. Cohan, whereabouts of tenant unknown. Door unlocked, no sign of forced entry."

The camera documented the inside of the apartment, foot by foot, starting first with the front door, which stood open, then carefully examining the contents of the room. Siggy tensed, not knowing quite why yet, except that the man's voice, for all its unrefined quality, still managed to convey the extreme seriousness of a situation that was still unknown. Suddenly the camera panned in on a red smear on the carpet, and things became a little clearer.

"Significant blood stain," said the voice, "source unknown, checking for species identification."

The camera stayed still while a man in a sterile suit walked carefully around the stain. He managed to bend over it without disturbing the area around it and touch it with a strip of white material. The material slowly darkened, and then the man inserted the strip into a small box with a tiny, glowing screen on its face. He watched figures dance across the screen, then looked at the camera.

"Human," he announced, with no apparent surprise.

"Let's move on," said the narrator. The camera went carefully around the stain, then zoomed in on a trail of the same substance leading to the kitchen.

"Oh God," Siggy heard Afrika whisper. This was like the part in the monster movie where the hero is going up the stairs, and you want to yell, *Don't go up there!*

but you don't because he can't hear you. She pressed her lips together, hard.

There was a lot more blood in the kitchen. The camera stopped at the doorway. The officers couldn't go in there without disturbing the crime scene, Siggy guessed. The camera spent a lot of time documenting the blood stains. The screen went black, and then some numbers appeared. Siggy just had time to figure out they were another date and time, and then the scene in the kitchen reappeared.

"Blood stains identified," said the voice of the narrator. "Confirmed, Ronald J. Cohan."

The floor had been cleaned up to a certain point, and the man in the sterile suit passed some kind of wand that flashed blue light over some bloody hand prints.

"Print identity confirmed," said the man in the sterile suit. "John Doe H117629."

They saw a lengthy montage of cuts and number blips, showing sterile-suited men performing various analyses, all confirming that Ronald J. Cohan's blood was all over the kitchen, often in the form of bloody fingerprints belonging to John Doe H117629. But Siggy was more interested in the shots she kept seeing of the trash compactor.

It was leaking blood.

She rubbed her head, wearily. She suspected what they were going to find in there. Couldn't they just get to it? But this was important police work, they had to document everything. On the other hand, what did that have to do with what she and the others were supposed to be learning? They weren't criminology students. The Director should have edited this part out.

Then finally, they did get to the trash compactor. Two sterile-suited men had to pry it open. It came with an awful squishing sound, accompanied by a fresh, if sluggish, flow of blood from the sides.

"Jesus," someone whispered with disgust, and Siggy felt her breakfast stirring again.

The camera walked over to the compactor and looked into it.

Siggy was so shocked, she forgot to close her eyes. The thing inside was still—somehow, horribly—human.

You could even make out the guy's face. His foot was crushed under his chin.

Siggy felt a surge of anger. How could they show a thing like this? But they had to, it was evidence, the police had to know exactly what had been done.

The scene shifted, and she saw sterile-suited men kneeling beside the compactor, trying to take it apart with power tools. While she was watching, one metal side was cut away and a limp hand plopped out.

Siggy closed her eyes and heard the Director's voice.

"Prisoner MS-12 committed two kinds of documented murders, each motivated by different stimuli. In the first example, he merely broke the necks of his victims, cleanly and efficiently, in order to rob them. These murders reveal no evidence of rage or malice, but seem expedient in nature.

"The second type of murder, as illustrated in this FBI footage from Philae, the murder of one Mr. Ronald J. Cohan, was apparently the result of rage. These murders follow distinctive patterns: evidence of death by severe bludgeoning, and then treatment of the body by crushing it into the smallest possible container."

This narrative was accompanied by a montage of ghastly stills, a collection of examples of prisoner MS-12's ingenuity for fitting people's bodies into very small places. Siggy heard someone gasp, then realized that she was the one who was fighting for breath. *Calm down* she told herself, but she couldn't do it until she took her eyes off the screen. She concentrated on the bland carpet.

"This treatment may be ritualistic in nature," continued the voice of the Director, "an example of a staged scene, characteristic of an organized serial killer; but it may also simply be the result of sustained rage, which would point to a disorganized type of serial killer.

"Prisoner MS-12 has been given a thorough battery of medical exams and brain scans since his arrival at the Institute; no physiological evidence of mental illness or of neurological disorder has been discovered to pertain to his condition. He refuses to speak with any of the doctors, and his observed behavior during his incarceration has been remarkably unrevealing. We have been unable to ascertain precisely what stimulus it would require to provoke a killing rage from Prisoner MS-12, and have been unable to gain any insight from the reports of the police agents who gathered and/or examined evidence at his various crime scenes.

"Prisoner MS-12 has no birth records. He was known by various aliases during the period in which he was committing documented crimes, but these aliases were not actively assumed by him; he merely used the credit cards and vehicles of some of his victims, and this use created false records. He has never once identified himself by any name, to any authority.

"Besides his lack of birth records, he is also undocumented by tissue or blood samples, pheromonal recordings, or retinal scans. Until various police agencies began to gather fingerprint records from crime scenes beginning one year before his arrest, there were also no fingerprint records for him on file. What records do exist are simply labeled 'John Doe H117629.'

"Prisoner MS-12 was remanded to our care by the federal court system when a panel of neuropsychologists were unable to ascertain whether or not he may have committed his crimes due to an existing or pre-existing condition of mental illness. We have undertaken to study the matter; but at this time his diagnosis is inconclusive. His prognosis is also inconclusive."

"They should have just put a bullet in the motherfucker's head," whispered Afrika.

Siggy was inclined to agree.

She waited to hear more about Prisoner MS-12, the man she and the others would later come to call the Professor; but the Director apparently had nothing more to say about him. The screen went dark, and then another test pattern appeared. Or at least Siggy assumed it was a test pattern. She refused to look up and make sure.

Light flickered on the carpet again, and Siggy heard voices. But they sounded mild and friendly; so Siggy risked a peek at the screen.

A young man in a military uniform was sitting across a table from a plump, middle-aged woman. The woman had an intelligent face and she regarded the man with a sympathetic, attentive expression. They both held themselves in relaxed positions, so Siggy wondered what was up.

"I couldn't feel any difference at first," the man said. "I mean I couldn't exactly see it or hear it, except that I seemed to be talking too fast for people. And when it was my turn to listen, I kept interrupting them. Other than that, I noticed that people seemed to *walk* funny. Their movements seemed jerky to me; but slow jerky, not fast. When they walked it was in sort of a slow-stop, slow-stop fashion, like a film that keeps getting stuck."

He grinned at the woman, and Siggy thought how handsome he was. He wore a starman's uniform, the same sort that David Silverstein would have worn some day. Siggy wondered why the woman wasn't smiling back at him. Her face looked sad. The camera was positioned on the woman's side of the room, and Siggy could see the woman's hand resting near a button underneath the tabletop.

"When were you sure that the restructuring had really changed your perceptions?" the woman asked, with no trace of nervousness in her voice.

"When I was in my fighter," said the man, still relaxed, still leaning back in his chair, and Siggy couldn't help but admire his build. He looked like he was in top physical condition. "Once they recalibrated the instruments to suit my speeded-up condition," he said, "there wasn't anything I couldn't make that baby do. You should have seen us, we were incredible. We were the latest thing, the secret weapon that was really going to make the difference."

The woman put her finger on the button, but didn't press it. The sense of tension was growing, but Siggy still wasn't sure why. The man seemed to be enjoying talking about his fighter, as any man would; any man would be proud to pilot a marvelous machine like that, lots of boys grew up dreaming about it. The whites were showing around his eyes a little bit, but that wasn't so odd was it?

"So you loved your fighter," said the woman. "That must have been marvelous, to be so much in tune with something so powerful. But when did you first begin to notice that you weren't relating as well to people?"

He shrugged. "I'm not sure. People started to act like they were scared of me. Like they thought I was going to do something bad." He grinned. "Like they thought speeding me up was the same thing as turning me into a Speedy. And Speedies are the enemy, right?"

"Are they?" asked the woman.

"They'd better be," he said, losing his smile. "Because if they aren't, I let a bunch of doctors rewire my head for nothing."

The woman almost pushed the button that time, Siggy was sure of it. Her finger had twitched. But she held back for some reason.

"You volunteered to be restructured," the doctor said, with compassion instead of accusation. "Do you regret that decision?"

He smiled again, this time slowly. "You're asking Mr. Hyde, sweetheart. You're asking him if he's sorry Dr. Jekyll drank the potion."

Mr. Hyde? thought Siggy. She had read the book in high school. She watched the woman, who had remained admirably cool and who still hadn't pushed the button. Siggy was pretty sure the man couldn't see the woman's hand from his position.

But he knew. With every passing moment, Siggy believed that more. He knew the woman was frightened of him. He was playing with her, enjoying himself, watching her struggle to keep control of the situation.

"I'll address my question to Mr. Hyde then," said the woman. "Are you sorry that Dr. Jekyll drank the potion?"

He smiled a dazzling smile, and Siggy felt her heart skip a beat. He was the sort of man that could break a woman's heart.

The woman pushed the button.

Two things happened simultaneously: four officers burst into the room and went for the man; and the man leapt across the table at the woman, moving so fast that Siggy and the others jumped in surprise.

The officers were moving fast, but not fast enough. The man grabbed the woman and the two of them toppled the chair over backward. Just before they hit the ground, the man put one hand out and stopped them, cold, about a foot from the floor. Then, in that impossible position, he bit the woman on her shoulder, in the bare place between her collar and her neck. He bit her so hard, blood spurted; but she didn't scream. She only gasped.

The officers were shocking him with their stun guns by then, but the shocks were slow to have any effect. Eventually the officers managed to pull him back far enough for Siggy to see his face. His teeth were stained with the woman's blood, and his chin was covered in it. He looked into the woman's eyes with such a languorous, amorous expression, Siggy was embarrassed to see it.

"You're good, baby," he said, thickly. "I want more of you."

To her credit, the woman didn't scream or cry then. She regarded him with the same expression of sad sympathy she had worn from the very beginning. Siggy admired her for it.

As they pried the man loose from the woman, her chair fell the rest of the way to the floor. There was a confusing moment as the officers grappled with the man and the woman tried to upright herself, and then the tableau was suddenly replaced by a static image of a military ID file. A photo of the man was in the upper right-hand corner. He was smiling; the picture had obviously been taken in a saner time. The difference between the man in this photograph and the man who had attacked the woman was startling; Siggy wondered how she could have thought he was sane before.

"Commander Joseph Bell," said the voice of the Director, "was the recipient of neurological restructuring, part of a top-secret military program designed to speed up human perceptions and reflexes. He was among the three percent of recipients to suffer brain damage as a result of the restructuring process.

"Commander Bell experiences two different mental states. The first is almost normal, with perceptions and reflexes only slightly speeded-up, and with normal functioning both of the limbic system and of the frontal lobes, which help mediate impulses from the limbic system. The second is characterized by perceptions and reflexes that operate close to Speedy capacity, but with overstimulation of several major brain centers, one of the results of which is an exaggerated sexual response.

"Commander Bell has *not* suffered mental retardation as a result of his restructuring; his mental capacity is as high as it was previously, possibly even higher in some regards. His reflexes also function perfectly, as was well demonstrated in the footage of his interview with the doctor; in fact, in that respect, his restructuring can be said to have been a complete success."

That figures, thought Siggy. *So now he can kill at the speed of light.*

The screen went dark again, and Siggy looked down. They were doubtless going to show images of what Commander Bell had done to his victims and then talk about his prognosis. But the screen stayed dark and the room silent, except for the sounds of the audience, coughing or moving around in their chairs, uneasily.

Didn't he do anything? Siggy wondered. *Maybe he was arrested as soon as he started to act weird. But you can't send someone to prison just for acting weird, he must have done something. How come they're not talking about it?*

Light suddenly strobed on the carpet, in regular beats that indicated yet another test pattern with a countdown on it.

Only one guy left then, Jerry Wolfe. What had she heard about him on TV? Wasn't he the guy with the messy house? With trash piled to the ceiling and rotting bodies. And wasn't there a kid who had escaped from the house? This part might even be interesting. Siggy liked stories about people who had escaped from monsters.

Sound exploded into the room, confusing Siggy, making her blink; someone pleading and sobbing, and the roar of an engine, and Siggy looked at the screen before she could stop herself.

She saw a naked man on a rack, his wrists and ankles tightly handcuffed, his arms stretched over his head and his legs splayed open. The rack was angled so that the man was almost upright, his feet almost touching the floor. He was obviously an athlete or a bodybuilder; he was

beautifully toned. But his body was burned, torn,
bruised, showing obvious signs of torture, and his face
was contorted in terror.

Jerry Wolfe was standing over him with a roaring
chain saw.

"Looka this!" Wolfe was shouting over the sound of
the engine, "You know what this is, asshole? Huh?
Whaddaya thinka this? You know what this could do to
flesh and bone? Whaddaya think I'm gonna do now,
huh? Guess! Guess, asshole! C'mon, guess!"

Wolfe lunged with the chain saw and then pulled back
at the last moment, giggling, and the guy's eyes widened,
he begged and pleaded, trying to reach Wolfe, trying to
get him to stop; but Wolfe wasn't going to stop, he was
in charge, he was the master, he was having fun, and the
machine roared and the pleading became so hysterical
that it was incoherent.

Siggy jammed her eyes shut and gripped the armrests
so hard she heard fabric tearing. Then Afrika was prying
her hand loose and holding it tight, and Jerry Wolfe was
saying "Oh yeah! Oh yeah! Here it comes, asshole! Here
it comes!"

And Siggy heard the roar of the engine, heard it
change pitch as it encountered something solid, heard a
scream that she would be hearing in her dreams for
years to come, screaming and the sound of Jerry Wolfe's
hooting laughter.

Siggy pressed her face against Afrika's shoulder; he
pulled his hand loose and wrapped his arm around her,
pulling her close as she jammed both hands against her
mouth, because if she didn't, if she opened her mouth,
she would scream until she was crazy, scream so loud
that she couldn't hear those sounds anymore, those
awful, pathetic sounds of a man dying.

And suddenly there was silence, into which the Director began talking again; but Siggy couldn't hear him, she
could only hear her companions sobbing, crying, cursing,
retching. She didn't open her eyes yet, she didn't want
to see them in pain any more than she hadn't wanted to
see Jerry Wolfe's victim that way. But she would have
to open then sooner or later, because surely that must
be all there was, there couldn't be anything else on the

mini, not after that. Could there? There wasn't anything else they needed to know about Jerry Wolfe.

But she was wrong, that wasn't all there was.

There was the little girl and the blow torch.

Then droning commentary from the Director.

There was the little boy and the power drill.

And more commentary, but Siggy didn't hear any of it, her capacity for listening destroyed.

What is he talking about? What could he possibly have to say after all that? The mini speaks for itself, a picture is worth a thousand words.

And a sound was worth a million.

When it was over, the TV screen switched off. Just like that, the end. Siggy didn't see it go off, she heard the *BLIP!* from the sound system. She felt Afrika stirring, hesitantly. Her eyes opened and she blinked, like a newborn, trying to adjust to what little light was in the room.

Everyone had been holding hands, right down the line. As Siggy watched, they all let go, reluctantly. Their expressions were all variations of the one Siggy could feel straining her own features; George looked madder, Thompson looked sick. The horror in Afrika's face was compounded by worry, for her.

He had to help her to her feet. Once there, she needed his help to stand.

"Are you okay?" George was asking Thompson.

Thompson couldn't seem to be able to bring herself to speak, so she nodded, instead; then she shook her head.

Siggy looked around until she saw the officer who had loaded the mini. The Director's Toady.

He looked right back at her. The first thing that she realized was that he was bored. The mini had bored him; other than that he had no reaction to it at all. But he seemed to have a reaction to the sight of their distress. His face hadn't changed that much, it was a subtle thing. But she was sure of what she saw there.

Smugness.

Rage washed over her, draining her remaining strength. Her legs went out from under her, but Afrika caught her on the way down. "Whoa!" he said, and picked her up as easily as if she were a small child. "We'd better get you to the infirmary."

He took her out of the room. The Toady went first, then stood on the other side of the door and watched them all file out. Siggy watched him over Afrika's shoulder, saw him take two steps back from the people as they passed him, out of reach of the hatred in their eyes, the promise that if he were any closer they would kill him with their bare hands.

If anything, his expression just got more smug.

What kind of creature . . . ? Siggy wondered, letting her head fall back on Afrika's shoulder, like a little girl being carried to bed by her father with the promise of a story.

You have to be nuts to want to be in charge of a prison full of crazy killers, Afrika had said.

Then what does that make us? she had wondered.

Desperate, he had answered.

Desperate.

Later, in bits and pieces, they would talk to each other about it. Siggy would learn all of their names well, though some of them left IFCI before she had a chance to really get to know them.

Afrika eventually confided that he had closed his eyes just before she had, and kept them closed. She would find out that Thompson had vomited in the hallway, and hadn't been able to stop vomiting for the rest of the day. The doctors in the infirmary sent Thompson home, and she stayed out for two days total.

Rode went into a trance, moving through his life and his job like an automaton, until he emerged from it three weeks later, dazed and confused.

Ashmarina suffered so badly from nightmares, she had to start taking Valium.

Calloway, Byrne, and Barbirolli found new jobs as fast as they could and quit the Institute. Metraux and Budge were not as lucky. They filed class action suits against IFCI, the Director, and the federal government. The suits were immediately dismissed—the Director had known exactly what he was doing when he called the mini "training materials"—and Metraux and Budge were summarily fired.

George never talked about the mini at all; you would have thought he hadn't even seen it. But Siggy noticed that he didn't laugh as much; and sometimes she would catch him looking into the far distance, an expression of bewildered disappointment on his face.

They treated her for shock at the infirmary. She recovered her strength pretty quickly, and seemed alert when they asked her questions, so they let her go back to work

But Siggy wasn't alert. She was numb. She wasn't crying anymore because it took too much energy. Afrika seemed in much the same condition, and she knew better than to ask him how he was feeling. She didn't even want to ask herself that question.

Siggy walked with Afrika and George back to the maintenance office, to find out what their duties would be for the rest of the day.

"You guys will be working Monster Row," said the supervisor, Mr. Morita.

Siggy stood and gazed at him as if he were a character in a movie. She was in the same movie, so she had to say "yes, sir" and "no, sir" at the appropriate moments because those were her lines. It was as if she were at home with Mom, sitting in her usual spot on the couch, watching herself with George and Afrika, all standing at attention as the supervisor told them what time they would each be braving the Monsters every day.

"Special duties are as follows," said Mr. Morita. "Mopping the row three times a day and cleaning up empty cells after a tenant vacates. You won't ever be going into a cell when a tenant is still in it, so don't worry about that. Every once in a while they move someone for treatment, and they might tell us they want the cell cleaned, but that's pretty rare. Most of the time, what it is, you'll just be mopping that hall when it's your turn and then you'll be doing regular duties in the north wing, where you'll still be working with von Holst, Gong, and Jimenez.

"That hall needs to be mopped three times a day?" said Afrika. "It's that dirty?"

Mr. Morita looked grim. "Mop it like it's dirty, even if it looks clean. Afrika, you'll have the morning shift on the row. Lindquist, you'll mop just before lunch, and George—you'll mop in the afternoon, just before you leave for the day. The whole job doesn't take more than ten minutes, and that's if you're being slow and careful. It's just that one narrow hallway."

"Who used to do it?" Siggy heard herself ask.

"I did," said Morita. "That area used to be off limits to regular maintenance workers, but I guess the Director's changed his mind about that. Anyway, it's no big deal, don't let it scare you. They're locked up, the guard usually opaques the cells so you don't even have to look at 'em."

"Oh," said Siggy, not believing him. They had shown the mini to her, and there had to be a reason for them to do that. There must be more in store. She didn't dare believe there wasn't. The blinders had been torn off her eyes.

"It's almost lunchtime, so you might as well come on down with me, Lindquist. I'll show you the supply room and take you through security. You two guys can head on over to the north wing now, just do your usual. I'll take you each through later."

Siggy felt George and Afrika looking at her, but she didn't look back. She knew that her face was as close to expressionless as it ever got; she could feel how slack the muscles were. She supposed that was a good thing; after all, they had their jobs to do, all of them. They couldn't afford to get bogged down by feelings.

"See you later," she told them calmly, and followed Mr. Morita out of the office.

They walked down the main hall until they came to the innermost checkpoint. There was a door there with a keypad beside it. Siggy had glimpsed it the day before and wondered where it led. Morita showed his ID to the little screen.

It blipped, and the door slid open.

It was an elevator. They got in, and the door closed behind them. Siggy felt a downward motion.

Mysterious realms, she thought to herself. *Special materials.*

When the door opened again, two officers were waiting for them on the other side. The officers shone a strobing light in their faces.

"Confirmed," Siggy heard one of them say.

Morita took her arm and ushered her into the checkpoint. The officers parted to let them pass, then followed them to the next door. One of the officers unlocked the door, and the supervisor led Siggy through, into a hallway that was transparent on both sides. There were rooms on the other side of those walls; one full of equipment, the other full of monitors. The room with the monitors also contained an officer. He watched Siggy's image on his screens, but didn't turn to watch the real Siggy just behind him.

There was a pressure door at the end of this hall, like Siggy had seen on the ship that had brought her to Agate. But she had a feeling that this door hadn't been built to prevent a sudden loss of atmosphere.

Just to the right of the pressure door there was a normal door. It even had a doorknob. Mr. Morita unlocked it and showed Siggy inside. It looked exactly like all of the other supply rooms she had seen so far.

He watched her while she prepared the mop and bucket.

"I can't stay in here any longer," he said as she wheeled the bucket to the pressure door. "Only one person is allowed in this hall when they open that pressure door. Any questions?"

"Yes," said Siggy. "If no one ever goes in there, how does the hall get dirty?"

He looked startled, then embarrassed. "Keep mopping it every day," he said, "And it'll stay clean. Okay?"

"Okay," echoed Siggy.

"See you later," he said. He handed her the key to the supply room and turned away.

"Okay," she called after him.

She watched him until the other door had closed behind him. Then she looked at the pressure door. It had a keypad and screen beside it. Siggy held her ID up to the screen.

She heard a distant buzzing and wondered if it had anything to do with her. She continued to hold her ID against the screen. She wondered, vaguely, what was taking so long. But she didn't really care.

The door began to open, releasing compressed air, as if it really were a ship lock after all. Siggy pushed her mop and bucket into the lock.

It was small in there, with room for just one technician, a bank of monitors, and a small control panel. One wall contained several storage lockers; another wall contained a door with a rest room symbol on it. The rest room looked impossibly tiny.

The Toady sat behind the control panel. He stared at her blandly.

Siggy's stomach turned at the sight of him. She was still angry at him, and she was surprised to know that. It was a feeling that would stay with her for as long as she knew him.

"My supervisor says that you're supposed to opaque their barriers before I go in," she said.

He didn't answer. He didn't touch the control panel.

Siggy squared her jaw and pushed the mop and bucket to the inner door. She waited there. She would wait forever if she had to, but she wouldn't speak to him again.

After a while, he opened the door.

Siggy peered out. The end of the row seemed a long way off. She could see transparencies from both sides of the hallway reflecting light from overhead banks; but from that angle she could see little else. There was a space of blank wall before the cells started.

She thought she saw movement flickering on both sides. The inmates must have realized the door had been opened and maybe they had moved to try to peer at the pressure door. But their angle of view couldn't be any better than hers was.

The Toady wouldn't opaque the transparencies. She knew it as surely as she knew her own name. But Siggy took a deep breath and pushed her bucket into the hallway. The pressure door closed behind her.

Mannequins, she told herself. *That's what they are. Just push this thing to the end of the row and work your way back, don't look at anyone, don't talk to anyone, just move. Like dancing, back and forth, back and forth, and then get the hell out of here.*

She saw the flicker of movement again, inmates straining to see her. She put her head down and kept pushing.

"Hey," someone said from her left. "Hey! I don't believe it! Look what they sent us!"

There was an explosion of sound as the men on the near end of the row caught sight of Siggy: whistles, howls, comments she tried not to hear. The hair on the back of her neck stood up, but she kept moving, like a dancer ignoring hecklers. Her muscles were true, they did their job perfectly. She kept her head down and kept moving.

"Hi there," said a friendly and perfectly reasonable

voice when she got about halfway down the row. It startled Siggy, she almost looked up; but then she recognized the voice as one she had heard on the mini.

Commander Bell.

"Nice to see a new face," he said.

A lump was forming in Siggy's throat. Somehow, the sound of the warmth and humanity in that voice was hurting her like none of the threats or catcalls could. *How am I going to face this every day?* she wondered, but kept on pushing the bucket, making her muscles do what they needed to do; and then another voice began to scream at her and she forgot Commander Bell for the moment.

"Hey!" it screeched. "Are you a nigger or a honkey?"

Siggy didn't know what either word meant, but she recognized this voice from the mini, too. The last time she had heard it, it had been yelling, "You know what I'm going to do with this, asshole?" over the sound of a chain saw.

Hate flooded into her, pulsing in her veins, rising in her cheeks and burning her eyes. She kept them on the floor and pushed the mop and bucket to the end of the row.

"Hey!" Jerry Wolfe kept screeching, on her right as she passed him. "Which one? Nigger or honkey, huh? Which one? Are you deaf or something? You dumb bitch, I'm talking to you!"

"Shut up, Wolfe," Commander Bell said, his voice weary but still full of the iron that had made him a commander; but Jerry Wolfe was well into his rant by then, and couldn't be stopped.

"Which one!" he demanded. "Goddammit, I'm the Antichrist you dumb bitch and I command you to answer me, you hear me? I'm going to burn you in hell for eternity and you'd damn well better answer me now because it's just going to get worse for you if you don't do exactly what I say and you'd better take off your clothes when I tell you to and you can suck my cock and—"

Etc., etc.

He was going like a wound-up machine. Now that he was well into it, his performance was almost awe-inspiring, but not for the reason he wanted it to be. Siggy was amazed at the energy behind the voice, the single-minded viciousness of it. A normal person would have been consumed by it, but not Jerry Wolfe. Rather, he seemed to *gain* energy from his rant, to feed off of it.

But in a way that was good. The other inmates had quieted, in respect for a better performer. And even better: Jerry Wolfe was speaking so fast now, Siggy could hardly understand him. It was much easier to tune him out. His voice became meaningless noise; it almost lulled her, brought her into an alpha state inside which nothing could touch her or move her.

She reached the end of the row and began to mop, swishing back and forth, back and forth, then pushing the bucket backward several paces when she dipped the mop in to rinse it. The fluid dried almost as quickly as it touched the floor, which, as Siggy had suspected, was already spotless.

Swish-swish, swish-swish, swish-swish, dip-push-wring. Swish-swish, swish-swish, dip-push-wring.

One-two-three, *one*-two-three . . .

Someone was standing to her left. She felt him as if he weren't behind a transparency at all, as if he were in the hall with her. But that couldn't be—they were all locked up.

Don't look up, she warned herself. *Keep your head down, keep mopping.*

And she did, without hurrying, without breaking her rhythm. She worked her way back to Jerry Wolfe again, and his voice picked up in volume as well as speed. She still wasn't listening to him; but his tone was beginning to annoy her, to distract her.

Why can't he just shut up? she wondered peevishly, and she almost lost track of where she was, what part she had just mopped. And then something seemed to rush at her, from ahead and to her left. She started violently, and looked up.

Right into the eyes of Prisoner MS-12.

He hadn't moved at all, he was impossibly still. His eyes transfixed her; her muscles stopped moving as if the machinery that ran them had rusted and failed. Jerry Wolfe stopped ranting; she heard a little gasp from him. She didn't look at him, though. She couldn't have looked away from Prisoner MS-12, not with those terrible eyes holding her so tight.

Her mind brought forth an image for her to consider. It was the man inside the trash compactor, seen with perfect clarity; the foot that had been crushed so tight under his chin, the blood that had leaked out the side of the compactor and onto the kitchen floor.

Prisoner MS-12 smiled faintly, as if he knew exactly what she was thinking. But his eyes didn't move or change at all.

What had it been like to see these eyes when the person who owned them was rushing at you, hitting you with so much force, breaking your bones . . . ?

"He can't hurt you," Commander Bell was calling. "He's locked up, kiddo. Don't look at him. Just look at the floor again. Yeah, that's right, you can get it done. One step at a time, back and forth, that's right. Just like a waltz, back and forth. You must be a dancer or something. You're halfway done now, you can get through it. No big deal . . ."

Siggy was back in step again. She could still feel Prisoner MS-12 looking at her and she was still terrified of him. But now she could almost stand back from it all and think, *Wow, that's amazing, I've never seen anyone like him.* Now he was almost interesting, just as a predator might seem fascinating to his prey as it watched him from a safe distance.

"Shit," snarled Jerry Wolfe, "Beelzebub is just a Demon! *I'm* the Antichrist! *I'm* the one you should be scared of, *I'm* the one who's going to burn your soul in hell for eternity!"

Commander Bell laughed. "Jealous, Wolfe? Just because our friend over there scared her without saying a word while you stand there and shoot your fat mouth off, all for nothing?"

"I'm going to rip your head off and shit down your neck!" shrieked Wolfe, and Siggy wondered if he meant her, or Commander Bell, or both. "You hear me? I'm going to *rip* your *head* off and *shit down your neck!* Shit down your fucking neck! I'm going to rip your head off and shit down your neck! You hear me?"

Jeez, thought Siggy, *What a spastic!* Wolfe just kept

saying the same thing over and over, like he thought the
repetition would intimidate her. Or maybe he just liked
the sound of it so much he couldn't stop saying it, making a complete geek out of himself.

But that was what people had always thought of Jerry
Wolfe: What a geek, what a spaz, what a dweeb, a nerd,
a scud, a schmuck, an idiot, a jerk. No one could take
him seriously, so everyone thought he was harmless.
Right up until the moment they woke up from a drugged
sleep and realized that he had tied them to a rack.

Siggy gritted her teeth and kept mopping. She left
Wolfe and the Professor behind. She passed silently by
Commander Bell, who had stopped trying to talk to her.
She thought he was still looking at her, or maybe she
just imagined that he was.

No, she wasn't imagining it. If she looked at him, he
would be looking back. She couldn't do that. Not ever.

She backed up all the way to the pressure door; then
stopped. She wondered if she was supposed to do the
last foot while inside the lock.

"Lindquist!" snarled the voice of the Director, and
Siggy jumped a mile. He was talking over the PA system,
trying to sound like the voice of God. "You missed several spots! I expect you to do your job adequately! You
will mop the floor again; and if you still haven't done
the job properly, I will *keep* sending you back until you
do! Do you understand?"

"Yes, sir," Siggy croaked. She looked at the floor she
had just mopped. It was so clean, it shone. There wasn't
one speck of dirt on it, anywhere; and she hadn't missed
one square inch with her mop. She had been very careful, very methodical, just like she had always been at
Mrs. Silverstein's house. He was lying, just to punish her.

The end of the hallway seemed twice as far away now.
Siggy sighed, until she thought she would cry. She
clamped down on the feeling until it had passed, then
began to push the bucket forward again.

Down the row, Jerry Wolfe howled with triumph.
"You don't know what you're doing!" he called. "You
can't even mop a damned floor right! What's the matter
with you? What's your IQ? You have to get every inch!
Every inch, you bitch, every inch of my big cock!"

"Shut up, Wolfe," said Commander Bell.

But he didn't have to tell Wolfe to shut up; Siggy couldn't hear him anymore. She couldn't hear anything. Inside her head there was just one big, ringing silence.

Dip, wring, Swish-swish, swish-swish.

One-two-three, one-two-three, one-two-three . . .

SECOND WALTZ

Okay everybody, let's dance!
—Championship Ballroom Dancing

Put your little foot
Put your little foot
Put your little foot right out
                    —*The Night Clerk*

Siggy finally caught up to Maxi in her dreams. This time she found herself in the backseat of his car. It wasn't where she wanted to be, but it was a significant improvement.

"Why can't I ride up front with you?" she asked.

"The new girl is going to sit there," he said without looking around.

"Who?" demanded Siggy, though she already knew.

"Leeza. I promised her I would show her how to tango."

Siggy tried to climb up front with him, but her seat belt held her down. The buckle wouldn't come undone. She stared at the back of his head in frustration. If she could just get up there, make him look her in the eye, things would turn out the way they were supposed to.

"It's no use, Siggy," said someone who was sitting in the back seat with her. It was Jorge La Placa. He gazed out his window, where Siggy could see the blackness of void. Enigma's G-star companion was there, its plume of hot matter spinning off to infinity. Jorge turned to look at her, his face shadowed. "You can step out of time, but when you step in again it's a new universe."

Siggy knew he was right, but she didn't want to believe him. She looked for Maxi again. He was gone; no one was behind the wheel now. And the car continued to drive, going forever because there was no one to stop it.

"You're not getting enough to eat," Afrika said the next morning.

Siggy looked up, startled. She had piled her lunch tray high with all the stuff she liked, but most of it was still there. She ate out of habit these days, her stomach clenched tight around something it couldn't let go of, something dreadful, something she saw mirrored in Afrika's eyes, and George's; and Thompson's, when she and the security guard met gazes as Siggy passed through the last checkpoint on her way out at night.

"Take another bite," said Afrika. Ordered, actually, and it was the same tone of voice he used with his children.

Siggy obeyed him. It was pot roast today, one of her favorites. It tasted good. Her stomach said, *Okay, I'm full now,* but Afrika's eyes said, *No, you're not.* So Siggy took another bite. It still tasted good. She chewed and let her eyes wander around the cafeteria, seeing the happy colors, the familiar people, hearing the sound of conversation but not quite picking up on what any of it meant.

Okay, I'm full now, said her stomach. Siggy took another bite.

Gong Li and Gustav von Holst watched her from the corners of their eyes. They were concerned, Siggy could tell. They kept looking to Afrika for cues.

He was eating, too. As was George. Siggy couldn't tell whether George's appetite suffered or not. He didn't seem any thinner than usual, and it would take years for her to realize just how much sadder he was.

Too much truth numbed a person. Or Siggy supposed it did if you were lucky. People could only stand so much. She and the others were still coming to work every day, they still spoke with friends and family, joked, laughed, watched TV, did their work. But Siggy's brain was doing something annoying these days. Every time something, maybe some little innocuous thing, reminded her of what she had seen from Jerry Wolfe's home movies, her brain would start blaring music at her, so loud she couldn't even think.

You're going crazy, she would tell herself. Then, *Don't be so melodramatic.*

Anyway, she was done mopping the Row for the day. She always felt so relieved afterward, almost the way she used to feel on Fridays when she was in school. After two weeks on the job, she didn't start getting nervous about mopping the Row until an hour or two before she actually had to do it. And after it was done, she ought to just let go of it, but today . . .

You shouldn't have looked at him, she told herself, sadly. *You should have kept your eyes down like you always do.*

She had established a good routine. As soon as the lock opened, she always pushed her mop and bucket to the end of the Row, keeping her eyes on the floor just in front of her. The things the inmates said often upset her—they came up with remarks that were sometimes so filthy and ugly she would never have been able to imagine them on her own. But once she had started the mopping she was always all right, the movement made her feel sure and confident again. Back and forth she would go, away from the Professor (George had christened him that), away from Jerry Wolfe (whose tirades were as ridiculous as they were ugly), and into Commander Bell's territory.

Commander Bell always had an encouraging word for her. She couldn't acknowledge him of course, shouldn't speak to him; and that often made her feel guilty. Mr. Hyde may have been a monster, but Dr. Jekyll was—a hero. He was a starman, every inch the sort of person David Silverstein had aspired to become someday; and every day when Siggy passed him by without a word or a look, her heart broke a little.

Remember the mini, she would remind herself. *Remember what he did to that lady. He's here for a reason. You can't break the rules.*

Today he had been silent. Siggy began mopping under the intense scrutiny of the Professor. She didn't want to look at him, either; though she would let herself look at his feet. That way she could tell where he was standing. When she came in to mop, he always stood right in front of the transparency, near the far corner where he could observe her for as long as possible. His regard felt like a physical blow.

Jerry Wolfe wasn't his usual self, though. Siggy looked for his feet, but they were nowhere in sight, and she could hear him near the rear of his cell, mumbling angrily to himself. She didn't try to catch what he was saying, but a few words stood out anyway: Apocalypse, bitch, and father, all said several times. Siggy backed away from his section.

Commander Bell stayed silent, though she could hear him moving, the sound of weight shifting on a bunk. She thought he was looking at her; she could always feel his gaze, too, a different sort of pressure than the Professor's glare. She hoped he wasn't angry at her. Or sad. But maybe it was better if he stopped talking to her. After all, she couldn't—

"Lindquist?" he asked, and she looked at him without thinking. She looked right into his eyes; and wanted to kick herself for doing it, because she knew she had been tricked into it. He looked back, hungry for the contact, and sorry he had to trick her into it, and that made it even worse.

"What's your first name?" he asked, and she was almost angry then, because he knew perfectly well he shouldn't ask it, just as he knew she wouldn't be able to turn away now without speaking, not when he was looking at her like that. Now she could see how he had been manipulating her for the past couple of weeks, earning her trust. And all because he wanted what she couldn't possibly give, had been trying so hard not to even think about.

And *damn,* but he was so handsome, so human now, seeming as sane as anyone. And he looked her right in the eye, not up and down the way she knew the others were doing. He just sat there, leaning forward with his elbows on his knees, his hands loosely clasped together, needing her answer, but not begging for it. *Asking.* And when someone asked that way, how could she tell him no? But she had to. She had to look away now and go back to work.

"I don't want to think of you as Lindquist for the rest of my life," he said. "Or even Lindy."

And suddenly she heard herself saying, "Siggy."

She hadn't said it very loud. But in another moment, someone repeated it back to her: "Siggy Lindquist." Spoken in a toneless voice that she had never heard before, yet she knew immediately whom it must belong to.

The Professor.

And Jerry Wolfe was stirring; he must have heard her, too. Commander Bell gave her a sad smile.

"I'm sorry," he said.

Now the Monsters knew her name. They could say it any time they wanted, they could put it together with other words, ugly ones.

"Commander Bell," she said, "We're not allowed—"

"Call me Joseph."

He knew. There wasn't anything she could tell him about the rules. He was risking a lot, trying to talk with her like that. He was risking for both of them, the loss of her job, the loss of his few privileges. But she supposed he was a man who was used to risks. After all, he had submitted to an operation that was supposed to save the human race.

"I'm pleased to meet you, Joseph," she said, courteously.

"I'm pleased to meet you too, Siggy," he said in a tone that revealed he was a hell of a lot more than just *pleased*.

Siggy felt the tips of her ears burning. She made herself look away and go back to work. She moved carefully, meticulously, praying that the Director wouldn't make her go back and do it all over again, as he did about fifty percent of the time.

Joseph hadn't said another word to her as she backed out of his area. He didn't get up and watch her, either, like he usually did. Siggy felt shyer and more vulnerable than she had ever felt in her entire life.

She was trying not to wonder how he felt.

You shouldn't have looked at him, she told herself again, in the cafeteria. *You shouldn't have.* She put down her fork and held her head.

"Hey, quit that!"

Siggy looked up, guiltily. Afrika waggled a finger at her.

"Don't you start feeling so miserable," said. "Forget about Monster Row and eat your lunch."

Siggy looked down at her plate again. She had made good progress, but there was still some left.

"What's eating you today?" asked George, whose lunch was long gone.

Siggy took a deep breath. "I think," she said, "I may have broken a rule."

"What did you do?" Afrika asked, the same way he would have asked his son.

Siggy felt their collective gaze on her, and was suddenly embarrassed. "I talked to one of the inmates," she confessed.

"Which one?" he asked, patiently.

"Commander Bell."

"Uh-oh." Afrika rested his chin in his hand and looked at Siggy as if he wasn't sure whether he should scold her or pat her on the head. Li and Gustav both looked like they weren't sure what the big deal was. George was carefully examining his coffee, as if he hadn't even heard her.

But it was George who spoke first.

"Yeah, I know why you talked to the guy. He's the one I would talk to, if I didn't know better."

Siggy swallowed, suddenly wishing she hadn't told them. It seemed like she just couldn't keep her big mouth shut, today.

"Listen, Siggy," Afrika said. "You wanted to be nice to the guy. But you have to remember something. Those guys on Monster Row are all smarter than you, you just have to assume that. Every one of them is there for a reason. Maybe it's not fair, maybe Bell can't help it. But you know for a fact if he was out, he would hurt you. Right?"

"Right," whispered Siggy. *He's hurting me right now.*

"All of those guys are going to try to trip you up, you can count on it," George said. "Sometimes they'll try to be nice, sometimes they'll try to be funny, and sometimes they'll act like bastards. You can't play their game with them. If they make a fool of you, just shrug and walk away. Don't try to out-think 'em, don't try to follow the convolutions in their heads or try to be a step ahead of them; and for Christ's sake, don't try to psychoanalyze them. The only thing you can do is follow the rules, to the letter, and don't *ever, ever* deviate."

"Right," Siggy croaked, then cleared her throat. "I know. I know you're right. That's why—I'm so upset. Because I know better."

Afrika clapped a hand on her shoulder and gave it a good, hard rub. "Okay," he said. "That's enough beating yourself up for one day. Now finish your lunch, we've still got stuff to do."

Siggy picked up her fork and obeyed. Chewing and swallowing helped fend off the tears she was afraid she might shed if they said even one more word about the matter. But they didn't. Everyone made small talk until Siggy had finished eating; and by that time she was feeling a lot better.

Siggy followed the others back to the supply room, where they all loaded up their work carts for the second half of their shift. She was just getting mop fluid when Mr. Morita suddenly appeared in the door, a troubled look on his face.

"Siggy," he said, "the Director wants to see you."

There was a deafening silence, in which Siggy could hear everyone thinking exactly the same thing she was. She was going to be fired. Siggy hung her mop back up, her movements stiff and awkward.

Those of you who do *see me will have cause to regret it,* the Director had said.

"Okay," she said, surprised at how calm she sounded. He edged away from the door and she followed, exchanging one quick look with Afrika as she passed him. *Don't panic until you know what it's all about.* That was what he wanted to tell her, she could see it as plainly as if he had spoken it aloud.

I'll try, she promised, and followed Mr. Morita down the hall.

She was surprised when they went into the same elevator that always took her to the Maximum Security block. "Where is his office?" she asked Mr. Morita.

"Two floors higher than you usually go," he said. "He's got most of the floor to himself."

"Wow," Siggy said. They rode down to a floor that wasn't even represented by one of the lights on the control panel. Morita had simply punched a special code into the keypad. Siggy hadn't tried to see what the code was.

The door opened into a vast hallway with marble

floors. At the far end were some massive double doors, which were shut.

"I can't go any farther than this," Morita said.

Siggy swallowed, hard. The whole scene was beginning to remind her of the scene in *The Wizard Of Oz,* when Judy Garland had gone to confront Oz himself.

Oz the Terrible.

"Listen," Morita said, suddenly. "This isn't the way he usually fires people."

Siggy looked at him, distractedly.

"I'm not saying he's not going to do that, but he's never done it this way before. I've been here for fifteen years, and he's never asked to see one of my janitors, personally."

"Wow," said Siggy, again.

"So—just keep your chin up and do your best, okay? I'll see you later. We'll see what we can do."

"Thanks." Siggy could see he had climbed out on a limb, saying that much to her. The Director was probably listening. She was grateful, and she didn't want to get him into any more trouble; so she stepped out of the elevator. She just had time to say, "See you later," before the doors whizzed shut again.

Siggy turned and looked down that long hall. It was outrageously elegant. It was like those beautiful buildings outside, the ones whose glittering tops touched the clouds on rainy days. The marble floor, the walls, the big double doors were all in tones of gold, subtle, rich, and utterly beyond her experience.

Siggy began to walk toward the doors.

Lions and tigers and bears, oh my! Lions and tigers and bears . . .

Stop it, said the mom in her head. *So he's going to fire you. That's not the end of the world! You can't let them think they've got you beat.*

It was true, this was not such a terrible thing. In fact, it was sort of a relief. She would never have to go down Monster Row again, never hear another tirade from Jerry Wolfe, never have to see Joseph Bell's sad face again.

Never feel the eyes of the Professor burning her.

Just one last time to say, "Yes, sir! No, sir!" And if

she was really feeling mad at the end of it she could say "Go to hell, *cabrón*!" Though her mother would never approve of that.

Siggy came to the end of the hall. She put her hand on the doorknob. It was made of crystal and platinum.

Pay no attention to the man behind that curtain!

Siggy took a deep breath and opened the door.

At the far end of the room, perhaps fifty feet away, the Director looked sharply up from his desk. The desk was at least twenty feet long, made of polished wood so dark it was almost ebony.

For heaven's sake, Siggy thought, scornfully, *there's room to waltz on the damned thing!* But she was careful to keep the scorn from her face. She used her years of dance class experience to school her expression into something pleasant and mild.

"I didn't hear a knock!" The director's voice barely reached her ears.

"With all due respect, sir," Siggy said, with perfect courtesy, "I doubt you would have heard a knock from this distance."

"Knock!" he demanded.

Siggy squared her shoulders. This *cabrón* was going to fire her, but he wasn't going to humiliate her, first. She shut the door behind her, and walked toward him.

Okay everybody, she thought, as if she were a guest on the Celebrity Ballroom show, *Let's dance!*

The Director glared at her. He looked every bit as mean as he had behind the podium, on that first day. He didn't look like he admired courage or pride the least little bit. He looked, in fact, as if he were about to spit on her.

Go right ahead, she thought. *I'll spit right back.*

But no trace of that thought had reached her face, she was sure of it. She was showing him the same face she showed rude or creepy dance partners. It was easy when she thought of it that way. She just had to put on her tango face.

She stopped at a respectable distance from his desk. It wasn't as wide as it was long, but it was certainly wider than it should have been. His papers, control pads, and monitors all sat in a pathetic little pile in front of him, dwarfed by their surroundings. He was dwarfed, too, but the malignancy in his eyes more than made up for his lack of stature.

"I was told that you wanted to see me, sir," said Siggy.

"Correct," he snapped.

Siggy waited. If he thought he was going to intimidate her with his stare, he was wrong. Siggy could look into someone's eyes all night long while dancing backward, in high heels; it didn't bother her.

"Tell me, Lindquist," he said at last. "Is there anything a man can do that you feel you cannot?"

Siggy thought seriously about her answer. She doubted he was referring to reproductive functions, so she thought about the other possibilities.

"I can't do heavy lifting," she said. "I doubt that I would excel in hand-to-hand combat."

He picked up a pen and began to tap it, hard, on a yellow pad of paper. Siggy wasn't fooled into looking at it.

Come on, she thought. *Is this the best you can do?*

"He spoke to you," said the Director, his tone almost mild now.

"Yes," said Siggy, but he shook his head.

"You think I mean Joseph Bell. I don't. I don't care what foolish pleasantries you exchange with him. The one I care about is Prisoner MS-12. He spoke to you today."

Siggy had almost forgotten about that. He had only said her name. What was the big deal?

"He never spoke a word to anyone before today, Lindquist. Do you understand? Not *one word,* not spoken, not written, not telepathically. For all we knew, he could have been a mute. But today, you proved otherwise."

He looked at Siggy as if he expected an explanation for it. She couldn't think of a thing to say. Was he accusing her of something?

Tap, tap, tap with the pen.

"Why would he speak to me, then?" she asked.

"That's the question, isn't it?" Again, almost with a tone of accusation. "I suspect it may have something to do with the fact that you are a young woman. You are rather striking, you have an interesting skin color. Are you descended from Africans?"

Siggy wasn't sure she liked his tone when he said the word *Africans*. "No," she said.

"In any event, he hasn't seen any women since he was incarcerated. We had no evidence that he was a heterosexual—he's never used his library terminal to access pornography, unlike the illustrious Mr. Wolfe; and he's never masturbated."

That was something Siggy didn't feel she really needed to know, but she kept her expression as neutral as she could.

"In fact," the Director went on, "he had never used his library terminal *at all,* not until he heard you say your name. After you left, he looked you up on the terminal—couldn't find any personal information about you, of course, we don't allow that; but he traced your ethnology. Every possible referent was pursued. I'll be interested to see what he does once you've spoken to him some more."

Abruptly, he stopped tapping. Siggy stared at him with her tango face. Inside, warning bells were making her head ring.

Do not become personally involved with the inmates, he had said. *Do no attempt to engage in dialogues with them, leave that to the doctors and the interrogators.*

Now he said, "It's very helpful to us when you talk to them. They won't talk to doctors, but you plain folk don't threaten them. They know you're not educated, so you can't analyze them. They can't use your personal information against you, because you don't have the keys to their cells. But they'll reveal things about themselves in their interactions with you. You can help us so much, Lindquist. I do hope you will."

This was not what she had been expecting, not in a million years. He wanted her to *talk* to them, all of them. The Monsters.

"I don't know—" she began "—if I can find—if I can possibly think of—what to talk about with them. Sir."

"Oh," he said, with a confidence that bordered on sarcasm, "you'll think of something. I'm sure of that. You seem to be graced with an extra measure of social skills. And in return, Lindquist, I can promise you a nice raise. Quite nice, in fact. More than any of your friends will ever make, I can assure you of that; so I wouldn't tell them about it if I were you. If you do as I ask, you'll see it by your next paycheck."

Siggy was beginning to feel dizzy. She took deep breaths, as if she were about to dance a polka.

"I'll try," she said, at last. "I'll do my best. To be honest, sir, I'm afraid of the inmates. I'm afraid of what they'll say to me."

"Very wise of you," he said. "You can be afraid, it doesn't matter. They might even like that."

She shivered. His request was beginning to take on some ugly angles. She couldn't let it be like that, she wouldn't prostitute herself. She would have to show him the limits of this agreement.

She would have to show *them* those limits.

She couldn't believe she was going to do it. But it was her job. And it had already gone too far, just as soon as she sat down to watch that mini. If she could stand that, she could stand this.

And the raise. She could save for vocational school, and some day she could get the hell out of there.

"Yes," she said. "I'll do it. I'll start tomorrow."

"Good," he said, and gave her the grimace that passed for a grin. "Here."

He scribbled some numbers on the yellow pad, tore the sheet off, and slid it across the desk toward her. She had to lean far over the ebony surface to retrieve it.

"My special code for the elevator," he said. "You'll be using it again. Memorize it."

Shit, thought Siggy. *Shit, shit, shit.*

"That will be all," said the Director.

Siggy folded the paper and put it in the breast pocket of her coveralls. She turned and walked back toward the distant doors.

"You really do move like a dancer," he called after her. "I wonder if that's what caught his attention first."

Siggy wondered, too. But she didn't really want to know.

*   *   *

There were a dozen sites on the information net, just for serial killers.

Siggy started combing through them as soon as she got home. Most of them were full of junk; some of them even seemed to cater to creeps who admired the killers. At first, Siggy had looked at some of these out of curiosity; but she quickly grew annoyed with them and tried to stick to leads that dealt with facts rather than sensationalistic conjecture.

She found a surprising amount of solid information, everything from police procedure to essays by criminologists, psychologists, and anthropologists; but even these were a waste of time, because Siggy needed something more specific. She needed to find out if there was anything about the guys on Monster Row that the Director wasn't telling her.

Finally, quite by accident, she found an alphabetical list. You could scan the whole thing and read a brief synopsis of crimes committed; you could also press on various icons to get other available information about each individual, everything from court transcripts to school records, to news or police footage.

Bingo! thought Siggy, and started to type in *Professor* until she realized her mistake. George was the one who had named him that. *Prisoner MS-12* wouldn't work either—what had they called him in the police footage? *John Doe* and a bunch of numbers. She typed in *John Doe* and got a list of several hundred names.

She couldn't remember what the numbers had been, but she did remember that there were a lot of them; so she jumped ahead to a place on the list with at least five characters following *John Doe* and began to scan the synopses.

It took her an hour to find the Professor. His story was unmistakable. Once she found him, she made a hard copy of the synopsis. He had killed twenty-seven people; thirteen of them by breaking their necks and fourteen through extreme blunt-force trauma. Extraordinary strength was inferred.

The story of his apprehension was interesting. The officer in charge of the investigation was an R-FBI agent named George H. Stine who had networked extensively

with local investigators on the seven worlds on which
the Professor had been known to commit crimes. Siggy
laughed when she saw the agent's photo; he had big ears
that stuck out like handles, and bushy eyebrows. He
might have been in his early forties, and his grin seemed
a little shy. She liked him immediately, and wondered if
she should trust the reaction. The eyes under those
bushy brows were very sharp.

Agent Stine had made a map of the Professor's movements and decided he must still be on Philae. He had
managed to work out a theory about where he would
go on that world, based on mass transit routes. This was
partly wishful thinking: The mass transit stations were all
monitored, and when Agent Stine was given the security
footage he programmed his computer to look for odd
and distinctive movement. He had guessed that the killer's physiology might be outside the normal human parameters. He suspected that the Professor could be a
modified soldier who had gone awry.

Like Joseph Bell, thought Siggy, and wondered if it
could be true. Somehow it didn't feel quite right. But it
wasn't a bad theory, and it paid off for Mr. Stine. He
managed to get a clear picture of the Professor from one
of the transit stations. And when he tried to get a visual
ID on that picture, his computer presented him with a
list of aliases—the names of the last several victims.

Realizing they'd finally found their man, Agent Stine
coordinated his team and the local authorities into one
group, and they planned a trap for the Professor.

They had never figured out a victim profile, so they
doubted they could lay bait for their killer. But they did
know he traveled on mass transit fairly often; he had
only stolen private vehicles twice, and had never taken
them very far. So they organized several teams to cover
his last known whereabouts; and when the Professor was
spotted in one of the stations, the teams moved in.

Siggy was able to look at the actual security footage
from the station. She thought it would make a wonderful
movie. The agents all wore civilian clothing—the Net
version had arrows pointing to each one, as well as a
narrative describing the operation.

"They were lucky that night," said the narrator, "because the rush hour had passed and the crowd was fairly thin; apparently John Doe H117629 didn't like to have too many people around him. Agents spotted him easily, due to his odd gait."

Siggy thought his walk had a jerky quality to it, but that could have been due to imperfections in the security footage. The quality of the image wasn't that great; she wouldn't have known she was looking at the Professor if he hadn't been clearly pointed out. On the other hand, maybe that was just a talent of his. . . .

"The agents carried tranquilizer guns, and were much more worried about what John Doe would do once he had been shot than about accidently shooting bystanders; though there was little chance of that, since the team was composed of sharpshooters. As soon as they had formed a loose configuration around him, they shot him with three darts, simultaneously."

The footage was slowed down so Siggy could watch the darts flying through the air toward the seemingly innocuous man walking across the train platform. She saw them hit. The man barely moved under the impact, and his face showed no pain or startlement.

And in another second he had vanished.

"The net restraint gun was deployed less than a microsecond after the darts, and should have hit the target before he could react to the first impact," said the narrator. Siggy watched the net ball expand and fly open to embrace a target that wasn't there anymore. It sailed out of sight of the camera. "The restraining net was later found on the tracks, just below the platform. But John Doe H117629 had disappeared, not only from sight, but from all security cameras as well.

"The station was immediately sealed and searched. John Doe H117629 was found within fifteen minutes, unconscious, inside an emergency fire stairwell."

The narrative ended there, and frustratingly, so did the footage. There were only a few stills, mostly of officers in the act of collecting evidence from crime scenes. There was only one photo to give Siggy a clue of how the Professor had been transported to IFCI.

It was a shot of Agent Stine and several uniformed men maneuvering a torpedo-shaped object into a truck.

Agent Stine was looking over his shoulder at the camera and his hand was blurred in the foreground, as if he were trying to fend off the reporters.

Siggy knew instantly who must be inside the "torpedo." It was big enough to contain a man. She stared at it with fascination. It looked extremely solid; in fact it looked like it might be constructed out of the same sort of material they used to build starships. From this angle it looked seamless and unadorned; but she saw one corner of something that might be a control panel peeking out from under Agent Stine's arm.

Where the heck would they get a thing like that? wondered Siggy. They couldn't have made it up just for the occasion, could they? It would have to be designed, and then they'd have to hire a contractor—unless they already had something like it on hand for extraordinary restraint. But who, other than the Professor, would need those kinds of measures? The answer suddenly hit her like a ton of bricks.

Speedies would. Speedy prisoners, taken alive.

"Your 'scientific community' is guilty of crimes against us and against your own kind," the Decider had said. Live Speedy prisoners, studied, examined, taken apart . . .

Siggy stared at the restraining box. A moment before, it had been comforting in its solidity. Now she could barely stand to look at it.

Agent Stine didn't seem like the sort of person who would inflict that kind of torment on someone, Speedy or otherwise. But what did Siggy know about it? What did good, ethical people do when confronted by an enemy who seemed so implacable, unstoppable, so capable of wiping you and all your kind right out of the universe?

A headache was beginning to radiate from the back of her neck, all the way up to her eyebrows. Siggy rubbed her head and closed her eyes, shutting out the image on the screen.

Listen to you, said the voice of the mom in her head. *Making a mountain out of a molehill. You don't know that any of this is true, Siggy. You're just guessing. Don't grieve over what you don't know. There's just too much of it.*

Good advice, thought Siggy. *I wasn't even thinking about the Speedies, I was supposed to be finding information that's going to maybe save my sanity.*

She opened her eyes again, took one last look at the terrible box, and then pressed the icon to return to the list of names. This time she typed in *Commander Joseph Bell.*

But there was no entry for that name. She was shown an alphabetical listing for *Commander, Joseph,* and *Bell,* but he wasn't in any of them. Siggy rubbed her head again, then called up a list for mass murderers.

He wasn't on that one, either.

So, despite the enormity of the download, Siggy called up the list for murderers and attempted murderers. With sudden inspiration, she added the specification that the computer select for members of any of the military branches.

But it didn't help. He wasn't there.

Commander Bell had been the recipient of some extremely high-end BioTech. She wouldn't have ever heard of him if he hadn't been on Monster Row. If she started asking questions about him, Siggy realized, there was only one thing she could get out of it.

A hell of a lot of trouble.

So, that left Jerry Wolfe. Siggy rubbed her head again, wondering if she even wanted to bother with that one tonight. But maybe she should. Just to get it over with.

On the other hand, she was starting to go cross-eyed.

The doorbell rescued her from any further debate. It had to be Afrika's son, Nathanial, come for his third dance lesson. She hadn't realized so much time had passed; she had worked right through supper.

When she answered the door, he was smiling; that was a good sign. Before, he had been so shy he wouldn't even look her in the eye. He was definitely coming along.

"Have you got the key to the auditorium?" she asked. He pulled it out of his pocket and held it up.

They walked across the courtyard, past the swimming pool, the barbecue area, the volleyball and tennis court,

to the building that housed the gym and the auditorium.
Siggy was pleased to see that Nathanial was wearing
slacks and good shoes this time. She had gently suggested that he should wear the sort of thing he would
wear to a dance, so he wouldn't feel uncomfortable in a
new medium.

Once he had relaxed a little more, she would start
wearing her fancy dresses. For now, she wore slacks and
dancing shoes. Tonight she was going to take the plunge
and teach him a dance that would involve holding a partner. It was a popular dance, "The Transit." He had
pointed it out to her when they were watching Dance
Parade together.

And while she was at it, since he was smiling tonight
and actually meeting her gaze from time to time . . .

"First thing I want to do tonight," she told him, once
they had locked themselves into the auditorium and the
music player had been deployed, "is get you to start
thinking about something important."

He regarded her warily, but she gave him her most
disarming smile.

"I'm going to teach you how to ask someone to
dance."

"Oh *that*," he said, and laughed nervously, because
this was the thing that always frightened boys the most.
And for good reason. Imagine having to go up to someone and put your pride and dignity on the line. Siggy
knew how to decline an invitation gracefully; but she
had rarely done that. Unless a fellow was very rude,
there was no reason to decline. But she had heard girls
say vicious things to boys.

"Listen," she said. "Let's get something straight from
the very beginning. When you ask someone to dance,
you are *not* asking them to make love with you."

Nathanial blushed.

"You aren't asking them to marry you," said Siggy.
"Or to go steady, or anything of the sort. Dancing is
social. You can dance with your mother, your sisters,
with a lady who's twice your age. You can dance with a
business associate, and have absolutely nothing romantic
pass between you. Dancing is a ritual; the minute you
start doing The Transit with someone, you both know

exactly what's going to happen, from start to finish. It's—it's communication, Nathanial. It's a way of getting to know someone."

He was starting to fidget, so she moved on.

"I'm your friend," she assured him. "I want you to practice with me. Here's what I want you to say, just this: 'Siggy, may I have this dance?'"

He coughed. "Siggy, may I have this dance?"

He had gone inaudible at the end of the sentence, like he usually did when he was uncomfortable. But other than that, it hadn't been bad.

"Good," she said. "Now here's how it looks. Watch how I walk."

She imitated the male gait as well as she could, and approached him until she was two feet away from him. He was already her height, so their gazes were level. "Nathanial," she said, with just the right combination of firmness and courtesy, "may I have this dance?"

"Sure," he stuttered, but then stood like a board.

"We'll practice that every night," said Siggy. "Right now, we're going to do The Transit. Don't worry about getting it exactly right this time, just do it the way you think it's done, and I'll follow. Let me get the music—"

In another moment, the music was playing and she was at his side again. "Let's go," she said, as if they were about to have the best fun in the whole galaxy.

Nathanial took her awkwardly in his arms, but in another moment he was moving more gracefully. His only problem was that he was looking at his feet, at the walls, out the window; anywhere but at her. Siggy waited until he seemed more confident and then started the real lesson.

"I'll tell you another secret," she said. "You can look right into someone's face without being embarrassed."

His lips tightened at that, and he gave her one panicked glance before averting his eyes again.

"It takes some time," said Siggy. "But you can look at someone without invading their space, without intruding; and without being intruded *upon*, Nathanial. It's just psychology. You can smile, and be pleasant, and keep a comfortable barrier firmly in place. I want you to try it tonight."

He looked into her eyes. He was terrified, embarrassed, and he stumbled a bit; but Siggy followed him so closely, he never stepped on her feet.

"Wish my partners could all be as good as you," he stammered.

Siggy smiled. "We'll teach them," she said. "You and I. You're good at this, Nathanial, you have a knack for it. All you need is practice."

"*Lots* of practice," he said fervently.

"Lots," she agreed, and kept smiling, until finally he was smiling, too.

We're halfway there, Siggy thought happily, knowing that in this case, at least, she had sovereignty, expertise, and no one could intrude upon that. No Director was going to tell her how to do *this* job.

For the rest of that evening, Monster Row seemed a million light years away.

The next morning, riding the transit to work, she was worried again.

"Is it worth the money?" George had asked when she told him and Afrika about her deal with the Director. She had never considered keeping the truth from them. It was just the sort of information that the Director could have used to blackmail her, later.

"That's what you've got to figure out," George said. "This could mess with your head, permanently, and then it won't matter how much money you've got in the bank."

"I can see why you'd say yes," Afrika said, though he seemed troubled by the idea. "You could invest the money, build a nest egg for yourself. But George is right, you can't let it go too far, Siggy."

"You want to know the truth," George added, "I don't like it. There's something ugly at the middle of this. Something rotten."

But Siggy couldn't see any way out of it, now. If she did nothing, the Director would certainly not like it. He wouldn't have liked it if she had said no in the first place; he probably would have found a way to drive her out of the job. Or he might have fired her outright, and he still could. Siggy couldn't see far enough into her own future to figure out what she would do if that happened.

She didn't know what she wanted to do with the rest of her life. She was just beginning to realize how sheltered she had been on Veil, despite her mom's attempts to prepare her. And now here she was, trying to figure out what sort of conversation she could make with a psychopath.

Nice day, isn't it?

Aren't the donuts yummy this morning?

How come you like to stuff people into little, tiny boxes?

All morning she was distracted. People had to ask her things at least twice before she answered, and she kept losing track of what she was doing.

"I don't know about this, Siggy," Afrika said, shaking his head.

And finally it was time for her to mop the Row. She was almost relieved, because she knew that for better or worse, she would be coming back out in fifteen minutes, a half hour tops if the Director made her go back again.

Maybe he would, so she could talk longer.

I'm going to have to work hard for that money, that's for sure.

Siggy left the elevator and walked down the security hall. She didn't try to wave at the officer behind the glass; he never waved back. She collected her supplies and buzzed her way into the inner lock.

The Toady stared at her from behind his station. She wondered if he knew. But she didn't try to decipher his expression; she disliked him too much to prolong the contact. He was still playing his mean games and probably always would. So she tried to pretend he was just another piece of machinery. One that didn't work very well.

He opened the inner door.

I'm not ready! thought Siggy, but she went in anyway.

The first thing she heard was someone crying. It was one of the guys in the cells near the door. The other guys watched her as avidly as usual, but they were quiet in respect for their neighbor's anguish. It was funny how they could be that way sometimes.

Siggy didn't look to see who the crier was. The sound was pathetic, like the sobs of a child. For one dreadful moment she thought of Commander Bell, and her throat closed up.

God Damn It! she raged at herself, *stop that!*

She glanced into Joseph's cell as she passed it, just to reassure herself. He was looking at her, dry-eyed, surprised to see that she was looking for him. Surprised also, when she sighed with relief. He got up from his cot and went to the barrier so he could watch her. Siggy started to tremble.

I can't believe this. I'm getting stage fright.

Then something slammed into the barrier on her right, making her start violently, and Jerry Wolfe started to chant, "Well there she is, that sweet little *cunt,* that dumb little *cunt,* that skinny little *cunt*—" kicking the barrier every time he said *cunt.* On and on he went, substituting a new adjective with every kick, making a crazy sort of dance with it.

"Shut up, Jerry!" Commander Bell roared, and there was a brief pause in Wolfe's routine; but then he started it up again, repeating words he had already used and kicking tirelessly at the barrier.

"You're just jealous because you don't have one yourself," snarled Bell.

Jerry Wolfe stopped. He giggled like a nasty child, but he didn't start up again. He didn't have to. Siggy was completely unnerved. Whatever half-baked script she had formed in her mind was now scattered and senseless.

She began to mop. She felt the Professor's eyes on her, but she had given up. She couldn't think of a thing to say.

"Where are you from?" he asked her, tonelessly. "What world?"

Siggy stopped mopping. She made herself look at him. The sight of him almost made her go dumb again. But she cleared her throat and said, "Veil. I'm from Veil."

He just stared. She wondered if she should ask, "Where are *you* from." But she had a feeling that would just cut things short. The interrogators must have asked him that a thousand times. They might have even tried to drug the answer out of him.

"Your ancestors are Scandinavian," he said.

"And from New Mexico," she added.

"Hispanic and Scandinavian," said the Professor, his tone so dull, no one would have paid him the least attention if they couldn't see his face, too, the intensity of his stare. "Your skin loves the sun."

"Yes," said Siggy.

"And your blood loves battle."

Want to bet? she thought, but didn't know if she should say that aloud.

"Hey!" Jerry Wolfe called, "Wanna fuck?" He asked it eagerly, as if he thought she might really say yes. Siggy ignored him. She waited for the Professor to say something else.

But he was done for the day. He just looked at her, until she couldn't stand it anymore. She lowered her head and started to mop again.

"Hey!" Jerry Wolfe was scurrying back and forth in his cell. "Hey! Will you suck my cock?"

Siggy continued to ignore him. She had said enough for one day.

"Hey, will you lick my butt? Will you—will you—bite my nipples? Will you—" His feet moved away from the barrier, and she heard him punching numbers into his library terminal. "Look at this!" hc called, like an eager child. He had dialed up something from the library; and from the excitement in his voice, it was probably pornography. "Look at this!" he demanded. "Look at this, you dumb bitch!"

But Siggy wasn't about to look. Let the Director look. Maybe he would learn something from it. Siggy was establishing the rules, drawing those lines that couldn't be crossed.

She mopped her way back to Joseph's territory. He was waiting for her. She looked him full in the face.

"Good morning, Siggy," he said.

"Good morning, Joseph," she answered.

He knew something was up. She studied him to see if she could tell what he might do about it.

He simply looked back at her, pleased to have the contact.

"Why did you leave Veil?" he asked, finally. "You must be homesick."

Jerry Wolfe and the Professor were listening, intently. Joseph knew that, but he hadn't meant the question unkindly. He was holding his breath, wondering if she would answer.

"I had to," she said. "To find work."

He laughed. "That's why I became a starman."

Siggy almost smiled, but she didn't want to do that where the others could see her. "Come on," she said. "You couldn't even attend the academy unless you were top notch."

"That's what *you* are," said Joseph, seriously. "But you still had to find work, right?"

"Right," said Siggy, the tips of her ears burning. She ducked her head and started to mop again. She was suddenly so flustered, she hardly knew what to do with herself. He had managed to do that to her without warning, make her feel like a girl at the ball, dancing with the handsome prince. She wanted to lean on her mop and talk with him some more, find out about his past, tell him about herself.

It was scary.

"See you later," he called, when she was almost out of sight.

"See you tomorrow," she promised.

She mopped the rest of the hall. The guy who had been crying had stopped now, and the others were beginning to stir. Maybe they thought they should all have their chance to talk with her, now that the Big Three had done it. But Siggy didn't let them harbor that illusion very long. She ignored them as steadfastly as she always did.

"Jeez," one of them snarled, "we're not good enough for you, is that it?"

The truth was, she thought they were dirt. She hadn't bothered to find out what their names were, or what they had done. She had already learned everything she needed to know about them from the way they had treated her, every day when she mopped the Row. She pitied them when they cried or suffered, but that was all.

Siggy keyed her code into the pad. She waited stiffly,

half-expecting the Director to make her go back and do the job over. But he kept silent. The door opened, and she pushed her bucket through.

She didn't look at the Toady as she pushed the bucket to the outer door. She stood in front of it and waited, anxious to be gone.

And waited. And waited.

"Look," she said at last, "I'm doing special work for the Director. If you're going to be an asshole, I'm going to have to ask him to talk to you about it. He isn't going to like you hassling me anymore."

"Want to bet?" he asked.

It was the first and last words he ever spoke to her.

Siggy looked at him. He had the same look on his face he had worn the day they had been forced to watch the mini. He made no move to open the outer door.

Siggy let her contempt for him pour out of her, right into his smug face. The Professor's words were ringing in her head: *Your blood loves battle.* Perhaps, in a way, that was true after all. She turned her glare into a hammer.

It seemed to have no effect on him. But he did, finally, open the door; and when Siggy turned away from him, she glimpsed a sheen of sweat on his upper lip.

Toady, she thought contemptuously, and dismissed him from her mind.

Finally she was riding down in the elevator, leaning against the wall as if she were weary from a full day's work.

How am I going to do this? she wondered. *How long am I going to be able to keep this up?*

One day at a time, soothed the mom in her head. *Just get through the rest of the day, Siggy. Worry about tomorrow when it gets here.*

The doors opened on Siggy's floor. It was time to find Afrika and go get lunch. She wasn't hungry, but she would eat, like she always did.

Let's see, she told herself, *how long I can do it. I did it today, I can do it tomorrow, that's all I need to know.*

She walked onto the main drag, into the crowd of people coming, or going, or halfway through their work-day. Their images and the sounds of their voices bounced off the polished metal walls, which were oblivious to the misery, the worry, the weariness, and the occasional joy of the human beings who came and went at IFCI. Siggy wasn't the only one there who took things one day at a time.

And she would have been very surprised to know that her time on Monster Row wasn't going to be measured in days. It would be measured in years.

If she had known, she would have turned left instead of right into the main hall, and she would have kept walking until she was out the front door, down the street, onto the transit, down to the starport and away to some other place. Any place but there.

Siggy was riding the elevator down to the Director's office. In her hand, she held a copy of a letter from Jerry Wolfe. Since it was a copy, she assumed the Director had the original and had sent the copy along to her. He already knew its contents. But there were some things she wanted to know, herself.

The doors opened on his floor, and Siggy stepped out, her tango face falling firmly into place. Even after a year, she was no more comfortable coming up here than she was about mopping the Row. It was an ordeal, every time.

She transferred the letter to her other hand; her palm was getting sweaty. She wished she could just throw it in the trash, or stuff it in a drawer and forget about it. What she supposed she really *ought* to do was send it along to the R-FBI; but the Director had made her aware, since they had begun their closer association, of certain rules at IFCI most janitors never had reason to know. Rules about disclosure of information to outside agencies.

Dear Siggy, the letter had begun, the courteous greeting penned in an amazingly small script, *You be my witness. I'm the Antichrist, and when I get out of here I'll bring about the Armageddon.* Lately he had preferred the word *Armageddon* to his old favorite, *Apocalypse.* Siggy assumed that eventually he would find and use every word that described the end of the universe. Maybe *Ragnarok* would be next.

Everyone I've killed will be my slaves in Hell, he continued. *I will torture and punish them throughout eternity. You will be one of my special concubines, with a place*

*of honor at my feet. You will kneel in front of my throne
and suck my cock.*

He went on to describe everything he thought Siggy
and his other concubines should do for him, in clinical
detail, a list of acts that no sane person would consider
pleasurable, even under the best of circumstances.

My father was the devil and my mother was a dog, said
the letter. *The numbers 666 have always been lucky for
me. When I get out of here, I will set the machinery in
motion. Time is waiting for me. You be my witness.*

Lately Jerry Wolfe had been saying *you be my witness*
a lot. The business about slaves in Hell and his alleged
parentage were nothing new, either. He had researched
the Antichrist from his library terminal, and it had crys-
tallized his existence for him. It had given him a sense
of purpose that made Siggy very glad that he was safely
locked up. The only thing that would make her gladder
would be his execution.

I wouldn't mind doing it myself, thought Siggy, as her
heels went tap tap tap on the marble floor. *I could pull
the switch, or push the button, or fire the bullet. And just
before I did I'd look into Jerry Wolfe's face and say,
"There aren't any slaves waiting for you in Hell, Jerry.
There's just the vengeful dead, waiting to tear you to
pieces. Have fun, good-bye!" Ka-blam!*

The double doors loomed large. Siggy knocked; she
didn't dare go in there without knocking again. To do
so would have been like spitting in the Director's face.
And if Siggy were going to pull a last act of defiance
like that, a take-this-job-and-shove-it sort of thing, she
would much prefer *real* spit.

It was one of the thoughts that helped her get through
the days.

"Come in!" snapped the Director's voice from the intercom. Siggy opened the door, and entered the
warehouse-sized office.

There he was, as usual, a small man sitting behind a
giant desk. He didn't bother to look up at her; he was
scribbling on his yellow tablet. He almost never used his
word processor to take notes, which made him look
more like Sigmund Freud than ever.

Siggy approached the desk. She laid the letter on its edge, but he didn't look at it.

"Why did you come here today?" he said. He sounded bored, annoyed, distracted. "I haven't observed anything in your interactions with the inmates on Monster Row that merits further discussion between us."

"I got a letter from Jerry Wolfe," she said.

"And?" he snapped.

"It worries me."

"Does it?" He didn't seem to care. He continued to scribble, and seemed inclined to forget she was there.

"I was wondering if I should send a copy to the R-FBI," said Siggy.

He glanced up, surprised. "Whatever for?"

"I just—" Siggy began to stammer, then steadied herself. "It seems like the sort of thing they'd want to add to their criminal profiles."

He sneered. "You've been looking at those serial killer websites again, haven't you, Lindquist."

She looked at him steadily, but she was thinking, *again?* Was he trying to tell her that IFCI wasn't the only place he had bugged? She didn't want to even consider that possibility.

"The R-FBI already has quite a lot of documentation for Jerry Wolfe," he was saying. "He's been quite prolific over the years. This letter he's written to you is superfluous, he's said it all before."

"No, he hasn't," said Siggy.

He glared at her. He didn't tolerate disagreement well. "Really?" he snarled. "What brilliant new insights do you have to add to the subject, Lindquist?"

"This is the first time I've ever heard him say, *When I get out of here*," said Siggy.

He frowned, furiously. "Why should that disturb you?"

"He sounds so confident. He believes it."

"He's wrong," said the Director, and went back to his scribbling.

Siggy calmed her breathing before she spoke again. He was trying to provoke her, and she had been very careful over the past year to make certain he didn't succeed. In fact, *he* had been the one who was prone to

losing his temper. Several times she had thought he
would fire her, or take away her raise.

"He must think he has some reason for hope," she
said. "If he thinks he can escape, people should be notified. Security, doctors, the R-FBI—"

"Leave those decisions to people more qualified to
make them," said the Director. "No one has ever escaped from our facility and no one ever shall. As long
as you follow our regulations to the letter, you shall
never have reason to fear a jail break from Monster
Row."

"But I'm *not* following the regulations to the letter,"
said Siggy.

He looked at her over the top of his glasses.

"I speak to the prisoners on Monster Row," she said.
"I tell them things about myself, my home world. I've
told the Pro—Prisoner MS-12 things that I've never told
anyone else."

"You mean the Time Pockets," said the Director, his
voice almost gentle.

Siggy had shared that information out of desperation.
The Professor had begun to ignore her a few weeks ago,
after almost a year of conversation that had been far
more revealing of her than it had been of him. She had
thought that might be a good cue to call the whole thing
off, but the Director had disagreed. He had even threatened to reduce her pay to starting level if she didn't
come up with something good, soon.

So Siggy had told the Professor about the Lost Boy,
and the Time Pockets. And that had done the trick. He
had grilled her for every piece of information she could
remember, every scrap of insight or conjecture, and
Siggy had shared it. Even Jerry Wolfe and Joseph had
asked her questions about it. It was odd, but out of all
of the people Siggy could have told, it was these three
men who most believed her.

She wasn't sure, but she thought maybe the Director
did, too. Because for a moment, he seemed more distracted than usual, as if he were thinking about possibilities. But finally he seemed to come back to his old
confidence.

"That's neither here nor there," he said. "Your personal life is completely irrelevant to their situation. You could not possibly help them escape, even if you wanted to. And believe me, Lindquist; there have been times in your interactions with Joseph Bell when I have wondered."

"I wouldn't make a mistake like that," said Siggy.

He glared at her, but nodded. "I suspect you wouldn't. My original assessment of your capabilities seems to have been on the mark. You will continue, and you may rest assured that this facility is safe."

Siggy was getting frustrated. Her instincts had been screaming at her ever since she had found the letter in her evening mail, with its tiny lettering and the childish drawings of inverted pentagrams on the envelope.

She hadn't slept well that night, after she had read it.

"Why did you let him send me a letter?" she asked.

Anger sparked in his eyes. It was never very far from the surface in him; Siggy had often wondered if there was a wife in his background, someone who could put up with the stress he would surely inspire in anyone who got close to him. She doubted it.

"What gave you the impression," he said, his voice a tight rasp, "that you were free to question my decisions, Lindquist?"

Siggy already knew she had stepped over the line. But she had committed herself. "I leave this job here when I go home at night," she told him, calmly. "Now it has followed me there."

"Oh!" he cried, mockingly, "you poor thing! How ever do you bear it every day? Well let me tell you something. *I* take my job home every day. I eat, sleep, and breathe my job; I would be useless as the Director of this facility if I didn't! I have studied criminally insane patients for thirty years, and there is nothing—*nothing*—you could possibly tell me about them that I haven't already guessed, years ago!"

Siggy's hands were cold. An awful thing had happened when he had said that. The Professor had come into Siggy's mind, the same way her mom often did. The Professor looked like he was made of electricity, like the cartoon image you sometimes saw on the sides of high voltage boxes, Voltage Man. His eyes burned into Siggy, and his grin was dreadful.

If that's the case, he asked her tonelessly, *what does he need you for, Siggy?*

"You don't know everything," Siggy said. "It's dangerous to think that."

The Director turned beet red. He jumped to his feet and marched around his desk, a considerable distance. He stalked right up to Siggy, clenching his fists. She watched him coming, amazed. He was the same height as her; he stopped so close to her she was almost cross-eyed with the proximity.

"Tell me, Lindquist," he spat, "do you plan to become a psychologist some day?"

I'm going to lose my job now, thought Siggy. "I have no plan to do so, sir," she answered.

"Really? Lack of ambition, is it? Or are you just plain lazy?"

"That has nothing to do with it," said Siggy.

He thrust his face forward, so that she had to lean back. "What's the problem then, Lindquist? Surely you'd like to join our illustrious ranks, you're so intelligent and observant."

"No, I wouldn't," Siggy said, steadily.

"Why?" he demanded.

Siggy thought about being diplomatic, but he was in her face, and after a year of his abuse, she was too fed up. She was almost curious to see what he would do with the truth. So she told him.

"Because you're a bunch of arrogant fools with your heads up your asses, sir."

She was rewarded with a spectacular display of the autonomic nervous system. His face went dead white, his lips drew back from his teeth in a feral snarl, and she realized that he might hit her.

"Is that so?" he said, his spittle flying into her face. "Our heads up our asses? And when we shit them out again, Lindquist, should we call you to clean up the mess? You're used to that, aren't you? Mopping up the dirty things? Is there anything you won't do, any job you won't stoop to? Yet *our* jobs aren't good enough for you, is that it? Is it?"

"Yes, sir," said Siggy. "It is."

For a moment he just trembled like a hound about to be set loose on a rabbit. Then he took several steps backward. He pressed his lips together, and turned stiffly away from her.

"Get out," he choked.

Siggy waited for half a moment, then pivoted gracefully and began to walk toward the distant door.

Ho boy, she was thinking. *Oh well.*

"Lindquist!" he suddenly shrieked.

Siggy stopped dead. She didn't want to look at him.

"About the Time Pockets," he said, his voice still shaking with rage.

He was waiting for her to acknowledge him. She just wanted to get out of there, but something told her to stand still. "What about them?" she asked, without looking at him.

"Stress reaction," he snapped.

Siggy waited. Was that it? Was he referring to the Time Pockets? Or was he just trying to tell her he was having a heart attack?

"It's why Mrs. Silverstein doesn't remember her son," said the Director. "Why *none* of them remember. It's a stress reaction. Their minds are trying to compensate for the changes in the time line. It's a phenomenon that's been observed before, Lindquist, did you know that?"

"No," she admitted. "I didn't."

"So there *is* something you can learn from me, is that what you're trying to say?"

Siggy took a deep breath and let it out again. "Yes, sir."

"Very good," he said. "You may go now."

She started toward the door.

"And in the future," he called after her, "do not come to this office unless I specifically call you here, is that clear?"

"Very clear, sir," said Siggy.

He didn't say anything else, which made her glad. She only wanted to be out of there. She was almost to the door when she realized she didn't have the letter with her.

And she wasn't about to go back and get it. At least

she wouldn't have the damned thing in her home anymore. But she really did wonder if the R-FBI should
have a look at it.

It's not your job to worry about that, said the mom in
her head.

But Siggy couldn't help it.

She was still thinking about it when she pushed her
bucket onto the Row just before lunch. She was thinking
about it so hard, she barely heard the mumblings of the
guys at the near end of the Row. Joseph didn't speak to
her as she passed him, so she forgot to look in; and she
wasn't about to look at Jerry Wolfe, not after he had
invaded her territory with his stinking letter.

Next time you send me one I'm not going to open it,
she vowed to the pigeon-toed feet that stood just at the
border of her peripheral vision. *I'm sending it right on
to the R-FBI. Screw regulations.*

That made her feel better, but her mind still chased
itself in circles. She kept thinking about her argument
with the Director. It was bad enough she had made him
lose his temper—she really wished she could have found
a way to avoid that. But his remark about *stress reactions*
had gotten her started on a whole line of thinking that
was leading her into unknown territory.

*It's a phenomenon that's been observed before, Lind-
quist. Did you know that?*

She had never heard of it, and when she mentioned
it to Afrika and the others, they were equally puzzled.
Stress reactions to changes in the time line. When had
anyone had the opportunity to observe such a thing?
Was it another one of those top secret projects of the
sort that spawned Joseph Bell? Or had people seen
something like the Time Pockets in other places in the
galaxy?

She mopped the first section of floor, working her way
backward, so deep in thought that she almost forgot
about the three inmates who sometimes haunted her
dreams. But the Professor's stare eventually broke
through her thoughts. She looked up at him, felt the
usual jolt of alarm, and then was struck by an inspiration.

"Stress reactions," she said. "To changes in the time line."

"Yes," he said. It sounded like an affirmation.

"How would people know there was any such thing?" she asked. "Why wouldn't they forget like anyone else?"

"You didn't forget."

She tried to study him, but the effort only hurt her eyes. She blinked, looked at his feet.

"Have you ever tried to contact Barry Silverstein?" the Professor asked. Since his questions never held the inflection you would expect to hear in a query, it took her a second to realize he was asking. And then she had to take another to be astonished at the idea.

Barry Silverstein, David's brother. She had never met him.

"Why?" she asked, aware that he liked questions even less than the Director did, and she had already asked him one too many.

But he must have been interested in the conversation, because he said, "The stress reaction may be a local phenomenon."

"Why would it be?" she asked, recklessly.

His eyes burned with unknown energies. "Time is."

She felt lightheaded. She had assumed that everyone, everywhere, would forget the people who went into the Time Pockets. But if the Professor was right, if she could find Barry Silverstein and if he remembered his brother, she would have finally found someone who could back up her theories.

" 'Round and 'round go the little gears," droned the Professor. " 'Round and 'round."

Siggy started to mop again. This was the most he had said to her in a long time, so she assumed he was satisfied. Besides, she wanted to think about what she could do to locate Barry Silverstein.

But the Professor wasn't finished.

"Halloween is coming," he said.

Siggy stopped again.

"You'll decorate the complex," he said.

Siggy told them all about last Halloween. When she had asked what the custom was on Agate, Afrika shrugged and said he used to take the kids around the neighborhood for trick-or-treat, but they felt too old for that now. So Siggy decided to throw a big party.

Her parties had started to gain quite a reputation by then. After a modest start, attendance had increased once the kids in the complex realized they would have another excuse to socialize with each other. When the news began to spread through the surrounding neighborhoods, people really started to take an interest in ballroom dancing (though Siggy had prudently decided not to call it that). So what started out as a small dance with twenty people or so, became an event that attracted at least two hundred.

But it was nothing compared to the Halloween bash.

"You'll have to work hard to top the one you did last year," said the Professor, his tone so flat the remark took on a sarcastic edge.

But he was right. Siggy would have to think up some new attractions to their Haunted Complex this year. Fortunately for her, Afrika's children and their friends had already volunteered to help her.

"Halloween is my birthday!" squawked Jerry Wolfe. "I'm the Antichrist! I used to eat babies on Halloween. I used to roast them over a slow fire. You should hear them scream."

Siggy had.

She didn't care anymore if the Professor wanted to talk. She mopped the floor, backing into Joseph's territory. She had done about four feet of it when she suddenly realized he hadn't spoken to her yet. There wasn't one day in the past year when he hadn't spoken. She glanced at him.

He was looking at her body. Slowly, his eyes roving up and down. And on his face was an expression she had seen only once, on the mini, when he attacked the woman who was interviewing him. Siggy froze as his gaze slowly climbed, to her face.

He looked pleased when he saw how scared she was.

But then he looked confused. He blinked several times. "What was that about Halloween?" he asked.

Siggy cleared her throat. "They were just—just wondering what I would do to top last year's party," she said.

He nodded, studying her face intently. He looked normal again, but Siggy didn't like the way he was watching her. There was something calculating in that gaze, something cold.

"I guess I'll just have to think about it," she said, and began to mop again. She did it very carefully, she didn't want the Director sending her back again, not when Joseph was acting that way.

She went back and forth, swish-swish, dip-wring, step by step. With every foot she advanced, a hard knot was growing in her stomach. *Stop it, you scaredy-cat,* she chided herself, but she knew that wasn't it at all, she wasn't scared. She was hurt. She had liked Joseph; and though she hated to admit it, she had sometimes basked in his attention. When he was himself he was so handsome, so smart and strong. Her heart had broken for him many times over.

But that was nothing compared to the way it was breaking now, because she had a feeling he would go away forever. Mr. Hyde would come to stay in his place.

Siggy finished the floor and waited by the door, her expression so neutral it hurt. *Come on,* she pleaded. *Don't make me go back. Open the damned door.*

She could tell the Director was thinking about it. She shouldn't have provoked him. She was starting to shake now; this wasn't going to be pretty.

And then the door opened.

Siggy practically leaped through it.

Afrika was waiting for her in his usual spot outside the elevator. He always took a moment to study her, to see how things were going. If she was okay, he just grinned and kidded her as they walked to the cafeteria together. Some days what he saw made him put his arm around her shoulders.

Today was one of *those* days.

They had gotten into the habit of sharing information later, when they were away from IFCI and its bugs, but today Siggy bent the rule a little bit.

"Mr. Hyde is coming," she told Afrika.

"Ho boy," he said.

The usual crowd was waiting for them at lunch:

George, Gustav, Li, Thompson, Ashmarina—Siggy thought it was funny how the janitors all called each other by first names and the security officers all called each other by the last. She got a healthy serving of meatloaf and mashed potatoes, which was still half the size of the serving on Afrika's plate.

Siggy had learned to eat properly over the past year. For a while she had been too thin, but now she weighed the same as she had when she had arrived on Agate. *If anything,* she thought, ruefully, *my appetite is too good.* Which was why she hadn't grabbed a dessert with lunch.

She felt a little better after she had eaten. The argument with the Director was beginning to seem unreal, and her suspicions about Joseph groundless. She didn't really believe that, of course. It was just her way of putting some space between herself and her worries. She joined Afrika and Gustav for afternoon duties in Wing B, the three of them supervising a group of inmates who did janitorial work in exchange for privileges. Afterward there were bathrooms to clean, and no inmates were allowed to help with that. The chemicals involved could be turned into weapons too easily.

Siggy worked diligently, burying herself in the activity, chattering with the others whenever her mind threatened to dwell too much on her fears.

Later that night, on the way home, she told Afrika about her argument with the Director. He didn't seem surprised.

"If I had gone in to talk to him, I would have strangled him for sure," he said. "Every time I think about you alone in there with that monster, it turns my stomach."

The Professor popped into Siggy's head again, an electrical ghost. *Time is a local phenomenon,* he reminded her.

"Right," said Siggy.

When Afrika gave her a puzzled look she shook her head. "I need to try to find someone I used to know," she explained. "Someone from Veil. A guy who was the brother of an—an old friend of mine."

"You can probably look him up on the address net," said Afrika. "You know, when you select for INFORMA-

TION, just take the clicker over to ADDRESS. If you know his name, his old address, the world he's from, that's usually all you need to find somebody."

"Good." This would be the first time Siggy had ever used that service. After supper she would tune in and start looking.

Siggy fetched the mail from her box on the way to her apartment. Mom wrote her faithfully, once a week, and it was almost time for another letter. Mom preferred a written note to electronic ones; and since ships went back and forth from Veil and Agate constantly, snail mail via ship was cheaper than using the fancy ComNet, with its millions of relays. Siggy and her mom exchanged weekly letters, photos, recipes, and minis (with Siggy's favorite movies on them, since her local TV stations didn't show the oldies). Mom also sent other niceties, such as Siggy's fancy dancing dresses.

Siggy sorted through the stack, was relieved not to see a letter from Jerry Wolfe in it. But then she saw the one on the bottom of the stack. The handwriting was neat and confident, the characters much larger than the ones Jerry Wolfe had so painfully engraved. She wasn't surprised to see that. Because the letter was from Joseph Bell.

Siggy unlocked her apartment and went to her overstuffed chair, throwing the junk mail aside. She sat down and opened Joseph's letter. Like Jerry Wolfe's, this one was also a copy of the original.

Dear Siggy,
The Director says we can write letters to you. I'm
sorry about the one Jerry Wolfe sent. I'm sure
it was full of the same old crap he always spouts.
I almost didn't write this one for you, because
there's just too much I want to say. I don't really
think I'd better, Siggy.
*   I'm only writing this so Jerry's letter won't be*
the last thing you read. Did you know that
when you blush, your skin turns a darker gold?
It's like watching a sunrise. If I were free and
didn't have the glitch in my head, I would court
you properly. I would make you forget

*whatever or whoever it was that made you so
sad. I have a feeling it has something to do
with that prom you told us about, the one where
you saw the Lost Boy for the last time. I know
that more must have happened than that, but I
won't try to pry it out of you.*

*The worst thing is not being able to give you
the happiness you deserve.*

*Well, that's probably not the worst thing, but
that's all I'll say. See you tomorrow, Siggy.
This will be the last letter, I suspect for both me
and Jerry.*

> *Sincerely yours,*
> *Joseph*

Siggy was crying when she put the letter down. He
was saying good-bye, that's why there weren't going to
be any more letters. When she went in tomorrow, her
ally would be gone. Her friend.

If his BioTech hadn't gone wrong, if she had met him,
she would have been in love with him. He probably
knew that. Even now, as much as she was afraid of him,
she cared.

She sat there for a long time, well past supper time.
She wasn't hungry. She supposed she ought to plug in
and find Barry Silverstein. After a while, she got up and
went over to her TV netlink.

The address finder found Barry in less than five minutes. He was still at Oxford. Siggy added him to her file.
She had planned to write him as soon as she found him,
but that would have to wait for tomorrow.

Joseph's letter was still sitting on the chair.

You're just making it worse for yourself, thought Siggy.
*If you hold on to it, you're just going to hurt more when
Mr. Hyde gets here.*

She picked up the letter and climbed up to her loft.
That was where she kept her notebook, *The Truth About
David Silverstein.* She scribbled lengthy notes about her
conversations with the Director and Professor, including
the theory of stress reactions. Before she closed the
book, she slipped Joseph's letter into it.

That's where it belongs, she told herself.

It would stay there far longer than she could imagine.

That night, Siggy dreamed she was Cinderella. Sort of.

It was another dream about the prom, but her mind kept trying to find new ways around the truth, to convince her that the past could be fixed again. She was back on Veil, and it was the night of the Prince's Ball. There was no prince on Veil, let alone a Prince's Ball, but Siggy could see the spires of the palace from her bedroom window, so it all made sense to her sleeping mind. She was waiting; Maxi was late. She knew he wasn't going to come for her, but she kept leaning out her window anyway, looking up and down Indianola Avenue.

Mom suddenly appeared at her door. "I can make a beautiful dress for you," she said.

"I don't need another dress, I've got this one," said Siggy, then looked down and realized she was wearing her coverall from IFCI. She really should have been in a white ball gown, with big hoop skirts and tons of lace. But it had to be the coverall, it was important for her to wear it.

"Come downstairs," said Mom. "Look at the Jack-o-lanterns we carved."

That sounded like a good idea. You could turn pumpkins into a magic carriage, that's the way it worked in the stories. Mom took her by the hand and pulled her downstairs, into the kitchen. The Jack-o-lanterns were sitting on the kitchen table. One of them was looking up, its mouth carved into a worried "O."

"That one!" said Siggy, pointing to the worrier. Mom picked it up and took it out back, into the garden.

But there were no mice to be found. "Must be too many cats in the neighborhood," said Mom, scratching her head. Then she snapped her fingers. "We'll make a spaceship, instead."

And suddenly Siggy was inside a Jack-o-lantern spaceship. The mouth, nose, and eyes had transparencies in them, just like the ones on the maximum security cells at IFCI. The walls, carpeting, and cushions were all a garish orange color, which Siggy thought was a little tacky.

She looked out the mouth to see where she was going. She was headed straight for the Enigma Nebula.

"Talk about taking the long way around!" she said. "The palace is just a few hops away!"

She zoomed through the stellar debris much faster than anyone had ever done for real. This made her nervous. What if she ended up going right to the middle of Enigma instead of jumping over the Fold? Her pumpkin would be torn to pieces.

Suddenly she saw it up ahead, a massive black whirlpool, bigger than a thousand solar systems. *I can see it!* she thought. *I'm the first one ever to see it!* But that wasn't true, the Speedies had probably seen it just before they got sucked into the Time Pockets.

The whirlpool seemed to tilt on its side, and Siggy zoomed toward it faster than the speed of thought. The pumpkin shuddered, Siggy screamed. The tidal forces were getting her! She was going to go into the singularity! She fell on the floor, feeling the pumpkin under her toss and shake as if it were a bucket going down the rapids. She closed her eyes and tried to wake up.

And then she was walking down the street, to the palace. She was relieved to have escaped Enigma, but she felt a little embarrassed that her ride had vanished. The people at the palace might have been impressed by her giant, flying pumpkin. Now she had to go like a beggar.

Oh well, she thought, *at least I have my glass slippers!*

But the slippers went clink clink clink on the pavement. Siggy hoped they wouldn't make that much noise on the dance floor.

Finally there was the palace, around the corner and up ahead. Siggy wove her way through hundreds of parked cars, trying to reach the front steps. It took forever. It took so long, the ball was almost over by the time she had made her way to the front lawn. Siggy tried not to cry about it. After all, she could still have the last dance with Maxi, and they would be crowned king and queen of the ball. They would live happily ever after if she could just get it to go right this time, if she could just get into the palace and find him. He wouldn't be able to resist her when he saw her glass slippers. That was how it always went in the stories.

Siggy ran up the front steps. The huge double doors were just like the ones to the Director's office. She tried to open them, but they were locked tight.

She could hear faint music coming from inside. It was "The Tennessee Waltz," her favorite. She pounded on the doors.

"Let me in!" she screamed. "I was queen for the last three proms! If Maxi dances with me, he'll change his mind!"

But no one opened the door.

Siggy started to prowl around the edges of the palace. It was huge, and she kept getting caught in vines and shrubbery. She could see some big windows along one wall, and some of them were open! She fought her way over to them. They were on a veranda, so Siggy had to climb dozens of steps to get up to them; really, hundreds of steps. They hadn't looked like that many when she had started.

But eventually she got to the top. The windows were thirty feet tall, reaching from the ground all the way to the ceiling of the auditorium. Or ballroom, it was supposed to be a ballroom. It sort of looked like the auditorium, only a lot fancier, with gold marble on the floor. Siggy could see men and women waltzing, the skirts of the fancy ball gowns sweeping back and forth across the floor. She ran to the first open window; it was only cracked open. The gap was too narrow for her to squeeze through. She tried to push it open farther, but it wouldn't budge.

"Hey!" she called to the dancers. "I can't get in!"

A few heads turned in her direction, but no one seemed to really understand that they should let her in. And then she saw Maxi. He was looking for someone.

Me, pleaded Siggy, but in another moment he waved at a blond girl.

Leeza. In white, which was only for weddings. Leeza smiled at Maxi, and he went to her. He wore an expression that made Siggy's heart twist in her chest. It was an expression he had never worn for her.

Maxi ran to Leeza and never looked back.

Siggy watched the ball whirl past her window.

I'm not getting in, she realized. *I've got glass slippers and everything, but I can't go back and fix it. Maxi isn't going to dance with me and he isn't going to marry me.*

She was aware of how poetic she must look, standing out there alone, unable to get in and join the ball. She thought it might be even better if a few tears slid down her cheek. But she wasn't sad enough to cry. This was already old, the hurt. She had gotten used to it. She was sad, but not surprised.

After all, she hadn't even cried the first time.

Siggy turned around, ready to go down the steps again, thinking that she'd better go find the spaceship. Instead, she found David Silverstein.

As if the Time Pocket had opened right into her dream. The steps descended from the veranda into a twisted place, and he was standing just at the edge, looking at her.

He mouthed the word *Siggy.*

"David?" she called, amazed. He looked exactly like he had the last time she saw him, only—was he really that young? She had thought of him as a man, but he looked like a freshman to her now. Was he always going to be fifteen?

Still in his ROTC uniform, his hair damp from the rainstorm. As hard as she looked at him, as many times as she blinked to clear her vision, or even to wake up, he stayed right where he was. Only the edge of the Pocket seemed to blur, as if the fabric of her dream were too fragile to support it.

"Can you come out of there?" she called, but she couldn't tell if he had heard her. He looked worried, strained; and he kept looking over his shoulder, as if expecting someone else to come out of the Pocket.

This is it, Siggy thought suddenly. *This is how I can fix it. I'll go into the Pocket with David. I'll step right out of the new future that I didn't want.*

But she was scared. The edges of the Pocket shifted. If she tried to step across, would she fall *between* somehow? Fall nowhere?

"You can't," said someone behind her. "It's too late to change anything now."

Siggy turned. A man was standing in front of the lighted windows, his form almost a shadow. She could just make out his starman's uniform. "Maxi?" she asked, doubtfully. "Jorge? David?" She couldn't imagine who this new intruder could be. Not until he moved into the light.

Mr. Hyde had come for her.

He grinned. The whites showed around his eyes.

"Joseph, how did you get out?" asked Siggy, then wished she hadn't spoken with so much fear in her voice.

"I'm speeded up, remember?" he said. "I ran right past the officers. I promised myself I'd come get you when I got out. We can get married now, Siggy."

"Okay," said Siggy, trying to humor him, buy some time; but he saw right through her.

"Why are you scared of me?" he asked.

"I don't want you to hurt me." Siggy started to back toward the steps. Surely someone in the ballroom would see she was in trouble, and come out to help. But he grabbed her wrist before she could move an inch.

"I wouldn't hurt you." He laughed, just like he had on the mini. "Not my little Siggy."

The smile fell from his face then, and he pulled Siggy close. She hung in his arms like a mouse in the claws of a blue hawk. *This is what it feels like,* she thought dazedly, *to know you're going to die.*

Then he sank his teeth into her neck, and Siggy screamed. She felt it as if it were really happening, felt the pain and the hot rush of blood, felt the dreadful draining of her life from the wound.

"I'm sorry, Siggy." It was Joseph's voice. Her eyes were closed, but she knew it was him holding her now, cradling her. "I'm sorry," he said again, and continued to say it as she drifted away from him. The devastation in his voice was the only thing in the dream that had been able to make her cry.

She wasn't crying when she woke up, though. She just felt glad to be awake. Her heart was pounding, she was still scared from seeing Joseph out of his cell. Her instincts had been looking after her all along. She had never been fooled into thinking she was safe.

Siggy sat up and rubbed her head until she felt calm again. She didn't feel like trying to go back to sleep. Instead, she went down to her kitchen and made some hot cocoa. She put a couple of big marshmallows in it, and after half a dozen healthy sips she was feeling better.

She had never dreamed about the senior prom the way it really happened; she thought that was funny. The only part that was true was the part about David Silverstein. And that one moment when Maxi had run off with Leeza. Since then, Maxi had never shown his full face to her in a dream. He was always moving away from her.

But she could see David Silverstein's face as clear as anything. He always did and said exactly what he had really done. Dreams about David always left her feeling hopeful.

But this dream about Joseph Bell was something else. It promised to teach her more about sadness than she ever wanted to know.

Don't grieve yet, soothed the mom in her head. *There's plenty of time for that later.*

And Mom should know.

Siggy suddenly remembered the Jack-o-lantern spaceship, and that made her laugh. Her version of Cinderella was pretty peculiar. And the glass slippers had been so noisy, how come the handsome prince hadn't noticed that in the story?

Maxi as the handsome prince, that probably wasn't so farfetched. He looked the part. The men in the storybooks had the same charming smile, the I-Know-I'm-the-Handsomest-Guy-in-Town confidence—and maybe the same emptiness behind it all.

Don't be so petty, Siggy chided herself. *Sour grapes.*

But after a few more sips of cocoa, she was wondering. For maybe the first time since her life had fallen apart, maybe even the first time *ever,* Siggy took a good hard look at Maxi. She dragged out every memory of him and looked at it from another angle. She asked herself, *Did he feel the way I thought he felt? Did he mean what I thought he meant? Was it all the way I've always pictured it, or was I building a castle in my head? I always*

*had such a clear idea about how things ought to be. But
how did everyone else see it? How did Maxi see it?*

She didn't come up with any definite answers.

But the questions were very disturbing.

Siggy was riding the bus to work the next day when
an idea suddenly hit her.

"A masked ball," she said.

"Huh?" said Gustav, who was sitting next to her.
Afrika and George were across from them, talking
about baseball.

"That's how we can do Halloween even better than
we did it last year," said Siggy.

Everyone was suddenly listening. "Better than the
pumpkin-carving contest?" asked Afrika.

"Or the mummy's tomb?" asked George.

"We'll still do all of that," promised Siggy. "But Halloween falls on Friday this year; we can have our
haunted complex that night. And on Saturday, we'll have
a masked ball!"

"Hey," said Gustav. "That might be fun." He had
begun to attend the dances about six months before. He
was shy, just like Jorge La Placa had been; but always
warmed up as the night wore on. He even lost that perpetually, tired look once you got him waltzing.

"We'll have to send the news out to our dance group
immediately," Siggy said. "We've only got twenty-seven
days before Halloween. . . ."

"Last year you pulled it all together in a week,"
Afrika reminded her.

"But this year it'll be even better. They'll be talking
about our Haunted Complex for weeks afterward! We'll
let people wear costumes if they want, or they can wear
fancy dance clothes and masks. We'll get a whole bunch
to hand out at the door, the kind you can get at any
party shop. I'll dig through my music library to find the
spookiest music I can. It'll be great!"

"Hey," said Thompson, "that sounds kind of interesting. I might come to that." She had brought her two
sons to trick-or-treat at the complex last year, but she
had never been to one of the dances. Siggy thought she
had been tempted, though. Maybe this time would be it.

"Siggy, you're the most holiday-crazy person I ever met in my life!" Afrika said teasingly, pleased with the way his kids had blossomed in the past year, the girls wearing elegant dancing dresses, Nathanial now more concerned about projects he was working on than TV, and all of them meeting new people.

I can't wait to send the photos to Mom, Siggy thought. They sent them back and forth to each other, pictures of friends, family, gatherings, scenery, anything they could think of. Mom knew what all of Siggy's friends and co-workers looked like; she had already exchanged several recipes with Afrika's wife and daughters. She joked with Siggy that it wasn't fair, as Siggy would have more holidays than her now that she was on Agate. Agate had a solar year and a rotation similar to Earth's, so it was on the Standard calendar.

Siggy was so excited, so lost in thought about her Halloween preparations, that she temporarily forgot about her problems on Monster Row.

It was too bad they hadn't forgotten about *her.*

"Hey Siggy," George called, "have you talked to Afrika? He's looking for you."

Siggy had been busy with Gustav and Li all morning, training new employees.

"I'm late for the Row," she said. "Tell him to meet me at the elevator after I'm done!" And she rushed off.

She was out of breath when she got into the elevator. The clock said she was five minutes late; the Director wouldn't like that. *I don't need trouble today,* she prayed. *Not when I was feeling so good this morning.*

But the Director wasn't her biggest worry. Once the glow had worn off of her excitement over the masked ball, she had started to think about Joseph again. What would he be like today? Would Mr. Hyde be so terrible when he was locked up? She shouldn't get her hopes up about it; she remembered Mr. Hyde vividly from the mini. The therapist had been so sad, even while she was scared. That was probably how it was going to go.

Joseph had gotten such a kick out of hearing about Halloween last year. He even had a suggestion for this year.

"You should do a Halloween tree," he had said. "You ever read Ray Bradbury?"

"You bet!" Siggy had said. Ray Bradbury was Mr. Halloween, read and honored for generations on Veil. But no one had ever done a Halloween tree there, as far as Siggy knew.

"I grew up in a small town," Joseph said. "Perkins' Pond, population twenty-five hundred and seventeen. There actually was a pond, and I guess this guy named Perkins found it. Right next to it was the biggest tree you ever saw in your life, a blue oak. It was so big, they should have called the place Perkins' Oak. Anyway, we used to hang our Jack-o-lanterns up there, put glow rods in 'em so they would be all lit up, over two thousand of 'em. You should have seen it."

Siggy *could* see it, she could picture it perfectly. She had been so swept up by the idea she had stopped mopping and had just stood there, carried away.

The tree in the courtyard of the apartment complex wasn't that big, just large enough to decorate for Christmas. But there was one at the very front that was a good twenty feet high, and its branches spread out bush fashion instead of going straight up. It might make a good Halloween tree.

There were lots of big trees back home in Red Cliffs. Maybe someday . . .

Siggy had planned to take pictures, if they could put together a Halloween tree this year. Mom would get one of course, but she had wondered if she should place a request with security to try to get a copy to Joseph.

Now she wasn't sure it would be necessary.

When the elevator doors opened, the officers weren't at their post. Siggy froze, suddenly sure that one of the prisoners had gotten out.

She touched the call button near the elevator door.

"Hey!" she said, "this is Lindquist! Everything okay?"

The seconds dragged by, and her heart began to freeze over. *Shut the door,* warned the mom in her head. *Run!*

"Yeah!" a voice suddenly boomed out of the speaker. "This is Lindquist. Who—"

"Yeah, it's me, Burke."

Siggy sighed. She recognized the voice.

"Go on in, we're just doing paperwork, giving our statements."

"Your statements?" asked Siggy. But he didn't elaborate.

The door to the hallway stood wide open. Siggy walked through it, still nervous, still sure something was wrong. She didn't feel like she was in danger anymore, but she knocked on the transparency until the man looking at the monitors turned and looked at her. He waved, cheerfully. Siggy waved back.

Okay. He's still there, so it can't be a breakout, no one is holding the guards hostage and making them say things.

Siggy got her cleaning supplies and buzzed the Toady. She was surprised when the outer door instantly zipped open. She stepped through and looked him square in the face.

She regretted that. His expression always made her angry. Today it was just a little smugger than usual, perhaps gloating over the fact that he knew exactly what was going on and she didn't. She gave him a brief glare and then turned her back on him, positioning herself in front of the inner door.

Don't ever look at him again, she told herself firmly. *Not ever. He's just a mannequin.*

The inner door slid open, and Siggy pushed the bucket through.

Silence on the Row.

The guys up front didn't say a word as she passed them. She never looked at them, but she could sense them; today they hardly seemed there.

She was almost halfway down when she saw the Professor and Jerry Wolfe pressed against their respective transparencies, waiting for her. Joseph wasn't at his. Siggy blinked, trying to see the other two without actually making eye contact with them. The Professor snared her anyway. The intensity of his gaze was impossible to ignore.

Siggy faltered.

She almost asked, *What's wrong?* But these two guys were the last ones she should ask.

She started to push the bucket again. She was almost to Joseph's cell. Her stomach clenched in a knot. She would have asked him what was going on if he had been himself. But Mr. Hyde was probably in there now. Mr. Hyde was probably the reason everyone was acting so strange today. Siggy knew it in her bones.

And then she saw the blood.

There was a long smear of it along the floor inside the cell. There were spatters on the transparency, too, but she hadn't seen them at first. The material must have been so slick, the blood had dripped down it and pooled on the floor.

"Joseph?" called Siggy.

No answer. There was never going to be an answer. Siggy pushed the bucket forward a few more steps, until she could see the entire cell.

Joseph wasn't there. But he had left a lot of blood behind.

It was everywhere, on the walls, the floor, his cot. It looked like he had exploded. Here and there, Siggy could see impressions of body parts: smeared hand prints; the outline of a torso; footprints, as if he had tried to kick his way through the walls.

Some roundish patches had hairs imbedded in them.

"They fought all night," called the Professor. "Dr. Jekyll and Mr. Hyde. Poor Dr. Jekyll got his head beat to a pulp. You should have heard them, tearing at each other. Dr. Jekyll stuck up for you, Siggy. He was in love with you. He wanted to hold you in his arms. It's all he thought about, night and day. Dr. Jekyll can't have feelings like that, they're not good for him. They make Mr. Hyde come out. He wanted you, too. But his dreams about you were a lot more lurid."

Siggy didn't look at him. She listened to his toneless voice and stared at the bloody cell.

"It was a demon!" shrieked Jerry Wolfe. "I sent a demon to possess him! He'll be my servant in Hell now, Siggy, he can suck my cock, too, he can take turns with you and Dr. Kenyon, and when he's not sucking me he can go out and be my Chief Tormentor. He had lots of good ideas, he told me! He knows all about burning babies, he knows how to skin people alive! I tried to do that a few times, but it's hard to get the skin off in one piece."

"Is he dead?" asked Siggy, but Jerry was drowning her out. She pushed her bucket all the way to the end of the row and went to stand in front of the Professor. She couldn't have been more than a foot away from him, looking right into the inferno of his eyes. She should have been burned at that distance, but she wanted an answer.

"Is he dead?" she asked again.

He didn't answer for a long moment. He looked like he would never speak. Siggy wondered if she could glean the answer from his expression. But he didn't have one.

"He wasn't moving when they took him out," he said at last. "They didn't say anything. The medical technicians."

"Did they cover his face?" demanded Siggy.

He gave her a faint smile.

"I think he was trying to beat it out of his skull," he said. "The glitch. He knew it was the BioTech that had ruined him. He went from being a hero to a monster. That's quite a fall, don't you think? You're bound to bust something open if you fall that far."

Siggy gazed at him. She was withering by the moment. She couldn't see into him any better than she could have seen past Enigma's event horizon.

She backed away, and began to mop.

When she had gone all the way to the end, she waited for the door to open.

Ten minutes later, it did.

Siggy didn't care.

It was a small town, said the Joseph in her head. *Twenty-five hundred and seventeen. I was number twenty-seven thirteen. They didn't update that sign for the longest time; the kids always used to scratch the numbers out and write in new ones. But the real number was never much more than that. People came and went. Eventually, I went, too.*

This was what Afrika had wanted to tell her. He had been there that morning, he was trying to warn her.

Leave a Jack-o-lantern on the Halloween tree for me, said Joseph. *We all hang there eventually, Siggy.*

Siggy put away her supplies and walked back down the hall, got on the elevator. Afrika would be waiting downstairs for her. At lunch, she would tell him about another holiday, one she wanted to observe the Sunday after the masked ball.

It was called El Dia De Los Muertos.

"**S**even years," Siggy whispered, "seven orientation speeches, and I still don't know the man's name."

She was sitting with Afrika and George for the yearly orientation speech in Auditorium D. The Director was saying the exact same thing he always said:

"You will address me as *sir*. You will say, 'Yes, *sir*,' 'No, *sir*,'" I hear and obey, *sir*.'

Siggy sighed. In his own way, the Director was as pathological as Jerry Wolfe. He repeated himself a lot, and with great energy.

Siggy let her eyes wander as the Director went through the rest of his spiel. She saw Gustav and Li sitting a few rows over. It was a shame they wouldn't sit with Siggy anymore. She suspected it was Li who probably was uncomfortable with that.

Siggy and Gustav had spent several nights together a few years back. In fact, Gustav was the one who had divested Siggy of her virginity. She liked him very much, but when he asked her for a permanent arrangement, she told him she couldn't do it. She was capable of sharing affection with him, but not anything more than that. So she and Gustav had drifted apart, and eventually he had started keeping company with Li, who was twice her age but didn't look it.

Siggy had a feeling their relationship wasn't going to work out, and Li's coolness toward her only confirmed her suspicions. It was a cliche for the older woman to try to control her young lover as if he were a child, but cliches existed because they were so often true.

"Those of you who *do* see me will have cause to regret it!" snapped the Director.

More than I could possibly tell you, thought Siggy,

whose tango face was firmly in place. She had spoken to the Director only twice during the last six years. The first time was shortly after Joseph was removed from Monster Row. As usual, it was Prisoner MS-12 he wanted to discuss.

"Did he seem different to you this time?" the Director had asked.

"How do you mean different?"

"I'm talking about feelings. You seem to be well in touch with your instincts, Lindquist; use them! How did he *feel*?"

Siggy wanted to scream at him. She wanted to tear his head off. But she was playing her cards close to the chest this time; she still didn't know if Joseph was alive or dead.

"I need to know something before I can answer that," she said, then quickly added, "Did Joseph talk a lot while he was banging his head on the walls?"

"Why?" snapped the Director, and Siggy could tell this wasn't going to be easy.

"I need to know if Prisoner MS-12's assessment of the situation was accurate. The battle between Dr. Jekyll and Mr. Hyde."

"He drew the same conclusions I did," said the Director. "The same conclusions, I suspect, that you drew yourself."

"I'm wondering," said Siggy, "if all that blood excited him. And the banging. His own murders must have been just as violent."

"Yes?" he prompted.

Siggy took a deep breath. "Seeing Joseph die must have caused him to feel agitated."

The Director glared at her, unhelpfully.

He hadn't reacted at all when she said Joseph had died. He wasn't going to confirm or deny it.

But who knew—maybe someday she would pry it out of him. So she gave him what he was after.

"The intensity of his gaze," she said, "was almost unbearable."

"Yes," he said, and then he had dismissed her.

Afrika had been the one who cleaned Joseph's cell. "All that blood, Siggy," he had said. "I don't want you to get your hopes up. The way he must have hit those walls with his head, he had to have done a lot of damage to his brain."

"Scalp wounds bleed a lot, don't they?" Siggy asked. "They always look worse than they are."

"Then where is he, sweetheart?" he asked. "How come he didn't just go to the infirmary and come back again, heavily sedated?"

"He would need a padded room," George had remarked. "We have those here, but they're not up to Maximum Security standards. If he's still alive, they'd have to send him somewhere else."

"Maybe they're going to operate," said Siggy. "Maybe they'll try to fix his BioTech glitch."

"Shoot," Afrika had said, "don't you think they've already tried that? If they could've fixed it—"

"They might have something new now!" Siggy pleaded. "He was here almost ten years, they could have found something new!"

"If they did," George remarked under his breath, "you can bet we'll never hear about it. This is military stuff, and you just don't want to be talking about that where someone can hear you."

And to prove him right, Siggy was called up to the Director's office the very next day.

"I hear you've been asking questions about Joseph Bell," he said, and he seemed unusually subdued. He posed the question to her while looking down at his pen, with which he was toying.

"I just—" Siggy had begun, but then he raised his eyes to her, his hands suddenly freezing.

"*Don't*," he said, more quietly than he had ever said anything, more quietly than she had thought he would be capable. It wasn't like him, and it chilled her blood. "For your own sake," he continued, his hands still frozen, his voice still low, "for the sake of your friends and your family, *do not ask any more questions about Joseph Bell. Do not even use the word BioTech. Do not pursue this subject, drop it now and forever.*"

He looked down at his pen again, and turned it over. He began to doodle on his yellow pad. Siggy, speechless, merely watched him.

"You must understand, Lindquist. The war we had with the Speedies was lost by us. They called it off for reasons we are still trying to fathom. When it was at its hottest, and we were all sure we were facing complete annihilation, there were things we did that had to be done. Things that we are *still* doing."

Siggy started to tremble. She was glad he didn't seem to require a response from her.

"I don't have to tell you any of this. If you were to disappear suddenly, it wouldn't reflect badly on me. But I don't want you to accidentally drag any of the rest of us down with you. You really must be careful what you say to Mr. Jones and Mr. Smith."

Afrika and George would not have been happy to hear their names being spoken in this context. Not at all.

"I understand that you felt pity for Commander Bell, but he is no longer your concern. Whatever his fate, you can be certain that he is in better hands, divine or otherwise. Let him go."

He raised his eyes, one more time.

"This is the only warning you're going to get," he said.

"Understood," said Siggy.

"Dismissed." He nodded as if he were a commander and she a soldier. Siggy turned and exited his office for the last time.

She knew why he had warned her.

He broke the rules! He wasn't supposed to let any of us near those guys on Monster Row, only the doctors are supposed to see them! We should never have met Joseph, and we should never have seen him in those "special materials" he made us watch.

His temper and his arrogance had led him down that road; and then his ruthlessness, when he had noticed how interested Prisoner MS-12 was in Siggy. He was taking a big chance, and Siggy had almost rocked the boat. It hadn't been concern for her, or Afrika and George, that had prompted his warning. He had been threatening her.

Siggy watched attentively as the Director finished his speech and stalked out of the auditorium. She watched the newbees stir uneasily, saw them looking around at the old-timers for reassurance. She wanted to tell them they'd only have to suffer the Director's poison once a year, but she wouldn't say anything about it within ear-shot of IFCI.

Today her newbee was a woman named Thora Frideborg, a youngster with white-gold hair who stood head and shoulders taller than Siggy. She was large, more muscle than fat, but surprisingly graceful and gentle. Siggy suspected Thora would make an excellent dance partner if any of the men could ever work up the courage to ask a woman who looked like she could snap them like a twig.

Thora was shy as well, probably not much more than eighteen, and her smiles were rare that first day. She only loosened up for a moment that morning, grinning and saying, "Sigrit Lindquist! That's a fine Teutonic name!"

Siggy had grinned back and said, "Why, thank you, Thora Frideborg!"

Thora would make a good co-worker. She was nervous because it was her first day, but she was strong, hard-working, patient, and calm. Siggy told her she was like a lot of the nurses who worked there.

"Oh no!" Thora said, emphatically. "You don't want to see me when I lose my temper."

"Oh," said Siggy "it's a good thing you left *Mjollnir* at home!"

Thora had tried to stifle a grin as the others looked at them oddly. Most people simply didn't get a joke about Thor's hammer these days.

"Hey," said Afrika, "knock it off with the Scandinavian humor. Otherwise I'm going to be forced to start punning in Swahili."

Orientation day was always a little more relaxed than usual, like the first day of school. It was also the day the new raises kicked in.

Not that she needed one. Her pay had been doubled seven years ago; she made more than anyone else on the non-professional staff, Mr. Morita included. She still got her raises anyway, and she dutifully invested the money in the company investment plan. Within a few years, she would probably go to City College in the evenings.

If she could only decide what she wanted to do.

Nathanial was studying accounting there. He had made the honor roll his first semester. His older sister Electra had moved on to university with the same major; and another sister, Sheba, was due to enter next fall and study biochemistry.

Sheba had confided in Siggy that a job in that field would probably take her to the edges of the known galaxy.

"I haven't told my folks that," she said. "I know it'll break their hearts. I might never see my family again, Siggy!"

Siggy had put her arm around Sheba, but she could see something behind the sadness: an excitement, a yearning for adventure.

"This is what you really want to do?" she asked the girl.

"More than anything!" Sheba said, and Siggy had envied her enthusiasm, her self-knowledge.

So, asked the mom in her head as Siggy pushed the button to ride up to Monster Row, *what are* you *going to do with your life?*

She had entertained the idea of pursuing psychology, despite what she had said to the Director. Lord knew, she spent enough time with crazy people every day. She knew more about the guys on Monster Row than anyone. She was the one who had seen the change coming for Joseph, the emergence of Mr. Hyde.

And she was the one who was worried about the changes she had observed in Jerry Wolfe. No one else seemed to be.

The Director didn't talk to her anymore, except to order her, from time to time, to go back and mop the Row again. But a couple of the other doctors called Siggy at home. They talked to her because they had found out, she suspected, how useful she had been to the Director. But they couldn't overcome their prejudice about her class, her lowly job. Ultimately, they dismissed her observations, and they had stopped calling her.

Meanwhile, Jerry Wolfe was changing.

It probably wouldn't be apparent to anyone who was intimidated by his blinding rages, his obsessive repetition of certain words and phrases. He still did all of that, he still ordered Siggy to perform sexual acts, made personal and threatening remarks, referred to himself as the Antichrist and made outrageous claims about his origins and his destiny, but there was something new that had been added to the mix, something that had been evolving over the last seven years.

He was starting to become *focused*.

It began just after Joseph was taken away. Siggy had come in a week later to find Jerry sitting in a corner, withdrawn, muttering to himself. She assumed he was reacting to Joseph's death. For all she knew, Jerry missed the man. He had lived next to him for several years.

That day she heard him say, very distinctly, "My Lord, why hast thou forsaken me?"

He hadn't said it with humility, of course, or with pain. Jerry's plea was wrathful, accusatory.

Threatening.

So who was he talking to, God or the Devil? She listened to him more carefully than she had before. Eventually, she found out that Jerry didn't differentiate between the two. The God he knew was the one who buried cities in sand, or great floods; who turned people into pillars of salt. Jerry had been obsessively researching the Bible, looking for stuff that would prop up the myth he was weaving for and about himself.

From there, his research spread into widely divergent areas; there were many days when he was too busy poring over his library terminal to harass Siggy at all.

The Professor watched it all without a flicker of reaction. His voice was as toneless as ever, and his eyes still watched her in a way that made her wake up in a cold sweat at night. He never did anything much in her nightmares, but he didn't really have to. It was enough for her simply to know that he was there.

I'll always be here, said the Professor in her head, his edges blurred, his eyes glowing. *If you're still alive, one hundred years from now, I'll still be here.*

Yes, he would. They all would. Some day Siggy might remember them better than she did her family or her friends.

The door slid open, and Siggy greeted the officers. They did their usual security check, and she was waved through.

The Toady took his usual time opening the door. As she entered the lock, she reflected that she wouldn't have known if his appearance was any different these days. She hadn't looked at him or spoken to him in years. He sometimes tried to play games with her, provoke her, but she steadfastly ignored him. He could be two hundred pounds heavier and completely bald, and she wouldn't know it. Or care.

She waited for him to open the inner door. She had discovered that he didn't dare wait longer than a few minutes. She suspected that the Director was impatient with the delays. At first, the Director had been annoyed enough with her to enjoy her discomfort; but that pleasure must have grown old quickly.

The inner door slid open, and Siggy pushed the mop through.

"Hey, Lindquist!" screamed the guy in the first cell. "Let's get married!"

He had been there a couple of years. He wasn't actually a bad guy, for a Monster; he never cursed at her. But she wouldn't answer him or look at him. Afrika told her that this guy had murdered his entire family and tried to blame it on his twin brother, a man who didn't even exist.

"You and me!" said Prisoner MS-01. "As soon as I get out of here. I'm serious!"

She believed him. She was glad he wasn't ever getting out.

Down on Jerry's end, things were quiet. She could see the flickering light of his library terminal.

Good, she thought, *he's occupied.* But the thought disturbed her, too. This would be one entire week when Jerry Wolfe had been too busy studying to talk to her. His ability to focus had increased, sharply.

Siggy pushed her bucket to the end. The Professor waited for her. When she got there, he asked, "Do you like the child-killer?" meaning Prisoner MS-01.

"I like the fact that he doesn't bother me much," said Siggy.

"Don't underestimate him," said the Professor, monotonously. "Perhaps he'll convince his doctors that all he needs is medication. Someday, he *could* get out. He could come looking for you. What will you do if he finds you?"

Siggy started mopping. She hated to admit it, but that was a good question. Guns of any kind were illegal on Agate. What would she do?

Somewhere behind her, she could hear Jerry typing something into his keyboard.

Better not be another letter, she thought, angrily. Since the first one, she had rented a secret P.O. box, rather than risk getting letters from Jerry. All mail that went to her street address was refused, but as far as she knew, he hadn't tried to send another one.

Jerry was typing up a storm. Siggy kept mopping, backing toward him, away from the Professor. She let her mind go calm, almost blank. After a while, she started to hum. By the time she had reached Jerry's territory, she was singing aloud, one of her favorite Judy Garland songs, "On the Atcheson Topeka and the Santa Fe."

"STOP THAT!" thundered a voice, so loud and with such passion that Siggy thought it must be the Director over the intercom. But one look at the Professor changed her mind. She almost dropped her mop.

He was glaring at her, his face twisted in an impossible rage. "Stop singing!" he shouted. "I hate that! It's bad enough when you hum, but don't ever sing, not ever again!"

"I won't!" promised Siggy. "I won't even hum anymore!" She hoped he was convinced of her sincerity. The face he was showing her now might have been the face his victims had seen, just before he had bludgeoned them to death. If he had been free, in the same room with her, he would have killed her then.

Siggy put her head down and started mopping again. Jerry Wolfe had come over to the transparency to see what was going on. Siggy waited for his usual obscenities.

"I thought it was a very nice song," he said. "You have a nice voice."

Siggy almost lost her mop again. She tried not to show it.

"You probably shouldn't sing in front of Beelzebub," warned Jerry. "He hates music. I like it, though. I'm the Antichrist."

And everyone knows how much the Antichrist loves music, thought Siggy.

She could still feel the Professor smoldering over in his corner. He wasn't going to forgive her anytime soon.

What did the others do, I wonder? It could have been anything, singing on the subway, playing music too loud, god only knows. Maybe something different for everyone, the only thing they probably had in common was music. And he hates it so much, he loses control. Otherwise, he just snaps their necks.

She mopped her way back to Prisoner MS-01, who whispered, "What got into that guy?"

Don't ask, thought Siggy, and pushed the button to be let out.

"Not so fast," snapped the voice of the Director. "You are losing your edge, Lindquist. I've never seen you do such a poor job."

Oh no . . .

"Go back and do it again!"

Siggy looked at the floor. It was shining, spotless. She debated arguing with him, but she knew it was useless. She pushed the mop all the way back to the end again.

He was waiting. His face was calm again.

"Just so we have an understanding," he said when she had started again.

"We do," said Siggy.

"Victory is such a two-edged sword," he remarked.

That might have been aimed at the Director. Siggy had accidentally tricked the Professor into revealing something about himself: a weakness, a motive. He wouldn't be likely to forgive that; not her, not the Director.

You'd better pray he never gets out, she would have liked to tell the Director. *Because when he does, I bet you're higher on his agenda than I am.*

"You'll be my concubine in Hell!" called Jerry, his greasy face pressed against the transparency.

And this time when he said it, she could have sworn he sounded just a little more sure of it.

When Siggy stopped off at her P.O. box on the way home, there was a surprise waiting for her. A letter.

Fortunately, it wasn't from Jerry Wolfe. But she was amazed to see it anyway. It was from Barry Silverstein.

She had received no answer to the two letters she had written him, six years ago. She had been certain she never would. She had tried to be careful; she had fussed over the first letter for one whole Saturday, uncertain whether to tell him the complete truth or to be indirect. Finally, she had just kept it simple.

> *Dear Mr. Silverstein,*
> *I am from Red Cliffs, in the Veil System, and*
> *I used to go to school with a David*
> *Silverstein. Are you his brother? Please forgive*
> *me for being nosy, but I live far from home*
> *now. I have fallen out of touch with David. No*
> *one seems to know where he is anymore.*
> *Would you mind sending me his new address?*
> *The one listed in the address finder is out of*
> *date.*

She wasn't totally satisfied with this version, but she figured at least she wouldn't scare him off by sounding like a nut. If he didn't remember his brother, he could say *Sorry, wrong number.* If he did, he might say, *I regret to tell you that my brother is missing.* Then Siggy could open a real dialogue with him.

But he hadn't said anything at all.

After six months, Siggy broke down and sent him a backup letter. She included a copy of the original letter in the envelope.

Did you receive this letter? was all it said. *I don't mean to be a pest, but I worry that it may have been lost.*

And maybe both letters had been lost. One way or the other, she never got an answer.

Until today.

Ho boy, she thought. *Here it is. After six years.* She might have been less surprised to hear from her dad.

Or Joseph.

Don't think that, she warned herself. It sounded too much like a prophecy.

Siggy took the letter inside. She held it up in the light from her kitchen window and tried to see through the envelope. Faintly she could make out the lines. Lots of them.

That was probably good. It could have just said three words: *Leave me alone.*

He wouldn't wait six years to tell me that, anyway.

Siggy thought briefly of making herself a cup of coffee before she sat down with the letter, but she couldn't wait another moment. She sat down at the table and tore open the envelope.

Dear Siggy, was written in clear, cursive script.

I know it must be surprising to hear from me after six years. The fact is, when I got your first letter, it knocked me for quite a loop. It hurt, too, and I think you know why.

The truth is, I've done some research about you over the years. I'm a lawyer now, and have some strong ties in useful places. I've asked my mother about you, too, and she thinks very highly of you. I must say, it was very clever of you to pass yourself off to her as a housekeeper. When I visited last year, I saw the blank space on David's wall, where his certificate of merit used to be.

There aren't very many of us left who remember that David ever existed. I spoke to your friend Maxi, and after some coaxing, he remembered your odd theory. I confess it's part of the reason I didn't get back to you. I was pretty sure my brother was dead by then, and I was in no mood for fairy tales. But several questions have haunted me over the years. Why is it that no one on Veil remembers David? It's remotely possible that my parents have blocked out his memory from grief and shock, but this has never seemed all that likely to me. So I posed your theory to some physicist friends

*of mine, and they did a little research of
their own.*

*I can't promise that we're ever going to solve
this mystery, but an inquiry has begun. My
friends feel that your suspicion that the
disappearances have something to do with
Enigma has merit. In fact, I was surprised how
quickly support was mustered for our research
once I mentioned your name. I'm not sure if this
is good for you or bad, but I want you to
know that you have friends you didn't know you
had. I hope you'll consider me one of them.*

*Once again, I apologize for taking so long to
answer you. Next time, my answer will be
more prompt, I promise.*

Take care, and keep talking about David!

Siggy stared at the page for several minutes. A few
things kept snagging her attention: *I spoke to your friend
Maxi . . . he remembered your odd theory; I was surprised
how quickly support was mustered for our research once
I mentioned your name;* and *you have friends you didn't
know you had.*

A chill crept up her spine as she remembered the last
time she had spoken to the Director.

I hear you've been asking questions about Joseph Bell.

She couldn't think of any other reason strangers would
know her name. And why would they have perked up
so much when they heard her theory about Enigma?

*The war we had with the Speedies was lost by us. There
were things we did then that had to be done. Things that
we are* still *doing.*

She was being paranoid. What did she have to go on?
Once, she had asked questions about Time Pockets.
Then she had asked questions about Joseph Bell.

We were facing complete annihilation.

Had Barry misunderstood what his associates intended? Had they lied to him?

*If you were to disappear suddenly, it wouldn't reflect
badly on me.*

Siggy put the letter down and rubbed her eyes, her

face, and finally the top of her head. When she picked up the letter again, something else struck her:

I'm not sure if this is good for you or bad. Followed by, *you have friends you didn't know you had. I hope you'll consider me one of them.*

Barry Silverstein had gone to Oxford, he was a lawyer now. He was no fool. He was cautious; that was why he had taken so long to write her. Once he had decided to write, he stated in print that he was her friend.

Maybe she wasn't the only one he wanted to see that statement. Maybe he was warning someone.

She read it one more time. Once she had finished, she took it upstairs and tucked it into her notebook right next to Joseph's letter. She had a feeling it belonged there.

Siggy waited at the bus stop in the cool spring air, with Afrika and Gustav and about a dozen other people who had become regulars over the past several years. On mornings like this, when Crazy Horse Mountain seemed so clear and close, Siggy almost felt like she had been there forever. But Afrika laughed when he heard her say things like that.

"I've been working at IFCI seventeen years now!" he said. "Don't talk to *me* about forever."

Siggy hoped she wouldn't be there that long. She thought she could probably stand a few more years, but she had been studying the local job net lately, looking to see what sort of education she would need for various things. So far it hadn't been too promising, but things seemed to be opening up a little bit lately. The economy was on the upswing.

And in the meantime, she had her friends, her dances, holidays to plan for. Mom had just sent her pictures of this year's Halloween on Veil. Their calendars had diverged widely in the past seven years.

George was already on the bus when they all climbed aboard; he lived just a few stops down the road. Thora was there, too; she lived a little further yet. Siggy sat next to her.

"Are you ready for your second day of work?" she asked the big, quiet girl.

"Sure," Thora said. She gazed out her window at the mountains. You could see hawks circling back and forth between them and the city. It was a beautiful sight.

Siggy was surprised to feel Thora shiver.

"What's wrong?" Siggy whispered.

"The birds," Thora said, quietly, so that only Siggy could hear. "I dreamed about birds last night."

"They're hawks," volunteered Siggy, but Thora only looked grim.

"Birds," she said, "circling a battlefield. It seemed to stretch for miles, and there were people, so many men— but they were dead. No one lived, no one moved."

"Thora—" Siggy leaned slightly into her. She didn't want to startle her; when a woman of that size and strength was startled, someone could get hurt.

Thora didn't react, mesmerized by the birds.

"It was a sad dream," Siggy whispered. "But why does it frighten you now?"

"It was a vision," said Thora. "Women in my family get them. It was a very *powerful* vision, the kind that warns of change and death."

Siggy shivered too. On Veil people took omens seriously.

Change and death.

"*You've* been through a big change," Siggy said. "Moving here from another world and starting your first job."

But Thora didn't answer her.

On the Row, things were suspiciously quiet.

Prisoner MS-01 didn't speak when Siggy passed him. She didn't notice at first, because she had been thinking about the Toady.

He had spoken to her.

"You'd better get it done extra good today," he had said in a poor imitation of the Professor's monotone. "The Director's out of town, so *I'm* the one you have to please."

Oh shit. The thought of being at the mercy of the Toady was an ugly one. While the cat was away . . .

The rat will try to make my life miserable. She cursed

her luck. *Maybe this is what Thora's bad dream was all about.*

And now it was quiet on the Row. The prisoners stood at the front of their cells and watched her. She passed them without a word or a look, as always. Soon she could see the Professor standing in his usual spot. Jerry Wolfe pressed his face against the transparency, trying to stretch his field of vision as far as possible. As soon as he saw her, he broke the silence.

"The Apocalypse has begun!" he trumpeted. "The fires of Hell will consume you! You will writhe and scream, you will beg for mercy, but Hell has no mercy!"

Siggy passed him. She went to the end of the Row.

"I have already created Hell in the living world," Jerry continued, as if he were acting out a prepared monologue. "I have tortured mortals in every way possible. I know I'm the Antichrist, because they feared me! You should have seen how frightened they were, Siggy, you should have seen!"

But Siggy *had* seen. And suddenly she was so fed up, she couldn't stand it any longer. She turned and pointed her finger at him, looking directly at him for the first time. He was an ugly, despicable sight, but she made herself look him right in the eye.

"You're just guessing," she said.

This momentarily derailed him. "Huh?" he said.

"You're just guessing about what those people felt. You have no idea. That's why you had to make the mini—"

He grinned like a vicious child, then looked confused.

"The fact is," Siggy said confidently, "you've never been able to figure it out."

"Figure *what* out, you dumb bitch?" asked Jerry, interested despite himself.

"What people are."

He made a rude noise, but he still looked interested. Siggy regarded him with contempt.

"You've never been able to grasp the fact that other people *are* people, Jerry. They walk and talk, but the problem is—they're not *you*."

"I'm the Antichrist," he reminded her. "No one is me."

"Yes," she said, dismissively, "but you've only decided that recently. All your life, you've tried to figure out what other people are feeling. Even when they tell you, you can't grasp it. That's why you made the mini. You had to keep looking at it. You thought if you kept looking at it, eventually you'd figure it out. But you never did, and now you've come up with a fairy tale to explain it away."

She resumed mopping. He spluttered for a moment, then became very thoughtful. As she passed him, he said, almost to himself, "I gave up trying to figure it out, because it doesn't matter. You're all going to die."

"Everyone dies eventually, Jerry," she said. "Even you."

"That's where you're wrong, bitch!" he said, triumphantly. "I'm immortal! I will reign in Hell!"

Wonderful, thought Siggy. *Fat lot of good that did. Now he's even happier with himself than he was before.*

She knew, without looking, that the Professor was watching it all. But today he didn't seem to have anything to say. He seemed less intense than usual, but it wasn't a relief to feel that.

He's holding it back, she thought, nervously. *Trying to seem like nothing's wrong . . .*

She finished mopping the Row, moving carefully so the Toady wouldn't have a legitimate reason to send her back. She got to the end, pressed the button and waited by the lock.

Nothing happened. That was no surprise, he knew he could draw it out today because the Director wasn't around to snap at him. Siggy stood there with her tango face on, waiting for him to get sick of the game.

The minutes dragged by.

They were all looking at her. The prisoners.

Siggy looked back toward the end of the Row. She wondered if she should go back and mop over. But no, she wouldn't do that unless he specifically told her to.

She shifted her weight back and forth. She fought the impulse to look at her watch. She stifled another impulse to call him and ask what was wrong, or demand that he open the door. None of it would do any good.

"Apocalypse . . ." Jerry Wolfe was singing to himself.

He sure loves those fancy Doomsday words, Siggy thought, wearily.

She was sure half an hour had gone by. This was ridiculous. He wouldn't try to make her stay until George's shift, would he? If he was even going to let George in. He could lock George out. Then Siggy might have to spend the night there. She wouldn't be able to eat, or go to the bathroom.

And the prisoners were still staring at her.

Shit, Siggy thought again, and then suddenly the lock opened and Afrika came through.

Siggy stepped back, astonished.

"What's going on?" they both asked at once, and then the door slid shut behind him, hissing as the seal engaged. Afrika whirled and hit the OPEN button. Of course, nothing happened.

"What is he doing?" Siggy asked, irritably, though she was glad to see Afrika. At least she wasn't alone in there anymore.

"He called me and said there was trouble in here, but he wouldn't say what it was," said Afrika. "Said it would take both of us to clean it up—"

He would have continued, but the lights went out in the hall, leaving only the lights inside the cells. Siggy gasped, and Afrika punched at the controls, trying to get the lights back on. They stayed off.

"You're in for it now," warned Prisoner MS-01.

"Son of a—" Afrika started to curse, and then the cell lights went off, too. It was pitch black on the Row.

Siggy clapped her hands over her mouth. The Prisoners all should have started yelling, complaining when that happened. But they were dead quiet, she couldn't even hear them breathing.

Afrika put a steadying hand on her shoulder, but he didn't speak. Somehow they both knew they'd have to stay quiet. She let him guide her to the door, then stood there with her shoulder touching him as he worked at the controls. If she had thought about it, she would know there was no way he could open the door from this side of the lock. But she didn't think about it, she only prayed.

And listened.

She could hear the clicks of the keys on the wall unit. There were a lot of them, and they weren't doing any good.

The bastard! she railed, silently. She knew he was doing it on purpose, the Toady. He had lied to Afrika to get him there, and now he was playing an ugly practical joke. But how far would he go?

The Director is out of town.

What was that noise?

Afrika heard it, too. He stiffened. He stepped in front of Siggy, motioning with his hands that she should stay behind him.

My god, a cell door just opened. He let somebody out!

Siggy was breathing so hard, she was sure she must be making a racket, drawing the inmate down the hall and toward them. She covered her mouth again and tried to stifle the sound. She tried holding her breath, but that just made her dizzy.

Was that another sound, closer to them? Afrika tensed again. The two of them searched the darkness, trying to make their eyes do what they couldn't.

He really did it, he let someone out. I can't believe he let someone out!

Afrika was sweating. Siggy could feel the dampness coming through his shirt. She was just the opposite, ice cold. She wondered how long the Toady would draw out their terror. What if the Professor was coming up the Row toward them? She wondered if he would just break their necks, or if they would be bludgeoned like the man in the trash compactor. Maybe he would try to fit them both into the bucket.

And then the lights went on. Siggy blinked, even more blind than she had been in the dark. When the hallway started to take shape again, she peered around Afrika.

Jerry Wolfe stood just a few feet from them, blinking, a mildly disoriented look on his face.

Siggy felt a jolt seeing him so close, but she was relieved it wasn't the Professor. "Jerry!" she snapped, "get back in your cell!"

He frowned, and his weasely eyes shifted to Afrika.

"You don't have your drugs to help you now," Siggy reminded him. "You can't put us to sleep, Jerry. Afrika could snap you like a twig! And he will, if you don't get back in your cell right now!"

He looked like he might believe her. He looked like he might go back. And that was the moment Afrika should have acted, should have punched Jerry Wolfe right on the tip of his chin and knocked him cold. Siggy had seen him do that to an inmate armed with a home-made knife. He had laid the guy flat before he could even blink. Now was the time to do that to Jerry.

But the only thing Afrika did was push Siggy behind him. His hand shook as he did it, and Siggy caught a glimpse of an ugly grin spreading across Jerry Wolfe's face.

"Afrika," she said, "what—"

She felt an impact against Afrika's body; he staggered back, pushing her into the wall, but she didn't feel him trying to hit back. All he did was keep pushing her behind, keep trying to shield her with his body.

"Fight him!" she cried, "hit him, he's just a skinny little man, he's not the Antichrist!"

But Afrika had never been quite sure of that. Later, Siggy thought about things Afrika had said about Jerry Wolfe; and more important, things he had *not* said. The subject always horrified and disturbed him, he never could quite get the tortured children from the mini out of his mind. Later Siggy would wonder, was there some small part of Afrika that really did believe Jerry's claims?

She heard him gasping, choking off cries as Jerry did things she couldn't see. She tried to squirm out from behind Afrika, to lay her own hands on the little weasel. But Afrika wouldn't let her, and the weasel was a lot stronger than he looked. He slammed Afrika into Siggy, whose skull fractured against the wall.

Her head seemed to fill up with yellow sand, and the noises receded from her, though they never went away entirely. She heard Afrika screaming. She also heard gunshots.

Then everything was quiet for a while.

Got to get up, thought Siggy. *Only halfway done with my work today. Thora must be worried.*

She felt Afrika's weight over her legs.

*My gosh, we fell asleep on the job! We're going to get
killed for this. Got to wake up.*

And she really did mean to, really did want to; but
every time she tried to open her eyes, her head spun
away into darkness and jumbled-up thoughts. She
thought she heard voices. Once she thought she opened
her eyes and saw the Professor standing over her. She
forgot to be scared of him. "What happened to Jerry?"
she asked, but he didn't answer.

Someone was calling her name. Sounded like Thompson. But it was Thompson's day off.

Siggy opened her eyes, people crowded close now. She
could hear again.

"Can you see me?" someone was saying. "Say yes if
you understand."

"Yes," said Siggy, and someone shined a light into her
eyes. "Ow!" she said.

"You've got a head injury." The person turned out to
be a pale-skinned lady in a jump suit. She had a voice
a lot like Thompson's. "We're going to take you to the
infirmary, just lie still for a minute."

Siggy watched the other people, officers, paramedics,
some people in business suits who turned out to be
staff doctors.

"Is Afrika okay?" she asked the Thompson sound-
alike.

"Everything is fine," said the lady. "Just lie still and
don't try to talk."

That wasn't what Siggy had asked. Afrika's weight was
gone from her legs. People crowded around something
a few feet to her left, but the lady paramedic blocked
her view. She was doing it on purpose. Siggy looked her
right in the eye.

"He's dead." She didn't ask.

The lady nodded.

A lot of people came to Afrika's funeral.

Siggy sat in the back of the church. It wasn't that she wanted to avoid Afrika's family, it was just that his family was so big. They formed a cocoon around Kalisha and the kids, protecting them, guiding them, taking charge.

Siggy watched Kalisha as she was ushered down the aisle and into her seat. She looked pale, composed, and utterly stunned. The girls were pretty much the same.

Nathanial looked as if he had been hit by a truck. He stumbled when he walked, and that wasn't like him. He had become the best dancer in Siggy's group, even better than Maxi had been. He had grown tall and strong and handsome, but today he was somebody else. Someone who didn't even know or care where he was.

The rest of the crowd had to stand outside the church and listen by loudspeakers. Siggy knew a lot of people from work had come. The Director wasn't there, of course. No one knew where he was.

There would be four other funerals that weekend. One for the Toady, of course; but Siggy found it hard to imagine that anyone would show up for that one.

Afrika's funeral was an open casket ceremony. Siggy wondered who had decided that, or if there had even been a debate about it. She watched family members filing past the coffin. Some reached in and touched Afrika.

When it was Kalisha's turn, she leaned over and fixed his collar, adjusted his tie. She had always done that when he was dressed up. Her face was so crumpled, Siggy wondered how the grief was going to get out.

Nathanial looked down at his father, but Siggy got a

feeling he couldn't see anything. He was just going
through the motions. When he was done, he stood to
the side without going back to his seat. The minister
edged over and whispered something to him, but Nathanial just shook his head.

Row by row, they got up to look. Soon, Siggy's row
was getting to their feet. She rose with them. They
joined the line and slowly filed past the coffin.

Nathanial was waiting for her at the other end, she
realized. She followed the line, and then it was her turn
to look in.

They had repaired his face. They hadn't done too bad
a job, considering the damage Jerry had inflicted. Siggy
noticed that they had put something under the closed
lids to prop them up, compensating for the eyes that had
been torn out.

The Afrika in her head looked a lot better. He was
quiet today, out of respect for the dead.

Nathanial was still waiting. Siggy walked up to him,
slowly raising her eyes; but he didn't look at her. He
turned his face a little to the side, and put his arm around
her. He walked with her up the aisle and sat her next
to his family. On her other side, Sheba took her hand.

That was good. Siggy had wondered if they thought
she was responsible. None of it would have happened if
it hadn't been for her, though she didn't think it was her
fault. She knew perfectly well who was to blame. She
even thought she knew why he had done it.

The Director hadn't been trying to murder them.
After all, the Toady had rushed in at the last minute
with his gun. He could only have done that because
things were going *wrong,* not according to plan. The Director had done it all, as usual, for the Professor, to
provoke him, get a rise out of him. Just the day before,
he had lost control; and after all, Siggy had been the
one to suggest that Joseph Bell's violence might have
agitated the Professor.

How would Prisoner MS-12 react if Siggy were threatened? Was he capable of attachment to people? Would
he be angry, frightened, amused? Afrika would save the
day, of course, before things got out of hand. Afrika had
taken down men twice Jerry's size; angry, crazy men.

But everyone has an Achilles' heel.

After the service, Siggy sat where she was. Nathanial and Sheba stayed with her; the rest of the family went off with an aunt. People were handing out maps to the open house. It was being held in the same auditorium where they had their dances.

Siggy, Nathanial, and Sheba piled into the back of a van with some cousins and rode over in silence. Once there, Sheba went off to find her mom, but Nathanial stuck to Siggy like glue. She saw Thompson, Gustav, Ashmarina, Li, and Thora all sitting on some chairs near the door, so she and Nathanial sat with them.

"We're going to keep having the dances," Nathanial said suddenly, as if picking up a conversation from before.

"I'm glad." Siggy felt a weight lift from her chest. She had thought, had worried, that because she had helped cause Afrika's death, all of the things they had done and planned together would just be let go, forgotten. Now she knew why Nathanial had waited for her and taken her to sit with the family. It had taken a lot of strength. He had thought of her at a time when most could only have thought about their own pain. Now she knew that someday he was going to be all right.

Someday.

"Next year," she said, "hang a pumpkin for me on the Halloween tree, will you?"

"Yes," he promised.

Neither of them needed to mention that Afrika would have one there, too.

We all hang there eventually, Siggy.

She had come very close. They had told her. Jerry had bent over her when he was done killing the Toady. He had almost touched her, but then the Professor had called something from down the hall. Just two little words.

"Your witness."

Jerry had stopped then. He had left her, and dragged the Toady into the security lock. The cameras in there were on the fritz; the Toady had told the outer officers he was running a diagnostic and not to worry. So Jerry had put on his uniform, and then he had gone on to kill the three men who Siggy had waved to five days a week for the last seven years. He had washed up in their bathroom, and changed clothes again, and taken an ID, and he had just walked out. Petra City was in an uproar now, looking for him.

Siggy's face was still swollen, bruised by the impact with the wall. She still got dizzy sometimes, but she suspected that was because she kept forgetting to eat. Afrika wasn't around to remind her anymore.

You be my witness! I'm the Antichrist!

"They should have just put a bullet in the motherfucker's head," whispered Nathanial.

"They will," promised Siggy.

Siggy had a small room on the ship back to Veil.

She had money now, but that didn't help in this case. Unless you were fabulously, outrageously wealthy, no one ever had a big room on board a starship. There just wasn't enough space for it. You could get lots of nice perks though, like fancy coffee and chocolates, a Net hookup, TV, and a well-stocked (if tiny) private bathroom.

Siggy surfed the news net for hours on the first day, ship time. By then, everyone was claiming that Jerry Wolfe had died on Tantalus. She found lots of headlines about him. What she saw didn't convince her he was dead.

He had keyed into the hotel room with his thumbprint—that was the main piece of evidence that the dead man was Jerry Wolfe. But no one had opened the door or the window to get out again. Lots of people theorized that he had turned a weapon on himself, but no weapon was found on the premises, and the burn pattern radiated from a spot across the room toward what was left of the body.

Siggy could picture one scenario: Jerry might have drugged someone, just like he did with his previous victims, and carried him into the hotel room. She just hoped the poor guy was dead before Jerry burned him. That wasn't Jerry's style, but maybe he was in a hurry.

All that remained was for him to get out again without being recorded.

The police said only someone with inside knowledge about locking systems could have fooled the sensor. They said Jerry Wolfe never had training in that field.

But Siggy kept thinking about the stuff that had been found in his house years before, the tools and the gadgets.

She leaned back and stared at her ceiling for a long time. She felt weird. She was both happy and sad.

On Agate, she had just been making the best of things. She had loved her friends, but now that Afrika was dead, she didn't want to settle there, beautiful though it was. She would never forget Crazy Horse Mountain. She, Gustav and Nathanial had hiked up there once—it seemed like a million years ago. She was glad to have that memory, but Veil was the world she would always call home.

Just thinking about Veil brought tears to her eyes. She would probably get there in time for Christmas. She could have visited before, if she hadn't been saving the money for college, but now she knew that the college fund wasn't the only thing that had kept her from going home. Maxi was there. He had married Leeza six months after Siggy had left. They had children now, Mom had told Siggy. She hadn't sent her pictures, but she didn't have to.

Mom had written to Siggy just before she had left.

Maxi wants us to come visit on Christmas Eve.
He's so excited to hear you're coming home,
Siggy. He remembers you as his best friend. I
told him we would, I couldn't explain my way
out of it. But if you can't do it, I'll think up some
excuse. I promise.

Siggy didn't know if she could do it. But on the other hand, she had two months to think it over. So much had happened in the past seven years, her break-up with Maxi almost seemed trivial in comparison.

Almost.

Siggy fell asleep on her bunk, the light of the Net shining softly on her face.

At almost the same moment, the Professor was in a hotel room in Petra City, breaking his doctor's neck.

The night before she got home, Siggy dreamed about her house.

She was walking up Indianola Avenue. Her house was a few doors up from the corner. It looked the same, except that the trumpet vine was back. Mom had taken it out years ago, because it attracted red wasps.

It was winter now, so the wasps were asleep. Siggy walked up the steps to her front porch.

So many years. I can't believe I'm home again.

Siggy opened the front door. She could smell enchiladas.

"Mom?" she called.

She hung up her coat and took off her galoshes. When she went into the hall, she could hear the TV. Mom must be watching her afternoon news. Siggy tiptoed down the hall, barely glancing at the photo gallery. But she stopped when she saw her prom portrait. It was enormous; it embarrassed her now. There she was with Maxi, bigger than life and with twice as much egg on her face. She looked so young and clueless in that photo.

The voice of the newscaster drifted down the hall.

Apocalypse, he was saying. *Doomsday has begun. The fires have already consumed Earth and the First solar system, and are spreading throughout the Republic in ever-widening circles. The death toll has reached the trillions. No system is being spared. In a statement this morning, the Antichrist promised that everyone killed in the conflagration would be his slaves in Hell. There is no hope. We are praying for salvation, but God is not answering our prayers. . . .*

That must be a movie or something, thought Siggy. She crept down the hall and into the parlor. Mom was sitting

on the couch, her back to Siggy. The TV was a red,
glowing furnace. Siggy could see entire worlds burning
in there, suns expanding to eat their solar systems, or
imploding and sucking everything in after them.

Siggy walked around the couch and sat down in her
customary spot. She was devastated. She had only just
made it home, and now it was all going to be gone.

"No one ever took him seriously," said a toneless
voice, and Siggy looked at her mom. But Mom wasn't
there. The Professor was sitting in her spot.

He turned to look at her.

Siggy whimpered in her sleep.

She scrambled off the couch and ran for the hall, but
the Professor was already standing there. The red glow
of the TV lit his face and the walls on either side of
him. His eyes were red too, like old, dry blood.

"Why didn't you stop him?" demanded Siggy.

The Professor shrugged. "It's not my universe." Then
he pointed at the TV.

Siggy turned to look at it. The scene had shifted to
the Enigma Nebula. It was beginning to glow.

"Here they come," remarked the Professor, just behind her.

Siggy covered her eyes and braced herself.

A buzzer woke her, releasing her from her wait for a
fire that had never come. It was a relief to wake up in
a cool, safe bed with everything still normal and intact
around her. Her itinerary screen was glowing with an
ETA just three hours away. That meant they were practically to Santa Fe Station, and were already braking.
Siggy flipped on the viewscreen function and saw Veil,
a small blue marble. Just beyond it was the sun; and
beyond that, (ten light years beyond it, in fact, but still
filling a third of the screen) was the Enigma Nebula.

Siggy's heart fluttered.

She would have time to shower, pack, and have breakfast. She could wait and eat at one of the thousands of
restaurants on Santa Fe Station, but Siggy had wanted
to spend a little time sight-seeing instead. Santa Fe was
the travel nexus for the whole solar system. It had muse-
ums and shops . . .

And shops! And she had money this time, and it was December 23rd, Veil calendar. She had just made it.

Her itinerary screen began to flash again. It had just hooked up with message systems on Santa Fe, and she had several waiting. Siggy punched in her code.

The first one was from Mom: *Call me as soon as you get to the station and let me know which shuttle you're taking down. Love you!*

The second one was from someone named Edgar Powell: *I'm a friend of Barry Silverstein's—would you be willing to have lunch with me some time soon? Would like to discuss physics and Pockets.*

The third was from someone named Special Agent Nicholas Liadov, R-FBI: *Please contact me at 234-254-775790 as soon as you reach Santa Fe Station. Urgent.*

The fourth explained the third. It was from IFCI: *Please regard the following as confidential information. We are required to warn you since your safety may be in jeopardy. Prisoner MS-12 has escaped IFCI and is no longer on Agate. Law enforcement officials will contact you with further instructions.*

Siggy blinked. She wanted to make sure she wasn't still dreaming. She wasn't like Thora, she didn't have visions.

But maybe it didn't take a clairvoyant to figure out what was going to happen. The Professor had never talked to doctors while the Director was still at IFCI. Once he was out of the way, the Professor had begun to toy with the doctors. They must have been so grateful when he had begun to speak to them.

He had it planned this way all along. But how could he? How could he know the Director would make such a dopey mistake?

Siggy shook her head. She didn't know what had passed between them when she wasn't present. She didn't know what happened on the Row the other twenty-three hours a day. Obviously, she had been pushed around like a pawn. And she wasn't the only one.

Would he come here?

That didn't sound very smart. Apparently, it was the first place they were going to look. If Siggy were he, she would go someplace where they weren't likely to find

him, and there were a lot of places like that on the
fringes of the Republic. Lots of fugitives disappeared
that way. Once they got far enough away from civiliza-
tion, there just weren't enough resources to track them.
Of course, it was a trade off, you probably had to give
up a lot of comforts. But the Professor had lived in an
eight-by-ten cell for fourteen years. Maybe comfort
wasn't his top priority.

Mom she thought, suddenly.

Three hours later, on Santa Fe Station, it wasn't Agent
Liadov she called first when she disembarked.

"Hello?" came her mom's voice, clear as a bell, and
Siggy almost cried with relief.

"It's me!" she said. "Is everything okay?"

It might have sounded like a weird question under
other circumstances, but Marta Lindquist was way ahead
of her daughter. "We've got a couple of R-FBI agents
watching the house for us," she said. "I hear an old
friend of yours might come to visit."

"I don't think he will," Siggy said. "But I'm real glad
someone is looking out for us."

"Me, too," said Mom. "So when are you coming
down?"

"I'm scheduled for a four twenty P.M. arrival, your
time. They're going to let me off on that pad right next
to the bus station. But I still have to meet a guy up here,
Mr. Liadov. He says it's urgent, so I might be delayed."

"I'll carry my portable," said Mom. "Besides, the bus
station is only fifteen minutes from here."

"Okay," said Siggy, breathlessly. People were rushing
past her booth, making their way up the claustrophobic
hall toward the big midway. Now that she knew Mom
was okay, she was getting excited again. "I can't believe
I'm here!"

"Me neither, sweetheart," said Mom. "But you are,
and you'd better save room for a good supper tonight!"

"You bet I will," said Siggy, who hadn't been able to
choke down breakfast. She was working up an appetite
again. "See you later, Mom. Love you."

"You, too," said Mom, and the two of them signed
off.

Siggy was about to call Agent Liadov's number when someone tapped her on the shoulder. She started, and turned to find a big man in a suit that was a little too small for him. He had black hair and eyes, and pale skin. He flashed an ID at her. "Sigrit Lindquist? I'm Nicholas Liadov," he said with a slight accent. "Will you come with me?"

"Where?" asked Siggy nervously.

"To our offices," he said. "It's not far."

Siggy took a hard look at his ID. "Okay," she said. "Lead the way."

The "offices" turned out to be a tiny suite just off the main drag. Liadov sat behind a desk with three monitors crowded onto it. Siggy thought suddenly of the Director and his huge desk, and almost laughed.

He motioned for her to sit in one of two chairs in front of his desk and folded down one of the monitors so he could see her.

"First," he said, "I have to warn you that nothing we say here should be talked about outside this office. Your own safety could be jeopardized, otherwise."

"I won't say anything," Siggy promised. "People would panic if they thought the Professor was coming here."

He raised an eyebrow. "The Professor?"

"Um," said Siggy, "Prisoner MS-12. John Doe number H1176 . . . something."

"Right." He was nodding. "You guys called him the Professor? Why is that?"

Siggy explained as well as she could. She ended up telling him Afrika's theory about how the Professor was a glass that reflected things back at people.

"Good observation," said Liadov. "He really fooled that doctor. He talked her into helping him escape."

Siggy swallowed, hard. "Who got killed, this time?" *Please, not George, or Gustav, or Thompson, or Thora . . .*

"The doctor," said Liadov. "She smuggled him out. She got him a passport, money, you name it. She was convinced he was brilliant and misunderstood. Like you said, a mirror."

"He didn't—" Siggy stammered, "you know, crunch her up into a box or anything—did he?"

"No," said Liadov. "Broke her neck."

"I guess she couldn't carry a tune."

That provoked a puzzled frown, and Siggy explained again. Liadov was fascinated.

"Did you look at any of the tapes they made of my conversations with him?" she asked him.

"We're still trying to pry those out of the IFCI. We had to get a court order, and they got it overruled by a higher court. So we've had to go right to the top. We should have them within a couple of weeks."

"They're scared," said Siggy. "And they damn well ought to be." She went on to tell him about the "special materials" she and the others had been forced to watch, and about her arrangement with the Director. She wondered if he was as surprised by the information as he seemed to be.

"We can't touch him," said Liadov, meaning the Director. "He was very careful to place himself in good circumstances."

"No, but you should talk to him about the Professor," said Siggy. "He probably knows more about the man than anyone alive."

"Except for *you*," said Liadov.

Siggy blushed. "I'm not a doctor."

"A good thing, in this case. I've learned a lot more from you in the last few minutes than my department ever learned from those so-called professionals in the past seven years. They couldn't even wager a good guess about where he's gone."

Siggy was struck by a sudden inspiration. "Have you thought of Tantalus?"

"No," he admitted. "Why?"

"That's where Jerry Wolfe faked his death."

He raised another eyebrow when she said *faked*, but didn't disagree. "And so—?" he prompted.

"The Professor has a weird sense of humor."

"Tantalus," said Liadov, musingly. "From there he could disappear, but he would have to go through some Speedy territories. They would mark him quickly."

"He's not an ordinary human being," Siggy reminded him.

"That is true," Liadov said, his hint of an accent returning again. It seemed to happen whenever he was thinking hard.

Siggy wondered if she should try to ask him about Joseph Bell. It was one of the things she had promised herself she would do that morning; but that was when she had assumed the R-FBI already knew what had transpired between her and the inmates on the Row. Apparently there was a lot they still didn't know, and she didn't want to push it.

"So," she said, "you'll be watching my mom and me?"

"We won't bother you," he said. "But we need to be careful."

"I understand," said Siggy. "I'm glad you'll be there. My mom would probably offer you the guest room."

He smiled, but shook his head. "I don't like my people to get too comfortable. It gets harder for them to stick to business when they're stuffed full of home cooking."

"This time of year it'll be tamales," said Siggy. "Chicken, pork, and beef. We make ten dozen of them for New Year's Eve. Big party."

"Save me some," said Liadov.

"You think I won't?"

He walked her up to the shopping level. "I've got work to do," he said, "but you'll be watched every moment."

"In that case," said Siggy, "I'm not going to the bathroom."

"Well," he amended, "maybe not *every* single moment. But most of them. I'll even be able to check up on you from my office. You'll be completely safe."

"I feel safe," Siggy assured him. And she did. But it wasn't just because the agents were looking out for her. She had a feeling the Professor wasn't headed for Veil. The more she thought about it, the more sure she was that he would go to Tantalus. She reminded Liadov of that, one more time.

"We'll have someone out there," he promised. "It's

a good thought. Have you thought of going into law enforcement?"

He meant it. Siggy was flattered. "For now," she said, "all I want to do is go home."

She spent the next two hours shopping. She bought so much, she had to hire a port-a-luggage to wheel along behind her, and her arms were still full. The hardest gift to pick out was the one she got for Maxi and Leeza. She still didn't know if she was going, Christmas Eve, but she knew she'd have to have a gift to send along, one way or the other.

Mom had said there were three children.

Who should have been mine, Siggy tried not to think. A boy and two girls. Siggy found it a lot easier to pick stuff out for them.

At last, much burdened, she fetched her luggage from its storage locker and labored her way down to the shuttle gate. She passed a view window, and stopped to gaze down at the world below her.

Veil was beautiful. Siggy thought it must be better than old Earth. It had everything Earth had; a somewhat larger land-to-ocean ratio, but with lots of rivers and lakes to make up for it. Mountains, valleys, deserts, forests, fjords, islands, reefs, volcanos—all the good stuff. The original settlers, from Scandinavia and New Mexico (plus a small Jewish contingent from New York) had found plenty to remind them of home.

Siggy watched the world turn beneath her. She scanned the mountain ranges for Red Cliffs, but gave up after a few minutes. The shuttle was boarding, and she had a lot of stuff to put up in the storage compartments. It was time to go home.

She hurried down the ramp, and into the open airlock.

So much happened in the first twenty-four hours, Siggy didn't even have time to get used to the fact that she was home.

She had just left springtime in Petra City, and simulated springtime on shipboard and on Santa Fe Station; winter rushed into the airlock of the shuttle as soon as it opened, and very few of the passengers had remembered to dress for it. Fortunately, Siggy's mom had brought an extra sweater for her.

As soon as Mom had brought her back from the bus station, there had been cooking, baking, wrapping, painting, decorating, card-signing, running back and forth to the stores for this or that forgotten thing, running to neighbors to borrow odds and ends, exchanging busy hellos and, "Siggy, you're home, how long are you staying? Do you have any nutmeg I could borrow?"

It wasn't until Siggy and her mom were in the TrollMart that it really hit her. They were pushing an overloaded cart down the aisle, arguing about whether they should grab another one, fussing over their list and shuffling through their coupons, and Siggy realized that this is exactly what they had always done. Ever since she could remember. It felt so good, she had to hide her tears from Mom.

On the morning of the twenty-fourth, after breakfast with Mrs. Silverstein, Mom asked Siggy, "What about tonight?"

Siggy was still thinking about it. Just before bed last night, she had lingered in the hall in front of the photo gallery. There were many pictures of her and Maxi there, and of course the big prom portrait. Siggy was dismayed to realize that her dream had been true in that respect. She looked too young in that picture. And too starry-eyed.

And she still felt bitter, seven years later.

But that wasn't necessarily an unmanageable thing. After all, she was going to live in this town for the rest of her life, and so would Maxi. It was a small place. She couldn't avoid him; and if she did, things could get chilly. People might feel compelled to divide into camps. Siggy didn't want that to happen.

"I'm going," she said.

Mom smiled. It was only when she smiled that she looked any older to Siggy; she had one or two more lines at the corners of her eyes. Otherwise, Mom was the same slender, youthful woman she had been before.

"I'm glad," Mom said. "He didn't do it to be mean, sweetheart. He just didn't see things the same way you did."

"I know," said Siggy. *But I wonder which of us was blinder.*

"The kids are delightful," said Mom. "I see them a lot. They've been looking forward to meeting you."

Well, that would be fun, anyway. Siggy had loved Afrika's children. She missed them terribly. She was beginning to have a sinking feeling that she wasn't going to have any of her own.

Don't start thinking that way. You're going to end up feeling miserable, and you still have the evening to get through.

So Siggy and her mother spent the rest of the day finishing the preparations. The tamales were done, and Mom had already been baking cookies for days. All of the packages were wrapped, and they finished decorating the tree. They stood for a long time in front of it, admiring. Dad's favorite angel was sitting on top.

Well, it wasn't exactly an angel. It was Daffy Duck with wings and a halo.

"Ready?" Mom asked, at last.

"Ready," said Siggy, and even sort of meant it.

Maxi lived in a fancy part of town. There were even a few houses there that looked like palaces.

Maxi's house wasn't a palace, but it was a lot fancier than his parents' house. Maxi's dad had a regular residence on Stockholm Station. He only came home for weekends, and apparently didn't feel the need for anything fancy. And Maxi worked for his dad now.

Perhaps it was Leeza's tastes that ran this rich.

Mom had told her Maxi's house was a restored masterpiece, three hundred years old and three stories high. It didn't look its age; it looked very solid and graceful. The lawn was perfectly manicured; the cars parked in the circular drive out front were new and luxurious.

Siggy thought of Maxi's old car with a pang.

"Do her folks have a lot of money?" she asked Mom when they were getting out of their car, which hadn't ever been luxurious, even when it was new.

"I think so," said Mom. "But I've never met them."

They were carrying two dozen tamales, a cake, tins of

homemade cookies and candy, and gifts. They made their precarious way up the walk, and about halfway there Siggy was beginning to suspect that an avalanche was imminent.

Then the front door flew open, and a small boy came bursting out.

"Dad, they're here, they're here! Marta and Siggy!"

"Hello, Jason," Mom called. "Come help us with all this stuff!"

Jason ran up to Mom, stealing shy glances at Siggy. He managed to slide a few of the tins off the top without making Marta drop the rest of her burden. Siggy tried not to stare at him, but she caught her breath as soon as he had come close enough for her to get a good look at him.

He looked exactly like Maxi had at that age.

"Dad, come help us!" Jason was calling. "There's lots more!"

Siggy looked over at the front porch again, and there he was. He was smiling. He hurried over to help Siggy with her packages, and then his hands were brushing hers, he was gazing down at her the way he had for so many years, when they had danced, or walked together, or done a million other things. With affection.

"I've missed you so much," he said, meaning it. "It hasn't been the same without you, Siggy. I'm sorry you got hurt at your job, but I'm glad it brought you home again."

And he was looking at her closely, looking for the bruises from Jerry Wolfe's attack. They weren't visible anymore, which seemed to reassure him.

She gazed back at him with eyes made of clear, hard crystal. He was even more handsome than he had been when she left. She hadn't seen him then, hadn't said good-bye. The night of the prom was the last time.

Didn't you wonder why? she wanted to ask him as the four of them went up the walk, onto the porch, and into the front door, into the warmth and the good smells, onto the hard polished wood floor and into the living room that was as big as Siggy and Marta's entire house. Maxi was taking the things from her and placing them on a table full of other Christmas goodies, full of china and crystal and fine lace. Jason put the presents under a magnificent tree which must have stood ten feet tall, yet didn't brush the vaulted ceiling.

Siggy knew she was staring at Maxi. She kept waiting for him to realize what had happened between them. He was wearing wool slacks and a sweater, and he smelled like aftershave. Siggy had never liked him to wear that. It tickled her nose.

A little girl was standing next to one of the elegant couches. Siggy could see her out of the corner of her eye. The little girl was perhaps four, and very shy.

"Dad said you've been living *off-world*," Jason was saying to Siggy. She looked at him with some confusion.

"I had to go away to work," she said.

"What was it like?" he asked, excitedly. "Was it very different?"

Siggy thought about it. "Agate was bluer," she said. "The light, I mean. The mountains had sharp edges, and the hawks were brown. The year was shorter, and so was the day."

"Marta showed us all your pictures!" he announced. "And the Halloween tree!"

"We'll make one here, too," Siggy promised, and then Leeza walked into the room. She had another child with her, a girl of five or so. Both of them looked at Siggy as if she were a delivery person or a maid; courteously, but with an utter lack of regard.

She never even met me, Siggy reminded herself.

"Siggy always carved the best Jack-o-lanterns," Maxi was telling Jason.

Maxi and Leeza looked like a perfect couple, the kind that should be standing on top of a wedding cake.

She watched them. Leeza unwrapped the food and brought out napkins. Maxi brought out wine, tequila, coffee, soda for the kids. Various chairs, among a multitude, were selected and sat in. Jason sat next to Siggy; Marta sat next to the little shy girl, Erin; Maxi sat next to Leeza, and the middle girl pulled up a chair by herself, where she could watch the guests with a perfect imitation of her mother's reserve.

Siggy could see gorgeous furniture from the corner of her eye, but she never looked directly at it. She was busy studying the two people who had ruined her life. Neither of them seemed to know it. Maxi was thrilled to have her there, he kept saying, "Remember this, remember that?" And Siggy would talk about it, laugh along with the others.

Jason was the only thing that distracted her. He adored her. She treated him the same way she had treated Nathanial, carefully and with respect.

Leeza was wearing a dark blue dress, a full-length A-line. Siggy had worn jeans and a sweater. Leeza's hair was pinned up into an elegant and deceptively casual knot. Siggy's was sticking straight up because she had been rubbing it so hard all day long. Leeza's manners were perfect, even though Siggy could tell that she was bored.

Siggy wasn't bored. She felt like she had been shot in the heart. No one was making a fuss about it, so she didn't want to either. If she acted normal, maybe no one would know. Mom was having such a good time, she adored the kids; even the middle one, April. Siggy could see that Maxi and her mom liked each other just as much as they always had, and it was really important to him that his best friend and her mom had come to visit on Christmas Eve.

"Will you show me how to waltz?" Jason was asking her. He asked it so shyly, she knew he had probably wanted to bring up the subject hours ago.

"He knows how," Maxi told her, "but he doesn't have any partners around here."

So Siggy and Jason found a clear space in the enormous room, and she waltzed with him. He looked right into her eyes, the way she had trained Nathanial to do. Siggy was thinking, *Leeza should know how to do this. She should have started teaching him when he was five.*

Leeza didn't seem to mind that Siggy was teaching him now. She didn't seem to resent Siggy, or feel any jealousy. Maxi still doted on Leeza, that was plain. He looked as smitten now as he had on that first night. It was like Siggy had never even existed. She waltzed Jason carefully around the room, paying close attention to him, being a good partner.

Her heart was breaking all over again, but this time

there was a finality to it. Now she knew, Maxi really
could forget everything. He could casually wipe away all
their promises and kisses like they had never existed.

Leeza took his regard for granted. She didn't bask in
it, she merely took it as her due. This seemed painfully
unfair to Siggy. Leeza was so beautiful, so graceful at
the homely arts, so at ease in her magnificent home.
So perfect.

You're a better dancer, Afrika would have said. If this
had been a party at his home things would have been
different. Siggy would have felt warm. The girls would
have danced with Jason, and shy Erin would have been
giggling with the youngest in a corner. But Siggy couldn't
picture Leeza at a gathering like that. Leeza probably
never moved through surroundings that weren't fancy
and polished.

*Who cares if she can't dance? She's so beautiful, no
one notices that she isn't perfect.*

Better dancers make better lovers, Afrika would have
reminded her.

Siggy laughed out loud, and fortunately Jason laughed,
too, thinking that he was entertaining her. He wasn't
entirely wrong. She liked him, he was helping her get
through an evening that otherwise would have been
intolerable.

"Come see our gallery!" he said proudly, pulling Siggy
across the big room and toward a large hallway.

Siggy noticed that Leeza stiffened when she saw where
they were headed. That was odd. *She doesn't want me
in her house,* she thought, but still thought it had nothing
to do with jealousy. It was too bad if Leeza felt that
way, because Maxi had dozens of pictures of Siggy and
him together; Siggy had always seen them in the gallery
at his parents' house. He treasured those memories,
though apparently his interpretation of them was vastly
different.

But Siggy wasn't in any of the pictures in this gallery.
Not *one.* Not even in the background, as a bystander.
All were of Leeza and her family, Maxi and his, the
kids. And then, of course, there was the senior prom
portrait. That was Jason's favorite.

There stood Maxi and Leeza, smiling in their prom outfits.

They must have had it taken afterward, Siggy thought numbly. *She must have thrown the other one out.*

"I don't really like people to come back here."

Leeza was standing at the end of the hall. She spoke sternly, in a tone that tolerated no argument. "I haven't had a chance to get this carpet cleaned yet."

"Mom!" Jason objected. "The carpet is *perfect*! Come *on*!"

Siggy took his hand. "Come on, I'll show you how to cha-cha. That's a hard dance, but I bet you can do it."

He came along, but he looked unhappy. "I've got pictures of you in my bedroom. Marta gave me lots. I wanted you to look at them."

"You can come over to my house and I'll show you more pictures. And next year you can help me carve Jack-o-lanterns."

"Okay," he said, his spirits lifting a little, but the look he shot his mother was hurt and puzzled.

Leeza and Siggy looked directly at each other.

She knows, thought Siggy. *She's rewritten history. She knows what she did to me, and she doesn't care, she's not even jealous of me. But she knows that I can call her a liar.*

Siggy was wearing her tango face when she and Jason came back into the living room.

"Jason was just showing me your gallery," she explained to Maxi. She watched him to see if he would realize that she had seen the amended prom portrait. But no such realization ever crossed his face.

"How about some cake?" he said. "It's your favorite."

"Thanks," said Siggy, squeezing Jason's hand.

She wasn't hungry, so she would have to take the cake home with her. It was getting late. They started saying their good-byes, and a full half-hour later, they were still talking.

Or Marta and Maxi were. Trying to make plans for the future. Erin and Jason were involved, too, many of the plans involved them. They had often spent after-

noons with Marta while Maxi was off-world and Leeza
was off doing . . . whatever it was she did.

Siggy floated on top of the conversation like a bubble.
She stood there with her cake-laden paper plate in hand,
waiting to be released. She could see through Leeza's
cold courtesy. Leeza was glad they were going, hadn't
wanted them to be there in the first place. Marta probably knew it, too, but she adored the kids too much to
let it bother her.

I guess that's how I'll have to look at it, too, thought
Siggy as they took four more steps toward the door and
got stalled out again. But she doubted that they would
ever have another Christmas Eve like this one. This had
all been Maxi's idea. Leeza would probably find some
excuse for taking them all elsewhere next year, somewhere that Marta and Siggy wouldn't be welcome.

And that's fine with me, thought Siggy. *I guess I love
the kids too, but Maxi . . .*

Her heart still ached. Even if she told him everything
now, how she felt and how much he hurt her, he
wouldn't understand. She had to just let it go.

"Wait!" Maxi said, "I've got another gift for you upstairs, I almost forgot it!" And he was tearing up the
stairs just like he was seven years old again.

Leeza was beginning to show visible strain now. Siggy
still had her tango face firmly in place.

"I'm going to go help Dad," said Jason, looking anxiously at Siggy. He was old enough to understand that
something was going on, and he was trying to help. Siggy
smiled at him, and he ran up the stairs.

Leeza sighed and rubbed her eyes.

"Siggy, why don't you go out and get some air," Mom
asked, gently. She knew perfectly well how hard it had
been for Siggy, and she didn't want her to have to suffer
through one more delay. "Maybe that will help get us
the rest of the way out the door," she joked.

"I think I will." Siggy hugged Erin. "Goodbye, lovey."

April was standing behind her mom, but rushed up at
the last moment for a hug of her own.

Good, thought Siggy. *Maybe there's hope for this one
yet.* "Thank you for having us, Leeza. Merry Christmas."

"Merry Christmas," Leeza replied, and gave her a sincere smile. Siggy tried not to be too warmed by it. She went out the door, into the cold, bracing air.

It stung her nose and her ears. She supposed she should have brought a hat, but it didn't really matter. She felt the cold, but was oddly removed from it. She held her plate of cake, which Maxi had wrapped up so carefully for her because he knew it was her favorite.

The street was beautiful at night. All the Christmas lights had come on. The houses had a lot more space between them, so there were large pools of soft darkness. Snow had fallen while they had been inside; it was still drifting down a few flakes at a time.

The neighbor across the street had a beautiful Christmas tree displayed in the front window just like Mrs. Silverstein liked to do. Siggy wondered where one could buy such fancy, ethereal lights. Mom and she always had the cheap multicolored ones from the drug store. The one across the street from Maxi's house had dozens of strands of monochromatic lights, blue and white that blended together in a mystical haze, nestling under silver and crystalline ornaments.

But we have Daffy Duck on our tree, thought Siggy. *No one can top that.*

She drifted off the porch, onto the walk. Beyond their parked car was a fence that bordered a little stream, which was frozen over for the winter. A tree bent over the stream, its branches thick with snow.

Siggy could hear Christmas music drifting from somewhere. She wondered when Mom was going to come out.

It wasn't my fault, thought Siggy. *It was just bad luck.*

In another moment, she wondered what she had been thinking about. She had almost fallen asleep, even though she was standing up. And it was so crisp and cold, though she felt it less and less. She wasn't going numb, there was just something odd about the night.

Timeless, thought Siggy. Maxi and the pain seemed so far away now. Years away. Siggy looked at the beautiful winter night and heard the music getting softer and softer, finally trickling into silence.

Someone was standing by the fence, under the tree, looking at her.

It was David Silverstein.

Siggy held her breath. She could see the Time Pocket curling away behind him. He seemed so far away, yet close enough to reach if she was careful.

Siggy moved quickly. She kept her eyes on him every moment. He watched her with growing excitement. He knew what she was doing. He looked worried, but not frightened. He was still fifteen, still wearing the ROTC uniform.

Siggy walked until she could feel the distorted space. She went right up to David, close enough to touch.

"You cut your hair," he said.

"I had to," she replied. She was studying him, trying to memorize every detail. She had been a child all the other times she had seen him. Now she was an adult, and she knew perfectly well the difference between an experience and a hallucination.

He was real.

"David," she pleaded, "where have you been?"

He shook his head. "I don't know. It's strange in here. Sometimes it looks like outside, in a street, and sometimes it's like being in this weird hallway. I've been stumbling around for hours."

"David—" she started to tell him the truth, but he knew it already.

"Years have gone by out there, I can tell. You're getting older. I saw you at your prom."

He looked over his shoulder. Instead of a stream, a crooked street angled away into a distorted jumble. Near the end of the street, a figure moved.

Siggy felt a thrill of terror. Something about the way the person had moved.

David waved to the person, then turned to Siggy again. "Listen," he said urgently. "I don't know how much time we have. The Lost Fleet is in here!"

This was so much like Siggy's theories, she was beginning to wonder if it was a dream after all.

"I went through a door, and I walked right onto one of their ships," he was saying.

"You went through a *door*?"

"It's dangerous in here. I was lucky I picked that door. Sometimes I wonder, if I pick the wrong door, will I get sucked out into vacuum, into space? Or will I find Enigma in there somewhere?"

Siggy shivered. David kept talking eagerly.

"I convinced them to send someone back with me, a Decider. She and I have been lost for a while, but I knew I would find you again. For some reason, you always seem to be near an exit. Anyway, I'm going to go get her, and I need you to stand *right here,* don't move. I want you to meet her. You're my proof, Siggy! They don't quite believe my theory about where we are, they think they're stuck in jump-time, but I mostly have the Decider convinced now. If she can talk to you, that'll *really* clinch it."

"And then you can both come out with *me,*" said Siggy. "And convince people out *here.*"

But David shook his head. "I can't. They need me. We have to go back and tell the guys on the lead ship, and then I have to be on the ship when they find a way out again, so I can tell people down here they're not attacking. I promised, Siggy."

He was so young. He was going to be a starman. He was what Joseph Bell had probably been like before his brain had been screwed up.

"I'll wait right here," she promised.

He was about to run up the crooked street when he noticed what Siggy was holding. "Can I have that?" he asked, and then blushed. "They love sweets. I'll share it with the Decider. We're kind of hungry now——"

"Sure!" Siggy pressed it into his hands. "Merry Christmas."

He grinned at her, and then ran away. She watched him going back and forth along the impossible angles. He seemed to go quite a long distance.

Is he ever going to get there? she wondered.

And then he was gone. Siggy was looking over the fence at the little frozen stream. The Pocket had withdrawn, leaving her on the street again. She couldn't feel it or see it anymore.

The music was playing. "Jingle Bells." It had begun to snow harder.

Siggy didn't call his name. He had gone again, for who knew how many years. She would have to tell his brother

Barry that David was all right. She would have to call
Barry's friend, the one who had wanted to have lunch,
and tell him about it. She hoped he would believe her.
It sounded so fantastical. She wasn't even going to tell
Mom when she came out. She had given up trying to do
that years ago.

What was keeping her, anyway? Siggy gave the street
one last look, hoping that perhaps the Pocket would
poke out again so David's friend could get a glimpse of
her. But it wasn't going to happen, and the snow was
coming down thick now.

She went back up the walk and onto the porch. There
were dirty smudges on the concrete, as if someone had
walked through mud. She hadn't seen that before. Had
someone come out while she was talking to David?

Siggy knocked lightly on the door, then pushed it
open.

"Hello?" she said. "Did you find the present?"

Maxi was sitting in the living room. He looked across
at her, thunderstruck. He got slowly to his feet.

"What's wrong?" asked Siggy. Maxi looked so strained.
She hadn't seen those lines at the corners of his mouth
before. Worry lines. Maybe he and Leeza had a fight.
The thought didn't make her feel good.

He didn't move, so she went into the room. When she
got closer, she could see even more lines in his face.
It was as if he had aged ten years in one night. Still
handsome, but . . .

Siggy froze. The Time Pocket.

"Maxi—" she said, but he shook his head.

"Jason," he told her.

Siggy swayed on her feet. She tried to focus on his
face. "How long . . . ? she asked.

He swallowed, hard. "Thirty years."

The edges of the room blurred. "I was only there for
a minute," she said. "I gave him a piece of cake."

"David Silverstein," said Jason.

Siggy nodded.

He moved closer. He acted as if he couldn't quite
believe she was real. She knew just how he felt.

"I saw you," he said. "I went out on the porch, and
I saw you walk into something that rippled. I saw some-

one else in there, too. I ran all over the street looking
for you, I was crying. When I told everyone who I was
looking for, they didn't know what I was talking about."
He swallowed again. "Siggy, your own mom. She didn't
know who I meant. My mom and dad still don't remember you."

"That's how it was," Siggy said, calmly. "That's just
how it was before. Stress reactions."

"That's what I've heard. I couldn't believe I just made
you up, because I still had all those pictures. I couldn't
let it go, just like you couldn't with David. And when I
was visiting your mom, I sneaked into your room. I
found this, and it explained everything."

He went back to the couch and picked up a notebook.
Siggy's handwriting was on the cover. It said: THE TRUTH
ABOUT DAVID SILVERSTEIN.

"I was looking at this tonight because it's the anniversary," said Jason. "I've got one just like it, Siggy.
About you."

Siggy nodded, automatically.

"I think you'd better sit down," said Jason, and he
took her arm.

"Okay," said Siggy, and then she fainted dead away.

INTERLUDE

After Man, the Horla. After him who can die every day, at any hour, at any moment, by any accident, He came, He who was only to die at his own proper hour and minute, because He had touched the limits of his existence.

—Guy de Maupassant,
"The Horla"

The last outpost before you got to the Enigma Fold was a station called the Skaw. It had been named after the finger of land that jutted from Denmark into the Sound, that channel of water between the North Sea and the Baltic Sea. Most of the people who lived on the station had never been to Earth; and if they had, they might have been disappointed to look across the Sound and see mere Earthly sights. Sweden was beautiful, but the Enigma Nebula spanned three light years; and at its heart, an invisible monster was eating a sun.

The Skaw housed a population of two million. It was primarily a science station; but like most of the large stations that challenged the space between the Veil System and Enigma, it accommodated other interests as well: mining, travel, and military.

Siggy sat on a bench on the Grande Promenade of the Visitor's Center, gazing out at the giant transparency that provided a computer-enhanced view of the Enigma Nebula. This close, you could see the plume of matter from Enigma's G-star companion curling off into nowhere, disappearing at the event horizon.

Just outside the window, clinging to a sharp abutment, was an exact copy of the statue of the Little Mermaid, that had been created to honor Hans Christian Andersen; but this one, rather than looking out from Denmark toward Sweden and Norway, yearned toward Enigma.

Poor thing, thought Siggy, regarding the forlorn mermaid. *Out there in the void, without any air or warmth.* She could relate to that story by Andersen much too well these days. Her prince had married someone else, and now she couldn't go home either.

She thought it was funny she had fainted. She had

never done that before in her life, never the whole time she was at IFCI, or even after she found out Afrika was dead. Jason had been very flustered, he wanted to call an ambulance, but Siggy wouldn't let him.

"I'm not dying," she said. And she sat there on the floor while he tried to explain the last thirty years to her. No one had been there to help him. Maxi and Leeza lived on Copenhagen Station now, and the girls were married and living in Desert Center. Only Jason had stayed in the house. He had been waiting for Siggy to come back.

"I'm the one who should have fainted," he joked.

"Be my guest," said Siggy.

That was six weeks ago. Today, they were guests on the Skaw. It had been a busy day so far. Siggy and Jason had spoken to a group of physicists and investigators for several hours. Everyone was already familiar with her notebook, *The Truth About David Silverstein,* a fact that embarrassed her, since most of it had been compiled when she was a kid and still sort of had a crush on David.

But they were fascinated when Siggy told them the rest of it. She had time to think about it on the trip over. There were three light years between Veil and the Skaw; some of the most densely populated areas of space you would find in the Republic, with approximately one hundred billion residents, many of whom were scooting back and forth between stations, moons, asteroids, other ships. If Siggy's ship had simply wanted to jump the Fold, it would have ridden one of the jump lanes and been across in a couple of weeks. But ships moving back and forth within the system made a lot of stops and observed many security protocols. So the trip had taken six weeks.

They only stayed on Veil long enough for Siggy to visit her mother. The encounter had been brief and devastating.

Marta Lindquist was still beautiful, but her skin was marked with thousands of tiny lines now. She was seventy-seven, and frail. For one moment, when her mother had gazed at her with such a quizzical expression, Siggy had entertained the hope that the sight of her would jog her mother's memory.

"Why, you could be my granddaughter!" Marta exclaimed.

"How many grandchildren do you have?" Siggy managed to ask her.

"None," Marta said, sadly. "My husband died when I was young, and we never had children."

Siggy had not been able to speak another word for the rest of the visit. Marta tried to put her at ease, the same way she did with all strangers whom she liked but who were shy.

"Please come and visit again," Marta said, when they were leaving, and she winked at Jason. "I've been wondering when this young fellow would find someone to settle down with."

Siggy hoped that some day she would be able to go back and tell her mother the truth. But she wondered if it wouldn't be cruel. Every time she had tried to tell people about David Silverstein, they simply hadn't been able to absorb the information. Marta Lindquist had thought of herself as a childless widow for thirty years. Maybe it was better to leave well enough alone.

There were other problems to consider as well. Like the fact that Siggy's settlement money was gone. From her perspective, she had been comfortably wealthy just a few days ago. But from the bank's perspective, she had been missing for thirty years. She was declared legally dead, and the money reverted back to IFCI.

Jason and Barry Silverstein were going to try to get at least some of it back for her. But Jason had warned her it would take time.

"We can prove your identity," he said. "But it could take some years to work its way through the courts, Siggy. We'll have to find work for you in the meantime."

Of course there was another option he would have liked her to consider.

She had leaned heavily on Jason once they left Marta's house, which once had been Siggy's, too. She broke down in the car and wept in his arms like a lost child, and he held her very close. He looked so much like Maxi, even smelled like him. The only difference was, unlike Maxi, Jason had been obsessed with Siggy for thirty years.

It might not have happened that way if she hadn't disappeared. He would have had his childhood crush on her; a genuine love, but something he would have grown out of as his life took its normal course. But when she disappeared, and when no one but Jason could even remember that she existed, his crush had become an occupation.

They booked separate rooms on the ship over, but always had private suppers together. One evening when they were eating in his quarters, he confessed to her.

"I saw the prom photo of you and Dad in your mom's hall, years ago," he said. "*Before* you disappeared, before I even met you. It was just like the one that hung in our gallery but with one pertinent difference."

He fell silent, and looked down at his plate, blushing.

Siggy considered, carefully. If she told him the truth, it wouldn't reflect too well on his parents. "Did you ever ask your dad about it?" she said at last.

"Yeah. His explanation didn't jibe too well with what your mom told me. She said you and Dad went together. She said my dad met my mom at the prom, and fell in love."

Siggy had to take a few sips of iced tea before she could say, "That's true. So—I've got to admit I'm curious—what did your dad say?"

Jason took a deep breath. "He said that he only took the picture with you so you would have one. He knew how important it was to you."

Siggy felt a rush of rage. *That's a lie!* she wanted to shout, but she was too angry to speak for several moments.

When she began to calm down again, she saw things a little differently.

"You know," she said, "he and I never talked about what happened that night. I think he had no idea how much he hurt me."

Jason looked away again. At first Siggy felt a little annoyed by his reaction, but then she understood that he wasn't doing it because he was embarrassed. He was *angry*.

Well I'll be darned! she thought. *Finally, someone is outraged on my behalf!*

"I know it's none of my business," he said. "But there's been a big mystery at the center of my life—" he looked up and smiled, heartbreakingly, "—named Siggy. Even before you disappeared, some important facts were being fudged. Would you mind—would you tell me—"

"You want to know what happened on prom night," said Siggy.

"Your notebook said you saw David Silverstein that night. But nothing about the prom itself. I wondered if that wasn't why there was so much mystery about the rest of it. But now I know better."

She told him the truth. She had never told *anyone* before, not even Afrika when he asked her who she was grieving over and how come she never got serious about any of the men who courted her. She never talked to Mom about it, because Mom had already known. Had known more than Siggy wanted to know, for that matter.

"After he left me standing there," said Siggy, "I didn't know what to do. I just walked around; you know, circled the place. I wasn't even thinking at that point, I guess I was like someone who had just been in an accident. Finally I wandered outside, and that's where I saw David."

She sipped her tea, examining her old, hurt feelings with the comfort of distance. David's Pocket disappeared quickly, leaving Siggy to wonder again if she had just imagined him; and she had gone back into the dance, only to circle it like a restless spirit until everyone went home and she had found herself sitting, dazed, on the front steps. Alone.

"How could he not realize?" Jason asked, at last. "You take a girl to the prom and give her a promise ring—he had to have known!"

"Do you think he did?" Siggy asked.

Jason frowned. It was painful for him. He loved his dad. He loved his mother, too, and Siggy had been careful not to paint Leeza in an unflattering light. Leeza had simply been there, like Cinderella.

He shook his head. "No. I guess not. My dad has always been kind of—clueless about certain things. Like other people's feelings. He used to step on mine all the time without meaning it. But then he would be so kind and loving the next moment, you always had to forgive him."

"That's Maxi," said Siggy.

She felt better. In fact, a strange thing was happening. She was getting over Maxi.

His son, however, was a serious matter. She watched him throughout the rest of the supper, and as they talked late into the night. She examined her feelings. She tried to guess his.

I've been wondering when this young fellow would find someone to settle down with.

He hadn't married, and he was thirty-seven now. Siggy harbored few doubts about the cause of that.

And yet, she couldn't really say that what he felt for her was love. Or what she felt for him. She was attracted, and so was he, but maybe that wasn't such a good thing. He didn't really know her.

And she could easily let herself think he was a replacement for Maxi.

If Leeza could remember who I was, she would be so pissed!

Later, when he had tried to kiss her, she wouldn't let him. He wasn't entirely surprised.

"I guess I never really got over the crush stage," he said.

"Me neither," said Siggy. "And I think it's high time I got over your father."

Jason was ten years older than her now. He had those things that were missing from Maxi's personality, those things that could have made it work. Siggy knew that if he pressed it, the two of them were going to make love. And if they did that once, they were going to do it again.

And if they did, they were going to be sorry.

He knew it, too. He took her hands and kissed them.

"See you in the morning," he said, and he left her alone.

There had been other moments, since then, when things had almost gotten too warm. But they seemed to be getting better at avoiding them. And in the meantime, there was plenty for Siggy to catch up on.

She still hadn't met Barry Silverstein in person. He had opened a practice in the Veil System a few years after Siggy disappeared. He wanted to be close, to keep tabs on the investigation. He was currently on Oslo Station, in the middle of a civil case. He and Siggy had only exchanged mail since she had reappeared.

He was very relieved to hear that David was all right.

I tried to have hope, he wrote, *but I couldn't get over the nagging fear that David was dead. My friends told me they've observed some interesting phenomena, but no one has been able to deliberately open a Time Pocket, or predict where one will open on its own, or enter one once it's been spotted. Apparently you and David are the only ones who have had experience with openings that are stable enough to let people in or out. I'm sure the investigators are going to want to ask you a lot of questions.*

They certainly had. Siggy and Jason had entered the conference room to find twenty-three scientists, doctors, and even some military personnel waiting for them around a large table. Siggy's first reaction was to be nervous; she couldn't get over the feeling she might have done something wrong. She remembered her interviews with the Director only too well.

But no one at this table acted like the Director. When they looked at her, they seemed almost awed.

"I've been hearing about you for years, seeing your photographs and reading your notes," one young physicist told her. "This is almost like meeting Santa Claus."

Siggy was flattered and embarrassed. When she had been a girl, she had hoped people would take her theory seriously one day; now that they did, she couldn't get used to it.

The first thing they wanted was to hear about her last encounter with David Silverstein, so she launched into a detailed account. She had already told Jason the same story, and she had written about it to Barry Silverstein; but this time people interrupted her for questions.

"Did the Christmas music just stop playing, or did it seem to fade away?"

"Did it actually get less cold, or did you feel like you were becoming less sensitive to it?"

"Were you aware of linear time while you were in there? Did it seem to pass the same way it does out here?"

Someone had thrust a pad of paper and a pencil at her and said, "Do you think you could draw what you saw?"

Siggy looked at the pad, almost picked up the pencil, but then shook her head. "I don't have the skill to show you what I saw. Besides, M.C. Escher has already done it. It was like one of his convoluted drawings, only—more!"

When Siggy got to the part about the Decider, she got the undivided attention of all military personnel present. The ranking officer was an iron-haired, middle-aged woman, Colonel Taima.

"You're saying that he opened a door, an ordinary wooden door—and found himself on one of their *ships*?" she asked.

"That's what he said. He said that sometimes it looked like he was in a crooked hallway, and there were doors that went places. He said he was afraid he might open one and vacuum would be on the other side."

"So that would imply," said the colonel, "that the Pockets extend into the space around the Veil System, perhaps even as far out as Enigma."

"Well," said Siggy, "if Enigma is the cause of the Pockets, they wouldn't be extending *to,* they would be extending *from.*"

This statement provoked considerable discussion among the physicists, most of which was not only over Siggy's head, but over the heads of many others present as well.

"People," Colonel Taima said at last, laughing, "plain Standard, please!"

"Siggy probably put it best in her notebook," said the man in charge of the team of physicists, a man in his late fifties. "Think of a giant tornado spawning little baby ones in its wake."

"Thank you, Dr. La Placa."

Siggy looked at him again. She hadn't realized, until she heard his name, who he must be.

"Jorge La Placa!" Siggy cried, right in the middle of

someone else's question. She couldn't help it, she was too thunderstruck. It had been a great jolt when she had seen her mom looking so much older, aging thirty years in one day. But somehow, she hadn't expected to see anyone else she had known. Her past had seemed dead to her.

Now here he was, sitting right in front of her and asking pointed questions.

"Didn't you know?" he said, smiling a little. "I'm sorry. I forget how much older I must look to you."

"You became a doctor," she said. "Your mom must have been so proud."

This time he laughed. He was Jorge, all right, still a bit reserved, but more relaxed now that he was older. No wonder he believed what she was telling him. She had told him about her theories when they were still in high school.

"Do you remember David Silverstein?" she asked.

"No," he confessed. "And I have a feeling that if I had been on Veil when you disappeared, I wouldn't remember you either. Whatever the effect is, it's very localized. But it makes me wonder who else may have been lost on Veil over the years, who may have been forgotten. We've got people combing through records, trying to find discrepancies like the ones you found concerning David. And let me tell you, the first time I saw David's room— "

"You saw his *room*?" asked Siggy, delighted

"Yes. We've checked out your story very thoroughly, Siggy. It's been fascinating."

"What a relief! Everyone used to think I was nuts!"

"Well, there are a lot of people here who think you have pretty good instincts," he said.

Siggy spent the rest of the meeting feeling flustered and self-conscious. People discussed everything she had written in her notebook, everything she could remember since. They asked her questions and listened carefully to her answers. They asked for her opinion. Physicists, psychologists, officers from the Star Force. It was overwhelming, but she put on her best tango face and told them what she knew, what she suspected.

Afterward, they thanked her. Siggy couldn't help but contrast their open-minded reactions to those of the doctors at IFCI. Those doctors did not compare favorably.

Most of them are probably retired by now, Siggy thought, as she and Jason wandered out of the meeting room.

"Siggy!" Jorge La Placa had caught up with them. "Excuse me, are you going to another meeting now?"

"Soon," she said. "I have to meet with the R-FBI in half an hour."

"This will only take a few minutes," he said. "Could I speak with you privately?"

Jason bowed out, quickly. He and Jorge already knew each other, and Siggy had a feeling Jason already knew what Jorge was going to say.

The two of them stepped into an unoccupied room. Siggy turned to Jorge, nervously; because he was nervous, too.

"Listen," he began, "I was never very good at talking to people, and I'm not much better now, but I couldn't go away without telling you some things. When I heard you had disappeared, I wanted to kick myself for not getting in touch with you before. We worried that you were dead at first; we thought that serial killer had gotten to you. We were relieved when we found out what really happened, but I still didn't know if I'd ever see you again. After all, the Lost Fleet has been in there for almost a hundred and fifty years . . ."

"Yes?" Siggy asked, encouragingly.

"To tell you the truth, I had a big crush on you, all those years ago when we were kids. I almost asked you to the senior prom, but I knew you were going with Max." He looked embarrassed. "Later, when I noticed he had left you on the dance floor by yourself, I almost asked you to dance with me. But you looked so cold Siggy, so remote—I didn't think you would hear me if I talked to you."

Siggy kept her eyes level with his. She was surprised to feel a pang. She had thought she was over it, when she talked it over with Jason. Now here it was again.

But she was also curious. She had never heard another

account of that evening, never been able to look at it from anyone else's point of view. Maybe other guys wanted to ask her to dance too, but her expression had frightened them off.

"Jorge," she said, "were you surprised when Maxi left me?"

She had thought it might be too personal a question to ask, but he answered immediately. "Surprised? I was *floored*. What was wrong with that guy, anyway? He was crazy, everyone thought so. To leave a gal like you—he would have to be crazy, Siggy."

Siggy smiled at him, sadly. His face softened into an expression she hadn't known Jorge could wear, becoming almost fatherly. "Look," he said, "I'm happily married now, I've got grandkids, so I don't want you to think I'm coming on, but there are some things I've always wanted to tell you."

"Please do," said Siggy. This was a rare opportunity. Most people never got the chance to look at their most painful memories from a different perspective.

"I didn't know you were going to have to go off-world for a job," he said. "If I had known that, I would have pulled every string I could to help you. Hell Siggy, I would have asked you to marry me. I know it would have been a crazy thing to do, I know you weren't in any mood to hear anything like that. But I just want you to know that other guys liked you, other guys would have been proud to have you. I've been happy for the last thirty-five years, but I never forgot you. I've always wondered what happened to you. I'd like to help now, Siggy—"

He broke off, looking embarrassed again. "—I hear you were working as a janitor."

"At the Institute for the Criminally Insane," added Siggy.

"You're too good for that kind of work, Siggy. I can get you something better. I can get you a tech job with opportunities for advancement. You'd have to do a lot of training, but you'd find it worthwhile. The best paying jobs for beginners right now are in the mining industry—would you mind that?"

"Not at all," said Siggy, astonished.

"Jason and I have been talking to some people. We can line up some interviews immediately if you want. I live on this station, so you can stay with my wife and me until you're settled somewhere, but to be honest, there are a lot of people who would make the same offer."

Siggy was overwhelmed. She took his hand, then kissed him on the cheek. "I would love to meet your wife," she said. "And yes, I'd like interviews as soon as they can be arranged."

"Consider it done," said Jorge.

Now all that remained was Siggy's interview with the R-FBI.

She wondered what Agent Liadov looked like now. He must have been very upset when she disappeared. He must have wanted to strangle his men; they were supposed to have been watching her.

On the other hand, the ones planetside might have forgotten who she was. She wondered what he had thought when he tried to talk to her mother about it, and found out that her mother couldn't remember her.

Her pager went off; it was time. She hurried away from the Grande Promenade and got onto elevator LL.

The government offices on the Skaw were just as tiny as the ones on Santa Fe Station. Or maybe that was only true about the R-FBI offices.

Siggy knocked, heard someone say, "Come in!"

The man sitting behind the tiny desk was perhaps seventy, but he was not Agent Liadov. Siggy took one look at his prominent ears and his bushy eyebrows and said, "George Stine!"

Those bushy eyebrows shot up. "Yes," he said, sounding both pleased and surprised. "And you are Sigrit Lindquist. I've read your notebook. Please come in and sit down."

Siggy did, blushing. Apparently just about everyone had read her notebook. If she had known that would happen, she would have used much better penmanship.

"Well," said Agent Stine, once she was sitting, "we meet at last." He was studying her with considerable interest. She couldn't help but return the favor. Here was the man who had caught the Professor. She couldn't believe it.

"I saw you on the serial killer website," she explained. "I mean, I saw the footage they had from the public transit station. I was looking at it because the Director had asked me to help him with the Professor—I mean, John Doe H116, um, 7—"

"John Doe H117629," said Agent Stine. "I know it by heart, but you can refer to him as the Professor if you want. Agent Liadov wrote up a full report. And we have copies of the tapes your ex-director made of your discussions with the inmates on the maximum security row—very interesting. When we visited him, he turned over some documents, including a letter Jerry Wolfe once wrote to you."

His eyes gleamed mischievously. Siggy felt somewhat put off balance. People were usually so grim when they talked about Jerry or the Professor. Her included.

"I'm told you've been in a Time Pocket for the last thirty years," said Agent Stine. "Please tell me about it."

So Siggy described it again, for the hundredth time. She was careful not to leave out the slightest detail, the slightest nuance of feeling or perception, but also careful not to embellish or exaggerate. He asked her to clarify several points. But he didn't get excited until she described the person who had moved at the end of the lane, the person she had assumed to be the Decider.

"You say the movement was odd," he said.

"Yes."

"Would you say it was *jerky*?"

She thought about it. "No. Not exactly."

"Perhaps blurred at times?" he asked.

"I don't think so. I guess—the feeling I got was that I was looking at the movement of muscles and tendons that weren't, you know—human."

He nodded. "Have you ever seen Speedies in person?"

"No," she confessed. "Unless I did that night."

"Ah," he said, "then you're not sure."

"I never saw the person's features or figure very clearly," Siggy confessed. "Speedies are pretty hard to miss, if you can get a good look at them. I've only seen them on TV, though."

She had a feeling Agent Stine had seen Speedies in person, but he didn't seem inclined to say so.

"You were scared," he said.

Siggy nodded. "I was terrified."

"Why?"

She gazed into those sharp eyes and tried to find the answer. She could see it all so clearly. David Silverstein was running up the crooked street, back and forth. She had watched him, not the other figure, because she had worried he would get lost inside one of those impossible angles. She had only glanced at the figure when David had waved. It had moved, and Siggy had felt that thrill of terror.

"Have you ever been that frightened before?" Agent Stine asked, gently.

"Yes," Siggy said, her thoughts still back on that snow-covered street, her eyes still watching David navigating inside the Pocket. And then that figure moved, and her heart skipped a beat.

"When?" Stine was asking.

"On Monster Row," said Siggy. "Only the Professor could scare me that much."

She looked at him, startled out of her revery. He gazed steadily back at her. She was beginning to understand why he had been assigned to chase the most dangerous man in the known galaxy.

"But," said Siggy, "I never saw the Professor move, not even an inch. It was his eyes that always frightened me."

Stine's brows shot up again. "Are you sure of that? Absolutely positive?"

Siggy had to think again, and she was taken back to her very first day on the Row. She had been so determined not to look at the prisoners, but then she had felt someone moving, someone rushing at her . . . .

"Okay," she admitted. "I guess I'm not positive."

"So then," said Stine, "the Pocket closed again, leaving you on the outside."

"Yes."

"Did things look exactly the same to you? Did you suspect how much time had passed?"

"I didn't suspect, but things weren't exactly the same. It was snowing harder, and the front porch looked a little shabby. It had been pristine when Mom and I had arrived, but now there were muddy footprints."

"How big were the prints?" Stine asked, his eyes glittering.

Siggy remembered her little feet walking over them. "Man-sized," she said.

He tapped a stylus on the desk, thoughtfully. Siggy wondered about the footprints. What was so important? She had thought they were Maxi's at the time, but they must have been Jason's.

Had he been out that night? She had never thought to ask.

She was pretty sure the mud had been fresh. . . .

"He's still missing, isn't he," said Siggy.

Agent Stine nodded. "But he showed up on Tantalus, just like you predicted. Thirty years ago."

Siggy swallowed. "What did he do there?"

"He died," said Agent Stine. "Can you guess how?" Again, that mischievous look.

Siggy *could* guess. "A plasma weapon?" she asked.

He grinned. "Same hotel, same room. Management was furious, they had just repaired everything. He's got his own sense of humor."

Siggy could see him in her mind's eye, his edges blurred like Voltage Man, his eyes so strange and unblinking, his smile so terrible.

"Where is he now?" she asked.

Agent Stine shook his head. "We don't know. We found a stasis unit on Thanatos. We think he was in it for most of the time you were missing."

Siggy tried to absorb that. She knew about Thanatos, but most people wouldn't have recognized the name. She knew it because she had lived on Veil all her life, with the threat of the Lost Fleet hanging over her head.

She knew that Thanatos was a moon that orbited a gas giant. It was roughly five thousand kilometers in diameter, had a primal atmosphere, and was scoured by winds that averaged three hundred miles an hour. It had been a scientific outpost once, housing a small orbital station and a ground installation.

Thanatos lay just inside Speedy territory. It was now forbidden to humans.

"As I recall," said Siggy, "you once thought that the Professor was a human who had been altered. Someone who had been speeded up by the war department."

"I think that's possible," said Agent Stine. "But there are no records to back up my theory."

"You're familiar with Joseph Bell?" Siggy asked.

"Yes. I saw him in your tapes. I'm aware of his case."

"Is he dead now? Did he die that day he injured himself?"

"I have no idea." His sincerity did not look forced.

I'll never know, Siggy thought. *I just have to face it. He's gone where I can't follow.*

"The reason I ask," she said, "is because I wonder if there are things the war department wouldn't be willing to share even with you guys."

Agent Stine laughed, shortly. "My dear, wonder no longer. There are *definitely* things the war department would not share with us; and furthermore there are things I would not *want* them to share with me."

"So," Siggy asked, "where do you think the Professor is?"

"I was hoping you might make a good guess," he said.

Siggy sighed. She hadn't thought much about the Professor since she had emerged into the future, and that had been rather nice.

"Did he go after the Director?" she asked.

"Not yet. We've had people watching the Director. But he thinks our man would be more interested in *you.*"

Ho boy. I didn't need to hear that.

"Maybe he would," admitted Siggy. "Though I'm not sure why."

"After watching those tapes," said Agent Stine, "I'm inclined to agree with your Director. You probably didn't know that the Director was monitoring the brain waves and autonomic functions of the prisoners while you were present on the Row. The Professor had some notable reactions."

Siggy hadn't suspected that, but it made sense. "Such as?" she asked.

"When you were absent, his brain functions were almost primitive. The midbrain structures were active, but he rarely exhibited activity in his frontal lobes. It was a mental state a Zen Master would have envied. But as soon as he could see *you,* there was a kindling. The frontal lobes became *hyper*active. Our experts have never seen anything like it."

"Which begs the question," said Siggy, and hoped that she could actually get an answer. "Was the Professor really human?"

"That's an interesting question," said Agent Stine. "Yes, we think he was. Physiologically, anyway. There were some anomalies in his DNA, but they weren't in places you would expect them to be."

"Then why did you use three tranquilizer darts on him when you captured him?"

He shrugged. "Just a hunch."

A hunch. The Professor had crushed people with sheer, brute force. Siggy would have been tempted to use *ten* darts.

"Now what?" she asked.

"Well," said Agent Stine, "We found the stasis unit a year ago—"

"How?" she suddenly thought to ask. "How did you know to look there?"

For the first time, he looked disturbed. "He sent us a letter. We got permission from the Speedy government to check it out. The stasis unit had just recently been vacated."

Siggy didn't like the sound of that. He had *told* them where he was. Like he wanted them to chase him. She didn't like to imagine what sorts of games he would want to play.

"One other thing you ought to know," said Agent Stine. "He didn't write the letter recently. He sent it to your old P.O. box, on Agate."

"Huh?"

"He mailed it to your P.O. box just before he left Agate. He also paid your box fee. He paid a lump sum, requesting twenty-nine years. When the time was up, the

postal service opened the box. There were only two letters inside, you had specified you didn't want junk mail.
When they checked you out in the address finder, they
found our tag. They forwarded your mail to us."

"Wait a minute," said Siggy. "Twenty-nine years?"

"Yes," said Stine his eyes glittering just the same way
they had in his old picture, the one that had been taken
just after he had captured the Professor. "Odd, isn't it?
As if he knew just how long you would be gone."

There had been *two* letters in the P.O. box.

Agent Stine had given her copies. The originals were sealed in a safe place, along with other evidence.

Siggy spread them out on the kitchen table in the little apartment Jason had rented for her. She had decided it would be better not to stay with anyone yet. It was all too overwhelming; she needed a private place to recover.

Though she wouldn't have complete privacy. Jason was a regular guest for breakfast, and she had plenty of lunch and supper invitations. She was booked solid for the next week.

But for tonight, it was just her, the letters, and her Net hookup. She had some research to do. The first letter was the one the Professor had meant for the R-FBI. Siggy was intrigued to discover that it was addressed specifically to Agent Stine.

I wonder how many strange letters he's gotten over the years, angry threats from monsters he's captured. . . .

But the Professor's letter wasn't exactly threatening. It was just weird. It didn't start with a greeting, merely had AGENT STINE: at the top.

> *Thanatos is off limits to humans, but you should request permission to visit. The ground station is still functioning. There is a stasis unit in the medical section. It has foiled time for twenty-nine years. Absent friends are waiting, and I have much to do before I sleep.*

The letter had been typed, and there had been no signature, but Siggy felt sure the Professor had written it. Agent Stine said that the letter had been typed on the word processor in the Professor's hotel room in Petra City. He must have done it right after he killed his doctor. Siggy could picture him sitting at the desk, the body cooling on the floor just a few feet away.

Why twenty-nine years? I was gone for thirty.

But maybe she was making a mistake in assuming that it had anything to do with her. The number twenty-nine might have personal significance for the Professor. What bothered her more was the last part: *Absent friends are waiting, and I have much to do before I sleep.*

By *sleep,* he might have meant before he went into the stasis machine. Before he could do that, he had to go to Tantalus and fake his death.

But who were the absent friends?

Me? wondered Siggy. *The Director? Agent Stine? Jerry Wolfe?*

"As far as we can tell," Stine had said, "Jerry Wolfe is dead. We've seen no sign of him, and he never had the intelligence or the resourcefulness to hide his activities. Jerry stuck out like a sore thumb, he was caught within the first two months after he began his killings."

"Only after some guy escaped and tattled on him," said Siggy.

"True," Stine admitted, "but the neighbors had already begun to smell something bad in the house, and relatives of the victims were searching for them. Jerry never bothered to cover his tracks, and at his trial he admitted everything. Bragged about it. It never *occurred* to him to try to hide himself."

"But he changed in those last few years," Siggy worried. "You saw the tapes."

"Agreed," said Agent Stine. "But consider this. Jerry really thought he was the Antichrist. That means he thought he was immortal, couldn't be killed. He also said he was going to live in Hell, talked about the fires. It makes perfect sense that he would immolate himself on Tantalus to prove it."

"Immolate *himself*?" Siggy asked, astonished.

Stine nodded. "I don't think there ever was anyone else in that room with him. He really thought he was the Antichrist. I think he believed he was going to ascend from that fire. Or I suppose in his case it would be a *de*scent."

That made sense. It made *perfect* sense. But Siggy couldn't quite let it go.

"Don't you have *any* lingering questions about the way he died?" she asked.

"Sure," said Stine. "But Jerry's not the one I'm worried about right now. Compared to John Doe H117629, Jerry Wolfe was in the minor leagues."

That was true enough. If Jerry were still around, he would be killing. People would notice him, even if only to say, *Who is that geek?*

Siggy looked at the letter again.

Thanatos is off limits to humans.

The ground station is still functioning.

He must have been there before. Siggy couldn't imagine how he had managed to sneak into Speedy territory; but if anyone could pull off a stunt like that, it was the Professor. And there was another possibility.

That the Professor had sneaked *out* of Speedy territory, not into it. Agent Stine would certainly have considered that possibility, though he hadn't mentioned it to Siggy. There were plenty of things he hadn't mentioned, and Siggy had thought it best not to ask. She had learned that lesson from the Director.

Which brought her to the second letter. It was from him.

He had managed to find out what her P.O. box number was, after all. Siggy supposed it wasn't that hard a thing to do.

The Director's letter must have arrived only a few weeks after Siggy had left.

Dear Ms. Lindquist,

I suppose it does no good to tell you that I regret the death of Mr. Jones. I should have anticipated that he might entertain certain fears concerning Jerry Wolfe's claims of demonhood. Mr. Jones was a religious man.

I'm afraid that my position at the Institute has become untenable, and very little information

was gained for the sacrifices that were made.
Prisoner MS-12 was truly a singularity; a great
deal of energy had to be expended to salvage any
information from inside that event horizon. I
hope you will view Mr. Jones' death in that light.
   In any event, I'm sure they've given you a
comfortable settlement. You won't be forced
to scrub floors anymore, at least. I don't suppose
that IFCI was ever the right place for you.
You are intelligent. But I think you will agree
that the work you did for me was somewhat
revealing. If Prisoner MS-12 does seek you out,
I don't believe he will kill you.
   Beyond that, I cannot speculate. I trust you
will stay well.

Sincerely yours,
Lawrence K. Spencer
Former Director,
Institute for the Criminally Insane

Lawrence K. Spencer. At last she had a name for him.
She didn't really care if it was his real name, she was
always going to call him the Director, anyway. And he
was right, it did no good for him to tell her he regretted
Afrika's death. The remarks in the rest of the letter put
those regrets in their proper perspective.

He must be in his eighties by now. Siggy wondered if
he still got apoplectic when he was angry with people.
He should have dropped dead of a fit by now. If he
could see her, so young while he had grown old, he
might just do that.

Or perhaps not. Perhaps, in his own way, he had
liked her.

Siggy slipped the letters into her notebook, along with
the one Joseph Bell had written. Jason had salvaged *The
Truth About David Silverstein* for her, along with photos,
dresses, and various other belongings.

This is one original I get to keep, thought Siggy. *Everyone else has to look at copies.*

She had made a new entry, on the trip over. Now she
sat and wrote down the questions everyone had asked

her about the incident, along with questions and specula-
tions of her own. When she was done, she laid aside the
book and turned on her monitor. It was time to plug in
to the Net.

She looked for John Doe H117629 first. She found the
John Doe list, and his name was there; but when she
tried to call up his file, it said ERROR, RETURN TO LIST.

Siggy tried it once more, but she knew she wasn't
going to get anywhere with it. She wasn't surprised. She
could tell that Agent Stine hadn't been happy with the
website. The R-FBI probably had some pretty good
hackers working for it.

There was still no entry for Joseph Bell.

So Siggy finally called up Jerry Wolfe's file. She had
never looked at it. Even now, she had to make herself
read the text and study the topics. She found one that
interested her right away. It said, THE ONE THAT GOT
AWAY.

She selected it, and more choices came up. All of them
seemed to be audio/video. So Siggy started at the top of
the list.

Right away, she could see that this was an excerpt
from Jerry's awful mini. She almost turned it off, but
then she remembered that this was the guy who had
escaped, he wasn't going to die.

What was happening to him was bad enough, though.
Fortunately, the clip only showed about a minute of the
torture. The guy was strapped to the same rack Jerry
had used for everyone else. His face and genitals were
deliberately blurred by censors, and so were the areas
of his body that Jerry was working on, Siggy couldn't
even see what he was doing. But she could see the blood.
The guy's upper torso and arms were covered in it.

There was audio, too, and the guy was screaming.
And cursing.

"You [BLEEP]er! You [BEEP]damn [BLEEP]er!"

"[BLEEP] my [BLEEP], [BLEEP]hole," Jerry said,
and continued to work feverishly on whatever he was
doing. Siggy was glad that at least it didn't seem to involve a power tool.

"[BLEEP] you!" screamed the victim.

"[BLEEP] my [BLEEP] and tell me you love it. Maybe I'll have mercy."

"Go to Hell you [BLEEP]er!"

Siggy was surprised when Jerry didn't take that as a cue to start talking about being the Antichrist. Didn't he know it back then?

"When I get out of here I'm going to break every [BLEEP]ing bone in your body you mother[BLEEP]er!" screamed the victim.

"Too much work," Jerry muttered. Siggy wondered if he meant the bone-breaking or his own current task. He didn't seem to be having much luck with it, and he looked frustrated.

In the background, a television was blaring. Siggy had heard it frcm the other excerpts as well. She wondered if Jerry kept his TV on all day and all night. What a madhouse it must have been. There were mountains of trash behind Jerry and his victim, you noticed it once you could get past what was happening in the foreground.

"My shows are on now," Jerry said, and abruptly walked away.

Siggy was amazed. He hadn't done that with the three victims she had seen. He had tortured them until they were dead. Why was he leaving a job half-finished?

The victim seemed to be wondering that, too. He had lifted his head, and was watching Jerry until (Siggy presumed) he was out of sight. Then the guy began to wriggle his hands. They were covered in blood, and they must have been slippery. Within a couple of minutes, he had one of them free.

Siggy cheered and pounded her thighs. "Come on!" she said. "Just one to go!"

In the background, the TV was blaring the audio from various cartoons. Jerry was flipping rapidly from one to another, not even stopping long enough to hear an entire sentence:

"[CLICK]—oh great Pharaoh, we have come from the future to—[CLICK]—elves and fairies are having a party, and you're not—[CLICK]—meet again, Dr. Quest. My flying fortress—[CLICK]—I have you now, funny-looking animal—[CLICK]—just oodles and oodles of boodles and boodles—[CLICK]—think so, Brain, but can we get the chocolate to stick to the—[CLICK]—*Arriba! Andale!* I am the fastest mouse in all of—[CLICK] . . ."

And in the meantime, the guy got his other hand free. He started to work on his feet. *He'll never get out of there,* Siggy thought, forgetting that he already had. He got his feet loose, tearing the skin off of his right ankle in the process, and fell onto the floor. From there, he crawled off camera.

The image froze, and the words: ELAPSED TIME TWENTY-SEVEN MINUTES appeared on the screen. Then the action started again. In the background, the theme song for an old sitcom was playing. Jerry walked back into the picture. Siggy noticed that he was so thin, you could see his pelvic bone from the rear, because there was little there to pad it. His hair was longer than it had been at IFCI, and greasier. Jerry looked like he needed a keeper.

He stood with his hands on his hips, contemplating the empty rack. Then he looked at the camera. Siggy started. It was as if he had looked right at her.

He walked up to the camera, going out of focus. The screen went blue, and then the mini-menu appeared again.

Right, thought Siggy. *He checked his own mini to see where the guy had gone. But his camera was stationary; once the guy moved, there was no way to tell where he was.*

She touched the next icon, which said HOSPITAL INTERVIEW.

The guy appeared again, only this time he was sitting in a hospital bed and his face wasn't blurred. He was a big guy, so Siggy was startled to realize that he was young, no more than a teenager. There was sani-gel sprayed all over both of his arms and part of his chest. The skin underneath it was beet red.

That was because there *was* no skin underneath it.

He knows all about burning babies, Jerry Wolfe had said, *he knows how to skin people alive! I tried to do that a few times, but it's hard to get the skin off in one piece.*

The kid was doped up with painkillers, but he could still talk fairly well.

"I was at the arcade real late, like one in the morning, and there was this really geeky guy playing the machine next to mine, and he was like, you know, trying to come on to me or something, real gross stuff—so—you know—I just walked away and I went over to the Mad Dog machine, and I was just getting into it, and then I felt something sharp on my arm, like a sting. I look over, and this creep is standing next to me, grinning real big, and he says, 'You're gonna be asleep in a second, and then we can have our fun in private. . . .'"

The kid shuddered. A hand came into the picture and patted him on his good shoulder. He blinked several times, and swallowed.

"And then," he said, "I think I was in a car trunk for a while, 'cause I could smell the spare tire, and it was hard to breathe. And I can sort of remember being dragged. And when I woke up, I was—I was, you know—naked. And—like . . ."

He started to cry. The hand reappeared, and this time it stayed put.

"He started," the kid said, through tears, "to touch me. And then he pulls out this straight razor, and he was trying to *skin* me, like he thought he could get all my skin off! And it was like being burned, it hurt so bad. And I was screaming, and I couldn't understand why someone didn't hear me yelling. But then I thought, you know, with all the crap he had stacked in there—I mean, you wouldn't believe all the stuff, and the *smell* was like, enough to knock you flat. And he was peeling the skin off my arms, and I thought *shit,* he's really gonna do it, he's gonna—*shit!*"

"Son . . ." warned a woman who was off screen.

"I'm sorry," sobbed the kid. "It was just the pain. The pain was so bad."

"I know," soothed the woman.

"And then suddenly he goes to, like, watch cartoons. He had the TV on the whole time, just blaring away, and then the cartoons came on, so he went away for a while, and that was my chance. I got loose because all the blood made me slippery, but it hurt so bad, you wouldn't believe it—but—I knew I had to go right then, because I wouldn't get another chance. I crawled under this huge pile of stuff, just *dug* myself into it, and part of it fell over on me, but I doubt he could even tell because there was so much of it. I just buried myself, and then I didn't move for hours. I know he was looking for me, and I couldn't move, and the smell made me pass out a few times. Then I woke up again, and it must have been hours later. That TV was still going, but I didn't hear him, so I took a chance."

He stopped, gasping for breath, and someone handed him a cup of water. After a few sips, he began again.

"I started to crawl. I tried not to make any noise, and that was hard, because I cut myself on stuff and once—once I—I found this—body—and I think it was a little girl—and she had—he had—cut—"

"Don't try to talk about that," warned the woman. "Not now."

He nodded, blinking and swallowing again. Siggy watched him, breathlessly.

"I found a window," he managed, at last. "But it was boarded up. And I started to cry because—because I could see—out this little crack in the wood. I could see the street outside. And I couldn't get there."

He clenched his fists. "And then I got mad, and I started to rip the wood off, I just ripped it with my bare hands, tearing my fingernails and stuff, I didn't even care, I didn't care if he heard me and came after me, because I wanted out of there. No way was I going to stay there, I would have torn his head off with my bare hands if he had touched me again."

You would have tried, anyway, Siggy thought, sadly. *And then he would have drugged you again.*

"But I guess he wasn't home, because he never came. I pulled the wood off, and then I got the window open, and I crawled out, fell onto the front lawn, and I screamed when my arms touched the grass. And then I was running down the street, trying to get as far away as I could. I wasn't even thinking about where I should go, I just knew I had to get away from that house, and I guess someone must have called the police, because they came and got me."

He stopped, taking several breaths, looking oddly relieved.

"And I showed them where the guy lived," he concluded.

There was more, but it was just repetition of stuff Siggy already knew. She pressed the icon that said A FIERY DEATH and got more of the same. Nothing new. And, thankfully, nothing about the attack at IFCI, and Afrika's death. When it had hit the news, IFCI had managed to keep the identities of the new victims secret.

Siggy turned off her screen. She made herself some hot cocoa and sat down with it, sipped it slowly.

Jerry Wolfe's not the one I'm worried about right now, Agent Stine had said. *Compared to John Doe H117629, Jerry Wolfe was in the minor leagues.*

If Jerry Wolfe qualified for the minor leagues, Siggy hated to think what that said about the Professor.

Thanatos. He was on Thanatos. I'll bet he looked real natural there, too. Like he belonged.

She had seen news footage of the storms on Thanatos. She had seen documentaries about the scientists who had worked there. They had been evacuated once the war had started. Siggy could picture the ground installation, empty now, its machinery still running. And then a figure appears in the storm, it opens the outer doors of the air lock. Then the inner doors.

The eyes. They look at things they've seen before.

Absent friends are waiting, and I have much to do before I sleep.

Me too, thought Siggy.

THE TANGO

Those not revealed shall remain concealed . . .
—Tor Age Bringsvaerd
Phantoms and Fairies
from Norwegian Folklore

When Siggy's sparring partner punched her in the head, she went down like a stone.

"Shit!" she could hear Oscar yelling. "Goddammit, Siggy, why are you such a sucker for that punch?"

"Idunno," she mumbled around her mouthpiece, watching the little stars dance around her head. She supposed she ought to get up and have another go at it, but somehow she couldn't work up the initiative.

Hands helped her to sit up. Her head didn't like the change of position, and the room spun around like a lopsided top.

"I'm taking you to medical," Oscar's voice said, somewhere close, and then Siggy was picked up. She felt locomotion, and closed her eyes to lessen the confusion.

It was Oscar; she recognized the smell and feel of him. She put her arms around him and rested her head on his shoulder, even though it jarred her skull with every step he took.

"Not supposed to get hurt this bad with your head protector on, Siggy," Oscar scolded. "You're not cut out for this."

Siggy spit out the mouthpiece. "I know," she said. It was an old argument, and she didn't have a leg to stand on. If it weren't for her head protector, she would have had a broken nose or jaw a long time ago.

After six months of training and hard lessons, she couldn't really say she was getting any better at it. She hated to hit people, hated to *get* hit, cried when it hurt, felt afraid, intimidated, embarrassed, humiliated. Fighting was completely against her nature.

But she came back every time and tried again.

"I can walk, now," Siggy told him. People were staring

at them, and she was embarrassed. Everyone knew what a crummy boxer Siggy was. Most people felt sorry for her. Some people, like the woman who had just knocked her flat in the sparring ring, didn't have any sympathy for her at all. Those were the people Siggy preferred to spar with.

Oscar set her on her feet. He looked into her eyes, to see if her pupils were both the same size. Siggy looked steadily back.

"Am I ever gonna be able to talk you out of this, baby?" he asked, softly.

"I've got to do it," Siggy said.

"Let me do the fighting." He cupped her face, head protector and all, in his hands and gazed at her with cool, hazel eyes. Oscar Montoya had olive skin, narrow features, the black hair of a bull fighter or a flamenco dancer. He had been a pro boxer before he had ditched a lukewarm career for a good, steady job as a miner. But he still practiced every day, and he looked it. Any woman would have been happy to have him as her defender. The woman who had just knocked Siggy flat, for instance.

Everyone knew Oscar and Siggy were lovers. It was officially against the rules, but people were willing to look the other way. The Belters took care of each other. As long as you did your job and kept your nose clean, it didn't matter to the bosses who you had consentual sex with. No one wanted to be accused of sexual harassment, of course, but that was a risk you had to take from time to time.

The corridors of Trondheim Station were narrow, not built for beauty or comfort. Siggy and Oscar were currently making their way through the one-gee ring, which spun a simulated gravity of Earth Normal. It was also the ring in which they both had quarters. Siggy had worked all over the station so far; she had been down to the surface of Astaroth, the moon to which Trondheim was currently connected via the *Trollstigveien,* the Troll's Ladder, which carried loads from the surface up to the refinery at the center of the station. Siggy was being trained as a heavy-equipment technician. Oscar was her supervisor during the day, her boxing instructor four afternoons a week.

At night, he taught her other things.

The doctor scanned Siggy's head, while Oscar stood by and looked grim. She could tell he had already decided what to do about her, and was waiting for the doctor's diagnosis before he spoke his mind. Oscar had a terrible temper; but over the years he had disciplined himself. He knew how to use anger as a weapon, a fine blade. He boxed the same way, always thinking, no matter how angry he got.

Siggy was awed by his control. Since she had started lessons with him, she had lost control of her emotions many times, making a fool of herself. She wasn't used to losing her temper, and when it happened, she didn't know what to do about it. She was trying to get used to the sensation, but it wasn't coming easily for her.

"I found the old fracture, but no new ones," the doctor announced at last, standing with her hands on her hips, unconsciously mimicking Oscar, regarding Siggy with the same grim expression. Her dark red hair was tied into a lopsided bun on top of her head; a stylus was poking out of the bun. She pulled out the stylus and made some notes on Siggy's record. "Looks like a temporary inner ear disturbance."

"That's it?" asked Oscar.

The doctor frowned, nodded. She had spent thirty years as an emergency ward doctor before transferring out to the Jotunheim Belt, the cloud of asteroids that lay just outside the Enigma Nebula. She had seen every possible injury the human body could sustain.

"I would switch hobbies if I were you," she advised Siggy, and then left the two of them to talk it over.

Siggy climbed off the exam table. "Let's get some supper," she said.

Oscar put his arm around her, and they went back out into the corridor.

Everywhere you went on Trondheim, you bumped shoulders and hips with people, waited patiently for people ahead of you to clear the ladders or the various intersections. It wasn't an easy place to talk privately. Siggy and Oscar went to their section cafeteria and passed through the food line together without speaking before they found a spot at a crowded table.

"From now on, you spar with Myrk," said Oscar. "She won't hit you like that."

"Exactly," said Siggy. "Myrk feels bad when she hurts me. It's got to be Szymanski. She wants to kill me."

"She's gonna do it someday," said Oscar.

Siggy shrugged and ate her dinner. She loved the food on Trondheim. You could get Scandi-Mexican fare, Veil style, but also dozens of other different cuisines, spicy and exotic. She needed the workout Oscar put her through to keep her weight down.

The dancing helped, too. Siggy had more students than she could teach by herself; she had been forced to enlist others in her cause. Oscar's uncle was a flamenco dancer, and Oscar had inherited his grace.

"If you can teach boxing," Siggy had told him, "you can teach dancing, too."

It was a wonder they had time to be alone together. They worked hard all day, trained hard all afternoon. Many nights, they fell asleep together. Another bent rule on the station. Who would have believed that it had taken a month for them to get around to their first kiss?

But then, once that was out of the way, it had taken about an hour for them to get into bed.

As they lay together in Siggy's narrow bunk, she couldn't help but think about Jason. She hadn't felt guilty; Jason and she had talked about their feelings before he had seen her off for Trondheim.

"I want you to call on me, anytime," he had said. "I'll always be your ally, Siggy."

"I know," she assured him. She had heard the same from Barry Silverstein and Jorge La Placa, not to mention several of the people on the Time Pocket Task Force, and Agent Stine of the R-FBI.

Outrageous, Siggy thought. *I've become the resident expert on serial killers and Time Pockets.*

But it wasn't her expertise that had drawn Jason, and it was hard for him to let her go. She could see it in his face, a longing for just one night together. So he could know what it was like, what he had been dreaming about for so many years.

And if it had happened, would she have called him *Maxi* in her moment of release?

She had written to him regularly since then. He was dating someone seriously now. Siggy had a feeling he would be married within the next Standard year, and she didn't think he was on the rebound. He was free now. He could get on with his life. In all of his recent photographs, the shadows had gone from his face.

But Siggy still had some dark places.

"Tell me the truth," Oscar asked her on that first night, his breath warm in her ear. "Who's gunning for you, Siggy?"

She had been warned not talk about John Doe H117629 or Jerry Wolfe. "Not any more than you have to," Agent Stine said. "I'm not putting a gag on you, but you need to be careful. It's not a topic of light discussion, understand?"

Siggy understood perfectly. But after a month with Oscar, working closely with him, depending on him, learning from him, teaching him on the dance floor, she knew that he had broken down the barriers that Maxi had built around her heart. She was going to be spending a lot of time with him.

So she told him everything. Starting with the attack of the Lost Fleet when she was seven and ending with her thirty-year visit inside the Time Pocket. It took most of the night.

She showed Oscar Jerry Wolfe's entry on the serial killer website. She wished she could show him the one she had seen about the Professor, but it was still off-line.

"Okay," said Oscar. "So they think Jerry Wolfe is dead, but maybe this Professor guy is still after you. From what you've told me, it's no good to fight the guy anyway. He would tear anyone to pieces, right? So why do you have to get yourself knocked silly?"

"I wouldn't try to fight the Professor," said Siggy. "I would try to talk to him. It's Jerry."

"The dead guy."

"I don't believe it." In fact, despite Agent Stine's reassurances, Siggy found that she believed it less every day.

"If he's still alive he would be how old by now?" asked Oscar. "Sixty-four?"

"Your Uncle Roberto is sixty-two, and he's still a top flamenco dancer," Siggy reminded him. Uncle Roberto moved like a man half his age; he was focused and passionate.

In his own way, Jerry Wolfe was, too.

It was difficult to explain. Jerry's attack on Afrika had taken her completely by surprise. Jerry was a little man, no taller than Siggy. He was scrawny, she hadn't thought he could hurt anyone, except perhaps for children. He used drugs to subdue people, and she had assumed he couldn't fight for real if his life depended on it.

But he had hit Afrika hard enough to knock Siggy cold, because she was standing behind him. He had been amazingly strong; and what was worse, he wasn't capable of fear or restraint. There was *nothing* Jerry Wolfe wouldn't do.

Siggy had never been in a fight in her life. She would have flown at Jerry if Afrika had let her, she would have punched, slapped, torn at him with her nails. She wasn't afraid of him, that wasn't the problem. The problem was that Siggy wasn't mean.

Maybe Afrika knew what he was doing after all. He knew I would try to come to his defense, and that Jerry Wolfe was a wolverine.

And that was why Siggy asked Oscar to match her up with people like Szymanski, people who would try to think up ways to permanently hurt her. God knew Jerry would.

But six months later, she was beginning to wonder if it was doing any good.

Oscar ate his entire supper and was having his one beer for the evening when he finally told her what was on his mind.

"Kickboxing," he said.

"Who, me?" said Siggy.

He nodded. "You're like most women, you can't hit worth a damn. You can strengthen your arms, improve your reflexes, maybe get over your fear of hurting people. But no matter how hard you work, Siggy, you're never going to be able to hurt someone with those little hands of yours. But your *legs* . . ."

He squeezed her thigh under the table.

"You've got dancer's legs," he said. "Strong, fast—you've always been good with the footwork. What you have to do, baby, is start *kicking*. I know a guy, he says he'll show you how. I wish I had thought of this a long time ago."

Siggy stared at him. It was a *great* idea. "No more fighting with Szymanski?" she asked, with profound relief.

"Nope," he said. "No reason to."

"But—" Her old fears didn't go away that easily. "I should still spar with her. I can't let myself relax like that."

"Siggy, don't you get it?" he said, not unkindly. "It's not helping. You can't change your spots. If you have to defend yourself, you'll just have to do your best. We'll teach you how to kick your way out of a clinch. The point is, you have to get away from the guy. If he has a knife, you can't fight him with your hands anyway. You just end up with fending wounds that way, believe me. I've seen it."

Oscar had grown up on Medusa, a world that barely fit within the parameters of "Earth Normal." Settlers on that world had been a tough and desperate breed, mostly from Spain and Eastern Europe. They had come out of the slums of Old Earth to scratch out a better place for themselves, and Medusa hadn't made them welcome. They had fought her all the way, and they were still fighting.

"People end up in the morgue with knife wounds on their hands," Oscar said. "It passes through on its way to the body, understand?"

"Yes," said Siggy.

"You kick out with your legs, you've got more reach, they can't get in close to your torso. You kick hard enough in the right spot, they're going to end up in a tight little ball of pain and you can get out of there. That's the strategy."

It made sense. But then, Jerry was more likely to use a hypo than a knife. On the other hand, he could zap her just as easily if she was using her fists to defend herself. In fact, if she kicked, she might have a better chance of avoiding a hypo prick altogether.

"First lesson tomorrow night. It's Ron Hoshi, you've got him in your tango class."

Siggy remembered the man. He was a good-looking older guy with an incredible build. He had told Siggy he did five hundred push-ups a day.

"Does he know I'm coming?" Siggy asked, nervously.

Oscar grinned. "He knows. He's got two daughters just your size, trained 'em both. So don't be nervous, okay?"

"Okay."

"You'll feel better once you've had a few lessons. You'll see."

As it turned out, he was right about that. She did feel better after having a few kickboxing lessons with Ron Hoshi; and that was just as well.

A few lessons was all she had time for.

Tovarish Mining had moved a lot of different ores in its twelve-hundred year history. It had hooked ore elevators like *Trollstigveien* up to moons and big asteroids, it had attached mass drivers to smaller asteroids and comets, it had even mined deep gravity wells the old-fashioned way. Its most common payload was water ice.

When Siggy signed onto Trondheim Station, it was busily processing a substance that had been in demand for millennia, a substance that had sometimes been more valued than gold or precious gems.

Salt.

On Trondheim, no one said, "Well, it's back to the salt mine," unless they were brand new. Everyone else had heard that joke too many times.

Siggy had been learning to use a scooper for two weeks; she was beginning to get pretty bored with it. But the salt mine itself wasn't the sort of place you could get tired of. It was too dangerous for that.

Astaroth was one of fifteen moons that circled the gas giant, Resheph. It had a core of rock and ice, an outer crust of water ice. Under the crust, water flowed. Salt water. Astaroth's orbit was elliptical; and when it came close to the other moons, the gravitational effects pulled and tugged at it, flexing it enough to cause earthquakes, forcing the salty water to the surface through geysers.

At the surface, the water solidified into an ash of salts and ice crystals. Large faults scarred the surface of Astaroth, thousands of kilometers long, black from precipitated salts. Tovarish had set up operations along one of those faults, and Siggy spent much of her day clinging to the slope, using an ice pick and a scooper to retrieve salt.

Astaroth was currently as far away from the other moons as its orbit could take it, but it was still prone to occasional earthquakes and spectacular geyser eruptions. Siggy had an open communications link with Project Control; when the cryovulcanologists warned her to evacuate the area, she obeyed. So far, that had only happened twice.

There were other challenges. The gravity on Astaroth was one-tenth Earth normal; you had to remember not to move too fast or with too much force. The miners' suits were bulky, and you had to check your gauges constantly. Once you did that, you were then supposed to check up on your teammates, in case they were suffering from anoxia and didn't know it. Insufficient oxygen caused dementia. Siggy had never seen it happen, but Oscar had warned her that she would, sooner or later.

She checked her gauges, looked down the line at Myrk, who gave her the thumbs up and then checked the guy next to her. They were spread across the slope in a loose line, periodically feeding the chunks into the conveyor that would take them into the Troll's Ladder and up to the station, where they would be put through evaporators to sort the water ice from the salts. The water would be conveyed to storage as another payload; and the salts would pass through more filtration systems and sorted by chemical compound, sodium chloride being the most rare and sulfur being the most common.

I like pepper better, thought Siggy, and wondered if it was time for lunch yet. She was about to start scooping again when she spotted Oscar making his way down the line toward her. Oscar's suit had brightly colored boxing decals on it; you couldn't miss him on the black slope. She turned off her drill and set it in its case, then signaled the team leader that she was leaving the line and met Oscar halfway.

"Come on," his voice came out of the speaker next to her left ear. "We've got to get up to the station."

"What's wrong?" asked Siggy.

"I'll tell you on the way up," he said.

He looked upset. Siggy frantically searched her memory, wondering if she had committed some grievous error recently. She was still a newbee, still prone to forgetting important details. Newbees were watched mercilessly, and Siggy was no exception just because she happened to be sleeping with her supervisor. Quite the opposite, in fact; Oscar was ruthlessly professional when they were on the job.

"What did I do?" she asked him at last.

"Nothing, baby," he said, which scared her more, because he never called her that during working hours.

They made their way across the surface, finally climbing into an ice buggy whose fat wheels carved a path all the way up to *Trollstigveien*'s massive feet. They waited by the personnel elevator until they could get a car by themselves. Once inside, they activated their magnetic boots. They were riding up to the zero-gee center of the station.

Once the car had pressurized, they removed their helmets.

Siggy was afraid to ask Oscar what was wrong. She had never seen this particular expression on his face before.

"There's a Speedy delegation here to see you," he said.

Siggy gaped at him. He looked back, just as dazed as she was, as if someone had sucker-punched him.

"Why?" she asked.

He shook his head. "They won't say. They're talking through an interpreter, a diplomat. All he's willing to say is that they need to talk to you *now,* and it's important."

"The Time Pockets," said Siggy. "It's got to be about the Lost Fleet."

"That's all I can figure," said Oscar. "Maybe they want to ask you about your thirty-year Christmas Eve."

He put an arm around her, and she realized how terrified she must look. How terrified she *was*. Her heart was pounding so hard, she wasn't even sure she could talk properly. Or stand—her knees were knocking together.

The *Speedies*!

"Are you sure they wanted to speak with *me*," asked Siggy, "not with someone *about* me?"

"*With* you, Siggy." Oscar looked grim. "No doubt about it. He made that very clear."

"Okay," said Siggy, and he gave her a squeeze. For a moment she was afraid she might cry. Then all of the feeling ran out of her, and she felt numb. *Shock,* she thought. *Look out.*

Siggy breathed carefully for the next several moments. When she felt steady again, she managed to give Oscar a smile.

He responded by kissing her, hard.

"What was that for?" she asked breathlessly, when he had pulled away again.

"I don't know," he said. "I love you, Siggy."

Siggy suddenly wished they could stop right there for a couple of hours. He had never said that before. She considered her own heart carefully before answering him.

"I love you, too."

He kissed her again, this time on the forehead.

"Knock 'em dead, kid," he said.

Two vice presidents were waiting for them at the top, magnetic boots covering their expensive shoes. Siggy thought she had never seen anyone look so serious in her life. It made her stomach flutter, and she quickly put on her tango face.

"Ms. Lindquist?" one asked, formally, but she could tell they already knew who she was. They might have even guessed why the Speedies wanted to talk to her.

"Yes, sir," she replied, politely.

"They're waiting in the executive conference room. We should go immediately."

"I'm ready," she lied.

The executive conference room was in the one-gee ring, but in a section Siggy had never visited before. Its corridors were far more spacious than the ones she normally moved through. Everyone had stopped to remove vacuum suits and boots, leaving Siggy and Oscar in work coveralls and the vice presidents in modified business suits. Their feet made no sound on the plush carpeting.

Siggy expected to see the Speedies sitting around the big, polished conference table. But one man was waiting for her, alone. He was human.

Oscar and the vice presidents left her at the door and closed it firmly behind her. The man stood when she entered the room. He had jet-black skin, rare in the Veil System, where most people were brown; but that was nothing extraordinary. What immediately caught her attention were his enhancements.

His eyes were artificial. They were silver, as reflective as polished metal, and impossible to read. He was wearing a g-suit, a black form-fitting garment that looked very much like the one she had seen the Decider wearing on TV those many years ago, except that this man's suit was reinforced with fine, silvery struts that hugged his body and climbed up his bare face, meeting in a grid on top of his shaved skull.

"I'm Mr. Ashur," he said. His voice had a slight rattle at the end, and Siggy guessed that his vocal chords were enhanced as well.

"I'm Siggy," she said.

"I know. I've seen your file. We don't have much time, so I'm going to prepare you as well as I can." He indicated the chair next to his. Siggy sat in it, and he sat next to her.

"What's going on?" Siggy asked him.

He smiled. Siggy was glad to see that his teeth were normal, anyway.

"I've been at this job ten years, and I still don't know how to answer that question," said Mr. Ashur. "I don't know exactly why they want to talk to you."

"They didn't tell you?"

He shook his head. "No. Look, here's how it is. I'm not happy they didn't tell me. I thought we were starting to break down some barriers, really starting to understand each other. My teachers at the academy warned me about that; just when you think things are going great, you run into a brick wall. But that's not your problem, you have to remember that. Here's my advice."

Siggy sat up straighter. Mr. Ashur had an accent that she recognized from the R-BBC channel, one of the accents people referred to as "British." His particular version sounded very cultured and proper.

"Just be yourself," he said. "Be perfectly honest and do your best. Take your time, go at your normal pace. Don't try to alter what you would normally say in order to please or placate them. Say exactly what you think, exactly as you would normally say it, and don't try to say it as fast as you can just because you think they're getting impatient with you. If you go too fast, you'll make a mistake, and Speedies hate mistakes more than they hate slowness."

He was watching her, maybe to see if she was frightened. She supposed she ought to have been, but he was making her feel more curious than anxious. "Is it really that simple?" she asked. "I thought it took years to learn to speak to them."

"It does. As you've noticed," the light reflected from his silver eyes, "it also takes some jacking around with the hardware. We're working on an interface now, something we can plug into, together. We've had some limited success, and I hope we'll keep trying. I hope they're not as upset right now as I suspect they are."

"Oh no," said Siggy. "Oh boy." A bad feeling was replacing her nervousness. Something was wrong, this wasn't a friendly visit. She rubbed the top of her head, vigorously.

"I've checked you out as thoroughly as I could in the limited time I've had," said Mr. Ashur. "I have some ideas what they may be after, but I don't understand why they'd be upset. At this point, we can only wait and see. They'll be here any moment, and I'll have to leave, so—"

"You're not going to translate for me?" Siggy was frightened again.

"They speak Standard," he said. "They won't let me stay. I'm sorry."

"I'm just . . ." said Siggy. "I never . . ."

And then the door was open, and the Speedies were in the room.

Siggy froze. One moment the door had been closed, and the next, it was open and six aliens were standing just inside, their head tendrils pulled flat as they clustered together. They were dressed identically, in black garments that hugged their lean, angular bodies, making their faces and hands seem all the paler in comparison. Faceted eyes looked at Siggy with an intensity that made sirens scream in her head.

They stood absolutely motionless. Like statues.

Siggy was vaguely aware that Mr. Ashur was speaking; or rather, he was making sounds. He was approximating their speech, using his throat enhancements. The Speedy who stood in the fore answered him, much more rapidly. The Speedy was deliberately slowing his pace, Siggy could see it. His mouth was hardly blurred at all.

Siggy felt a warm, human hand touch her shoulder, briefly. Then Mr. Ashur got up and walked to the door. As he neared the Speedies, Siggy realized that he towered over them; they must be no taller than she was. That surprised her—she had thought they were giants. As Mr. Ashur passed them, he moved very carefully.

He doesn't want them to think he's going to attack them on his way past, thought Siggy. *Ten years with them, and he still has to prove it.*

Mr. Ashur went out and closed the door behind him. The Speedies stayed where they were.

Siggy was barely breathing. Her hands had gone cold, but she was afraid to move them. The Speedies were so still. In her whole life, only one man had ever been so utterly motionless.

My god, just like them. He was just like them.

There was a sudden ripple of movement within their ranks, and Siggy started, violently. She gripped the table, and they stopped again. The movement had been indescribably odd, almost like stop-motion animation.

They moved again, but this time much more carefully. Siggy watched them, transfixed, as each Speedy made his way to a chair and sat in it. One sat right next to her. Her breath was taken away by the control they displayed as they moved. They managed to get almost all the way across the room at human speed; only blurring at the edges once or twice in a way that reminded Siggy of the motion of hummingbird wings.

They regarded her from their various positions around the table. They still didn't speak.

"I'm Siggy Lindquist," she said, thinking that perhaps they weren't sure they had met the right person. "I'm pleased to meet you," she added when they didn't respond. She only said it because that was what she would normally say to people. Mr. Ashur had said to be herself. But in the silence that followed, she wondered if that was going to be good enough.

"How can I—" she began again, but suddenly the man next to her was speaking. "I'm sorry, what—?" she said, but he was still speaking, snapping at her impatiently. She shut her mouth and tried to listen.

"—for you." he finished, and placed a mini-disc and a business-sized envelope on the table. He slid them toward her with fingers that ended in hard points, as if they were made of bone instead of flesh. "Look," he ordered. "Then questions."

Siggy was intimidated by his tone. He was acting like she had done something wrong. But she looked at the disc; it was of human manufacture, the sort anyone could buy to make home movies or record stuff off the TV or the Net. She wondered if she was supposed to slip it into a viewer, she didn't see one in the conference room.

So she picked up the envelope, instead. Across the front it said: FOR SIGGY LINDQUIST, VEIL SYSTEM in tiny, precise letters.

Jerry Wolfe's handwriting.

"Where did you get this?" she asked the spokesman. "When—"

"Read," he snapped, before she had even finished speaking.

She glared at him. He didn't have to be rude, *they* were the ones who had asked to speak to *her*, not the other way around. But she controlled her temper. Maybe Jerry's letter would tell her what she had wanted to know anyway. She started to pull it out of the envelope, which had been slit precisely along the top—someone else had already opened it, of course. And then her eyes fell on the disc again.

Home movies.

Images played out in front of her mind's eye, various people chained to a rack. She could hear the begging and pleading again, as if she had just heard them yesterday. She closed her eyes and pressed her hand against her mouth, trying to stop the sobs before she could humiliate herself. When she opened her eyes again, she had to blink away the tears, and her hands were shaking so badly she could barely get the letter out of the envelope.

> *Siggy,* said the obsessive little characters,
>   *You're my witness. Armageddon has begun,*
> *just like I told you at the Institute. That was*
> *where I learned my destiny. The demons of Hell*
> *came to me in my sleep. They told me who I*
> *was and what I had to do. They taught me many*
> *things, they showed me the Gateway. I've*
> *done my work now, and I need you to meet me*
> *at the Crossroads. That's where you will watch*
> *me cross over into my kingdom of Hell. It's al-*
> *most done now, I'm just waiting for you.*
> *Don't delay, or your punishment will be terrible.*
>   *Once you know the trick, Speedies come un-*
> *done just as easily as humans. They have*
> *some nice tools. Hurry.*

The last word was underlined six times. There was a date at the bottom of the letter. It had been written only two Standard months earlier.

Siggy put the letter down and looked at the mini-disc again. It wasn't that she thought she could learn anything from it at this point, but she didn't want to look at the Speedies yet. She was trying to drive certain images from her mind, first.

Finally, she was able to look at the spokesman again. His eyes were dark, sable, beautiful things. If she looked closely, she could see hundreds of facets. From a distance they had looked as hard as the jewel-like tendrils that grew from his head, but close they looked soft, like something that would be pleasant to stroke.

She wondered if Jerry had touched Speedy eyes. It wasn't a good thought to entertain at precisely that moment.

Those eyes were unfathomable, but the tightness around his all-too-human mouth was revealing. Jerry Wolfe had written about Armageddon, and how Speedies came undone.

"Where did you get this?" she asked, her voice trembling.

"He left it," spat the spokesman. "With the last one."

"How many?" she enquired, suspecting the answer.

"Thirteen. Six adults. Seven children."

With the peace so fragile, relations between the two races still so precarious. Speedy technology was vastly superior, their reflexes and perceptions so much faster. Siggy was amazed that Jerry had found a way to hurt them. But he had bragged about starting Armageddon.

Agent Stine would be so surprised. Jerry Wolfe, underestimated again.

Siggy folded her hands on the table, to stop their shaking. She regarded the spokesman as steadily as she could. "Are you a Decider?" she asked him.

"Yes."

Siggy was tempted to look at the others, she could feel the weight of their stares; but she had a feeling that would be bad form. She swallowed. She tried to keep her chin up.

"Have you spoken with the R-FBI?" she asked the Decider.

"No," he snapped.

Siggy wondered what to say. She suspected that if Mr. Ashur had known what this meeting would be about, he never would have left her alone to say the wrong things, to make matters worse.

"Why *you*?" demanded the Decider. "Why is your name on the envelope?"

Her answer could have taken all night, but she decided to keep it simple. "He was a prisoner at the Institute for the Criminally Insane," she said. "They put him there because he tortured thirteen humans to death, six adults and seven children."

There was no flicker of a reaction from the Decider.

"I was a janitor at the Institute," Siggy continued. "He used to speak to me while I was mopping the hall in front of his cell. One day he started to say that I should be his witness. I always tried to ignore him. But he escaped. They thought he was dead."

"He is going to wait for you," said the Decider. "At the Crossroads."

"He was bragging," said Siggy. "He did the same in his other letter. The R-FBI has a copy of the other letter, you should—"

"We will wait with you," said the Decider, cutting her off.

Siggy clenched her hands. "But—I don't know where the Crossroads are!"

"Best guess," he said, "inside our territory. No humans have gone so deep. None but him. And now, you."

Siggy could hardly believe what she was hearing. "You're asking me to come with you?" she said.

His mouth pulled into a thin line.

"We are *telling* you," he snapped.

Siggy couldn't really tell what he was feeling, what he thought of her or the rest of the human race at that moment, but she could make a darn good guess. Her first impulse was to give in, to meekly do whatever he said.

To placate him, which was just what Mr. Ashur had warned her not to do.

"Ask me," she said. "Don't tell."

He didn't answer, but he and his companions leaned forward in their chairs, their tendrils so tight against their heads they looked almost like helmets. They placed their sharp fingertips on the tabletop, and Siggy thought, *My god, they could launch themselves at me from that position, they could tear me to pieces.*

But that wasn't the real danger. These people were too disciplined to attack Siggy. The real danger was that they would leave the room with war on their minds.

"Listen," begged Siggy. "You don't understand. This man hurt me. He killed my best friend. I've seen parts of the other mini he made, how he tortured other people to death. I have tried to forget what I saw, but I can't. Jerry Wolfe is my *enemy*."

"And so?" demanded the Decider, as if nothing she had said made the slightest difference.

"So ask me," said Siggy. "I want to be your ally. Let me."

The word *ally* was a carefully chosen one, and risky. Siggy remembered it from the newscast she had seen over forty years before, how Dr. Ngoni had used it with that other Decider. Like that other man, this Decider knew perfectly well what she was trying to do when she used that word.

"You ask too much," he said.

"If I'm not your ally, then I'm your prisoner."

He considered that for half a second. In Speedy time, that was lengthy.

"If you insist," he said, but didn't say which it was to be.

Siggy was getting a very unhappy glimpse of what Mr. Ashur's job must be like. He was beginning to look like a saint to her. And a genius. But she wasn't ready to give up yet.

"You want to catch him, yes?" she said. "You want to stop him. So do I."

"That isn't all," said the Decider. "You don't understand."

"I know," admitted Siggy. "But neither do you. That's the problem."

His next pause, for a Speedy, was a veritable eternity.

"We ask, then. Come with us."

"I will," agreed Siggy.

Around the table, head tendrils began to float loose. They didn't come up into a relaxed position, but it was a marked improvement.

Is it possible? wondered Siggy. *Did I actually manage to say the right thing?*

"I'll have to pack my things," she started to say, but the Decider cut her off again.

"No time. Come now. Mr. Ashur will explain."

And suddenly they were up and at the door. They didn't look back at her as they opened it and vanished.

Siggy sat there, stunned.

Mr. Ashur poked his head in. "Good job," he said. "We'd better get going."

"Now?" Siggy was horrified. She wasn't ready. She needed to say good-bye.

What was Oscar going to think?

"Your bosses already know you're leaving," said Mr. Ashur. "Believe me, we've managed to convince them how important this is. And it won't do you any good to pack. You're going to be living in two gees for a while. You'll be wearing a suit like this."

"Can't I at least get a message to my boyfriend?" Siggy was almost in tears again. "He'll be worried if he doesn't know where I've gone."

"He'll be even more worried if he *does* know," said Mr. Ashur. "But you can send him a message from the ship. I'll see to it."

Siggy got shakily to her feet. She picked up the letter and the mini. "Well," she said. "Then I guess we'd better go."

"You're right," said Mr. Ashur. "We'd better."

The g-suit felt weird. It was a two-piece garment, though it looked like one piece when it was on.

"You should only take it off for brief periods," said Mr. Ashur, "for hygienic purposes. You'll even sleep in it. I know two gees probably doesn't sound like much, but it starts to tell on you. If you weigh one hundred twenty pounds, your weight becomes two-forty. It wears you out after a while."

"I hear you can end up with internal problems," Siggy said, still too dazed to really grasp what she was about to do.

"That would take a long time," he assured her. "Especially if you wear your g-suit like you're supposed to."

They stood in an air lock together, in zero gees, waiting to be admitted into the Speedy side of things. Siggy hadn't had a chance to exchange more than a few words with anyone but Mr. Ashur since she had left the conference room. He was showing her the various features of the suit.

Support filaments hugged her face and head. Her short hair poked out through the grid on top of her skull. She kept wanting to take the gloves off. There was a control pad on the inside of her left forearm where she could adjust the support system.

"Up to four gees," said Mr. Ashur. He had already showed her how to turn on the magnetic soles of her boots. While docked, the Speedy ship was at zero gees. It wouldn't spin up to two gees until after it had jumped over the Enigma Fold.

The outer lock opened, and Siggy looked through the coupling section and into the Speedy lock, which was six-sided. Two armed security officers were waiting in there. At the sight of the humans, their head tendrils settled tight against their bodies.

"They're starting to hurt my feelings," Siggy whispered to Mr. Ashur.

"Get used to it," he said, softly. "If it makes you feel any better, we upset them just as much. Maybe more."

"It doesn't make me feel better," said Siggy. "It makes me feel worse."

"Good. I'll feel better about having you along, then."

The two of them walked across the coupling section and into the six-sided lock. Behind them, hatches closed and sealed. It was comfortably warm in there, and almost odorless except for a faint woody smell, almost like sandalwood or cedar.

Siggy tried to imitate what Mr. Ashur was doing, even the way he was moving. Her ballroom experience was paying off again. The officers didn't point their weapons at her, but Siggy knew she was thoroughly covered. She noticed that one of the officers was a woman. The woman had breasts and her pelvis was wider.

Mammalian characteristics, just like we learned in school. But those insect eyes . . . and it doesn't help to see this six-sided architecture, either. Like walking into a giant honeycomb.

But that impression was dispelled somewhat when the inner hatch opened and they were escorted into a wide hallway, constructed with only four sides. Siggy hadn't had a chance to look at the Speedy ship from any of the viewports. She had no idea how big it was, but if the size of its hallways were any indication, it must be enormous.

Because of the head tendrils, she suddenly thought. She sneaked glances at their escorts, calculating. Fully deployed, the tendrils must take up three feet of space on all sides. *I wonder if they ever get tangled up with anyone else. And if it would hurt.*

Four pairs of magnetic boots made soft clicking noises on the floor, connecting, releasing, connecting, releasing again.

"Where are we going?" Siggy asked Mr. Ashur.

"Our jump station."

"So soon? I wanted to send my message—"

"Our station is in my office. We'll get it off, don't worry."

But Siggy was worried. And scared, and dreadfully homesick already. The Speedy ship was beautiful, full of graceful geometries and subtle colors; but it wasn't an inviting beauty. It was cold, elvish, like being in one of those faery hills the Professor had warned her about.

"I'll need to review that mini as soon as we're under way," Mr. Ashur was saying. "I'll have a lot of questions."

He had been horrified when she had told him what was going on, but pleased that she had agreed to cooperate. She could tell that he wasn't prepared for what he was going to see on that mini. He was worried, angry, and sad; but the full impact of what had happened, what Jerry had done, wouldn't hit him until he actually saw it.

"I can't watch it with you," she warned him.

He didn't answer. He was frowning. Not looking forward to it, she could tell.

"I saw part of the first one he made, years ago," she said. "I still haven't gotten over it."

"I can't believe he managed to trap Speedies," he said. "That just doesn't seem possible."

"You have to know Jerry Wolfe," said Siggy, wishing to God that she didn't.

"He must be a genius."

"No way," she said. "If anything, he's retarded."

"You don't understand," said Mr. Ashur. "*I* couldn't trap Speedies, and I've lived with them for ten years."

Siggy was very aware of the officers, who moved at human speed with flawless control. "Have you always lived with military personnel?" she asked.

"And government officials, yes." He looked sideways at her, wondering what she was getting at.

"Trained professionals," said Siggy. "But what sort of Speedies did Jerry kill? Were they civilians?"

"We'll know when I look at that mini," Mr. Ashur said grimly.

Every door they passed was pressurized, just like you'd find on a human ship, but these were all six-sided. They went through an open one, past more guards, and into Mr. Ashur's office. Siggy could tell he spent a lot

of time there. It looked like the bridge of a ship, it had
so many work stations. It had no human touches that
Siggy could see, which gave her another pang. She
couldn't imagine what it would be like to spend ten years
so far away from everything that made her feel comfortable and warm.

"You might as well sit here for the jump." Mr. Ashur
directed Siggy to a station with a keyboard and monitor;
she could write her message to Oscar from there. She
sat in the chair and fastened herself down. But she felt
a jolt of anxiety when she looked at the keyboard. It
had more keys; and the characters were, quite naturally,
from the Speedy alphabet.

Mr. Ashur pressed a key, and the characters momentarily vanished, to be replaced by human Standard script
in the usual pattern, leaving some of the keys blank.

"Type fast," he warned.

Siggy was suddenly at a loss for words. But this was
her last chance, so she did her best.

> *Oscar,*
>   *I have to go with the Speedies. I can't tell you*
> *why. Please believe that I really do love you,*
> *and I'm doing what I have to do. Please hold*
> *my things for me, especially The Truth About*
> *David Silverstein. I don't know how long I'll be*
> *gone. Wait for me if you can.*
>
> > *Love,*
> > *Siggy*

"Sent," said Mr. Ashur. "We're on our way."

Done, Siggy agreed. *And I'm glad Oscar and I had
that kiss in the elevator. And we got a chance to say "I
love you." I hope it's not the last time we'll ever say it. . . .*

Mr. Ashur sat at another station, one that looked like
it got a lot more use than Siggy's. He tucked Jerry
Wolfe's letter into a drawer and almost put the mini in
there, too. But he hesitated, looking at it speculatively.
He really wanted to get it over with.

"Not while I'm in the room," Siggy begged.

He put it away and turned on his own monitor. He
began typing notes, at an astonishing rate, his fingers

almost blurring. Siggy looked at his screen to see what he was writing, but it was the Speedy script again.

Wow, she thought, impressed.

The officers were watching her. She tried not to stare back; she didn't know if that was polite or not. She couldn't ask Mr. Ashur just then, because *that* might not be polite, either. She wondered what the Speedies thought of her. Did they hate her because she was Jerry's "witness"? Did they think she was somehow to blame?

Siggy turned back to her keyboard. She looked for a HELP key, but this system didn't have one. It must have been built specifically for the diplomatic corp. Siggy doubted that it had any games on it.

She leaned back in her chair and closed her eyes, but she couldn't keep them closed. She was too wide awake. She swiveled her chair 360 degrees and studied the room. It was full of baffling stuff.

I wish I could have brought some books. Or some music. Or anything.

The Speedies watched her. She watched Mr. Ashur. He seemed to have forgotten that she existed. And she was starting to go nuts.

After she had spun on that treadmill a few times, she remembered something. They were a light month away from Enigma. It would take at least twenty-four hours to get there.

"Mr. Ashur," she said, tentatively.

"Yes . . ." He didn't stop typing.

"Since we have such a long time to jump—"

"We've got about an hour."

"What?" Her tone made him look over for a moment.

"Forget everything you think you know about Speedy technology," he said.

"But their ships," Siggy argued, "when they're over here, they never go faster than—"

"Something's changed," he said flatly, and he tapped the drawer where he had stashed Jerry's mini. "They don't care if we know how fast they can really go now. That should scare you."

"It does," Siggy said.

"Good." He turned back to his keyboard, and Siggy

watched him, and the Speedies watched her, and the ship sped onward at a distressing rate.

An hour later, reality blinked.

"What was that?" Siggy asked, startled.

"The Fold," said Mr. Ashur, unperturbed.

"Are we going to jump now?"

"We just did. We'll be spinning up to two gees now."

Siggy wasn't sure if she was disappointed or just disturbed. She had never been across the Fold before, she hadn't any idea what it was like. That blink had been so strange, so difficult to describe. It had been like nonexistence.

She wondered what it had been like for that first human ship, *The Heimdall*. They had blundered across the Fold accidently. They had been hauling ore to the newly built Alesund Station and had suddenly ended up in an entirely new solar system, discovering Tantalus. If it hadn't been for their navigational computers and automatic systems, they might not have been able to find the Fold again.

As far as Siggy knew, when a ship jumped over the Fold, it was traveling through that place *between* space and time, that place Siggy could never describe adequately on her science tests. The blink that happened for the Enigma Fold might happen during jump-time, too, but maybe that blink was so brief you weren't aware of it.

"What happens," Siggy couldn't resist asking, "during that *blink*, when you go across the Fold?"

"I don't know," he admitted. "My brain turns off, even with its enhancements. But I think the Speedies know."

He thinks. But he can't ask them, even though they're standing right here?

And Siggy couldn't ask them how come they could get places faster than human ships. Human ships made many thousands of jumps during a ten to twenty light-year trip, so many that the time dilation effect was minimal. Did that mean that the Speedies made millions? Or was it something else she couldn't even guess?

"I guess you'd better go to your quarters now," Mr.

Ashur said, and sighed heavily. "I'm going to look at the mini. Get it over with."

"You probably won't be able to watch the whole thing," Siggy warned him.

He looked at her with his machine eyes.

"I have to," he said. "It's my job."

Siggy suddenly felt sick. "I'm sorry," she said. "I wish I could tell you how sorry."

He shrugged. "I wish it mattered."

That wasn't very encouraging. But he had a terrible task ahead of him. Siggy tried not to be hurt that he wasn't offering more human comfort.

She unstrapped herself from the chair, and got up.

"You can turn off your boots now," Mr. Ashur said.

Siggy could feel the gravity increasing. She supposed it would become uncomfortable soon, but for the moment she liked the feeling.

"This way," said the female officer. Siggy was interested to note that the female's voice wasn't any different in timbre from a males'; at least, this one's wasn't. Every Speedy's voice she had heard, in person or in a recording, had been low by human standards, though there was variance between individuals.

She followed the officer out of Mr. Ashur's office. "See you later," she called on the way out, but he didn't answer.

The officer had taken her lightly by the arm. Siggy was surprised at how gentle the woman's grip was. Her sharp fingertips didn't prick at all; they didn't even tickle.

The walk was a short one. Evidently, the Speedies wanted the humans to be in the same general area. That was okay with Siggy, though she was beginning to suspect Mr. Ashur wasn't going to be very good company.

Especially after he saw the mini.

Her room was spacious. It had its own work station, a bunk built into a wall, an immovable table and chairs for meals.

"Thank you," Siggy told the officer, and went to sit at the work station. She didn't look to see if the woman was going to stay or leave. She was unutterably tired.

She heard the door open and seal behind her.

I wonder if they'll lock me in.

The work station was pretty much like the one Siggy had just vacated. She pressed the proper key, and the keyboard changed over to Standard. She started to poke around, hoping she could find out what the functions were.

Mr. Ashur was probably viewing the mini now. She tried not to imagine what he was seeing, but the images from Jerry's first mini were still fresh in her mind.

Eight years now, she thought. *I should be able to get over it.* But she knew that wasn't true. You would have to have a memory-wipe to get over something like that. At the moment, Siggy would have jumped at the chance for one.

She pitied Mr. Ashur. For most human beings, watching torment was almost as bad as suffering it. For some, it might be worse.

Damn you, Jerry. If I ever see you again, I'm going to kick the crap out of you.

In the two weeks since Oscar had talked her into taking kickboxing lessons, she had been to Ron Hoshi's class four times. That wasn't much, but she had learned enough to entertain herself, imagining the kicks Ron had taught her, her feet connecting with Jerry's skinny, smelly body with loud and satisfying thumps. Eventually she got tired of it, and of trying to decipher the keyboard. She decided to explore her quarters.

The bathroom, at least, was pretty easy to figure out. She used the zero-gee privy, which was fancier than the ones she was used to. *Everything* in her quarters was fancier. Or maybe it just seemed that way because it was alien and beautiful. But not everyone would find it so, she suspected; Speedy designs were much more mathematical than human sensibilities would normally contrive, much more functional. You didn't quite grasp the deeper aesthetic quality until you moved and saw the hidden designs on surfaces that had previously appeared plain. Siggy spent several minutes finding hidden geometries in the walls, the floor, the fabrics covering the furniture, even in the g-suit she was wearing.

She had a feeling it looked really great on her. She

wished she could look in a mirror. But that didn't seem
to be something Speedies ever did.

When her eyes began to feel like they were going to
fuse shut, Siggy lay down on her bunk, thinking she
would rest before supper. Maybe Mr. Ashur would eat
with her. If he had the stomach for it after the mini.

Her eyes were tired. She could still feel the gravity
increasing, but her suit seemed to be doing its job. She
had no trouble breathing. She was relaxing pretty
quickly. In fact, she might fall asleep. She wondered how
much time she would have to nap.

They must be deep in Speedy territory now. Where
had they gone? For some reason Thanatos came to
mind. It was a thought that could inspire nightmares, if
she let it. But Thanatos wasn't in a hub system. And it
wasn't *deep,* like the Decider had said. They were going
deeper than any human being had ever been, except
for Jerry.

Meet me at the Crossroads.

What were the Crossroads? Siggy had never heard of
any place in particular by that name. She wondered
where Jerry had heard of it. Maybe it was from the
Bible, some obscure reference.

She was drifting off to sleep. She hoped Mr. Ashur
didn't need her. Some of her friends had been ill after
seeing the mini. Afrika had held her hand. She could still
remember the pressure of his grip, could almost feel it.

She fell asleep, comforted.

Someone was in her room.

In her nightmares, this had happened many times, and
she had struggled awake, expecting to see a man with
terrible eyes bending over her. She woke instantly, her
heart pounding.

The Decider was standing by her door. His head tendrils had stirred slightly, had been curled at the ends,
but as she sat up they flattened against his body. His
mouth was a thin line.

"Get up," he said. "Eat quickly."

Siggy sat up. There was food on her table. Had he
brought it himself? How long had he been in the room,
watching her sleep?

When she stood, her head spun. She felt a mild strain in her lower back. "How long have I been asleep?" she wondered aloud, and the Decider took it as a direct question.

"Six hours, human Standard."

Six hours. Some nap. Siggy sat down at the table and looked the fare over. It smelled good. There was some sort of fruit juice and a variety of small cakes. Siggy ate one, decided it was something like krummkaka.

I don't suppose I should ask for the recipe. It's a little too sweet anyway.

The Decider seated himself at the opposite side of the table and watched her. It was unnerving to be studied so closely while she was trying to eat. And it felt weird to chew with the support filaments on her face, though they gave her complete freedom of movement.

She wondered if he thought she was taking too long. She tried to hurry, but it was hard to shift gears when she had just awakened. In fact, even thinking seemed harder. And why did her lower back keep twinging like that?

The gravity, she suddenly remembered. She took a moment to adjust her suit for two gees, just like Mr. Ashur had shown her. The pain in her back eased.

The decider's sable eyes followed her every move. He had no eyelids to blink. Siggy couldn't see herself reflected on the surface of his eyes, yet she could still feel the intensity of his regard. His attention was unwavering, and once again, she couldn't help but be reminded of someone else.

"You are afraid," announced the Decider.

Siggy almost choked on the cake she was eating. She started to cough. She had to wash it down with some juice, and that was too sweet, too.

"I'm worried," Siggy managed to say at last.

"Feeling guilty," he snapped.

Siggy glared at him. He seemed to have a talent for infuriating her, just with his tone of voice. The Director would have admired his finesse.

"Why should I feel guilty?" she demanded.

"Murder. Torture. Lies."

"I haven't done those things."

"You are not responsible," he said, and Siggy was silenced by confusion. Did he mean it wasn't her fault, or that she was irresponsible?

"Who is responsible?" he demanded, changing his approach.

Siggy still felt so sluggish. Six hours hadn't been enough, and now this unblinking statue of a man was trying to nail her down on the semantics of serial killers. Her brain wanted to lurch in several directions at once.

"Some people are malformed," she said. "I mean their minds. They don't know the difference between right behavior and wrong behavior. Sometimes they do terrible things, and all the rest of us can do is try to identify them and—"

"Answer the question!" he shouted, as if she were a slow child.

"I'm trying to answer the question!" she yelled back.

He didn't wait for her to finish. "You are wasting my time!"

It was as if he hadn't even listened to her. His mouth was a thin line, and his head tendrils were pulled down tight. His hands were curled into claws, the sharp fingertips resting on the tabletop. Siggy felt tears filling her eyes, but she fought them back.

"Do you want to hear my answer or not?" she asked, as calmly as she could.

"I would not ask if I did not want to know," he snarled, putting more space between each word than was really necessary, as if to imply, *how impossibly slow you are!*

"Then stop interrupting me," said Siggy.

He was silent then, so she decided to take another stab at his question.

"Jerry Wolfe is responsible for his own actions," she said. "He is to blame for his own crimes."

"You told Mr. Ashur Jerry Wolfe is retarded," the Decider said.

Uh-oh, thought Siggy. She had meant that, too, but few experts would have agreed with her.

"Not in the usual sense of the word," she said, carefully. "I was referring to his emotional development."

"Retarded individuals are not responsible," stated the Decider.

Siggy sighed, an action that wasn't as easy in two gees as it was in one. She gazed unhappily at the Decider and wondered how much damage she was doing every time she opened her mouth and spoke her mind to him. Mr. Ashur would be very disappointed in her, she was sure.

"Mentally retarded individuals are not responsible," she agreed. "But emotionally retarded people must be held responsible for what they do, because the way they are is partly based on decisions they have made in the course of their lives."

He frowned. "Specify."

Deep water, and she was fudging like crazy. She didn't honestly know if what she was about to say really applied to Jerry Wolfe, but she had already committed herself.

"All human children," she said, "are confronted with moral dilemmas as they're growing up. Big ones and little ones. Often, doing the right thing is harder than doing the wrong thing. Some people do what's easy. But most people try to be strong, and do what's right."

He was silent again, and this time when he watched her he seemed weighted with heavy thoughts. He was quiet so long that Siggy was calming down again, and she reminded herself that she had not seen what he had seen, a recording of innocent Speedies being tortured by a monster. She couldn't bear to imagine what he had done to them any more than she could stand to remember what he had done to humans; but her grasp of the universe had not been drastically changed by the experience. For the Speedies, this must be a new and terrible thing.

When she had finished eating, he stood.

"Turn on your boots," he said. "We are spinning down."

Siggy realized he was right, she could feel herself getting lighter. She bent over to turn on her boots, and the Decider watched her. He did not seem unduly impatient, and Siggy felt a pang of guilt.

"I'm sorry I lost my temper," she said, softly.

"As I said," he snapped. "You are guilty."

Siggy flushed. So that's what he had meant. She *felt* guilty, which was infuriatingly true. Her temper was threatening to run away with her again. Didn't he care that she was far from home, that she had no human company? He probably didn't even know what that was like.

"Have you ever been alone among humans?" she challenged.

"Yes," he said, and he took her arm and pulled her toward the door, his patience at an end.

Mr. Ashur and the security officers met them in the hallway. Siggy looked anxiously for any sign of reassurance from the only other human who lived within tens of thousands of light years; but Mr. Ashur wasn't up to it, she could see that immediately. He looked as if he hadn't slept for days. If his eyes had been made of ordinary flesh and blood, she was sure they would have been red and haunted.

He fell in beside Siggy, and they continued briskly up the hallway.

"I see what you mean about Jerry Wolfe," he said.

Siggy wished she didn't have to ask him. "You've watched the whole thing?"

"Yes."

It was funny how one word could say so much.

"And you were right," he went on. "They were all civilians."

The victims. Not trained professionals, like the individuals who moved so carefully beside them now. Siggy wondered where they were going. Ashur probably knew, he didn't look particularly worried. Or rather, he seemed too worried about other matters to spare much anxiety for a simple walk down the hall.

They walked for a long time, passing Speedies who didn't blink or move, walking at a pace that was so brisk Siggy was practically running to keep up. Several times she almost lost magnetic contact with the floor. Her dance experience was helping to keep her on an even keel, but zero-gee locomotion was something that had to be experienced to be mastered.

At last they turned right and went through a massive, six-sided doorway, into a room that dwarfed the human imagination. It was sparsely populated by Speedies at various work stations and dominated by a view screen that made the one on the Promenade of the Skaw seem puny in comparison. The image on the screen took Siggy's breath away.

It was the surface of a world. But that wasn't exactly true, because you couldn't see the surface. It was covered in supertowers that extended out of the atmosphere, and out of the gravity well. They had to be miles tall, and they shone with a gold and amber splendor that would have put the Director's office decor to shame. Siggy knew about such things—you could find launching towers on some human worlds—but nothing on this scale.

"It's three gees inside the gravity well," Mr. Ashur said. "They built towers like these when they started their space program, millennia ago."

Siggy didn't tell him she already knew something about the beginning of the Speedy space program. People on Veil knew more about Speedies than most other humans did. But she was still awed by the scene on that giant screen. She decided that the sight of these supertowers was worth all of the fear and discomfort she had experienced so far.

She might change her mind about that later, but right now it was true, and that was enough.

"Mr. Ashur," she said, as a sudden thought occurred, "this isn't their *home* world . . . ?"

"No," he quickly assured her. "I doubt we'll ever see that. But this is an old colony. I could tell you its name, but you wouldn't be able to pronounce it."

Siggy had already made up her own name for the place, anyway. At the sight of those towers, and all of the structures that linked them together, the first name that occurred to her was *Hive*.

Strange sounds managed to pull her attention away from the screen. The Speedies on the bridge were talking to each other, moving at Speedy-normal. The sounds raised the hairs on the back of Siggy's neck, but they were fascinating. When Speedies spoke at their own speed, the sound came to the human ears as buzzing, chirping, whistling, short barks, purring, brief roars, croaks, and vibrating sounds that were almost like the noises insects could generate with their wings or cara- paces, or back legs. These latter noises seemed to be produced by Speedies with their head tendrils.

We must seem deaf and mute to them, or almost com- pletely so, Siggy thought with wonder.

"Here we go," said Ashur, and Siggy looked up to find the room tilting on its side; or at least appearing to do so as the image pivoted and the ship began to descend toward one of the towers. Siggy caught her breath, marvel- ing at the complexity of the geometries below them. The tower toward which they were moving was six-sided. Siggy wondered why six seemed to be so important— why not eight, or nine, or five? As they pulled closer, her sense of perspective was sent reeling.

She had thought the platform that topped the tower might be the size of ten football fields, but every passing second revealed new details, tiny dots that became large structures, bugs that became machines, lines that became gaps large enough to swallow whole ships; and still the image grew until Siggy knew she was looking at a plat- form so large that Santa Fe Station could have rested there without hanging over the sides of the tower.

And how many levels lie below it? she mused, dazedly. *How large is this world? Is it bigger than Earth, or denser, or some of both? And what kind of engineering wizards must they be to build structures that could stand tall under such crushing forces?*

The supertowers that humans had built hadn't been challenged by more than one-and-a-half gees. Siggy was sure that there were many human engineers who would give a limb or two to be able to see what she was seeing. The square mileage of living space had to be astronomi- cal, yet the Speedies probably didn't fill it the same way humans would. They needed room, perhaps psychologi- cally as well as physically.

And maybe that's one of the things Jerry exploited in order to capture individuals, Siggy thought, with dawn- ing horror.

"There's our spot," remarked Mr. Ashur, indicating

the six-sided area, outlined in black, that was rapidly
filling the screen. As Siggy watched, those black edges
suddenly flashed a purple so dark, it was almost black
itself. The golden image on the screen swelled, became
unsmooth, marked by the sorts of designs Siggy could
find in the walls of her quarters if the light hit them in
the right way. But these weren't just designs, they were
a working part of the structure, and looking at them
made Siggy feel odd.

"You can't see this," Mr Ashur said, "but there are
lights flashing too rapidly for the human eye to follow.
I'm sure it looks beautiful anyway. I'm surprised that
they invited us up to watch."

Siggy glanced at him and was startled to see bitter,
cold anger in his face. For a moment she thought it
might be directed at the Speedies, but then she remembered where she had seen it before. Afrika had worn an
expression like that after he had seen Jerry Wolfe's mini.
Siggy supposed she had, too.

She knew Mr. Ashur must be worried. She couldn't
imagine how he was going to manage damage control
for such an impossible situation. Siggy hoped he wasn't
angry with her. She hoped it for selfish reasons; he was
her only human connection. But she had stopped expecting him to comfort her, he had too much resting on
his shoulders. All she could do was try not to make his
job any harder than it already was.

So stop arguing with the Decider! she told herself,
sternly, and hoped she would have the strength to follow
her own advice.

Colors and lights throbbed in her eyes until she had
to close them against the overload of her brain's slower
processing systems. She envied Mr. Ashur his enhancements. It must be marvelous to be able to see what was
really happening.

She felt a slight jolt under her feet.

"Come," said the Decider, almost at the same instant.
Siggy pried her eyes open and lurched after him.

They were inside the supertower, ship and all.

Mr. Ashur and Siggy made their way down a wide
ramp, into a shipyard so gigantic that nearby vessels

were tiny things in the distance. It was warm there, and
Siggy marveled at the energy it must take to regulate
that kind of temperature in such an enormous space.

Mr. Ashur and Siggy were escorted by the Decider
and three officers. At first, Siggy couldn't see anyone
else near them. They were walking away from the ship,
at which she sneaked a few backward glances out of
curiosity, breaking off the attempt when she realized
they were still much too close to it for her to get a good
view of it.

It was all too outrageously, staggeringly big, and too
complex, too fast, too—alien. *Mr Ashur,* she wondered,
*how do you do it? I'm already overloaded, ready to go
home again.* Part of her also longed to explore, but she
was afraid. How lost she would feel, even if she encountered people and could ask them questions. The idea of
trying to do that made her feel unbearably shy and
awkward.

But Jerry did it.

Right, said the ghost of Afrika in her head, *but to
Jerry there's no difference between a human city and an
alien one. He's an outsider everywhere he goes.*

They followed lines that Siggy couldn't decipher, past
pillars, buildings, machinery whose purpose Siggy didn't
have the experience to guess. After some time, she saw
people up ahead. A crowd of them, perhaps a hundred.
They were waiting close together, their head tendrils
pulled in tight.

What is this? wondered Siggy, with a twinge of apprehension.

Once she got closer, she could see that very few of
these people were wearing uniforms. She couldn't quite
make out individual expressions, but there was no mis-
taking the avidity with which they stared at the humans.

"Mr. Ashur—" Siggy began, but he shushed her.

"Don't panic," he said, curtly. "Copy what I do."

The crowd stood in an open area. The Decider's group
escorted Siggy and Mr. Ashur to within ten paces of the
waiting crowd, then stopped.

The Decider turned and said, "Go."

Mr. Ashur obeyed immediately, and Siggy forced her
legs to follow him, but it was against all of her instincts.

She was beginning to suspect who these people were, and that vengeance was the order of the day.

A crowd of humans, under similar circumstances might tear them to pieces.

Well, thought Siggy, as she and Ashur went into the crowd, who parted for them and then closed ranks again, encircling them, *if that's what they're going to do, it shouldn't take them more than a few seconds to do it.*

Faces rung her in, sable eyes and hard, shiny tendrils, bodies quivering with what surely must be extreme emotion. Siggy was surprised she wasn't shaking, herself; she was so tense, her breaths came in short, painful gasps, which she did her best to mute. Her tango face was firmly in place, but she doubted it was doing much good at the moment.

The civilian Speedies had a body odor she hadn't noticed on the ship personnel, not unpleasant, really almost like cinnamon or even allspice; and each face differed, not only in appearance, but in expression. Some mouths were pulled tight, some were softened, lips slightly parted to reveal teeth that were perfectly square and even, with no incisors. Siggy even glimpsed someone's tongue, as black and soft as the eyes. They stared hungrily at Siggy and Mr. Ashur for what seemed an eternity, then all faces were suddenly turned toward the Decider.

Mr. Ashur didn't turn, but Siggy couldn't help herself. She looked over her shoulder at the Decider. He was looking directly back at her, his mouth a thin line.

Siggy held his gaze and tried to look brave.

He moved, his hands a blur, and his tendrils erupted into a cloud around his head, blurring and throwing off prisms of color as the light hit their hard, shiny surfaces.

The press of bodies around Siggy suddenly pulled in tight, bodies blurring and seeming almost to teleport toward, then away from her as people touched her. Siggy felt a blow as one woman's hand came too close to her cheek, glancing off with bruising force. Siggy cried out and fell back against the people behind her. But in the next micro-second, the woman was touching Siggy's cheek with gentle fingers. Siggy couldn't read her face, but she understood the touch. The blow had been an accident. Most of these people were civilians, untrained to interact with humans.

Just be yourself, Mr. Ashur had instructed her. And that's what the Speedies were doing now. They were speaking in normal Speedy tones, and Mr. Ashur was trying to answer them. They stopped and listened, but they also interrupted him, unused to having to wait so long for information. Siggy didn't think they were being deliberately rude, they were just out of sync.

They spoke to Siggy, too, and she felt bad that she couldn't make them understand her. "My name is Siggy," she said. "I'm sorry about your loved ones."

But it was as if she weren't speaking at all, they acted as if they couldn't hear her. They would stop for an instant, as if listening, but then speed up again, buzzing, whirring, blurring.

Like bees, Siggy thought; unwillingly, because in school they had tried to discourage that notion. The Speedies weren't insects, they had many mammalian characteristics. They didn't live in honeycombs and obey the orders of a breeding queen. Yet face to face, the comparison was irresistible.

Head tendrils began to move in ways she hadn't seen before. They had been pulled in tight, but now they began to creep up Siggy's body like snakes, moving and entangling with each other until Siggy was completely covered from her waist to the top of her head. By this time she really was shaking, and a tear spilled down one of her cheeks, to be instantly absorbed by a quivering tendril.

Some people might pay good money to get a massage like this, gibbered a tiny voice in Siggy's head, and then the tendrils began to slip into her mouth.

Panicking, she bit down; but it did no good. The tendrils were too hard, they simply slipped right past her teeth. Siggy would have screamed if her mouth hadn't been so full.

But they didn't go any farther, they didn't try to slip down her throat where they surely would have choked her. They stayed in Siggy's mouth until she was forced to swallow the saliva that had pooled at the back of her throat.

They tasted sweet.

The tendrils withdrew, and the people stepped back from her. Their speech clattered and rattled to a halt. They stared at Siggy and Mr. Ashur for a little while in silence, and then they were suddenly gone, speeding away like a swarm of dragonflies. Siggy gazed after them, her heart in her throat.

She turned to Mr. Ashur. His expression made perfect sense to her. He was profoundly moved, so much so that he was close to tears.

This has never happened to him before, Siggy realized. *He's always been with professionals like the Decider. These were ordinary people, and he got to talk to them.*

But why? Had they only been curious about humans? What had they wanted to learn about them?

Afrika's voice spoke softly inside her head. *They want to know if all humans are like Jerry Wolfe.*

"Come back to the ship," commanded the Decider. He and his guards turned and walked away at human speed. Siggy and Mr. Ashur followed. Siggy had to wipe away tears as she walked. She had new appreciation for the Decider and his crew, who took such trouble to communicate with her, to slow themselves down for her.

Shame haunted her as well. "Those were the families of the victims, weren't they?" she asked Mr. Ashur.

"Yes," he said, his voice harsh with emotion.

Siggy glanced at him, touched his arm. He looked at her distractedly and gave her a pat on the shoulder.

Siggy was tired by the time they got back to the ship, and she didn't think it was entirely because of the zero-gee two-step she had been doing for so long.

So now what? she wondered.

"That is all we require for now," said the Decider, and he left them in the hallway outside Mr. Ashur's office.

"Well," said Mr. Ashur, "I have work to do."

But Siggy followed him into his office, where the officers did not follow.

"What happened?" she asked him. "Why weren't those families angry with us?"

He put his hands on his hips and sighed, deeply. She could see he didn't want to take time with her right now, he had other concerns. But she had asked a good question.

"You can't be certain they weren't angry. I think some of them were. But Speedies like to have the facts before they act. They can be very aggressive, but I don't think they enjoy hurting others, they get no satisfaction out of it. This is why Jerry Wolfe's actions are so puzzling to them."

He rubbed his face, looking unspeakably weary.

"This is such a horror," he said.

Siggy couldn't agree more. "Did they ask you questions?"

"Yes. I answered as well as I could. But there are some areas where there's no common ground." He shrugged, then looked at his work station longingly.

"Will you be able to ask the Decider about this?" asked Siggy, hoping that if he could, he would then share answers with her.

"I'll ask. But they don't always answer."

Siggy's shoulders sagged. And it wasn't just because of the returning gravity, which was spinning back up to two gees. "How do you know what's true, then?" she asked.

"They don't lie," said Mr. Ashur. "They are very disturbed by the fact that *we* do, sometimes. If you ask them a question they don't want to answer, they stay silent."

Siggy remembered that old TV interview again, when Dr. Ngoni had asked the Decider why Speedies weren't sharing information with humans.

"So it's as difficult for them to share information they don't want to share as it is for us to stop lying," she mused.

"Yes," said Mr. Ashur. "I think it is. It might even be harder."

Siggy took a deep breath, let it out again. "Okay. Thanks. I'll see you later."

He nodded, and at least had the courtesy to wait for her to get most of the way to the door before he went to his work station.

Siggy went back to her quarters, where the first thing she did was rush to the privy. She had been too tense to realize just how badly she had to go, but now there was no ignoring the need. When she came out again, she noticed lunch was waiting.

More cakes. She ate them, but had to force herself to finish.

Who would think I could ever get tired of sweets? she wondered, then went back to her own work station to struggle with the computer.

Hours later, she had figured out how to get into the word processing system. She took extensive notes, hoping she could add them to her notebook, later. But when she tried to save them, she accidentally lost them.

Oh well, she thought. *That'll give me something to do when I wake up from my nap.*

When she lay down, she was tired but not sleepy. She thought that perhaps she had better start exercising, so her body would feel more grateful for rest. Her g-suit gave her complete freedom of movement, so it shouldn't be too hard to work out.

Her mind drifted back to the Speedy civilians. If they had tasted sweet, then Siggy supposed she and Mr. Ashur must taste salty. Or smell, rather. And like dust, and perfumed soap, and who knew what else. The tendrils that grew from Speedies' heads were sensory apparatuses that handled both smell and hearing; they were much more sensitive than human senses, able to take in much more information. Given this fact, Siggy was surprised that she and Mr. Ashur hadn't seemed disgusting to the Speedies. She was glad this was the case. Things were already bad enough.

Siggy's weary thoughts circled around and around. Jerry had come to Hive by himself, had managed to enter and do his work, then escape again, undetected. How could he have accomplished it? Was it just because he was so obsessive, so unpredictable? Was it because the Speedies never expected to see humans so deep in their territory, so they didn't look for them?

Siggy turned on her right side, facing the wall. The pillow wasn't quite big enough to support her neck in that position, but she was sick of being on her back. She was getting sore just from lying down. If Oscar had been there, she could have wrapped an arm around him and cupped herself against his back; or he might have been the one who was holding her from behind. When they slept together, they usually alternated back and forth all night long.

She had gotten used to having him there. She would have loved to tell him everything that had happened, to ask his opinion and tell him her own theories, her doubts. She would have loved to see his handsome face and to feel his warm hands. He liked to kiss the back of her neck, right up near the hairline. She liked to kiss his bare shoulders.

The Professor grinned at her from the darkest places in her mind. *It was good while it lasted, wasn't it? But you always end up alone again, don't you, Siggy. And everyone you touch suffers in the end. It doesn't pay to make friends.*

Shut up, she told him.

Careful, he said. *That's something you would never dare say to me in person.*

You're not in person. I'm just dreaming about you.

His eyes burned in the dark. *You haven't thought it*

all the way through. Joseph Bell should have given you the clue.

He went nuts when they tried to modify him, said Siggy.

Yes. And do you think the Speedies ever used modified agents? They're so much cleverer than humans, much more advanced.

Siggy didn't like where that was going. She didn't like the feeling that was creeping up her back, like someone was watching her.

Turn around Siggy. Look at me.

She rolled on her back and slowly turned her head, as if struggling against ten gees.

There he was. He was pale now, and in Speedy clothes, and had head tendrils that were pulled tight against his body. His sharp-fingered hands were curled into claws, but his eyes were the same as they had always been.

"Time's up," he said in his monotone. "Let's dance."

And Siggy fell out of bed.

She hit the floor with a nasty jolt, with two hundred and forty pounds of force. It knocked the breath out of her, but it helped to wake her up. Unfortunately, it also made her feel like she was having a heart attack.

Siggy looked frantically around the room, gasping for breath. The Professor was nowhere to be seen. She had dreamed him, and she hadn't even known she had fallen asleep. She sat up on the floor and panted until the sick, dizzy feeling left her.

Finally she got up and went into the bathroom. She had a moment of terror as she peeked around the doorway, half-expecting to find the Professor in there. That's the way it would have happened in some cheesy movie. Siggy thought longingly of the musicals in her movie collection, left behind on Trondheim with her life and her love and every other good thing.

She used the privy again. She wondered if that was any indication of how much time had passed, not that it mattered when there was nothing to do.

She decided to use the zero-gee hygiene system. Her bathroom had been stocked with the usual human varieties of gels, along with plenty of towels to rub with. Siggy took off her g-suit, carefully undoing her face and head struts in the process, and opened a tube that smelled like peaches. She rubbed it on her skin, then scrubbed herself thoroughly with a towel. It felt marvelous. She applied the human-style deodorant under her arms and put her g-suit back on.

Her skin tingling pleasantly, she felt a little better. She wandered back out to her work station, but decided she didn't feel like staring at a monitor just then. She decided to go out for a stroll.

Her door was unlocked. There were Speedies out in the corridor, but they didn't look upset to see her. They only watched her, silently, professionally.

Siggy walked down the silent hallway, with its officers that stared like living statues. She felt like she was in a faery tale; surely this was what it was like to live with the *huldrefolk,* the hidden folk of the old tales.

Siggy found Mr. Ashur's door, but it was sealed tight. She couldn't make any sense of the controls at the door, wasn't even sure they *were* controls. If they were, they were designed to be touched by those sharp fingertips, not by Siggy's blunt pads.

She turned to one of the officers who stood nearby.

"Is Mr. Ashur still working?" she asked.

He didn't answer. Perhaps he thought the answer was too obvious. Mr. Ashur was working, or sleeping, or something else; whichever it was, he was not available.

"Can you tell me what time it is?" she asked, then felt foolish. What time by whose calendar? Of course, he was silent again, his expression unfathomable.

"I could really use a chronometer in my room," Siggy explained. "I never know what time—I mean, I'm going kind of crazy trying to . . ."

This was pointless, he wasn't going to speak, couldn't help. She doubted he would talk to her even if he understood her. He stood there with his feet in a square, martial stance, his posture erect, his lips closed tight.

"Mirror, mirror on the wall," said Siggy, "who's the fairest one of all?"

In the silence that followed, shame crept up on her, making her cheeks hot, burning the tips of her ears. She knew better than to be so petty, to say things he couldn't possibly understand.

"I'm sorry," she said, and was horrified to hear how her voice trembled. She was close to tears. Of course he had no reply, she had known he wouldn't, but she had needed so much to hear him say *It's all right,* which of course it wasn't.

She fled back up the hall, past the silent sentries and back into her own quarters, sealing her door behind her, feeling rejected and misunderstood.

The female officer woke her up, hours later.

"I have brought breakfast," she said.

Siggy sat up, feeling disoriented. Breakfast. So it must be the ship's version of "morning." That was ridiculously nice to know.

"Mr. Ashur would like to speak with you once you've eaten," said the officer.

Siggy perked up. "Okay," she said. "Please tell him I'll be right there."

The officer left with her message, and Siggy jumped out of bed. She barely nibbled the food—sweet fare again—then cleaned up and brushed her teeth. She didn't want to waste too much time.

Look at yourself, she scolded. *Don't get so excited. He's probably going to be grumpy and strained again.*

But he wasn't. He smiled at her when she came into his office. He was sitting at a table that didn't appear to be for work, and he was eating his own breakfast. He offered her some, and coffee as well, which she had feared she would never taste again. The cups and saucers were of human manufacture, delicate china, red and gold, the sort of design her mom would have called Russian.

"This food isn't as sweet as the usual," said Mr. Ashur, holding his cup in one large, elegant hand and the saucer in the other. "You get tired of that pretty soon."

"And how," said Siggy, sampling some of the fare on his table. It was good. Some of it was hardly sweet at all, and some of it was salty, a taste she hadn't known she had missed until it tickled her tongue.

But I still like pepper better. Pepper on scrambled eggs, and papas fritas con chorizo, and butter on rye toast . . .

Mr. Ashur still looked a little tired, but he seemed much more relaxed. He was handsome when he was in a good mood, with chiseled features and skin that gleamed like ebony. His silver eyes were striking in that context, and the silver filaments that hugged his face made him look like some sort of superhero.

"Well," he said, "those other minis are very illuminating; they've answered a lot of the questions I had."

"Other minis?" Siggy asked as she alternated sips between coffee and a drink that was more like iced tea than juice.

"The R-FBI sent them. From IFCI, the ones you told the Decider he should get when he first interviewed you."

Siggy blinked, trying to catch up. "When did they send for them?"

"Before we boarded this ship."

"Wow. The Speedies sure made their minds up about that quickly."

He smiled again. "Hence the name."

Siggy was pleased. The Decider *had* listened to her, he had taken her advice. Maybe he didn't think she was such a fool after all.

Mr. Ashur was studying her over his coffee, his expression much more friendly than she'd ever seen it. "I feel like I know you now," he said. "After watching hours and hours of you talking with those . . ."

"Monsters," Siggy finished for him. "We called the Maximum Security block 'Monster Row.' The janitors, I mean. Though we never said it in front of the inmates."

"Monster Row is a good name for it. I must say, I have very little experience in the field of abnormal psychology."

"They weren't crazy," Siggy said, firmly.

He raised an eyebrow.

"Really," she said. "Most of them weren't, in my opinion. I only saw a few who were crazy in the classical sense—you know, paranoia and schizophrenia. But most of the guys on Monster Row were just so screwy, no one knew what else to do with them."

She thought he would disagree, most people did; but instead he said, "You're too smart to be a janitor. How did you end up there?"

Siggy blushed. She hadn't been ashamed of her old job, but sometimes it bothered her that people seemed to think it was so lowly. "I was a B student," she told him, feeling lame.

He shook his head. "It isn't fair. Smart people should have more choices about what they may do with their lives."

"My sweetheart, Oscar, never even finished high school," said Siggy. "He had to get his GED, later. Now he's a supervisor with Tovarish Mining, with authority over two hundred people."

"Grades don't always measure how smart people really are," agreed Mr. Ashur.

"Most of my co-workers at IFCI were smart, too."

"Yes. George and Afrika." He would have seen them on the minis too. "I like them. Good men. And it's so interesting to know that some people are named after Africa. I'm from Kenya, you know."

"Which one?" asked Siggy, thinking he meant the planet Kenya, or one of the Kenya stations, or the many countries, cities, or towns named Kenya.

"Kenya, Africa," said Mr. Ashur.

Siggy's eyes grew wide. She had to set her coffee cup down. "Old Earth," she said.

"Yes." He sipped his own coffee.

Fabled Africa. A place that most people only dreamed of, the place where the human race had been born and where the first great civilizations had emerged. The place that some regarded as if it were Asgard, the home of the Gods. The place you had to get on a waiting list to visit, a list so long that most people would die before their name came up, and they had to will their spot on the list to their children, who often had to pass it down themselves.

"You grew up there?" Siggy asked him, astonished.

"Yes." He was beginning to look abashed. "Went to university in Timbuktu. Then straight into the Diplomatic Corp."

"And you'll never go back to Earth again," Siggy realized.

"I hope not," said Mr. Ashur. "This is where I belong. This is what I have wanted to do for as long as I can remember."

And he continued to sip his coffee, as if he didn't know how extraordinary he was. It was amazing enough to meet a person from old Earth; it was even rarer to meet an ambassador to the Speedies. You had to be absolutely top notch, and dedicated, and talented beyond normal human standards.

"Your conversation with Jerry and the others," he said, studying her with an intensity that almost rivaled Speedy parameters, "was extremely perceptive. I confess I think your talents were wasted as a janitor, but on the other hand—maybe that was exactly where you belonged. You were placed, inadvertently, in a position where you could do the most good."

Now it was Siggy's turn to raise her eyebrows. She had never thought of it that way.

"But they escaped," she reminded him. "And Joseph hurt himself so badly, I don't even know if he survived."

"Yes," he said, unhappily. "I saw it. They recorded the whole thing."

Siggy seized his hand, suddenly. He had seen it. He must know.

"Listen," she said. "Did you see whether or not he died? Joseph, I mean. I've never known."

It was his turn to look surprised. "I don't know," he said. "But it didn't look good. The force with which he hurled himself against the walls, head first—"

"Did they cover his face when they carried his body out?" she interrupted.

"No," he said.

Siggy relaxed again. She remembered to let go of his hand.

He used it to refill his coffee cup, then to add cream. No sugar, of course.

"Commander Bell was a sad case," he said.

Unfortunately, this gave Siggy another dangerous idea, another forbidden subject about which to enquire.

"You know," she said, "speaking of Commander Bell . . ."

He was silent, politely waiting for her to finish.

"You've seen the Professor, of course. Prisoner MS-12."

"Yes," he said, with no trace of guile. "A baffling man. He had extraordinary reflexes, you know. Or maybe you never saw him in motion. The minis cover a lot of things that happened when you weren't present."

"Right," said Siggy. "So maybe you have an opinion. Could the Professor have been a modified Speedy?"

He frowned. "Modified?"

"Like Joseph Bell. A Speedy version of him, modified to look human."

He still frowned, seemed to be seriously considering the idea.

"The possibility never crossed my mind," he said at last. "Why would you think that?"

"You've seen how fast he is."

Mr. Ashur leaned his elbows on the table and bowed his head, considering his next statement carefully. It occurred to Siggy that he probably had to struggle in both directions, to explain humans to Speedies and to explain Speedies to humans.

"That's not enough," he said. "His reflexes, I mean. The differences between humans and Speedies amount to much more than just timing. When I watched the Professor, I never felt the slightest suspicion that I was watching a modified Speedy. I have doubts that they even exist—you can't assume that they would take the same steps we have. For one thing, they aren't the ones at a disadvantage, technologically speaking."

Siggy thought about that. He studied her.

"I must confess," he said, "the man frightened me. Even the very sight of him. Those eyes. I applaud you for being able to sustain a dialogue with him for so many years. It's truly amazing."

"He's been on Thanatos," Siggy told him.

He didn't like that. She saw a shadow of his old anger.

"Yet another human invading Speedy space, when it isn't even supposed to be possible," he muttered.

"But he's *not* human," said Siggy. "Is he?"

Mr. Ashur shook his head. But he said, "I honestly

am not sure. Jerry Wolfe hardly seemed human either. Perhaps even less so. An appalling man."

Siggy poured herself more coffee and drowned it in cream. "I don't envy you," she said. "Having to explain the Antichrist to the Decider."

"Yes," agreed Mr. Ashur. "And Armageddon. Such happy subjects."

"And the sheer volume of material. Eight years of it."

"I've been watching it speeded up. My enhancements," he reminded her. "I should be done soon."

"I'd better warn you," Siggy said, quietly. "Afrika was murdered. You'll see it near the end of the tapes."

"Oh, Christ." He sighed. "Before this I had never witnessed a person's death. I was rather hoping I never would again."

"Jerry killed him when he escaped."

"Ah."

Siggy was rather sorry about the direction the conversation had taken, but she supposed they both had better get used to it. This was no vacation, and the circumstances hadn't grown any less dire since she had been there. Mr. Ashur was beginning to look worried again, but at least he still seemed friendly toward her. He seemed more like an ally than he had before.

But she wondered how objective he could really be about the Speedies. He admired them so much, he had sacrificed a home in Africa to be with them.

"I have to get back to work now," he said.

"Okay." Siggy tried not to sound disappointed. She would have liked to sit and sip coffee for a while longer, chat about happier subjects, get to know him. But Mr. Ashur was obviously not a man who had much time to spare for social activities.

"I hope we can have breakfast together another time," she said as she rose.

He smiled again, a cheery sight.

"Of course we will. We would have done it sooner, but I've been unduly swamped. We'll meet again tomorrow, if you like."

"Yes, very much," said Siggy. "See you." And she beat a hasty retreat before he could change his mind.

*   *   *

The next few hours were spent trying to figure out how to save things on her computer. She didn't get very far, but this time when she lost her notes, they only consisted of one sentence: *Let's see if I can make it work this time.*

She couldn't.

After that, she did some stretches and calisthenics, and after that she did a zero-gee peach scrub.

After that, she didn't feel much like taking a nap.

Another walk? she asked herself. She was still a little sore about the last one she had taken. But she couldn't think of anything else to do in her quarters, so she opened her door and ventured out again. The sentries were in their usual spots. Siggy didn't try to talk to them this time, and hardly glanced at them as she passed. It was easier that way, she didn't mind the weight of their stares as much. She only worried that she would get lost. She hoped that someone would give her directions back to her quarters if that happened, that she wouldn't have to simply sit down wherever she was and wait for the Decider or Mr. Ashur to find her.

She occupied herself for a while by memorizing the surrounding corridors. She tried to make a little game of it. It helped, but soon she was wishing something would happen, or that she could find something more interesting to look at. Another one of those big view screens, perhaps.

She turned another corner and heard music.

She walked farther, and it got louder. At first she thought it might be something from a Speedy composer, but within a few steps she recognized it. It was an orchestral piece, something she had heard during Music Memory in school. It was "Variations on a Theme of Thomas Tallis," by Ralph Vaughan Williams. Siggy followed the sound until she came to a big door, which stood open. She looked inside. What she saw made her stare in wonder.

The Decider was sitting in a chair, listening to the music. He had a music box of human manufacture sitting on a small table beside him. The tendrils on his head stood up and around him, but they weren't moving at blurring speed. They were undulating, slowly; and the expression on his face took her breath away. She was pretty sure she knew what it meant.

He was moved by the music. He was enjoying it to a degree that Siggy would never have thought possible. He knew she was standing there, he saw her clearly. He let her watch.

Those tendrils weren't just for hearing, Siggy remembered. They were for smell, too. Both senses were processed by the same areas in the Speedy brain. *So,* wondered Siggy, *what does music smell like?*

She was moved, too, not just by the music that evoked so many human emotions, not the least of which was homesickness; but also by the sight of him, listening that way. And suddenly she knew, beyond a shadow of a doubt, that Mr. Ashur was right. The Professor wasn't a Speedy. He couldn't be. It wasn't just the music. His face didn't know how to express this much emotion. His *heart* didn't know.

The music ended. The Decider reached over and tapped his music box off with his fingertips. His tendrils drifted down to lie about his shoulders again, but didn't press flat. He seemed to be waiting for her to speak.

"Do you like the music of Mr. Vaughan Williams?" she asked, at last.

"Yes," he said. She couldn't detect any of the hostility, or impatience, or suspicion she had thought she had heard in his voice on previous occasions.

"I like music, too," she said, tentatively. "But I like dance music the best."

"Dance," he said, and his tendrils stirred. "Dance for me, please."

Siggy blushed. "The kind of dance I mean is the kind of dance you do with a partner," she said. "Ballroom dancing."

"Two people?" he enquired.

"Yes."

He stood and walked over to her at human speed. "Show me, please," he said.

Siggy was intrigued. Was it possible? She didn't see why not, he had marvelous control.

"I'll teach you," she said. "Ballroom dancing is a social ritual. People do it when they're trying to get to know each other better."

She paused. He was listening with more attention than he had ever shown her before.

"In all of the forms I'll show you," she said, "one partner leads and the other follows. We must touch each other, but this touch is not supposed to be romantic in nature."

"Not *supposed* to be," he said, carefully.

"Right," Siggy admitted. "But some people who are less socially adept often mistake ballroom dancing as an invitation to fondle someone for whom they have a sexual attraction. This is a mistake. Flirtation is allowed, but nothing more than that."

He might not have understood what she meant by *flirtation,* but he was still listening intently.

All right, thought Siggy. *Here goes.*

"The first thing I'm going to teach you," said Siggy, "is the most important thing. I'm going to teach you how to ask someone to dance."

He was the best dancer Siggy had ever seen. He was better than Maxi, than Oscar, even better than Nathanial. And what was better, he really seemed to enjoy himself. His head tendrils floated off his shoulders several times in the next few hours.

Siggy had to sing and hum the dance music.

"My collection is mostly orchestral," he told her. "No dance music."

She sang until she was hoarse, and then she hummed. She taught him each dance by taking the lead herself, while he followed perfectly. Then he would take the lead, dancing each form like an expert. He wasn't wooden like she feared he would be. His body felt incredibly hard—it was like dancing with a statue, except that *this* statue moved with grace and wit. Siggy hummed until she began to cough.

"Oh dear," she said, and they had to stop.

Hours must have gone by, she wasn't even sure. And during that time she had taught him twenty forms, including the waltz, the polka, the cha-cha, and both strict and flamboyant versions of the tango.

"I like tango the best," he informed her. But he surprised her by preferring the flamboyant versions. She
would have thought just the opposite.

She was enjoying herself so much, she didn't notice at
first that he had a tendency to answer her questions
while they were dancing.

"Haven't you ever heard of ballroom dancing before?" she said, breaking off her humming for a moment
and then picking it up again. He wasn't disturbed by the
break, his sense of rhythm was flawless.

"Never," he said. "I like human music. I like to watch
human dancers and athletes. They move well."

"But don't you find the music too slow?" she wondered.

"It doesn't matter," he said, without interrupting her.
When they were dancing, his conversation was more in
sync with hers. "Beauty is still there."

Beauty. She had wondered whether the Speedies
thought everything about humans was awkward, slow
and ugly. It was nice to know that this wasn't necessarily
the case. Of course, this man was a Decider. He was
even more extraordinary among Speedies than Mr.
Ashur was among humans. He said he had spent time
alone with humans, and he had bothered to compile a
music library.

"You're fascinated by the slow universe," she guessed.

He didn't answer, probably because he didn't have to.

"It's the same way humans feel when we look at star-
fishes," she told him. "Or sea anemones. They're creatures who move very slowly, too slowly for human eyes
to follow. But we admire them, we wonder what they're
thinking, how the universe seems to them."

"I wonder," he said.

And Siggy was so happy to be dancing, she didn't
realize until later how much he had admitted.

When she could hum no longer, she had to stop.

"I wish you had some dance music!" she rasped.
"That was such fun, I've missed it."

"I would like more lessons, soon," he said.

"Yes," Siggy agreed, and she looked speculatively at
his music box. "If you wouldn't mind," she said, "I can
use your music box to modify some of your orchestral
pieces so we can dance to them. I can make recordings

of my voice, too, so it won't get tired. Do you have extra minis?"

"I'll have them sent to your quarters," he said. He picked up the music box and handed it to her.

Siggy smiled at him. "I'll start right now."

"Good," he said, more enthusiastically than she had ever dreamed he would. "I'll see you later."

Siggy blinked and he was gone.

She didn't mind that he had left at his own speed, he had to attend to his own business. She hated to admit it, but she liked him better now. She was looking forward to seeing him again, to teaching him more dances. She hoped he would want to keep dancing, once she had taught him everything she knew. It would make her time on the ship pass much more happily.

"Have you ever danced with a Speedy?" Siggy asked Mr. Ashur the next morning at breakfast.

"Only metaphorically," he replied.

Siggy bit into a piece of pastry that tasted like sopaipillas without the honey or the powdered sugar. "I've been teaching the Decider ballroom dancing."

"You what?" He sounded as if he weren't sure he had heard her correctly.

"He likes music and dance, and yesterday I told him I like to dance, so . . ." She smiled at him. "He's *excellent*. I spent the whole evening making minis for his box, using the music library stored in his hard drive. He had over five thousand entries! And this morning when I had my voice back—I had to sing for him yesterday—I sang some songs into the recorder so we could dance to those, too."

Mr Ashur looked like he could be knocked over with a feather. "How ever did you get such an idea?"

Siggy shrugged. "I love to dance. I've always given dance lessons, wherever I've gone. Would you like some?"

He raised an eyebrow. "From what you say, it would seem that some lessons are definitely in order. Apparently I've been remiss."

Siggy blushed. "Well, you know, now that I think of it, Speedies do seem to combine movement with speech.

The Decider and I talked much more freely when we were dancing together. And now that you mention it, there are many dances that men can do together. I know some Greek and Jewish wedding dances, some Scottish and Irish ones, too."

He was smiling now. "I'm just trying to imagine this. At the next summit, the ambassadors form a line, and we dance our way through all the meetings."

"They would be a lot more interesting that way. . . ." Siggy suggested.

"It's a thought," said Mr. Ashur. "A very good thought. I'm done with my first go-through of the tapes now, so I'll have more time. But I want to review some of the material again before compiling my report for the Decider. I don't have to tell you how important it will be, I'm sure."

"Nope," said Siggy.

Mr. Ashur poured cream into his second cup of coffee. "I've noticed something odd about Jerry Wolfe—I mean, other than the obvious points. Really, I wish I had more training in human psychology. I could swear that there are times when he seems to go into trances. They're preceded by extreme agitation, almost seizure-like in its intensity."

"Oh yes," Siggy said. "I remember seeing him that way sometimes. He would get stuck on words or phrases he liked, and he would—we had a saying on Veil: *spaz out.*"

"Yes, I'm familiar with that one, and it fits the picture perfectly. After having reviewed all of the material, including reports from before the time of his incarceration from doctors and police personnel, I think that it's safe to say that as mad as Jerry was before he went into IFCI, he was far madder by the time he broke out again."

"Maybe he would have gotten that way anyway," said Siggy.

"Yes, perhaps," mused Ashur, "but being on Monster Row, interacting with the people there, I can't help but wonder if . . ."

Siggy was suddenly unable to meet his eyes. "Do you think I was partly responsible for the change in him?" she asked, quietly.

"Well I—" he sounded a little unnerved, perhaps he hadn't meant to imply anything at all. "Yes, certainly everyone who came in contact with him on a regular basis had some effect on him. He certainly seems to have fixated on you, but that's probably for the best. It gives us a lead to follow."

He leaned his chin on his hand and fixed his machine eyes on some middle distance. "But there's something else, something I can't quite put my finger on. Something that had a profound effect upon him."

"The Professor," Siggy said, suddenly.

He nodded. "Yes, I've thought of that. But during most of the trance-like episodes I've mentioned, the Professor was asleep. And if he wasn't asleep, he wasn't doing anything at all. It's very puzzling."

Asleep, Siggy was thinking. She could still hear the Director telling her that the Professor had never spoken once before he had seen her. *Not one word, Lindquist. Not spoken, not written, not telepathically.*

"Are you sure he wasn't a telepath?" Siggy asked.

"Who, Jerry?" said Mr. Ashur.

"No. The Professor."

He frowned. "*They* seemed to be sure he wasn't. I have no expertise in that area, myself."

Siggy ate another one of the sopaipilla-type pastries. The taste was making her homesick again. She had never been hit so hard by it before; not even the first time, when she had gone to Agate.

"Telepathy isn't a topic with which Speedies are very comfortable," Mr. Ashur was saying. "I've the impression that they simply don't recognize its existence. And since I've never met a real telepath myself—or I'm pretty sure I haven't—I can't argue the matter effectively."

"What are you going to tell them?" Siggy asked. "About Jerry Wolfe?"

"That he is a defective human. And I'll have to provide details concerning defects, a sort of profile for them to keep for future reference."

"That's something else you could get from the R-FBI," said Siggy. "They've compiled the most comprehensive collection of criminal profiles in existence."

He sighed. "I know. But I was hoping to put that off

indefinitely, at least until we had improved the dialogue we've been working so hard to achieve all these years. From what I've learned, the spectrum of Speedy behavior is much more narrow, much more confined to what we could consider ethical behavior. I hate to suddenly present them with a catalog of monsters."

"There are angels, too."

"Perhaps they're not unaware of that," said Ashur. "For instance, have you noticed that since our encounter with the victim's families, we haven't been as closely watched? We've had breakfast alone two mornings in a row."

Siggy cocked her head, remembering something from long ago. "The student exchange program—what ever became of that?"

"It was going quite well," he said sadly, "but it's been suspended. In view of recent developments."

"All because of Jerry Wolfe?" Siggy asked, dismayed.

"Yes. Believe me, what he's done is quite enough. I doubt anyone could have contrived anything much worse, short of an all-out attack on a Speedy colony. In fact, even that would not elicit this kind of reaction; because of the Lost Fleet, you know."

Siggy *hadn't* known. No one on Veil had ever had the slightest clue as to whether the Speedies regretted what had happened to them at the hands of the Lost Fleet. Her head filled with questions she wanted to ask, questions she had always thought would remain unanswered.

"Mr. Ashur," she began, "why—"

And then the door was open and an officer was standing by their table.

"We have arrived," said the officer. "If you are finished eating, come with me."

Siggy looked apprehensively at Mr. Ashur. "Arrived *where*?" she asked him.

"Someplace I've never been before," he said. "I can't explain. You'll have to see it."

They followed the guard down the long hallways, up the lifts and to the bridge. The Decider was already there, standing on the viewing platform, dwarfed by the image on the screen.

Siggy gasped. She had thought the world of supertowers had been an incredible sight. But this was something straight out of Jorge La Placa's wildest dreams, something from another universe. It filled the giant screen, yet they were still at such a distance that only gross details could be seen.

Roughly, it looked like a soccer ball. But the six-sided black spaces on this ball were empty, and large enough that several suns could fit inside them.

Siggy and Mr. Ashur joined the Decider on the platform. On the screen, the ball grew larger, until more of its details became apparent; yet they were still a considerable distance away—Siggy couldn't even guess how far. The struts that constituted the "white" part of the ball began to look less smooth, more machine-like.

"That thing," Siggy gasped, "must be *light years* across."

"Yes," snapped the Decider.

"What is it?"

"The Nexus," he said. "The Crossroads." He pointed a sharp finger at the screen. "Those are the Gates. In the letter, he spoke of the Gate."

"But which one?" Siggy couldn't even count them, from where they were. "How do we know which one?"

"You will tell him you are here," he said. "We will broadcast throughout the Nexus."

"Wait a minute." Siggy squinted at the screen. The structure that framed the Gates was looming ever larger on the screen. Each segment had to be millions of miles long. "People *live* inside those things?" she asked, incredulously.

"Some people," he admitted. "Not many. Most of the structure is uninhabited. A good place to hide."

I'll bet! thought Siggy. *You'll never find him in there! You could look for centuries!*

That was intimidating enough, but another thought was dawning on her. This machine was far beyond human capabilities. If the Speedies could build something like this, what chance did humans ever stand against them if they decided to go to war?

"How could you build such a thing?" she asked, fearing the answer. "This incredible—impossible thing!"

He was silent, and for once she didn't mind it.

But then he said, "We didn't."

Siggy had to let that sink in for several moments. She looked at the image on the screen. It reminded her of Speedy designs she had seen elsewhere, especially the six-sided gaps, the Gates.

"Then," she asked, "who *did* build it?"

"We don't know," said the Decider.

And Mr. Ashur said that Speedies didn't lie. Which meant that this thing was so old, it had influenced Speedy culture.

Siggy shook her head. "That is one fabulous contraption. What—wait a minute." She suddenly knew the answer to the question she had been about to ask, about what was *inside* the thing. "Enigma's in there, isn't it," she stated.

"Yes," said the Decider.

"This is a hub system?" One of the ones Dr. Ngoni had accused them of hiding from humans.

"It is the Nexus of hub systems," said the Decider.

Siggy had to think again. "You mean that it only takes you to hub worlds?"

"Yes."

That didn't seem very practical. Something this big for just a few hub worlds? But that notion didn't very last very long in the face of those massive, six-sided Gates.

"Six to the power of six," said Siggy. "Is that the key? Is that how many hub worlds there really are?"

"No," said the Decider, making her feel foolish. But then he said, "Six to the power of six, six times. Do you understand? Six to the power of six, to the power of six, and so on."

Well, Jerry would love that. The number of the Beast, if you wanted to look at it that way. Siggy didn't even try to calculate the number in her head. It amounted to a whole heck of a lot, that's all she needed to know. Through this Nexus, you could go anyplace in the galaxy. In fact . . .

"You can get to other galaxies from here, too, can't you." Once again, she stated rather than asking.

He didn't answer. But that seemed as good as a yes.

"Speak now," he said. "Tell him you have come. Ask him where he is."

So they could broadcast the message across light years? Obviously, they knew things about communications that humans had yet to learn.

Siggy took a deep breath. "Jerry," she said. "It's Siggy Lindquist. I've come, just as you ordered. Where are you? I'll meet you there. Just tell me."

She could feel tension on the bridge. She looked away from the screen. Every Speedy there had stopped moving. They were waiting, listening. Did they believe they'd get an answer so soon? Was their communications *that* fast?

But they waited in vain. There was no answer. Siggy had a funny feeling, one she was afraid to express just then. She would wait and see what happened. It could take days.

"We will leave the channel open," said the Decider.

The Nexus loomed larger on the screen. Siggy wondered if they were going to land on the outside of the structure. It must be built at the very brink of the Fold, so the inside would have to be inches from it, almost touching it.

There you have it, Jorge. Your Tipler Transporter. I wish you could see it.

But Mr. Ashur hadn't even seen it before. Things were truly dire for them to risk bringing two humans to this secret spot. To reveal so much of themselves, to share information when their instincts rebelled against it. . . .

The Professor grinned at her from the darkness inside the Nexus. *Do you get it now, Siggy? The end of your story?*

"What are you going to do to Jerry Wolfe when you catch him?" she asked the Decider.

"Kill him quickly," he said.

And to a Speedy, that must be fast indeed. Jerry probably wouldn't even know he was dead until he found himself standing at the gates of Hell. Siggy could imagine him there, hammering at the door, screaming, *Open up, Dad!*

"Once you've killed him," she said, "what will you do with us?"

He returned her gaze. "You will stay with us," he

said. "You and Mr. Ashur. We will make you as comfortable as we can."

Like the inmates on Monster Row. Now Siggy was going to know what it was like to live on the other side of that transparency.

The Nexus loomed closer, but she could tell it would be a long time before they reached it, even at Speedy velocities. And maybe they didn't plan to go much farther until they heard from Jerry.

Which you never will, thought Siggy. *Not here. Not by your rules. Only Jerry knows the rules to his game, and he's not talking.*

She turned and left the bridge without waiting for permission. No one tried to stop her. She continued down the halls and all the way to her quarters, her tango face firmly in place.

The Decider was in his music room. Siggy had brought his box.

"I have music for us to dance to," she said. "We can have some more lessons."

He sat very still in his chair, his tendrils lying inert over his shoulders, his mouth a thin line.

Yes, thought Siggy, *you're right to be cautious, Mr. Decider. Let's see what you're really made of.*

"Mr. Ashur tells me that you will teach him group dances for men," said the Decider, so smoothly that Siggy wondered if he had been faking his earlier awkwardness with human speech. Maybe Speedies didn't come right out and lie, but that didn't mean they wouldn't try to give you the wrong impression.

"Later," she said, "when he's not so busy. For now, there are still many ballroom dances I'd like to teach you." *And another thing or two, while we're at it.*

She set the box and the minis she had made on his table. "What would you prefer first?" she asked. "A new dance? Or one that you've already learned?"

He didn't turn his head, but she knew he was watching her. His peripheral vision was probably just as good as his frontal.

"The tango," he replied.

Siggy selected a mini and slipped it in. He stood, turning to her.

"May I have this dance?" he enquired, politely.

"Yes," replied Siggy.

The music started, and he took her smoothly into his arms. He kept his eyes on hers, his face neutral. Siggy didn't mind. When dancing, she could match gazes with the best of them. As far as she was concerned, *he* was the one at a disadvantage right now.

But he danced beautifully. She marveled at his grace.

"Well," she said, "I suppose you'll have to be my dance partner from now on."

He kept silent, but she didn't let that bother her.

"We should have dance parties," she said. "We'll teach all of the crew to dance, and Mr. Ashur. And anyone else who'd like to learn, that would be fun."

"Many would like to learn," he said.

Despite herself, Siggy was glad to hear it. She followed his lead, letting herself enjoy it.

But she had been sneaky. She had looped the song so that it would run longer than usual. She wanted to talk to him.

"You know," she began, "in all of our travels, we humans have never encountered another intelligent race, except for yours." *As far as I know, anyway.* "Isn't that funny?"

"Amusing?" he enquired.

"Strange, I mean. But that Nexus of yours, it's taken you to other galaxies. You must have encountered other races."

He didn't respond. He didn't seem surprised by her line of inquiry, either.

"Mr. Decider," she said. "The void between the stars is an empty place. But it's not *that* empty."

He moved her into an extravagant dip, bending her almost to the floor; which at two gees was a move that left her gasping. Even with her g-suit on, at three or four gees he probably would have broken her back.

Touché thought Siggy.

"What are they like?" she asked him. "Like you? Like us? Have you fought with any of them? Or made friends?"

"You know everything already," he snapped. "No need for me to speak."

He was trying to make her angry, but she was ready for that. She might not know everything, but she knew enough.

"One of these days," she said, "you're going to meet someone faster than you. Then you'll know how we feel."

"Some faster," he said. "Some slower. Some the same."

And then it was another extravagant dip. Siggy thought he was altogether too fond of those. But if that was the price she had to pay to get answers, so be it.

"Do you have as much trouble understanding them as you do us?" she asked, sweetly.

"Always trouble," he said. "Understanding. Mr. Ashur told me something today. About Armageddon."

Siggy would have shivered if her muscles hadn't already been involved in movement. His mouth was a thin, hard line.

"He explained it?" she asked.

"Yes. I tell you now, you want answers, Siggy. Here is my answer. We can give you Armageddon."

She kept her chin up. "Please don't," she said.

"That's what they said on the mini."

"What?" She was trying very hard to keep up with him.

"To Jerry Wolfe," he said. "Please. Don't."

The music had reached the first loop. Siggy felt herself moving inexorably into deeper water.

"Don't let him make you do what he wants," she said. "Don't honor his wishes. That terrible, defective little man."

"The human spectrum," said the Decider. "Siggy Lindquist and Jerry Wolfe. Angels and monsters."

Siggy was taken aback at being called an angel. Apparently this Decider had learned much more about human culture than he was letting on. She still knew so little about Speedies, but she believed that Mr. Ashur was right, they didn't vary as much as humans did.

They didn't vary, but they had their extraordinary members. Like this man.

"And all of the other races you've met," said Siggy. "Are they equally mysterious?"

"Most we leave alone," he said. "Most do not have spacegoing technology."

"What about the others?" pressed Siggy.

Abruptly he stopped dancing. He stepped back, his head tendrils pressed so hard against his body they looked like one solid piece.

"You should join the Diplomatic Corps," he said, his voice so soft it frightened her. "You have talent."

He walked out of the room, slowly, at human speed.

Siggy gazed after him, her heart pounding. He had been angry. This time *he* was the one to lose his temper. *Well I'll be darned,* she thought. *Maybe he's right. Maybe I* do *have talent.*

She turned off the box and ejected the mini, then placed it in its case and closed the lid. She went into the hall, choosing the opposite direction to the one the Decider had taken, and went to Mr. Ashur's office.

The door was closed again, and a sentry was posted.

"Please," Siggy said, politely. "I need to speak to Mr. Ashur. It's very important."

The sentry stepped carefully aside and opened the door. Siggy entered, trying not to look too surprised at the promptness of his cooperation.

Mr. Ashur was sitting on a chair in front of a large monitor, watching images that would have looked comical at that high rate of speed if Siggy hadn't known what they were. He glanced up at her entrance, looking startled.

"We need to talk," she said.

He froze the image on the screen. Jerry Wolfe stood in an impossible position, standing on one toe, the other leg stretched far over his head as he kicked the transparency of his cell, his body bent over almost double, his face twisted into a crazed rictus.

Siggy pulled a chair up next to his. She was aware that the sentry hadn't closed the door behind her. She hoped that didn't mean they were going to return to their old status of constant watching.

"I have a very bad feeling," she confessed.

He waited, looking concerned.

"I don't think Jerry Wolfe is anywhere on the Nexus," said Siggy.

"Where is he then?" asked Mr. Ashur.

Siggy stared at Jerry on the screen. "I don't know," she said. "It's just a feeling. We've missed something. Probably something right under our noses. It doesn't *feel* like he's here. And we're running out of time."

Mr. Ashur drummed his fingers on his knees. "As you can see, I've been looking at the minis again. At Jerry. Look, here he is in one of those seizure states I told you about."

He turned the mini back on, only this time at normal speed.

"*Fuck* me!" snarled Jerry, kicking, "*Suck* me. *Fuck* me. *Suck* me," and on and on, ad nauseam, with boundless energy, never seeming to grow tired of either the words or the kicking. Siggy flushed with anger at the sight and sound of him. It was as if she were back on the Row again, listening to his poisonous rants. But she forced herself to watch and listen, trying to pick up anything new.

Jerry paused for half a second, looking confused. A fly was buzzing around him.

Don't listen to Beelzebub, he's just a demon!

"Beelzebub is the Lord of the Flies," said Siggy.

"I beg your pardon?" said Mr. Ashur.

Jerry started kicking with renewed vigor. Siggy listened hard for the buzzing. It was still there, under the noises Jerry was making.

The demons of Hell came to me in my sleep.

"Do you hear that?" asked Siggy. "The buzzing?"

"Sounds like a fly," said Mr. Ashur.

"No. We didn't have flies. We didn't have bugs of any sort, the Director was an obsessive clean freak. I never saw or heard a fly the whole time I was there."

He touched a control, isolating and amplifying the sound.

"What a minute," he said. "I didn't hear this the first time, because it was speeded up. This sounds like language."

"What's the Professor doing right now?" asked Siggy.

"Sleeping," said Ashur, and he changed scenes so

Siggy could see. The Professor was lying on his bunk, facing the wall, his back to them.

"He knew where all the cameras were," said Siggy. "Hear the sound?"

It was louder in the Professor's cell.

They told me who I was and what I had to do. They taught me many things.

"Can you understand what he's saying?" she asked Mr. Ashur. "Is it in a Speedy language?"

"No," he said. "Definitely not."

"Then what is it?"

He frowned, listening intently.

"It seems . . ." he said, "almost . . ."

"It's human Standard," said the Decider. Siggy started, violently. He had come in silently. He was standing right behind them.

"Look," she said, "at the man on the screen." She turned to look herself. The Professor was lying in his bunk. Then he was suddenly standing, wide awake, his eyes right on the camera. Siggy's heart turned to ice. It was as if he could see her.

"You told me," said Siggy, her voice shaking, "some were slower, some were faster, and some were the same. What about this man? Have you seen anything like him before?"

"No," he said, quickly. But then added, as if unwillingly, "I have heard legends."

The eyes burned, even on a monitor.

"What is he saying?" asked Siggy.

Mr. Ashur ran the tape back, and played it at human speed. The Decider listened for a long time, his mouth a bloodless line.

"Detailed information," he said. "About drugs that disable Speedies."

They taught me many things. So this was how Jerry had known so much about his victims, how to trap and disable them, how to hurt them.

"Go forward," Siggy told Mr. Ashur. "Let's listen to something else."

He found another spot on the mini. The Decider listened to the buzzing.

"He speaks of the Gateway," he said.

"Gateway," said Siggy. "Not *Gates*."

The Decider frowned, listening. "Thanatos," he said, at last.

Mr Ashur looked excited. "In human circles, Thanatos is often referred to as the Gateway to Speedy territory. Maybe that's what he meant."

But Siggy was trying to think. She had read the Professor's letter to the R-FBI several months before. What was the exact wording?

There is a stasis unit in the medical section. It has foiled time for twenty-nine years.

He never said *he* had used the unit.

Siggy looked at the image of Jerry on the screen. He was lying on his bunk now, his hands, feet, and face twitching, his eyes half open. The seizures Mr. Ashur had mentioned. The buzzing had intensified.

"Mr. Ashur," she said; quietly, because the Decider was still listening, "How old would you say Jerry Wolfe is? How old did he look on the mini he made of himself and the Speedies?"

"I don't know," said Ashur. "Perhaps thirty Standard years."

"Then he was the one who used the stasis unit on Thanatos."

"And that must be the Gateway he referred to in his letter. He must be waiting for you on Thanatos!"

"But wait—" Siggy paused again, because the Decider had raised his hand.

"He speaks of you now, Siggy," said the Decider. "And the Time Pockets. He says you have an aptitude for finding them and opening them."

That was a revelation. Siggy hadn't thought she had any special talent. On the other hand, the Time Pocket Task Force had told her that they hadn't been able to enter one themselves, even to send a robot probe in; so how come Siggy had seen them so many times?

Because David is looking for me.

That was the only explanation she could think of. David was inside, and he was looking for her because she was the last one he had seen before he fell in. He was probably walking up that same crooked street right now, trying to get to his Decider, trying to bring her back to where he thought Siggy was still standing. Up and around all the crooked hallways and streets that tricked and looped and crossed . . .

I need you to meet me at the Crossroads.

"I know where he is," said Siggy.

Hours later, Siggy lay on her bunk, trying to sleep. She had argued with the Decider for a long time.

"He's on my world," she had pleaded. "We're almost out of time. When he says Crossroads, he means the Time Pockets. If I don't come, he'll start killing again. My friends, my neighbors. My mother still lives there!"

He had seemed like stone. Not angry, not cruel, but immovable.

"We don't want to be your enemies," Siggy had argued. "We aren't perfect, I know that. We move slowly, maybe we're not even as smart as you. But we aren't to blame for what Jerry did. He never would have touched you if the Professor hadn't told him to."

"You said *he* is to blame for his actions."

"Yes, I know, but he's not alone, Decider. There's something more going on here. You know things you're not telling us, so ask yourself this: Who would profit from a war between Speedies and humans? Certainly not either of us."

She had fallen silent then, and looked at the image of the Professor on the screen, staring at her as if he could really see her. The Decider had looked, too. The image disturbed him, she was sure of that.

"Go back to your room," he had said, at last. "I will consider."

And for a Speedy, he was taking a long time to do that.

We have to do something, thought Siggy. *He must be hiding right there in my hometown. If they won't let me go back, they have to get in touch with Agent Stine. They have to warn people. Maybe they'll let me write a letter—*

Her door opened, but it was Mr. Ashur who came in. He stood, a human silhouette in the doorway.

"Are you awake?" he asked.

"Yes."

"I thought you'd want to know right away. We're going back to Veil."

Siggy couldn't answer him. She was too busy trying not to cry.

"Everything okay?" he asked softly.

Siggy took several deep breaths. "You bet," she said. "Thank you. Thank you so much."

"You're the one who should be thanked. We'll talk about it in the morning, okay? Over coffee."

"Okay," said Siggy.

He left, sealing the door behind him.

Hope that wasn't just a dream, thought Siggy, then fell promptly into real sleep.

Jason's house was crowded with guests, but the living room was still large enough for Siggy to give the Decider his dance lesson. He had almost exhausted her repertoire; she'd consulted the Dance Parade channel once they re-entered human space. Oscar had been helpful, too; he remembered dances his uncle taught him from Medusa, dances that Siggy had never even heard of.

"These Latin dances," said the Decider, as they did the mambo. "I think I like them best."

"Me, too, said Siggy. "Except for the waltz."

"The Tennessee Waltz," he said.

Siggy had made a recording for him back in Speedy territory, singing into the recorder because she needed a good waltz for them to dance to. He liked it so much, she bought a copy of the original Patti Page recording for him on Santa Fe Station, where they also picked up Agent Stine and his task force.

Planetside, there had been little question as to where they should set up their headquarters. Jason cleared a dancing space for them, right in front of the Christmas tree. It was December twenty-first, Veil calendar, and they had been there for a week. Upstairs the R-FBI were working with the Time Pocket Task Force at their observation post, and neighbors were cooperating by allowing surveillance equipment in their homes and on the street as well.

Siggy had worried the Speedies would balk at letting so many people know what was going on. But they understood why Agent Stine and Siggy were both worried about what Jerry Wolfe might be doing, might already have done on Veil. The local police coordinated with the R-FBI, and all of Siggy's old associates were being carefully guarded. Anyone who had ever seen or heard of Jerry's home movies knew why that was necessary, including, fortunately, the Speedies.

Jason managed to talk Siggy's mom into spending the holiday at his house. It had been Siggy's first priority, as soon as they got within message-sending distance.

Jerry Wolfe is on Veil, get my mother!

Mom had been completely cooperative. She helped in the effort to advertise Siggy's presence on Veil, even though she still didn't remember Siggy was her daughter.

Jerry probably knew she was there by now. He hadn't been spotted, but several anomalous readings had been taken in the vicinity in the past few days. He might be watching Siggy mambo with the Decider at that very moment.

Those anomalous readings suggested Jerry was using some unknown technology to conceal himself, equipment that may also have helped him conceal himself while inside Speedy territory. There was little doubt about where Jerry had acquired that technology.

"The Professor must have left it for him on Thanatos," Siggy told them at the big pow-wow on Santa Fe Station, where they met to share information and discuss strategies. It was a historic meeting, involving some very odd and diverse groups. The Decider had brought an elite team from his own ship, a group of combat technicians. Agent Stine had his own Task Force, made up of R-FBI specialists and local law enforcement officers. The Time Pocket Task Force was there in full force, headed by Jorge La Placa. Mr. Ashur came with some officials from the Foreign Department.

And Oscar Montoya was there, with Siggy.

"We have made a full transcript of everything the Professor said to Jerry Wolfe at IFCI," the Decider told the assembly. "Much of it is redundant; repetition was used to ensure that Jerry Wolfe absorbed all of it while within his trance state. This programming went on for most of the thirteen years the two of them were confined together on the Maximum Security Block; therefore the details were very specific."

Agent Stine raised his hand. "Are you familiar with the technology Jerry Wolfe is using now?"

"Not familiar," said the Decider. "We must coordinate to ensure that many possibilities are considered."

They had been doing so for a week now. The interface was surprisingly smooth. Siggy was sorry that the Director had given her the impression that all government agencies concerned with Speedy studies were peopled by ruthless, unprincipled monsters. The Specialists from the Foreign Department reminded her of Mr. Ashur in their dedication and their respectfulness. Not to mention their effectiveness.

The music was ending. "It's almost time," the Decider told her.

"I know," she said. "I have a feeling about tonight."

"That's what you said last night."

"Tonight, even more. We've got to be ready."

He was a changed being from the one Siggy had met—how many short weeks ago? In relativistic terms, how much time had passed, in jump-time and out of it? Days on the Speedy ship had been months on Veil, impossible distances covered at unheard-of speeds; but not much time dilation when you considered the light years traversed. If their current interface was successful, in the next few years human technology would see changes that might have taken centuries to evolve.

The Decider might even let Jorge travel to the Nexus. Some day. When he gave Siggy permission to talk about it again. For now, she had given him her word.

Since the hour when he had decided to return them to Veil, his head tendrils no longer clung close to his body. At this sign, his guards had relaxed as well. Some of them even asked Siggy for dance lessons. But the Decider was the one who got first choice. Tonight they had danced the waltz together, the cha-cha, the tango.

And now the mambo was over.

Barry Silverstein watched them from the arch that led to the hallway, where all of the photos still hung, including the bogus prom photo. Barry had been at the powwow, too, but his questions were about David. Siggy was glad that he didn't know what she suspected.

Jerry Wolfe cheated time inside a stasis machine. But the Professor must have had something else in mind.

Absent friends are waiting, and I have much to do before I sleep.

He had been on Tantalus, had faked his death there—a practical joke, Siggy thought at the time. She thought he had gone from there to Thanatos. Really, it must have been the other way around.

Agent Stine had achieved quite a feat, capturing a creature so advanced, so well equipped. He must have taken the Professor by surprise. That was a comfort, anyway, knowing it might be possible to surprise the Professor. He didn't leave Agate on any outgoing ship.

Any outgoing *human* ship.

Some of the information he passed to Jerry had been *very* specific.

Yes, the maximum security block hadn't been so badly constructed after all. It was too bad human beings were part of the security system. Otherwise, the Professor might be there still, waiting with inhuman patience.

Barry Silverstein waited for her to turn off the music box. She knew what he was worried about. He didn't know what she knew, but David was in danger. He sensed that much.

The Professor must have followed her into the Time Pocket at Christmastime, thirty years ago. He must have used the same technology to conceal himself that Jerry Wolfe had been using. He might have been the person she had seen at the end of that crooked street, the one whose movements had frightened her so. And if that was the case, David had been making his way directly toward him. . . .

"We don't have just one killer to look out for when we go in," she had warned Agent Stine. "We have two."

"They're ready to deploy the probe," Barry told them when the music had been turned off. "All systems are go, everyone is in place."

Siggy and the Decider looked at each other.

"Ready for our stroll?" she asked him.

"Ready," he agreed.

It was cold outside, and Speedies didn't like the cold very much; but they could stand it if they were dressed properly. He was wearing a modified version of his usual uniform, one that generated extra heat. His uniform con-

tained other features as well, carefully hidden and
deadly.

Siggy appeared to be wearing just slacks, a sweater,
and thermal boots. Under that, she was wearing an outfit
much like the Decider's. Both outfits were marvels of
human/Speedy sensor technology; it was even possible
that the Task Force would be able to track them inside
the Time Pocket. Siggy hoped so, but she wondered.
Chances were, they would be completely on their own.
So Siggy had been meticulously drilled in the various
features of her uniform.

And Oscar had given her more kickboxing lessons.

"I want to go with you," he kept saying.

"You can't. He won't contact me if people are with
me. He may not come out if he sees the Decider. But
I'm thinking he will. I'm thinking he's overconfident
about Speedies now. The symmetry might appeal to him
in his current state of mind."

Besides, no way they were going to let Siggy go completely alone.

They opened the door. Barry stood at the threshold,
smiling and calling after them to have a good walk, as
if he were just a holiday houseguest. Upstairs, Jason and
Mom were watching the monitors with Agent Stine, and
Jorge, and a crowd of agents, scientists, and Speedies.

If neighbors hadn't been clued into the situation, they
might have thought Siggy and the Decider were having
a romance. As it was, they dutifully spread rumors all
over town about the Speedies who had come to visit,
and gosh, what could they be doing here? Wasn't it all
fascinating?

If this worked, they were going to have to hand med-
als out to a lot of brave people.

Siggy and the Decider strolled down the front walk,
into the crisp night. Snow had fallen, but not very much
of it. A few flakes were still drifting down. Siggy heard
Christmas music.

Just like that other night, she thought.

She took the Decider's hand, which was warm and
incredibly hard; really, like living stone. It was a gesture
that would continue to inspire gossip, but Siggy wanted
to make sure they didn't get separated if a Pocket swal-

lowed them. They strolled together down the lane, toward the fence that bordered the little stream, and the tree that overhung them both.

"The lights are pretty," said the Decider.

He wasn't just making pleasant conversation—besides, Speedies didn't lie—but Siggy was surprised that he liked Veil as much as he did. He liked the bright colors that decorated the houses; and the folk designs, the flowers, animals, elves and trolls that covered so many roof beams and crawled up so many braces, peeked out from under eaves and stared from shutters. He loved the gardens and the streams, the rain storms that must have moved with infinite slowness past his eyes.

Siggy had thought her world would seem too garish to a Speedy. They surrounded themselves with subtle colors and designs. For a century and a half, they had refused to send an ambassador to Veil, and Siggy assumed it was because they couldn't bear to live in the slow universe. Her world.

But you never knew about people. Even other human beings.

"We have contact," whispered Agent Stine's voice inside Siggy's left ear, where her receiver was concealed. Sensors had picked up movement near them, but no one was in sight.

Siggy and the Decider continued to stroll. Siggy had been nervous a few nights before, the first time they picked up the readings. Now she was getting used to it. As long as she didn't think too much about what was going on, she felt pretty calm.

"We'll meet the other Decider soon," the Decider said, softly. "I'll give you a name to call me, for human ears, to spare confusion. A short one, like *Siggy*."

She held her breath. Mr. Ashur had told her that Speedies usually didn't try to teach their names to Humans. He had only learned a few.

"Call me Mr. Rathasmasdas," said the Decider.

Siggy laughed, gently. "That's a *short* version?"

He emitted a brief purr, the Speedy version of laughter.

"May I call you Ratha?" she asked. "It's nice and short, nice and—*speedy*."

"Agreed," he said.

They passed the fence with its overhanging tree. Siggy could hear the stream trickling; it wasn't completely frozen over this year. The Christmas music was still playing somewhere.

She thought she heard a noise behind them, the scuffle of a shoe on wet pavement.

Ratha's tendrils twitched. They drifted a little higher, but did not deploy anywhere near to maximum exposure. That would have given them away. His hand was steady in hers.

"Dreadful flowers," he remarked casually. That was the code phrase he used to let her know he could smell Jerry. Siggy was sure Jerry still didn't bother to take care of himself, other than to cram food in his mouth and to eliminate periodically.

Which meant he had to be more than ten feet away, or she would have smelled him even with her human nose.

If you could forget the circumstances, it was a beautiful night. The Enigma Nebula could be glimpsed through breaks in the clouds. Christmas trees shone from windows, lights twinkled on shrubbery and under eaves. There was one big tree about halfway down the block that had been done up in hundreds of strands of white lights, blinkers that ran in sequence so the lights chased each other like tiny trains. The tree was at least thirty feet tall, its branches trimmed so that it was fat and round. Siggy loved to stop right in front of it and watch this cloud of light.

To Ratha it must look very different, but he seemed as inclined to stop as she was. Often she was ready to go before he was finished looking. Tonight when they stopped, Siggy thought she heard an exhalation behind them, perhaps a snort of impatience. Jerry wouldn't be able to keep quiet forever. A few more nights of waiting, and he might deviate from the Professor's plan.

She watched the faery lights chasing around and through the branches.

You were in there thirty years the last time, Oscar had said. *And that was just when you were having a quick conversation with David. What's going to happen if you really take your time in there? One hundred, two hundred years will go by?*

I don't know, Siggy confessed. *That's why I asked them to offer you a stasis unit if you—if you would be willing to wait . . .*

The lights went around and around, completing each circuit and starting over again. Siggy listened for footfalls behind them. She glanced at Ratha, saw rainbows skimming across the surface of his eyes.

We'll see, baby, Oscar had promised. *I'll give you ten years in there. If you don't come out by then, I'll think about it.*

Another sound behind them. This time a snuffle. Maybe Jerry was catching a cold. Served him right.

Okay, maybe I'll give you five years, Siggy. Or hell, maybe I'll just pop right into a unit tomorrow.

Something odd about the lights.

I don't want to lose you.

The lights had broken their pattern, they weren't chasing each other anymore. Now banks of them were blinking together, in tandem with other banks. Siggy had never seen them do that before. Maybe that was one of the options you could get with these particular strands. But it was odd. They were already losing that pattern and finding a new one that made even less sense.

Siggy dropped her gaze to the trunk of the tree.

"There," she said, and pointed.

The Pocket was just behind the tree, in shadows that shouldn't be there with all of the lights shining down on them. It was just like the others Siggy had seen, big enough for several people to go through.

She and Ratha stepped forward, together.

Before they could get halfway there, something flew past Siggy's head, something about the size of a bird except that it was round and had a much more sophisticated method of propulsion. It flew into the Pocket, and Siggy watched it fly off at an impossible angle.

"Probe deployed," whispered Jorge's voice in her ear. "Good luck."

Siggy and Ratha walked up to the opening in time and space. They could feel the warp as they crossed over. For Siggy, it was a moment of disorientation, a prickliness that wasn't completely physical in nature.

Ratha stopped dead on the other side.

"What's wrong?" Siggy asked.

He looked at her, startled.

"Time," he said. "Timing. You're the same speed as me."

"I am?" Siggy didn't feel any different. But now that he mentioned it, he didn't seem quite himself.

"I can't hear and smell as well," he was saying. "My eyes—"

"Can you see?" Siggy was really worried now. Should they go back? Where the heck was Jerry? Had he come in yet, had the Pocket stayed open for him? She glanced back and saw the normal world sitting there, Winter Night, a lovely, remote picture. As she watched, it twisted in on itself and disappeared.

"My god," she said, suddenly terrified. "H.Q., can you hear me? Are you still reading me?"

There was no response, not even static.

Big surprise, thought Siggy, butterflies bumping frantically against the lining of her stomach. She hadn't really expected that they would be able to stay in touch, but for that moment when she realized they were really *in* and the known universe was really *gone* . . .

She tried to scan their surroundings. "David was right," she said. "This is totally confusing."

"I can see," said Ratha, "but I don't understand what my brain is receiving."

She squeezed his hand. "You sound exactly like a human being when you talk now, except that your voice is deeper."

He studied her as if he were seeing her for the first time. "Interesting. Your color is different. And your voice. This isn't so bad, once you get used to it. It is worth studying."

Siggy supposed he was right, but her brain kept wanting her to scream. It looked like they were about to fall—every time she tried to get her bearings, the world angled off in a new definition of up/down/sideways. They were standing on a patch of grass that stretched perhaps a hundred yards under their feet, then towered over them and curled like a lollipop. Around them were trees, pavement, flowers, houses, all of the elements you could find on a normal street, but everything was twisted around, jumbled up. The arrangement didn't make sense, she couldn't tell where they were; and worst of all, she couldn't tell where *Jerry* might be. He could come at them from just about any direction, and he probably wasn't even all that upset by this topsy turvy universe. It was might be a lot like the inside of his head.

"David?" Siggy called. "Hello, are you here?"

They listened carefully. Ratha deployed his head tendrils into their maximum exposure range. It was interesting to watch in "slow" motion.

"I hear something," he said.

Siggy strained her own ears. Was that someone calling? Could she just make out the tail end of her name?

A sharp pain struck her in the middle of the chest; simultaneously, she heard Ratha gasp. His hand spasmed inside hers, then began to lose strength. Siggy reached for him, but it was as if he were melting. He started to fall, and she tried to catch him.

But then she looked past him and saw Jerry not two feet away moving fast, human speed, his figure distorted by the colorless fabric that hugged his thin body. She saw a gleam from a hunting knife in his hand.

Without thinking, she let her body drop back. She grabbed Jerry's knife hand at the wrist and pulled, hard. His grimace of triumph turned to surprise as his momentum carried him right into her fall. Most people tried to push an attacker away, not pull him toward themselves. Siggy let herself fall on her butt, keeping her legs curled tight against her the bottom of her feet aimed at Jerry's midsection. He teetered over her awkwardly then began to fall. Still pulling him forward, she rammed both feet into his crotch as hard as she could. He emitted a *WHOOMPH* of agony and outrage and his legs stiffened reflexively, striking Siggy's butt without much force as she continued to roll back with him, flipping him up and over to land, hard, on his back.

She started to get up. Now was the time to kick with full force at his stomach and kidneys; not a nice thing to do, you could even kill someone that way, but Siggy was prepared to take that chance. She got to her feet and the world dropped sideways. She staggered, went down on one knee.

Something was sticking out of her chest. She looked down, saw the dart sticking there, and plucked it out.

He nailed us. Oh no. He drugged us.

She looked for Ratha. He was lying just a few feet away, on his side, looking at her. He could see her, but he couldn't move a muscle.

Jerry was lying a little farther away, groaning and cursing, curled up in agony.

"You *bitch*!" he hissed, between groans. "You goddam *bitch*! I'm gonna cut—your tits off! I'm gonna cut—pieces off you until there's—nothing left, and—I'm gonna leave—your eyes for last—so you can watch the whole—thing!"

Siggy struggled to her feet. The drug wasn't getting her as fast. Maybe it was a drug that worked better on Speedies; because he would have been more threatened by Ratha than he would by her, he would have taken the Speedy out first. She struggled to stay upright, managed to take a few steps. If she would get Ratha up and help him away from there, down the twisty street, out of sight where Jerry couldn't see them, maybe they could hide. . . .

She went down on both knees this time. She couldn't get up again. She started to crawl. Ratha seemed farther away now. He should have been within reach, he looked like he was ten feet away.

"Crawl, you bitch!" Jerry howled. "You bitch-dog!"

He had managed to roll onto his side, and was starting to get to his knees himself, but a new spasm of pain sent him down again. She must have made him pull something vital when she had thrown him. Good.

She fell on her side. She needed to rest just a second. Just to catch her breath. She could see Ratha, staring helplessly at her. She couldn't see Jerry anymore.

"I'm going to do him first, Siggy!" screeched Jerry. "You're gonna watch it! I'm going to take his eyes out for you! Your Speedy boyfriend. Hey, it can't be that much fun to fuck a Speedy, is it? They must finish really fast!"

He giggled at his own joke, but it was a sickly sound. He was still hurting.

But if the energy of his diatribe was any indication, that condition wasn't going to last for long. Siggy's muscles were shutting down. Moving even an inch was a monumental effort. In another moment, she was going to be completely paralyzed, while Jerry . . .

"When I get done with him I'm gonna fuck his eye sockets," said Jerry, gleefully.

The last of Siggy's energy drained away, leaving her muscles like so much dead meat. Red rage rushed into the void, filling her head, blurring her vision. It was a rage that harkened all the way back to her Viking ancestors, a rage for killing. If she had been free at that moment, she would have picked up his knife and chopped him to quivering pieces.

But she wasn't free, and she could hear Jerry coming closer.

In another moment, he was standing over her. She could see the details on his outfit now, filaments so fine you could only spot them when light gleamed along their surfaces. They covered his body and ran up his face and over the top of his head. He grinned through the delicate web, a cross between a smile of triumph and a grimace of rage. It suited him.

He spit on her. The globule splattered on her right cheek, then slithered down to her nose. He watched it make its slow way, finally dripping off onto the grass, leaving a trail of slime behind it.

"Go to hell," Siggy told him, and was surprised to realize she could still talk. Her vocal cords felt almost normal.

Yes, Jerry liked to hear them scream.

"I'm going to—" he started, and began to rant at her. What he was going to do, how he was going to do it, how she was going to die so she could be his slave in Hell. "I have Speedy slaves, too," he said. "You'll all be in the stew, and I'm going to eat you!"

"Why didn't you just kill me at IFCI when you escaped?" Siggy asked, derailing him.

He frowned. "I had to have a witness. Someone's got to be a witness to Armageddon, or what's the point?"

"So you still think you're the Antichrist."

"Of course I am, you dumb bitch! What are you, blind?"

He kicked her in the face. She saw stars of pain. Siggy could feel blood trickling out of her nose, but it didn't feel broken. He hadn't aimed very carefully.

"There's something you don't know," she said, as if he hadn't touched her. "The demons lied to you."

He kicked at her shoulder, rolling her over onto her back; but screamed in pain himself as the movement strained the muscles he had pulled in his groin. Siggy stared at her new perspective, the twisted jumble of streets over their heads.

"They set you up," she said. "All that stuff they left you on Thanatos was so you could do *their* work."

"Shut up," he hissed, still clutching his groin. But she had captured his attention when she had mentioned Thanatos.

"They played you for such a fool," she pressed on. "They knew you would believe anything they said. They wanted you to start a war so they could come storming in here when it's all over and take whatever's left. And you know what'll happen to you then, Jerry? Do you think you're going to be king of Hell? Well that's true, because they'll kill you when they don't need you anymore. And that's now, Jerry, they're in here right now, looking for you."

"Bullshit!" he snarled, but he was looking around. He was licking his lips.

"They told you where to find the ship that would take you to Tantalus, they showed you how to stage your death," Siggy said, disdainfully. "They told you how to use the stasis unit on Thanatos, and how to use the other equipment they left there. Then they got you to be their little errand boy, go do their dirty work for them with the Speedies, and you fell for it, Jerry. You fell for it because you're a pathetic, half-baked little creep who just doesn't get it. Without your home movies, you're not sure of anything, are you."

"I'm sure what I'm gonna do to you," he panted.

"Yeah, right, like you've really got time. They're watching you right now."

"Are not."

She laughed, and she wasn't entirely feigning it. He was ridiculous, even in this moment when he had absolute power over her. No matter what he did, he was still a geek in the end.

"Any minute, Jerry," she warned.

He didn't answer. He picked up his knife. He looked around, his eyes wide. But then he dropped to his knees, next to Siggy.

"Stupid story," he said, petulantly.

Oh, crap, she had time to think.

Then Jerry's knife was flying out of his hand, and his arm was bent from the elbow at an impossible angle. He screamed like a girl.

Jerry made it all the way up on his feet again, just as his other arm snapped. Something flashed past him, too fast for Siggy to see. Another two flashes, and his arms were broken at his shoulders. Each flopped over to the opposite side of his body, as if he were a shirt someone was folding.

His knees were snapped backward, and he was on the ground, eye level with Siggy.

"Decider?" she called. "Ratha?" No one answered. She was hoping it was he who was attacking, but she couldn't see. This should be payback for the mini, for the outrage perpetrated on innocent Speedies. But why didn't he answer her? Whether he was still on the ground, or he was the one killing Jerry—why didn't he answer?

"I'm the Antichrist," Jerry said, almost conversationally, as his legs were snapped and folded back at the hips. "You're my witness!" His eyes looked at her, but he couldn't see her anymore. They were clouding. Was it a moment of revelation for him? Did he finally understand what his victims had suffered?

"I will rise again," he whispered, and then his back was snapped at the waist.

Siggy closed her eyes and desperately fought the urge to vomit. In her current state, she might choke on it. She heard more snapping bones and thought, *For heaven's sake, he's dead already! Finish it!*

Finally the snapping sound stopped. There was a moment of silence, and then Siggy felt careful, hard hands on her face. Someone wiped away the blood and spittle. A moment later, she felt a sting in her upper arm.

"The antidote," said a toneless voice.

Siggy tried to breathe normally. Her limbs began to tingle. As soon as she could, she rolled onto her side, where she could see Ratha. He was still paralyzed, but now he was watching someone behind her.

Siggy climbed onto her knees. There were splashes of Jerry's blood on her clothing—she could see the edges of a red pool slowly creeping toward her. She didn't feel inclined to look for its center.

In another moment, she was able to sit back on her heels and lift her head.

Gray eyes looked back at her.

"I always carry some of the antidote on me," said the Professor. "Wolfe was unpredictable."

"He did your work well enough," said Siggy.

The Professor didn't shrug. He didn't move at all.

"By the way," he said, "I ran into your Lost Boy. He says hello."

Her heart contracted with grief. David Silverstein was dead. For a moment, she wanted to beg for Ratha's life, but a little voice warned her, *Don't mention him, don't look at him.*

The Professor stared at her exactly the same way he always had at IFCI, but this time there was no transparency between them. Siggy was going to die, maybe the same way Jerry had.

"Tell me now," she said, thinking that it would be the last thing she ever heard. "Who are you, really? Why were you here?"

He smiled that old, dreadful smile. Siggy wondered how she ever could have suspected he was a Speedy. His speed was the only thing he had in common with them. Even inside a Time Pocket he was fast.

As if he were at home in there.

"Enigma," he said.

"What?" Siggy wondered what she had missed.

"My name. Call me Enigma. Sometimes I consume, sometimes I spew. If you cross my event horizon, I will crush you." He glanced at Jerry's mutilated body. Siggy couldn't help but do the same. She wished she hadn't.

"You will always know I'm here," said the Professor. "But you will never know what I am."

"Some day they might," said Siggy. "They might figure out *exactly* what you are."

"You understand," he said. "I thought you might. I'm not like Jerry Wolfe, I don't need a witness. But you might as well understand."

Siggy heard something then. She heard a voice, calling.

"Siggy! Where are you? Siggy!"

It was David. The Professor watched her. He saw the struggle she couldn't keep from her face.

"Time is fleeting," he said. "Find the door with the Christmas wreath. It's your exit."

Siggy twitched. She didn't want to die, but she wasn't going to leave Ratha and David behind.

"Pick up your friend, Siggy. I'll watch you."

Siggy lifted her chin. The Professor wasn't a psychopath, but he did have some traits in common with them. He didn't respect anyone who was afraid of him and acted like it. Not anymore than the Speedies did. She wasn't dizzy anymore, and she felt stronger. She stood, only staggering a little.

He watched her. But now he was standing farther away.

Siggy glanced at Ratha. He was moving, too. Had he been given the antidote, or was it pure chutzpah that moved his limbs?

"Your Lost Boy has to find his own way out," said the Professor. "Hurry, Siggy."

She stumbled over to Ratha and helped him up. He wasn't recovering as fast as her, but he was doing his best to help her. She dragged his arm over her shoulder and propped him up. He was looking over his shoulder, at the Professor. Siggy couldn't tell if there was recognition in his expression or not.

"Follow the pavement around the corner," called the Professor, as if he were halfway down the street by now. Siggy resisted the urge to look at him. She and Ratha stumbled toward the corner that twisted down and to the right. Siggy concentrated on keeping her feet on the pavement; she closed her eyes as they crossed the threshold into the new angle.

When she opened them again, the street was gone. They were in a twisted corridor. It was lined with doors of every size, shape, and color. The doors wore the bright colors of Veil, and the fey designs; but these dwarves and trolls almost seemed to watch you as you passed them. They almost seemed to beacon, *Try this door, this is the one!*

Some of the doors were twisted into vortex shapes. Siggy wondered what was pulling on them like that, but she never felt tempted to try them and find out. She looked for the Christmas wreath. She thought she saw a spot of green up ahead.

"There!" Ratha pointed. It was suddenly closer, just six doors down. They staggered toward it in the closest approximation they could make to a beeline. It loomed ahead, and Siggy wondered if it would suddenly jerk away from them at the last moment, teasing, promising, then evading while the centuries zoomed by outside.

Siggy reached for the knob. She felt the cold brass under her fingers. She twisted, and heard the click. The door swung open.

She head a buzzing, then the shouts of humans.

"Here!" she cried, "We're here! We need help!"

But she didn't wait for it. She and Ratha fell forward into a crowd. Hands caught them, Speedy and human hands. The man who held Siggy was wearing the uniform of a local police officer. He was looking past her with wide eyes.

"My god!" he said. "What did you just fall out of?"

Siggy looked over her shoulder. The door with the wreath was slowly swinging shut behind her. She could just make out the corridor beyond, twisting and turning. Someone was standing at the edge of her sight, watching her, his eyes burning across the distance like the light of an ancient sun.

"Good-bye," she whispered.

And then the door swung shut, swallowing itself.

Questions were being asked, faces were swimming in her vision, but Siggy was looking for one in particular.

She saw him suddenly, pushing his way to her side. He didn't look older, but this could always be his son, his grandson, or his great, great . . .

"Jason?" she said, cautiously.

"Yes!" he said laughing, and then he was hugging her.

"How long this time?" she asked as soon as she could catch her breath.

"Just seven years, this time." He looked down at her as if he couldn't quite believe his eyes. "But seven years is a hell of a long time to hold your breath!"

Siggy woke from a terrible dream.

She had seen the Professor again. He had been going away from her, down that twisting corridor. She had only seen him from the back, but she knew it was him. He wasn't so much walking as he was *moving;* standing one place for a moment, then instantly vanishing and reappearing farther down the corridor.

He was looking at the doors. He kept moving until he found one of the distorted ones, that had looked as if something massive was pulling on them from the other side. He touched the knob to one of these and it was sucked away from him, into the void. Siggy saw him smiling into the crushing darkness.

"I'm home!" he called.

She opened her eyes in the darkness of her own room. Oscar was lying next to her, snoring softly. She searched the room with her eyes, looking for the Other. But he wasn't there.

Siggy got up as carefully as she could, trying not to wake Oscar. He was running his own gym these days, but also pulled duty as a dance instructor. He had inherited his uncle's habit of graceful aging. He had never climbed into a stasis unit while she was gone, so he was forty-five to her thirty-five.

He was also a light sleeper, a habit learned on Medusa. Over the last five years, Siggy had become an expert at noiseless movement. She tended to wake in the middle of the night, to go to the window and ponder.

That's what she did now. The Enigma Nebula had climbed to the top of the sky, looking down on her. She could just see its edges. If she wanted to, she could go out on the balcony to see it better; but she didn't want to wake Ratha, either. His room opened onto the same balcony. He was trying to change his sleep cycles to fit the human pattern better now that he was ambassador to Veil. He was adapting, but still needed regular naps.

Los Dias and Halloween had passed; it would be Thanksgiving soon, and then they could start getting ready for Christmas. Ratha loved Halloween and Christmas best of all, because of the candy. He had become an expert at carving Jack-o-lanterns, and a genius at devising costumes for the children of friends. Jason's boy Rory had worn Ratha's creations for the last several years, though now he was feeling too old to go door-to-door. Ratha was forced to enlist the help of Rory's younger sister Linda to help him procure candy these days.

He negotiated treaties and trade agreements with an iron fist, but the children adored him.

Siggy wondered if she should go downstairs and make hot cocoa. That might wake Ratha too, he could smell cocoa from down the block. He needed his sleep tonight; tomorrow they would be negotiating another trade agreement. The human delegates who were housed down the street dutifully attended dance class in the afternoons; they knew it would be essential for communication.

Siggy could hardly believe it. So much time had passed, inside and outside of Time Pockets; yet it also seemed like only yesterday that she had been a janitor at IFCI. Everyone told her she could do better, and now she was head dance instructor and liaison to the Speedies on Veil. Not that anyone would have ever believed that such a job would eventually exist. Some still accused Siggy of making it up for her own convenience.

These same individuals were not too happy that the Speedies insisted on referring to Veil as "Siggy's World."

"My full name is Sigrit, if you think that would sound better," she had suggested, helpfully, keeping her tango face firmly in place while they fumed.

And now she and Oscar lived in one of the fancy houses, the big restored places in Jason's neighborhood, four doors down from him. Siggy never wanted a big house, especially, but her home was often full of guests from both sides. Ambassadors, Deciders, scientists, specialists, agents, officers, politicians, exchange students— Red Cliffs was on the map these days. After the town got used to the idea, and after they had seen with their own eyes that Siggy wasn't ruining the place by letting all these visitors in, they asked each other how an outsider like her could be so much like a hometown girl.

Because they still didn't remember her, and they never would. Not even Mom, who was ailing these days. Siggy hadn't tried to tell her the truth, but they had become fast friends. Marta Lindquist loved Siggy's little girl as much as she would have loved her own grandchild. She often marveled aloud how much little Gerda looked like the photos of the children in her own family gallery.

"We must be distantly related," she told Siggy.

"Maybe not so distantly," was all Siggy would say.

Gerda had nut brown skin, white hair, and gray eyes. Oscar adored her, but shared her willingly with Ratha, who was waiting impatiently for Gerda to reach trick-or-treating age.

During Los Dias, they took Marta to the graveyard to visit her husband. Marta could hardly walk anymore, but she always enjoyed herself. She never asked why the visit meant so much to Siggy. Gerda had asked, though, last year; and it was Ratha who came up with the answer.

"He must remind her of her own father," he told the little girl, who was perched on his shoulders at the time, peering through a forest of tendrils. Afterward they all had a picnic together at Tivoli Park. The whole town turned out, Speedies and humans together. The people of Red Cliffs were used to the blurred movements of Speedies who were off duty and simply enjoying themselves. Some people had even gone so far as to exchange names.

It's working out pretty well, Siggy told herself, watching the stars on the horizon as they struggled to compete against Enigma's glow. *Slower than a lot of humans would like, but faster than they know.* So much had changed in the last twelve years.

Agent Stine was retired. Siggy still got Christmas cards

from him, but he never asked about the Professor. He had
reluctantly let that chapter of his life be closed by Intelligence agents who had nothing to do with the R-FBI and
everything to do with the Security of the Republic.

Jorge La Placa still ran the Time Pocket Task Force.
He had plenty to do, because the probe he had deployed
into the Pocket was still sending back signals. It took a
supercomputer to sort them out of their distorted state,
but Siggy assumed some useful information was being
gathered, because Jorge was still working closely with
the Speedies who helped him build the probe.

All of them wondered why the Professor had seemed
so familiar with the inside of Time Pockets.

Barry Silverstein was still waiting for David to reap-
pear. He was also retired, and was living in his parents'
old house, by himself. Mrs. Silverstein died while Siggy
was facing Jerry Wolfe for the last time. Mr. Silverstein
had passed three years ago. He had been happy to have
his only son move back in with him.

After his father died, Barry went into David's room
and cleaned it from top to bottom. "When my brother
gets home," he told Siggy, "he'll need to see some familiar sights."

I saw your Lost Boy. He says hello.

Siggy shivered. She hoped David had made his way
back to the Lost Fleet before the Professor found him
again. She tried not to hope that the Professor would
show mercy. She wasn't even sure he had shown it to
her. He let her go, but Jorge had given her reason to
wonder what the Professor's real motives had been.

Jorge told her that time didn't run evenly inside the
Pockets. It ran much slower in there than it did outside,
but it didn't always flow in a straight line. "We think
that sometimes it might loop back on itself. At least we
hope that's the case, because that's the only way some
of these data are going to make any sense."

When he told her that, Siggy remembered her last
glimpse into the Pocket, just before the door swung shut.
She thought she saw the Professor, and he saw her. But
she was fairly certain he hadn't followed them down the
corridor. He was headed to another destination. That
didn't necessarily mean he wouldn't end up in the same

spot as them, not with the way things twisted inside the Time Pockets; but maybe he really had gone somewhere else. At least, *that* version of him had, the one who already knew Siggy.

An earlier version of him might have been setting eyes on her for the first time.

Maybe you reminded him of someone, Ratha had said.

Like myself, Siggy thought. *That first day on Monster Row, maybe what happened was that he recognized me. That's how he knew I could help him.*

It still didn't explain why he had let her take Ratha out. Jerry's death made sense of course; he might have become a nuisance and had outlived his usefulness. But why let Ratha go?

"Because you wouldn't leave without me," Ratha suggested. "And he would need you later."

"A sensible answer," she agreed. "But maybe there's more. Maybe the Time Pockets aren't accidental things after all. We've always assumed Enigma was the device for travel. But what if the Fold is the side effect, and the *Pockets* are the device? In that case, he might not be too anxious to let other races get a good look around in there."

"Which is why he should have killed me," Ratha reminded her.

"Except that I wouldn't leave without you."

This reasoning was as convoluted as the inside of a Time Pocket, but Ratha liked it. "Then," he said, "if he knows where your Lost Boy is, what do you suppose he will do to him.?"

Kill him, Siggy thought miserably. But she clung to one faint hope. "It might be less trouble to show the Fleet the way out than to get rid of all those ships. He's alone, Ratha, maybe he doesn't have endless resources. He could send David back to them with a message and get rid of them quickly, no fuss."

"Unless he likes fuss," said Ratha. "But if your theory is true, one day David will come out."

Siggy hoped he would do it in her lifetime.

But for now, she had to admit, she was happier than she had ever been. Her husband loved her, Gerda kept reminding her of her own happy childhood, and she had finally found her calling in life.

And she was home, on Veil. It had waited for her.

Something streaked across the sky. It would have looked like a meteor shower, except that these streaks moved in unison. There were twenty of them.

Siggy heard the siren then, rising, falling. She was across the room in a fraction of a second, shaking Oscar.

"Get Gerda!" she shouted. "It's the Lost Fleet! Head for the basement!"

He didn't stop to question, was out the door in a flash, Siggy close on his heels. She dashed for Ratha's room, but his door flew open before she could pound on it.

"It's all right," he said. He was holding his portable phone. "They've already communicated with Planetary Defense. They're standing down."

Speedy time. Siggy leaned against the wall, her heart pounding. Oscar came back carrying Gerda, who was not happy about being pulled out of her warm bed.

Siggy and her family regarded Ratha, who stood there calmly, almost cheerfully. "The Lost Fleet isn't attacking," he explained. "Not this time. They know that the war is over."

"Who told them?" Gerda asked, sleepily, but Siggy already knew.

"David Silverstein," she said. "The Lost Boy has come home."

"Don't shoot, don't shoot!" David had shouted, his voice conveyed to all corners of the Veil System by the communications array, whose technology had been significantly boosted by the Speedies. "We're standing down, don't shoot!"

Ratha and Siggy were shuttled up to Santa Fe Station within the hour, only waiting long enough to collect Barry Silverstein.

David looked a little lost among the crowd of human and Speedy officers. His ROTC uniform looked a bit rumpled. Someone was explaining to him that a lot of changes had occurred since he had fallen into his Time Pocket. He was trying to absorb it all, but he was looking

for a particular face in the crowd, hopefully. When he
finally spotted Siggy, he looked like he might cry for joy.

She hugged him, hard. "I was so worried about you,"
she said. "When we went in to look for you, we couldn't
find you."

"We heard you calling," he said. "The Decider and I
were trying to find our way back to you, but we just
kept getting more lost. Then we ran into this strange
guy—"

The noise from the rest of the crowd faded away, until
Siggy could only hear David.

"He was standing at the opposite end of the street,
and I didn't recognize him. I thought maybe he was from
our town. He called to us, told us to look for a door
with a troll door-knocker on it. He said that would take
us back to the Fleet. I asked him if he had seen you,
and he said you were already on your way out, that you
were looking for us on the other side."

David looked exhausted. He was talking like a teenager, excited, happy to be home, anxious to make sense
to the adults and to have them believe him.

"Then he talked to Decider in her own language! She
said that he told her how to get the Fleet out. She said
we'd better try his advice, we weren't making much
progress on our own. She believed me by then. It's easier
to talk to them in there, Siggy; they go the same speed
as us in there. Otherwise, I don't know how I ever would
have made them understand me!"

David looked ready to drop. Siggy could bet that he
was hungry, too. Barry Silverstein was standing with
Ratha, just outside the crowd. There were tears on his
face, but he didn't want to approach his brother too
soon. He had told Siggy on the way up.

"He remembers me at nineteen. I'm seventy-one now.
He doesn't need a big shock right off. We'll tell him I'm
Uncle Meyer. I look like him."

David was looking at Siggy wistfully now. He was using
her as a gauge for how much time had passed, a false
impression. She braced herself for a difficult question.

"I saw you at your senior prom," he said. "You
looked wonderful! I've only been to my junior prom,

and I didn't dance very well. I should have had more lessons, but I was always too busy studying."

"You'll go to one this year," Siggy promised him. "And you'll know how to dance."

"Really?" He blushed. He reminded her of Nathanial just then, and their very first lesson. Nathanial who was a grandfather now, who had sent Siggy pictures of a Halloween tree just last year. "I've got two left feet, I warn you," David was saying.

Siggy hooked an arm in his and started to walk him out of the room, past officials who would have to wait a while to ask their questions. Ratha and Barry fell in behind them. "Don't worry," she said. "I'm an expert at teaching people with two left feet. The steps aren't even the most important thing you have to learn, did you know that?"

"No," said David, mesmerized.

"The most important thing to learn," said Siggy, "is how to ask a girl to dance."

"Oh, that!" David laughed, so relieved to be home that he didn't care anymore whether he looked brave, or strong, or like someone who was going to be a star-man. Soon Siggy was going to have to tell him the truth, about the time that had passed, the people who had forgotten him, the loved ones who were dead. But first, she was going to teach him to waltz.

Even outside of Time Pockets, there was time enough for that.